SONGBIRD AT MIDNIGHT

JOHN McDONOUGH

For Dad.

I see the top of the mountain.

For we wrestle not against flesh and blood,
but against principalities, against powers,
against the rulers of darkness of this world,
against spiritual wickedness in high places.
—*Ephesians 6:12*

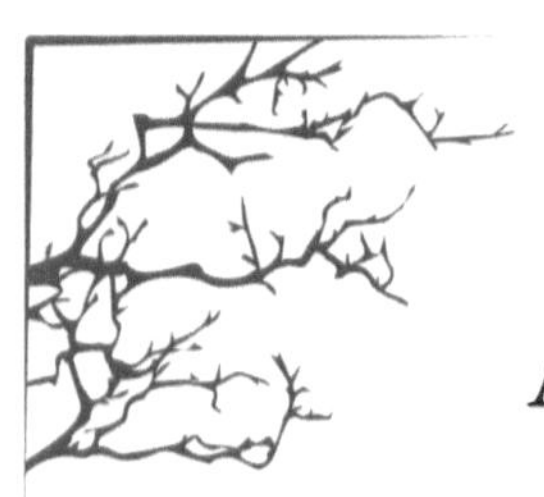

Acknowledgments

The following amazing people helped me bring this book to you. Thanks to:

Andrea for the first eyes and her inspiration.
Ian and Martha for the fixes.
Holly for her kindness and checking my words.
Stephanie for wondering about the rules.
Ashley and Diedra for reaching The End.
Julie, Jeff and Lauren for those early chapters.
Annie for the advice.
Hannah for giving me stage directions.
Sanya for checking my French.
Jessica and Abigail for being in my corner.
Billy for his enduring friendship and the generous contribution of his lyrics.
And to Maria for her bravery.

SONGBIRD AT MIDNIGHT

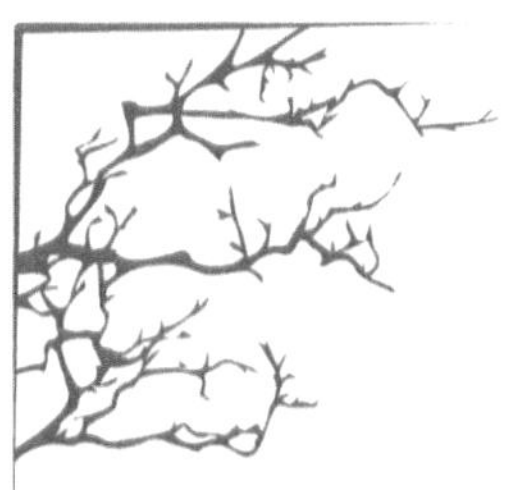

Chapter 1

The Man Upstairs needed a monster.

What he got was a musician.

I'm a singer and sax soloist, which means I travel light. Show up to the gig, swing open a case, get a sound check or two, and presto, ready to rock. But unlike a lot of horn players—and most vocalists—I do my part and pitch in to break down gear.

I also *like* my bandmates. And it was my turn to buy the java that morning, so I had a good walk ahead of me from the Church of Coffee to Austin Music Hall.

All over Austin, the cafes and streets crawl with hipsters, joggers and dog walkers. Rich California transplants. If you're expecting redneck cowboys and caballeros, you'll be sadly disappointed. There are newer arrivals though. Headscarf-wearing women. Communist brats. Diversity so diverse it hurts.

But the toned gals pacing into the cafe in their tight shorts and yoga pants didn't hurt my mood. Downtown Austin is flooded with gorgeous women, day and night. This morning was no exception.

I inhaled the mingled scents of feminine sweat, perfume and antiperspirant, roasting coffee and baked goods.

Bored out of my mind in the long coffee line, I tried to guess how many of the surrounding ladies were lesbians, like counting cars on a road trip. It was tricky to tell nowadays, Austin being Austin. Unfortunately, with any eye contact, I sensed which way the wind was blowing, and a rigged game isn't much fun.

Not soon enough, I was up to a familiar hipster cashier. His name is Larry, and he comes complete with piratey, waxed beard.

"Hey, Loch. Heard you guys were playing down the street last night," Larry said with a smile that made his mustache twitch.

"You heard right. Was a fun show, and you shoulda been there. Now I'm back to load the wagons. But not without coffee first."

Larry laughed. "What a life, dude. What'll it be?"

I ordered the usual rack of large roasts and a bag full of pastries and doughnuts, plopped down way too much cash for the entire haul, and then made my way over to the carafes for the pouring.

Minutes later, I was leaving the shop. There were laughs as I walked away.

Why? Well, I was wearing one of my favorite t-shirts. On the front it says **Stroke a genius.**

On the reverse: ***200 IQ***.

Sometimes I just can't help myself. Sorry.

Practically nobody strolled that part of town so early on a Monday. A handful of cyclists and one gay-guy couple carrying a red plastic clothes bin between them passed by. The tree-lined walk up Willie Nelson Boulevard took me past swanky shops, a couple more cafes, a restaurant, Violet Crown Cinema—I'd parked behind it—and Austin Rocks on the next corner. From there, I took the side street route toward Margaret Moser Plaza and my destination.

Austin Music Hall is a sprawling, warehouse-sized building with blue and white aluminum siding and cement walls. Glass ticket windows and exits line the front.

I walked around to the rear of the Hall, coffees out in front of me in their cardboard tray and the bag of doughnuts dangling from a hand beneath.

The load-in area consisted of a rickety metal walkway about half-a-story up via some cast iron stairs, and this platform stretched behind a long series of steel loading doors. I gingerly made my way up the steps, noting again, as I did every time I played there, that the damn walkway felt like it would collapse under my weight. It was just a trick of the mind really, those planks being made of alloy and not wood, but they *clicked* and *clanked* so damn loudly as I moved over them that I cussed. I got through a door without incident though, and my eyes adjusted to the darkness inside.

Not surprisingly, I was the first band member to arrive back on the scene. Several thousand square feet in size, the interior of the Music Hall was basically a giant square with one massive stage along the south side and liquor bars directly across from that.

One cute and familiar face greeted me though, stage left. My newest friend, Lois Thelwell.

Lois closed the distance between us, then gave me a hug under my out-stretched coffees. "Morning," she murmured. I noted a sleepy tone to her voice.

Like so many Austin residents, Lois is a mishmash of weird and cool. I'd met her a few months back when my rock band first played the Music Hall, and that had been Lois's first week as stage manager slash sound engineer. No way anyone could forget her either. A shock of long, white-dyed hair contrasted beautifully against her dark skin and mirrored her bright smile. Straight out of high school, she was tough but personable, with a run-the-ship-my-way command far beyond her years, all tucked into a five-foot-nothing frame.

This wasn't the *Keep Austin Weird* stuff though. Lois sported a prosthetic right leg. It was air-brushed to a deep purple cast, sometimes even adorned with a white and black garter, like it was that morning. No, I'm not kidding. Boating accident when she was thirteen, she'd told me.

Lois was my kind of people. And she definitely made playing the Hall a helluva lot easier on me and the band.

"Hey, Lois." I grinned down through the gap between the tray and my chest. "Please don't make me spill these."

"Oops!" She let out a burst of laughter, then her head bopped the dough-nuts as she pulled away, making her laugh even more. "Dang! Sorry, I'm still drowsy." Lois has a sweet Tennessee accent.

I lifted an eyebrow. "Did you even go home last night?"

"Um—no, I *didn't*. No big deal. I always bring a change of clothes, in case. Classes are *over*."

"Ah, this is true. Well, take one of these. We can share." I lowered the tray so Lois could grab a cup.

"My hero," Lois purred, popped off the plastic lid, then breathed in the hot aroma.

"Thanks for being here to open up."

Lois looked up at me while taking her first sip, swallowed, grinned, then said, "Welcome. Cute t-shirt, *genius*."

I chuckled as I looked down at the letters on my chest, then nodded toward the paper bag. "There's sugar and creamer in this. And *doughnuts.*" I gingerly loosened my fingers so she could take the bag from me, then I searched around for a logical spot to place the tray. The drum riser looked good, so I moved to center stage, and set things in front of the kick drum.

Through a mouthful of pastry, Lois said, "You guys kicked *ass* last night. *Again.*"

I caught myself eyeing Lois in a way I hadn't before, in part because I was still waking up, and also because some daylight was streaming into the Hall, giving me a fresh view. In Nikes, skin-tight jean shorts, and a half-T, that enticingly showed some matching ink peeking out just above her hips, she sipped coffee again. I'd never been with a black girl, as far as I knew, but I'd definitely never been with a one-legged girl. It struck me, had anyone been with her? My mind wanders to strange places sometimes.

"Huh?" I blinked, then lifted my eyes to meet Lois's across the stage. "Oh. Yeah. Always a blast here, right? Crowd was into it. But—was it really us? Classes are out for Summer."

"Most of the crowd was digging *you,* of course. I shouldn't pump up that big head of yours some more, but you know the buzz you've got going on. My hand—you know, Rick—said two music producers approached him after the show, asking a ton of questions. He must've given them the heads up you'd be breaking down." Lois lifted her black eyebrows at me, then put her nose into the over-sized cup again. She sat her curvy butt on the keyboard riser, swallowed another sip, then smiled wide. "They're on their way right now."

I snorted. "Well, damn. That's strange." I pulled my phone from my pocket to check the time. "I've had label people sniff around before, but usually half drunk or talking bullshit at South-By. Never at ten in the morning."

"Get used to it." Lois stood, walked over, and held out our coffee. "Drink. You gotta be awake when they get here."

"One sec." I lifted my phone. "Need to make a quick call." I pressed a contact and listened to the dial.

After four rings, a groggy but richly feminine voice answered. "This better be good."

"Sorry, Jaz. But can you get your shiny self to the Hall? ASAP? I wanna prep for a showcase. Some label reps are comin' down, and I just got word."

There was silence on the other end. Two breaths. "I'll be there in twenty." She hung up.

I slipped my phone back in a pocket. "There we go," I said and reached for the coffee Lois still held out. "*Now* we're ready."

ABOUT FIVE MINUTES ticked by before the rest of my band started trickling in.

First up was Dasan 'Running Bear' Workman, our talented bass player.

Lois was drinking from our shared coffee again as I stepped up to greet him.

"Morning, boss." He glanced past me. "Hi, Lois."

Running Bear unslung an empty guitar bag from his back, then gently tossed it onto the stage near his bass.

I told him the news about the producers.

He looked at me quizzically. "Odd place and time, but okay." He stared at his bass. "Should I keep this handy?"

"Yeah. Let's be ready to blow it out," I replied.

"You got it. Any more of that?" He nodded hopefully at the cup in Lois's hand, and she promptly handed it to me before picking up a coffee for Running Bear.

Right then, drummer Kat Hixon walked through the open stage door, so Lois got a second coffee. Kat wore a signature flatcap, the sort you'd see on British cabbies.

Running Bear nodded at her, turned to gratefully take his cup from Lois, then sat on a corner of the drum riser.

I clinched hands twice with Kat. "Mornin'."

"Hey," she responded, simply, and smiled at Lois. "Morning."

Lois just handed her a coffee.

I filled Kat in on what was happening.

She glanced at the center stage drum riser. "Hmm. I'll warm up a bit. They might actually show." Kat's seen her share of the bad side of the music biz.

Agreeable chuckling cracked from Running Bear. Not for the first time I huffed, "Guys. They seem pretty invested, coming out this early. We'll find out soon enough. *Try* to be positive." I sipped the coffee I'd been sharing with Lois, and she and I exchanged smirks.

Lois chimed in. "The woman on the phone didn't come off like a bullshitter. Sounded French. And very excited to meet y'all."

I grinned at helpful, little Lois.

Clanking of metal and more laughs came from outside the stage doors. Seconds later, in came a trio of band members—Tabor, Lindie, and Pack.

These three showing up together was standard. Half a year ago, they'd decided to roommate up in a small house and had become thick as thieves, often practicing at the place when the whole band wasn't rehearsing out of our shared storage unit off of I-35.

"Hey! Long time no see," shouted Tabor. He walked just ahead of Pack and Lindie as they entered the back of the stage and waved over at Kat, who smacked greetings on her snare drum with a *brat-tat-tat*. The band's youngest member, eighteen-year-old lead guitarist Tabor Sergio Tamayo.

"Oh my God, tell me that's coffee I smell," Lindie yelled above the growing drum rumble and percussive snaps. Our keyboardist removed her sunglasses to reveal sparkling, green eyes, then searched for the source of the aroma.

Pack grinned and pointed toward the coffee cups. "Over there." Paz 'Pack' Mack—say that three times quickly—is our percussionist and an old friend of mine. He'll run around shirtless on stage, and yes, as you've already guessed, that's how he got his nickname. He's also in charge of the band when I'm not around.

Lindie bolted for the tray as Tabor and Lois exchanged a hug.

"You better leave one. Jasmine's coming. You know the way she gets about spit," I warned. (Lead vocalists hate germs even more than regular folks do.)

Pack shook my hand, chuckling, and moved closer so we could talk over Kat's drum barrage. "Jaz is coming to break-down?"

"Don't be crazy," I told him. "She's coming because I *asked* her to." I paused for effect. "There's a label coming to see us. I wanna be prepared, and since we're all here..."

Tabor turned around to face me, wide-eyed, apparently having no problem eavesdropping over the drums. "What? Seriously?"

I faced him. "Yeah. Probably here any minute."

"No! My best guitar's at the house!"

"And none of my saxes are here. Don't worry about it." I pointed at a reserve guitar Tabor had left near his stage monitor. "You'll do fine with *that*. These folks were here last night. If we play at all this morning, it'll just be icing."

"Woo!" Tabor bumped fists with Running Bear, ran over to his guitar stand, then started checking the strings and looking for his tuner. Running Bear, a smile on now, stood over his bass amp and began the same process.

Pack and Lois stood to either side of me for a moment before Lois appeared to have a thought, then said, "I'll be right back. I think I forgot to unlock the front doors." She hesitated. "Here." She handed our cup back, then half-ran down the stage-left stairs, in the direction of the foyer.

Lindie returned to my spot with a coffee in-hand. She finished a sip, then said, "Sounds pretty exciting. Know anything about the label yet?"

"Nothin'," I admitted. "Lois barely knew. But if they're coming this early in the morning, I know one thing about 'em...they aren't wasting time."

Kat stopped warming up, then twirled her sticks twice before sliding them into a leather holster on the side of her drum kit.

There was a brief pause, then: "I'm not sharing this coffee," Lindie said matter-of-factly. Our eyes met, and she gave me and Pack her trademark devilish look, with her nose in the cup, then strolled over to the keyboard riser. I couldn't help but laugh.

Pack said, "I doubt Tabor needs any caffeine. But me, I could go for a doughnut."

"Same," I agreed, realizing my stomach was grumbling.

We shuffled over to the coffee tray. I set my cup down to pick up the nearby paper bag so Pack could get an easy view inside.

"Take your pick. The powdered ones are jelly."

While Pack made his choice, I got hit by more than just hunger pangs. We needed a *win*. You bet Pack knew it too but wouldn't say it.

He grabbed one of the jelly doughnuts, then a napkin, and I snagged a plain, fried one and scooped up my half-empty coffee to go with it. We sat down in front of the drums to munch down our fill.

It helped to act like it was just another day in the life.

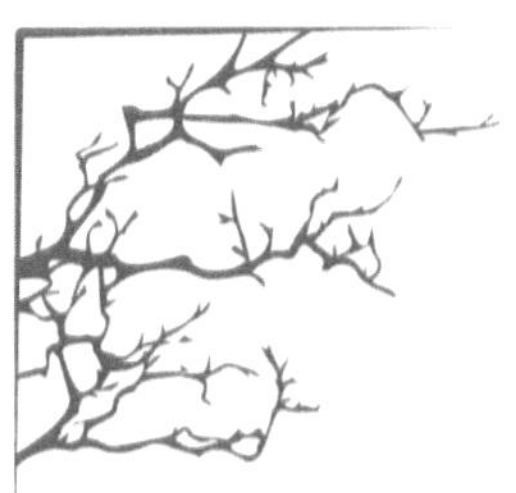

Chapter 2

No sooner had Lois walked back up the stage steps and grabbed our mutual coffee again, than two figures appeared at the end of the foyer near the main hall. One male and one very obviously female, silhouetted by the sunlight shining through the glass entrance doors. The pair walked out to where dimmed overhead lights shone down to reveal their faces.

They wore business clothing I'm sure cost what I make in a month and had a confident bearing and an air of anticipation about them.

"Good morning," said the mustached man, grinning.

His companion had high cheekbones and long auburn hair, and when she smiled it became very clear just how beautiful she was. She appeared older than me by a few years. If I'd had to guess, I'd have said the two were in their thirties, but extremely well-kept and athletic. They both stood arrow straight, not a hint of fat on either of them, almost like soldiers or two gray-clad pillars of roughly the same height. That last thought struck me odd, and I looked down at the woman's feet. She was wearing three- or four-inch heels.

The band was as quiet as that time in San Antonio when we'd stumbled into a bar full of Hells Angels. I moved quickly toward the lip of the stage and waved. "Hi!"

"Hello, Lochlan Nohr, I'm Conrad Wiprut." A German name, but the mustached man spoke perfect English. He gestured to his left. "And this is my associate and companion, Silana Michaux." *Silana Mish-OH*, I noted. "We've looked forward to meeting you for too long." The man and woman both walked toward me, expensive heels clicking on the concrete floor.

I crouched, swung my legs over the stage's edge and dropped down.

The three of us met near the center of the Hall and shook hands. Silana never lost her smile.

"Happy to meet you. Pretty unexpected though, I gotta say." I nodded over at Lois. "I'm told you're label reps." It wasn't really a question.

Silana answered in a musical voice, colored by a French accent. "*Oui.* We have seen your band perform several times. I'm sure you've guessed. We wish to know more. About you, and the other members. To get a feel for your artistic direction. Whatever you share will help us decide if we are a good match." She stared at me. "I have every reason to believe we are, but it would be bad business to make assumptions. Without some...*personal* discussion."

I noticed the emphasis on the word 'personal.' It wasn't a come-on though. Instead, I got the impression of some urgency.

"Um." I paused, trying to sort all the thoughts churning in my head. Realization that these people were seriously interested in the band—and appeared to have the finances—made me jump to the next logical phase. *Verify.* "Yeah. Yeah, of course. You have a card?"

Conrad barked a short laugh at that. "Sorry, sorry. Yes." He reached into the lapel of his suit jacket. "Here you go."

"We've been so excited to meet you, we've clearly forgotten ourselves," Silana said.

I read the card aloud: "Lucent Music Group." The shock took a second. "Holy fuck." I looked up and met Silana's blue-eyed gaze. "I mean..."

Silana laughed, but with no hint of being offended. "We did not mean to surprise you. 'Holy fuck' sounds about right."

Conrad laughed and smiled at Silana. "Indeed."

I swallowed and stood up straighter, pulled out my wallet and tucked the business card safely away. It was time to close the deal.

On cue, the sound of a front door drew everyone's attention away from me.

Into the Hall walked Jasmine, who stopped short at the sight of our visitors. She tugged some big, orange-framed sunglasses off her face. "Oh!" Then she took another step. "Good morning!"

"Morning, Jaz. *You're right on time*," I said.

"Um, I doubt that...but okay." Jasmine walked forward again.

"Conrad. Silana. I'm sure you remember our lead singer, Jasmine Medved. Jaz, they represent...*Lucent MG.*"

Conrad strode four long steps to greet Jasmine, with Silana not far behind.

"A great pleasure, Jasmine." Conrad put forth a hand that Jasmine shook warily, but she managed an awkward smile.

"Hello," offered Silana, along with her own hand.

Jaz reached up to check the pink ribbon securing her long, black hair. The ribbon matched the short boots she wore. The rest of her outfit consisted of a cut-off, faded yellow blouse, gold navel ring and jean shorts. By comparison, Jaz was a couple of hands taller than Lois, and about a half-dozen years older. She was the prettiest girl in the room—with one new, notable exception.

"Wow. You're *so beautiful*," Jaz said to Silana.

Silana only laughed. "You are adorable. *Merci*." She lightly touched Jaz's cheek and our lead singer stood transfixed.

I hated to break up the girl-girl moment, I have to admit, but business was business. "I invited Jaz down here this morning." An apparently genius move. "What I mean is—maybe you wanna hear a couple songs?" I looked back at the rest of the band, who watched intently, silently, except for the occasional staccato screech or whir from Tabor's fingers, nervously stretching over the strings and frets on his axe.

Silana's smile practically sparkled. "Music? Absolutely! But we'd love to meet your band first, please." She turned to the stage, still holding Jaz's hand, perhaps to reassure her. It appeared to be both genuine *and* working.

Jasmine smiled in my direction and nodded, so I approached the band and made introductions all around, hands being shaken from stage to ground level.

First, I introduced our guitar players. "This is our bass player, Dasan. Otherwise known as Running Bear. And this fast-fingered guitar prodigy next to him is Tabor."

For a frightening second, I thought Tabor would fall off the stage right onto Silana, he was so smitten with her, but luckily Running Bear pulled him back by his guitar strap in the nick of time.

If LMG sought to entice, Silana was definitely the right bait. However, as I stood near the stage, I noted that both our guests wore wedding rings.

Next up was our drummer. "This is Kat. She's the senior member of the band, but people have already mistaken her for Lois's sister."

Kat gave me some side-eye for that, but smiled at Silana and Conrad and politely shook their hands.

I moved on to keyboards. "Lindie here's the one with the piano chops, but she can tear up a dance floor, too. Used to do it professionally, right Lindie? Oh, and she practices at the gun range with me sometimes like every good little Texan should."

Lindie playfully fired a finger gun at me.

I came to Pack. "And this is my old chum and co-founder of Trip the Shark, Paz. But fans just call him Pack."

I also introduced Lois.

With all the introductions out of the way, I quickly grabbed two tall stools from one of the bars and set them near the agents, smack dab in the Hall's center. The pair nodded gratefully and sat.

Once Jaz and I were on stage, I pointed at her untouched coffee. She made love to the brew for a full minute. Finally, Jaz gave me a satisfied grin, and in-turn, I gave the band a series of reassuring looks, and a thumbs up to Lois, who'd made her way to the sound engineer's booth. I called out one of our vocal duets. A ballad called "Take A Minute."

Lindie began the song with a solo piano intro. The rhythm section kicked in on the fifth bar.

Then it was Jasmine's turn:

You can take a minute baby
You can take an hour maybe
You can take a day to get away
While I think of things to say

Jaz has a beautiful soprano. We co-composed "Take A Minute" along with Lindie, and Jaz could wrench your guts out with the soul she poured in. This morning, with just an audience of two, she sang as if the future of her and her son depended on it. That wasn't much of a stretch but the reactions coming from the LMG reps were all rainbows and unicorns.

Silana swayed on her stool to the slow beat, her eyes closed, and Conrad had his phone out recording. A huge, toothy smile stretched across his face.

That's when I first felt it was really happening. The dream of catching that musician's big break. The record deal, the tours, the studio sessions. *The fame.* Your music heard by millions.

I came in on the second verse, pulling my microphone off its stand and belting my baritone. I fixed eyes on Silana as lyrics intensified:

> **I know that I don't have much money**
> **But sometimes I am kinda funny**
> **And the way that you look in a smile means the world to me**

Jaz and I blended harmonies on the chorus:

> **Ya do me just fine**
> **You're like a sweet drink of wine**
> **Ya do me just fine**
> **You're like a sweet drink of wine**

Then the band pushed into the bridge:

> **I'm just a poet inside, born to make rhymes**
> **About life's beautiful ride**
> **But sometimes I get scared and hide**
> **Because it's so real, and I have so much feel**
> **So I set myself right**
> **And adjust my tie**
> **And look ole life straight in the eye, and ask:**
> **Forgive me, forgiveness please**

Tabor crunched a sweet guitar solo, and Shark finished out strong, until the song ended just as it had begun. Four beautiful bars from Lindie's piano steadily dwindled into silence.

I snapped my eyes open.

Silana and Conrad were already off their tall stools and applauding.

"Nice job," I whispered to Jasmine, who had walked over for a one-armed hug, though we never turned away from Silana and Conrad. She shook nervously, so I gave her a second squeeze.

Jaz sighed. "Jesus," she breathed. "Think we did it?"

"Looks that way." I smiled at her and then stepped forward, pulling Jaz with me as we took a bow. I waved an arm around the stage to acknowledge the band.

"You gave me goosebumps," said Silana, rubbing a forearm beneath her jacket sleeve. "See?" She raised both brows at Conrad. "*Oui?*"

"Oh, yes. No doubt about it." Conrad stepped toward us. "We've heard enough, my friends. *Please.* Pack your things and join us for lunch, because it'd be our great pleasure to treat you all, where we can talk properly about your future—" Conrad raised an imaginary stein in his right hand "—over beers!"

That did it. Whoops and affirmations burst out of Trip the Shark like a breaking of the proverbial dam. I calmed down and said, "You heard the man. Get the gear loaded up. I could use a beer right about now!"

More laughter reverberated around the hall.

Grabbing Jasmine's hand, I said low, for only the two of us, "Please keep our big shots happy. This'll be quick."

Jaz stood on tiptoe, pulled my head down by the scruff of my t-shirt, and kissed me on the cheek, then retreated—just about floated—down the steps to the agents. Lois joined them.

After what had to be the record for quickest breakdown of drums, congas, racks, monitors, and instruments, we had our cars loaded up and ready to caravan to lunch.

Conrad told us to meet up at Z'Tejas, a restaurant-grill converted from a 19th century Victorian home, three streets over from the Hall. I knew the place well.

I insisted Lois join us, so she jumped into my ancient—*but paid for*—four-door Volvo.

The Bomber, as I call her, is a dark green sedan with leather seats, in remarkably good condition for a vehicle with well over three hundred thousand miles on it. I keep waiting for her to quit, but she just keeps on going. The old girl has hardly any electronics onboard, and that appeals to my paranoid side. I don't much relish the idea of some hacker drone-steering me off a road, so I end up on YouTube—or worse—in the local morgue.

The band caravaned it in a hurry, and we were valet parked behind Z'Tejas within ten minutes, not only to keep our gear-packed vehicles safe, but because Conrad had insisted. If you've ever tried to find a parking spot in Downtown Austin, you can appreciate just how happy this made everybody.

It was still morning when Trip the Shark and our new, favorite reps funneled up through the double doors into the colorful Southwestern stylings of Z'Tejas. The mingled smells of jalapenos, roast chicken, fried pork, and baking corn made my mouth water.

LMG had thought ahead (no surprise) and reserved a pair of large tables in a corner of the restaurant's open-air porch, and we were led to our seats without delay.

"Welcome to Z'Tejas! My name's Cindy, and I'll be your server today."

Orders were made—beer on the way. We were the only group on the porch.

Above the bar was one large, flat-screen television. The guy bartending flipped its power on by remote, and the black screen blinked the current time in white before switching to some full-color program: 11:43 a.m.

The waitress returned with a full tray of salsa, queso, and tortilla chips. Down the line of the two connected tables, Tabor bantered with Running Bear, scooping up mouthfuls of salsa at the same time. Lindie and Kat sat across from those two and were both quietly checking text messages on their handhelds. Lois smiled at me and crunched chips in her hands before dipping the halves into a bowl of queso.

Silana spoke to me first.

"I was disappointed. You did not play your saxophone...but you sing so very well. It is shocking really, how powerful your voice is. You've had...vocal training?"

"Yeah," I replied. "At North Texas, all part of the music program. I took vocal lessons my senior year. Was told I had a good voice. Shocked me too. I was too used to having an instrument in my mouth all the time. Singing was just an afterthought, right? But Macey, my coach—Macey *Woodward*—pushed me hard. *Real* hard. Range between tenor and baritone is 'outrageous.' Macey's words, not mine. As far as lungs go, no surprise, I've got hot-air-to-spare."

"You're a mutant, Loch," teased Jaz. "Just look at him, Silana. Is there anything about him that isn't 'outrageous?' "

Her comment drew amused snorts and tittering from the room, especially from Silana, Pack, and Lois.

"All right, all right. Ha-ha. You get there's a *brain* in here, right?" I tapped my temple with an index finger. "I didn't ask to be this big. But I don't care about football." I reached out for a corn chip. "And believe me, there're coaches all over Texas still crying about it." I crunched the chip loudly.

Paz patted my back. "My secret plan from the moment we put Shark together? I'd never have to carry the heavy gear again." He gave me a mockingly surprised look. "What I never told you?"

Everyone laughed, including me. "You see what I deal with, Silana?"

"To be honest, I just see friends who make great music together. Future stars. *That's* what I see," she answered. "And a man with extraordinary gray eyes, if I'm being frank."

My lips curled into a half-smile at that last remark, and Silana showed me all of her pearly whites.

"And we mean to work with you. *All* of you," Conrad added. "Look around." He gestured. "You're a marketing team's dream. Beautiful songs, good looks, personality. Stage presence. Your reputation is well deserved. That's why we've come out this morning...we didn't want to give the competition a chance to steal you away." He paused for effect. "You should be recording with us. You should be on LMG."

I blinked. The tables grew quiet, and Kat and Lindie briskly put their handhelds away.

Thankfully, the waitress brought us our drinks, which broke some of the tension. She put beers in front of us, except for Tabor and Lois, who had to suffer with Cokes.

Cindy the waitress put on her biggest smile yet. "Can I get y'all anything else before your orders come out?" asking only me really.

I looked around the table and got nothing but vacant stares and negative nods. "We're good, Cindy."

Cindy fluttered her eyelashes. I'd seen it before. "Your food'll be out soon. Just holler if you need me."

"I might scream," I joked.

Cindy laughed, bit her lip, and walked away.

Jaz elbowed me in the ribs. "You are *so bad*."

"What?" I mustered my most innocently indignant tone.

"Just stop. You keep flirting with her, she might drop our food," Jaz poked.

"Or worse." Pack lifted his bottle. "My next beer."

More laughter.

"Point taken," I conceded. "I'll behave."

I looked expectantly at Silana and Conrad.

Conrad took the hint and reached down into a leather brief he had brought with him. He pulled out two copies of what I presumed were recording contracts. They looked more like manuscripts, or short phone books. He handed one to Pack and one to me. "Scan the first few pages please."

Pack and I each hefted our copies.

"Holy shit," gasped Tabor.

Running Bear whistled.

And Jaz let out a nervous giggle.

"Yeah," I agreed.

Silana said, "What you have there are binding recording contracts guaranteeing you at least six albums with our company, in exchange for exclusive rights to Trip the Shark for the period of time it takes to make and release those CDs." She smiled at me when I looked up from the novella of a contract. "Of course, we do not expect you to sign anything before you consult an attorney."

Conrad continued: "Take those home with you. Go visit your attorney as soon as you can. Hopefully both of you will sign. After all, you two are the founders." He looked around the tables. "After that's done, we'll have smaller contracts for the rest of you."

I doubt anyone in the band was even breathing at that point.

"And that will be that. I'm sure you'll find this agreement to your liking, gentlemen," Silana said.

"To making great music together then," Conrad said, lifting his beer.

Silana also raised hers. "And buckets of money," she added in her delicious accent.

Like the finale at a high school graduation, the sound of joyous hoots and howls reverberated off the metal roof of the restaurant's porch.

Everyone shook hands with Silana and Conrad, except for Lois, who was getting hugs from the band, including me.

Once Trip the Shark had hugged one another at least once, we managed to calm down again.

I saw the bartender and Cindy standing together near the bar, watching us with bewildered smiles. The television above them swapped from a floor cleaner commercial to the News at Noon from KXAN Austin.

It was the intense joy in the room that put me on edge first. When things go too right, I tend to get paranoid. Blame it on broken parents probably, but whatever my reasons, I have learned to take no good turn without watching my back.

But sometimes—*sometimes I just get a feeling.*

I had to call Harry when I got out of there. Harry Bruckman. An entertainment lawyer I met in between sets a couple years back. He became a fan first and a friend later, and as it turned out, his reputation in musician circles is stellar. He handles a lot of heavyweights in the Austin movie and music scenes.

I looked at the television but didn't really see it. My eyes were unfocused. My mind was still on the legalities and ramifications of success.

Unfocused, until I saw the name Victoria appear on the TV screen, inside a stark white-on-black word box. Victoria Ann.

My vision snapped sharp. The last name. Bold, white letters again.

Lott.

Victoria Ann Lott. Above the name hovered her photograph.

I walked a few steps toward the television, away from our crowd. "I'm sorry, but can you turn the sound up?" I made eye contact with Cindy for just a second.

She appeared startled, again, but hurriedly reached for the nearby remote. "Sure," Cindy replied.

Our waitress moved away from the bar so she could get a clean angle to aim the remote, and then there was volume up on the flat-screen.

"Hey. *Guys...*" My voice wasn't quite a shout, but it was definitely a command. I needed to hear.

I heard Lois shushing everyone on the porch behind me.

"...missing since Friday evening. Victoria Lott was last seen on campus security camera footage, here" —a petite woman with medium length hair was shown on the television screen at some distance— "walking through a parking garage located near University of Texas, Austin's Communications building—presumably going to her car. Miss Lott is a speech therapy professor at UT, in her second year. NBC's Michelle Sneeringer has the latest. Good morning, Michelle."

The television switched views away from the surveillance footage, back to a blonde reporter standing next to a screen scrolling various images of Victoria.

"The search began today with police, co-workers, and friends retracing Victoria Lott's steps. Nobody realized she'd been missing until she failed to show up to work earlier this morning. That's unfortunately valuable time lost, as investigators and family begin to look for answers."

I was distantly aware of bodies gathered around me. Gentle hands touched my back.

Lois walked in front of me and peered up at the flat-screen.

But it was Silana's voice that broke me out of my trance.

"You know her, Lochlan?"

I took a deep breath.

"Yes."

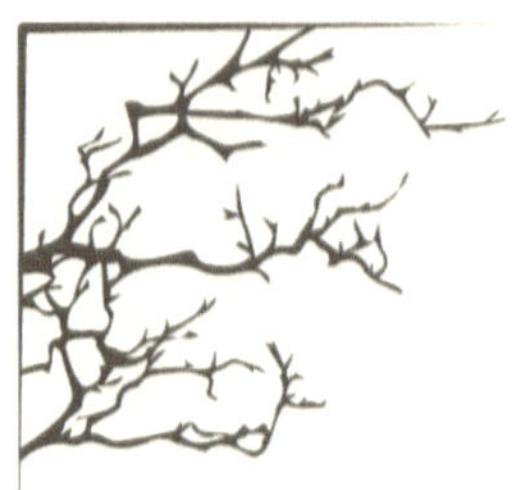

Chapter 3

"Hi, Mom."

My mother, Tressa Nohr, was sitting in an aquamarine-padded, metal chair—the sort you'd expect to find in a hospital hallway—facing a white wall and looking wistfully out of the only window in her spartan room. There was a large pond about a football field's distance beyond the window, with a giant fountain in its center spouting gouts of water in all directions.

On a single-sized bed tucked into the nearby corner, a white and gray cat with black paws, barely an adult, played happily with a fuzzy, red ball. As I showed myself fully in the doorway, it froze and locked eyes on me.

"Hey, Mittens," I said to the cat in a high-pitched tone. She popped onto her four paws and padded expectantly around on the bed's orange blanket, not making a sound and never taking her eyes off me. I sat on the bed close to my mother and scratched Mittens behind the ears.

The cat purred and rubbed against my fingers.

Mom turned to look at me, and her face cracked into a long smile, warmed even more by her moist, brown eyes. My mother had gained more weight, I noticed. Her brown hair was tied back.

"Sweetheart!" My mother reached out to squeeze my hand. Her hand was cool, but the grip was strong.

I leaned over and kissed her cheek.

"Mittens is bigger every time I see her," I said.

Mom petted Mittens briefly down her furry spine. "I refill her bowl, and the food just vanishes. She has your appetite."

"Oh-oh." I ruffled Mittens on the head. She swatted at me happily. "If she gets big enough, we can parlay that into getting you a larger room." I didn't dare mention my mother's own added pounds. A guy learns a few things along the way.

Mom laughed lightly. "I'd rather just bring her home," she said.

A tightness in my chest wrestled with my words trying to come out. "Me too."

My mother gazed into my eyes and read my mind the way mothers do. "What's wrong, Son?"

I smiled tightly, breathed in deep once, and then out through my nose in a rush. "Crazy day, Mom. Crazy day." I looked down and poked Mittens in the belly. The cat gently nibbled my left index finger. "My band got offered a record deal this morning."

Mom's eyes went wide, and her mouth dropped open a notch. "Lochlan! Oh, my boy! That's *wonderful*!" But she caught my mood and shook her head. "Isn't it?"

"Yeah! Of course. I mean...it should be." I pulled my hand away from Mittens and then pressed all my fingers briefly against my temples. "I mean. It is, but..."

"Tell me," Mom urged.

"I wasn't sure if I should say anything... Victoria—Vicki *Lott* is missing. Police are searching for her right now."

Mom gasped.

I looked resignedly at my mother. "You remember me talking about her, right? We met at North Texas. She was in my class that day—"

"Oh my God—yes, of course I remember! You were in *love* with her, Loch." My mother gazed out the window again. "My God, the poor girl. How can this be happening to her? Something so horrible twice?" She paused. "You don't think it's related to the shooting, do you? What do the police say happened?"

"I hope to hell not. But there isn't much to go on yet. Cam footage has her walking through a parking garage. Her car was found locked. And no signs of a struggle anywhere. But she hasn't been seen since Friday. Nobody even knew she was missing until this morning." I shook my head. "I didn't have a clue she was a teacher at UT!"

My mother stared at the water fountain.

"I'm really sorry, Mom. I shouldn't have told you. You—"

"Go find her, Lochlan."

"Mom, what—"

"I know you. You're already planning to search for her. Stop worrying about *me*." She turned in her chair and faced me with a stern glare. "I'm doing better each day, but that sweet girl is in real trouble again. And you're so smart, Son. You still love her. You can help her. You know it and so do I."

I smiled at my mother, beaten. "You're amazing, you know *that*?"

"I love you, and I'm so proud." Mom pointed toward the exit from her room. "Now get going. Let me know when you find her. *Then* we can talk about all the good news."

I petted Mittens farewell. She tried to wrestle my hand to the bed, but I flipped her over lightly so that she failed to get a grip, and then I stood, bent over, and kissed my mother on her forehead.

"I'll be back as soon as I can. Love you, Mom."

Mom patted my hand reassuringly. "You too."

I began to leave, but stopped as I neared the door and asked over my shoulder, "Have you had any other visitors this week?"

"Yes. Your Uncle Conor. And Jerry visited again yesterday."

I grimaced but made sure to not let her see.

"Good. That's—good." I felt my eyes watering. "Bye, Mom. I'll be back soon with news."

"Good luck! I'll be praying."

I left Mom's room, turned right and walked down a long hall dotted with a few elderly men and women in a mixture of robes and casual clothes. The smell of bleach was strong in the air.

I hate hospitals even though my own mother is a registered nurse. Or maybe because she is.

I recognized the two nurses near the visitors' arrival station for the Elderly Ward. They wore semi-casual attire with name tags, not white uniforms. Both waved at me as I approached.

"Hi, George. Hi, Lateisha."

"Hello, Loch."

"Hi, Loch."

"How's your mom today?" Lateisha asked.

"Seems in good spirits. She's gained some weight—but I'll take that any day over her starving herself."

"The food is pretty good here," said George, patting himself on the belly. George was definitely no string bean.

I chuckled but cut it short. "Um, look, she said 'Jerry' visited her again yesterday." I put out my hand expectantly. Before I'd arrived to visit, I'd been hopeful that Mom would be released soon, but the whole 'Jerry' thing had made me unsure again.

George clenched his lips and reached down under the standing desk he was next to. He handed me a clipboard with the signed visitors log for Sunday.

I gave it a once-over and pressed my lips together tightly.

"I'm sorry, Lochlan," offered Lateisha. George nodded.

I nodded back and handed the clipboard to George.

"Bye, guys," I said.

The somber pair waved goodbye at me.

A minute later, I was back in the Bomber and exiting the parking lot of Austin Waters Mental Health Hospital, out onto East 32nd Street.

As always, 'Jerry' hadn't signed the visitors' list.

I WOULD HELP SEARCH for Vicki, like Mom had told me to, but I had other responsibilities I couldn't ignore. Harry Bruckman, Entertainment Lawyer, was expecting me.

I'd left Z'Tejas earlier that afternoon, after I quelled everyone's concerns for me first. I explained that Victoria Lott was an old college friend I'd lost touch with, that I was worried, obviously, but that our deal with LMG was my current priority.

That last part had been a lie, but it had worked enough to calm everyone down. I'd then called Harry Bruckman and made a same-day appointment.

I'm pretty sure Lois knew I was in pain when I dropped her off at her car back at the Music Hall, but she hadn't pushed the subject. She made me promise to call her with updates though.

Mondays, just after lunchtime, are my most regularly repeated visits to see Mom, and I had dropped in on her right on schedule.

So, it was almost exactly 4 p.m. by the time I fought my way through Austin rush hour traffic to the parking garage behind the Bruckman and Myers law offices.

When I exited the garage elevator on the eleventh floor of Harry's office tower, Pack was waiting for me in the tiled lobby, only a few yards outside the glass walls that showed off Bruckman's suite entry. He moved like a decathlon athlete getting ready to high jump, arms crisscrossing, while bobbing up and down excitedly from heel to toe.

Pack put a hand on my shoulder as we walked together to Harry's office. The brunette receptionist behind the glass doors flashed us a smile. "How you doin', man?"

"Keepin' it together," I responded. "This should be a happy day, right?"

"Yeah," Pack agreed. He slapped me on the shoulder. "Fuck yeah it should be!" He stopped me with a firm grip on my arm. "Yo, but listen, hermano. I can see you're upset. Just let me know if I can help out. *Help find her.* Whatever you need. I'm there."

I smiled at Pack and nodded. "Thanks, man. 'Preciate it."

Pack laughed. "Now, let's go get rich!"

HARRY BRUCKMAN SAT hunched forward in his tall-backed, leather executive chair, one hand scratching well-groomed stubble on his jaw, the other hand strafing across a contract, before he turned a page. He looked like a balding, suit-clad college professor—sans his jacket hanging in a corner—grading an A plus paper from a C student. Confused, happy, and a little concerned. His shirt sleeves were rolled up.

Pack and I stayed quiet but kept nervously looking at one another, like someone had called us into the principal's office. What can I say? Harry's office reminded me of high school. The only thing that canceled the overall effect was the incredible view overlooking Downtown Austin, stretching out behind Harry through a series of large windowpanes.

Finally, Harry spoke up.

"This contract...is pure *win*." Harry shook his head and scrunched his face. "I mean, they're giving you *everything* you could want. Bonuses. Huge points. Merchandising. High per diem. Travel costs." Harry paused and raised a gesturing hand, his eyes still scanning the LMG bibles. "I don't really get it. Don't get me wrong—you guys are terrific. It's just that I've never seen a deal as sweet as this before. I sure as hell wouldn't give it out, and I like you guys."

I glanced at Pack and raised my eyebrows. In return, he showed me a greedy, Cheshire Cat smile. I laughed silently, feigned disgust, and then locked my eyes to the top of Harry's bald pate. He was sweating. I don't think I'd ever seen Harry Bruckman sweat.

After another minute, Harry looked up at us and grinned, tossing both hands up in surrender. "Congratulations, Loch. Paz." He pushed the almost identical contracts back toward us across his desk. "*Sign* them. Before they self-destruct."

I stared at the stack of papers, my full name typed inside a space near the top. **Lochlan Donatello Nohr**. They'd even researched my middle name.

Pack grabbed a pen from a wire cup on Harry's desk and I followed suit. We both signed our respective contracts. I signed my name in big, semi-cursive sweeps, added the date, and blew once across the black ink to dry it fast, then sat back in my chair holding the heavy, world-changing contract before me.

"Wow," I said.

"Ha! *Boy!* Look at us!" Pack punched me on my left arm. "*Rock stars!*"

I laughed and forgot about Victoria for a moment. I reached over and shook hands with Pack.

"To think I almost turned down that runway gig the day we met."

"Thank God you were just that fucking broke," Pack replied, laughing.

I nodded and said, "Speaking of money, how much we owe you, Harry?"

Harry looked at me and put up his right hand, index finger to thumb. "Zip," he told us. "Like I said, the contract is generous. LMG's covering my fee."

"Damn," I replied. I thought about that. "Well, in that case, consider yourself our attorney for-damn-near-ever, Harry."

I stood up. So did Pack. I offered my hand to Harry Bruckman. "Thank you."

Pack shook hands with Harry, too.

"My pleasure, boys. Very happy for you. Tell the rest of the band to come see me with their contracts. Once they have them, which should be soon."

"Will do," I said.

Pack and I left the office of Bruckman and Myers.

Back outside the elevator, in the parking garage, I reached into my wallet and fished out the business card that Conrad Wiprut had given me that morning. "Did you get a card?"

Pack looked embarrassed. "*Mierda.* No!" He took out his phone.

I read him the number from Conrad's card, and Pack quickly punched it into his contacts. "Got it," he said.

"Okay, good. I'm calling in that favor right now. Arrange dinner for the two of us with LMG. For tomorrow night. Handle whatever else they might need." I put Conrad's card away. "I'll be busy the rest of today—and probably most of tomorrow."

"No problem," Pack replied. He gave me a serious look. "You sure you don't want me to tag along?"

"Yeah. Yeah, I'm sure. I need to figure out where to even start."

With no warning, Pack grabbed me into a bear hug, his book of a contract slapping me on my back. I narrowly avoided getting a knock on my jaw from the top of his head. "Good luck, 'mano." He squeezed harder. "Be careful. I will say a prayer."

I gave him a gently crushing hug back. "I'll try, man. Thanks."

We stepped apart.

I grinned at Pack and chuckled. "All right. Don't go gay on me. Let's get shit done! Make those calls and spread the good word. I'm sure everyone's dyin' to know what the fuck is going on."

Pack let out a loud, "Woo!" and waved his contract overhead in farewell.

As I watched Pack leave, I took a deep breath and stared out across the crowded rows of cars.

All I could think about was Victoria Lott.

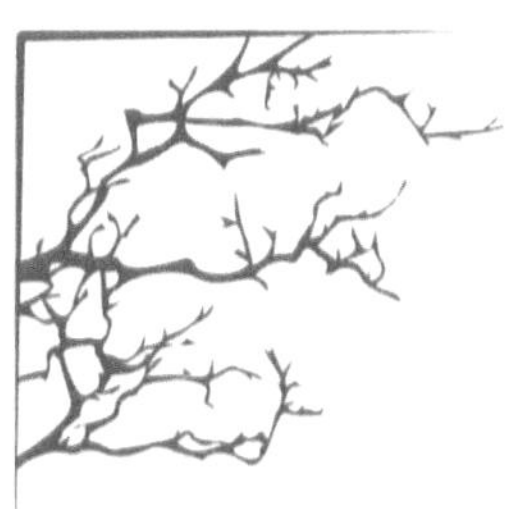

Chapter 4

In the Bruckman and Myers parking garage, I started up the Bomber and let the engine idle with the AC on. Then I dropped a few keywords into an anonymous search on my phone.

Although it was almost five o'clock in Austin, I knew I still had a few of hours of daylight left and meant to use them wisely. Reasoning I was an amateur about to go snooping after a missing person, there was no better place to begin than at the beginning. That meant, based on what little I knew up to that point, I needed to head to the University of Texas campus and find the parking garage where Vicki had been last spotted. Better yet, I hoped to find her car there and possibly some cops watching over it.

In mere seconds, my first web search pointed me to a campus map of UT. I was only vaguely familiar with the campus from a few visits, so my memory of it was foggy.

I opened my phone's browser to search up speech and language pathology, therapy, and communications. Vicki was a speech therapy professor, so logically her garage would be near the building her office was housed in. I assumed a communications department building, but I needed to be certain.

Department of Communications Sciences and Disorders. Sounded right. Professor Victoria A. Lott; Moody College of Communication. Jesse H. Jones Communication Center. *Bingo!*

I scanned a campus map and found the block housing the communications buildings wedged between Guadalupe and West 25th streets.

Another search and I found what I was looking for. San Antonio Garage. It was due west of the communications college. Not a sure thing, but it was the garage closest to Vicki's office.

My freshly signed contract with LMG lay on the floorboard of the passenger's side. I stared at it for a few seconds, almost expecting it to chastise me for being such a gigantic idiot.

But the contract was just a contract. I snapped on my seat belt and got the Bomber rolling.

I REALIZED, AS I WAS crawling north through rush-hour traffic, that I was bound to end up on the suspects list. 'Old friend' comes creeping around the scene of the crime. The same day Vicki goes missing. No cop *wouldn't* suspect me.

So, I decided I couldn't disclose more about myself than was necessary. I'd *be the ninja*. Part of my mission to the parking garage would be to assess the security scheme there. And the failures especially. This meant I'd be looking for cameras, scanners and drones. It also meant I'd have to avoid the damn things if I could.

Yeah, nothing suspicious about me at all.

The harsh reality about life in the United States was that every 'authority' I might run across would be just as suspect as any random college student or campus employee. Police violence against civilians and criminal violence against police was commonplace, so I'd learned to avoid confrontations. You stayed alive if you did.

Not to say there aren't good cops out there. There are. I'd dealt with plenty of upstanding police and sheriff's deputies while playing my gigs. But in recent years, the 'Police State of America' mentality had washed down even into independence-minded Texas. You had to watch your ass, keep aware, or end up in a jail mighty quick. After that, you stood a decent chance of getting dead.

AFTER TWENTY MINUTES of traffic I reached the exterior of the San Antonio Garage. The parking facility was sturdily built of gray concrete floors and red brick walls, punctuated with glassless windows on the sides, so I could see vehicles within. I counted seven parking floors, including the rooftop.

Students were walking the sidewalk outside, but not too many. I expected the garage would be fairly vacant. Spring classes were out, and the summer session hadn't started up either.

Along Nueces, parallel to the sidewalk, was a line of parked cars. Among those were a campus police car and a Channel 42 news van. The van had an opened side-door, and several crew members milled about.

Just past the van, I stopped the Bomber in the road and carefully scrutinized the entryway. Luckily there was no traffic behind me.

There weren't any security cameras evident at the entrance. That was a surprise. There had to be cams somewhere inside, and I knew that, by law, there would be signs warning of video surveillance. There were plenty of signs on the exterior warning about towing—shocker—but none outside about monitoring my every move.

I silently cursed the fact that security wasn't tighter. That had contributed to Vicki's disappearance, but I also recognized one big advantage for *me*—that I might drive into the garage without being immediately recorded on a campus-cop DVR.

But I got an even bigger break. I noticed a sign on the corner building straight to my left, next to the parking garage, so I drove up to read it. Fricano's Deli. With a parking lot. More cop cars and news vans. And a car vacating a parking spot!

I drove in and quickly grabbed the parking space directly in front of the deli, then locked the Bomber, despite the cop presence. Yeah, I'm the cautious type.

The small corner plaza also had a Smoothie King and a Starbucks. So, three places in total where I could easily ask questions, without attracting the attention of the cops. I couldn't believe my good luck.

"What is hip?"

My text message ringtone sang at me from a jeans pocket.

I fished the phone back out. The text was from Tabor. It read something like:

OMG OMG OMG!1! Yes yes yes!!

Punctuated with a half-dozen emoticons.

And so it began. I put my phone away.

In the lot behind me there was a mixture of UT cops, Austin PD uniforms, plain-clothes detectives, and journalists with the occasional cameraman in tow. I wasn't ready to deal with any of that crowd, so I marched straight for Fricano's.

The deli was fairly busy with a happy-hour crowd of almost a dozen people. It was the humble, homey, college hang you'd expect. The Specials dry-erase board behind the counter had a Che Guevara face sketched in green on it. Because Marxist ghosts make everything taste better.

"What is hip?"

Another text. I grimaced but ignored it.

I approached the lighted, glass deli display and the lone cashier in the far corner. A round-faced, middle-aged woman walked up behind the register.

"What can I get you, handsome?" She offered a welcoming smile, but with a nervous edge. Not surprising, considering the action in the parking lot.

I eyed a short spinner-rack of chip bags.

"I'll just take some salt and vinegar chips. And an ice tea, please."

"Black or green?"

"Black, thanks."

The cashier rang me up then poured my tea into a Styrofoam cup. "Go ahead and grab your chips," she told me.

I plucked potato chips from the rack and then tore the bag open. I *was* hungry. "Have they had any luck finding the missing teacher?" I kept my tone casual.

"No." The woman stopped pouring. "Word's getting around. Talk of a volunteer search being put together."

"Anyone from these shops see her on Friday?"

"Um, Vicki stops in here sometimes. Such a sweet girl. But I didn't work that day. Haven't heard of anyone around here talking to her recently. But like I said, word is spreading. So someone might have." She pointed at my tea. "You want this sweetened?"

"Yeah. Any raw sugar?"

She picked up a brown packet and then shook it at me.

"Yep, that's the stuff. One packet's fine." I ventured more questioning. "So, you know Victoria…"

"Uh-huh. But not very well. I've worked here for *years*. Meet plenty of professors. Vicki's one of the newer ones." She stirred the sugar into my cup.

Something tempted me to tell this nice lady a little more about my personal relationship with Vicki, but I reminded myself to shut-the-hell-up. Word was spreading. And I didn't have time—Vicki didn't have time—for hassles best avoided.

"I think I'd like to help out with that search. Any idea who I'd talk to?"

The cashier popped a lid on my tea then placed it on the counter. "That'll be two seventy-eight. Sorry, I don't know much else. You could go ask one of the cops outside?"

I handed her three dollars.

"Yeah, I'll do that," I lied.

"*What is hip?*"

Text message of insanely happy misspellings number *three*, I assumed. Again, I ignored it.

The cashier lady must have been very used to phones making odd and unexpected noises. She didn't flinch and handed my change back. "Have a nice night. Come see us again. You should try one of our subs."

"Thanks, I will." I dropped my change into a beer pitcher marked 'Tips.'

I headed for the exit and glanced around the deli one more time. Couples and singles, mostly of student age, but with a couple gray-hairs mixed in, hardly noticed me. They were either engrossed in a handheld device or reading one of the local newspapers. I took my chips and tea outside and headed around the corner, back toward the San Antonio Garage entrance.

The sun had dimmed, and some rainclouds were moving in. Brisk air left little doubt it'd get wet soon, so I hustled into the parking garage.

There was no guard kiosk. Instead, everything was automated with the standard ticket dispenser and seesaw gate. I adopted my best impression of a college kid with his drink and chips—okay, a college *football player* with his drink and chips—and began my exploration. Floor by floor.

Besides the yellow crime scene tape I expected I'd run into eventually, I looked for anything unusual and paid extra attention to stairway doors, elevators, and surveillance cams. The cameras were placed predictably on each floor, and, unlike at the entrance, I started spotting metal signs warning about video recording on the property. Each floor had an elevator in one corner, stairs in the opposing one. Security cameras were near the elevators and were angled out to take in the area in front of the shafts, as well as a good portion of the garage floor itself, especially the driving lane. I made sure to not get too close to the cams and didn't stop walking. This made it tough to calculate the field of view of the cameras, but I got it done in my head anyway.

And I didn't like my conclusions.

By the time I reached the mostly empty third floor, with only one car exiting past me, I noticed the cameras were all angled in such a way that the stairway entrances weren't in view. The same thing held true for floors four and five. I mean, the cameras *could* have been pointed out across one half of each garage floor, in a straight shot between the elevators and the stairs. They just weren't. And whether or not that was nefarious or status quo, it meant that if I wanted to, I could walk up or down those stairs and wouldn't be recorded. *Son of a bitch*.

On the fifth floor, I entered the stairway. No camera greeted me inside the shaft. I walked down a floor. *No camera*. Up to the sixth floor. *Nada*.

I took a deep breath, and the hairs on the back of my neck stood up. I was sure I'd just solved part of the mystery.

I exited the stairs on the sixth floor. All that was left from here was the rooftop, so it was no huge surprise when I practically tripped over yellow and black tape attached to orange cones all surrounding a single car and blocking off two adjacent, empty parking spaces. I was willing to bet a million bucks, not a camera in range either.

I moved around the perimeter of the police tape a few feet. Then I saw the police car.

The driver's side door opened on the police cruiser. A thirty-something, Hispanic woman in University of Texas Police Department uniform stepped out. *Shit*.

"Hi, can I help you?" She sounded friendly enough.

I feigned surprise. "Ah! Hi, officer. Didn't expect anyone up here." I meant to divert her from asking the questions. "What's happened? Something I should be worried about?" I waved my iced tea in the direction of Vicki's car, which was a new-looking silver, four-door, Kia sedan.

The policewoman relaxed her stance a little. To help her along, I donned my best expectant puppy dog gaze and waited.

"Abandoned vehicle. A faculty member in a missing person's case."

"That's awful. Who? Hope not one of my old profs." The implication was that I was a UT student. Again, to calm her. But I wasn't lying. I *wasn't* a UT student currently. It allowed me some outs if I had to do any dancing around the hard truth.

"Professor Victoria Lott," she said. "Report came in this morning."

"That explains why I haven't heard about it," I lied. I glanced at the Kia. "Looks practically new. So, not a carjacking…" I took two casual steps closer to the officer to get a look at the driver's side. The policewoman didn't appear to mind. In fact, she'd been more talkative than I would have expected. Being stuck at the top of a parking garage, I could imagine why.

My phone chirped, "*What is hip?*"

I rolled my eyes and swore silently to Jesus Christ.

I gave the policewoman a sheepish look and held out my bag of potato chips. "Would you mind? I need to check this text."

The officer laughed and held the bag for me.

I smiled, reached into my left hip pocket for my phone, and said to the officer, "Feel free to have some of those."

The text messages were each from Tabor, Lindie, Jaz and Running Bear, in that order. I would read them carefully later, but a quick scan showed me they were all basically along the same emotional high as Tabor's had been, the exception being Running Bear, who was always pretty chill.

I tucked my phone into my jeans and used yet another opportunity, and my free hand, to my advantage. I introduced myself.

"I'm Lochlan."

The campus policewoman nodded. "Alejandra Gomez—Allie." We shook hands. Then she handed my chips back. She hadn't eaten a single one.

I ventured another line of questions: "How long has Professor Lott been missing?"

"Last known whereabouts…right here in the garage. Friday night. So, over forty-eight hours. She was on video walking from the elevator to her car." Allie pointed at the Kia.

"Were you working Friday night?"

"No. I'm off on Fridays and Saturdays. Usually."

"But these garages are pretty safe. Campus police patrol, right?"

"Uh-huh, in cruisers or carts. But sometimes on foot."

Sometimes on foot. I wanted to bless Officer Gomez. I looked over at the stairway entrance. My mind was racing.

I sipped some iced tea and gave Allie a sincerely serious look. "I wanna help. Any volunteers getting organized?"

"Nice of you to offer. Don't know of any *civilian* search yet. But talk to campus PD. They'll have an email list. Or ask the Austin officers. Some of them are downstairs. Near Starbucks."

And there was my exit strategy, neat as you please. But I wasn't quite done.

"Sorry, my criminology professor would punch me if I didn't... There doesn't appear to be any sign of foul play around this Kia. Did you manage to check the insides?"

"Austin PD did, when the detectives were here. It was a pain in the ass—the battery's dead. No Onstar."

"Dead battery? Really?" I looked at the Kia again. If I had to guess, it was last year's model.

Allie shrugged. "Yeah, probably a defective unit."

Probably not.

I took another shot. "Nothing of real note in the vehicle?"

"I can't discuss much, but there weren't signs of a struggle or robbery."

"So, Professor Lott somehow vanished from this parking garage without a trace, on a Friday night, and nobody figured it out until today. Damn, that's not good, is it?" A rhetorical question, but I had to keep selling my detachment.

Officer Allie Gomez frowned. "No, not good at all."

"Well, I'm gonna take your advice, Officer Allie, and go volunteer at the campus PD. You sure you don't want the rest of these?" I held up what was left of my bag of chips. "I won't rat on you, I swear."

Allie looked around, then grinned and nodded. "Okay. I'm *starving.* Thanks, Lochlan."

"My pleasure. I'll see you."

"Adios."

With that, I waved at Officer Gomez and made my way back down the stairs, checking for cameras every floor, until I reached the bottom. There were no cameras.

I walked back out of the entrance without incident, then turned left, back toward Fricano's Deli and the Bomber.

Next up was Starbucks. I was searching for a Friday night cop. Where else would they go around there for coffee?

When I reached the parking lot outside the deli again, a light rain pelted the blacktop. I hurried down the corner plaza sidewalk, watching police and reporters in the lot scramble for cover from the downpour. A few of them marched straight for Starbucks. Not exactly what I had in mind, but I could work with it. I hoped.

I killed my tea then dumped the cup in a trash can before entering Starbucks. Some Austin police and reporters reached the doors just ahead of me. We bunched up and filtered inside in an awkward and fruitless attempt to avoid a few raindrops.

Once inside the shop, I hit the men's room to relieve myself of the iced tea and to kill a little time.

I reentered the long shop and then scanned a menu. Two Austin cops were in line ahead of me. Outside, the rain was light but still steady. A few more damp people, none in police uniform, straggled in.

I wasn't sure what band was playing over the shop's PA speakers, but the music calmed me down some. My thoughts cleared, and I focused on my next move...to inconspicuously collect more info from the night of Vicki's disappearance.

I could've worked the police inside Starbucks for clues, but I'd decided to treat law enforcement as suspect after conversing with Officer Gomez. In fact, I'd already scratched Allie off my list. She hadn't worked Friday.

Applying Occam's Razor, I sliced away the idea of focusing on the student body too. Obviously, there were far more students at UT than campus cops or Austin police. I didn't have the resources to tackle all that, so I'd have to rely on the police to do their jobs.

Also, I reasoned out that Vicki's vanishing late on a Friday, a Friday that had been the closing day of dorm housing for the season, dramatically cut chances that students would be hovering around campus—not when they'd likely be moving out or celebrating in good-old college style. Like they'd done with my band on Sunday night.

The security cam footage I'd seen at lunch backed up my theory. The San Antonio Garage had been fairly empty of cars. That held even more true when I'd done my sweep of the facility.

But I'll just call it what it really was. *An old-fashioned hunch*.

The two cops ahead of me ordered coffees then went to join the former parking lot crowd that had taken over the round tables between the shop's line of booths. The noise from all the chatter going on at those tables helped me out considerably. Nobody gave me a second glance, which was a welcome change.

I approached the Starbucks dude at the register. Upon his green apron, his name tag read 'Owen.'

"Welcome to Starbucks," he said.

"Hey—" I made a point of reading his name tag again. "—Owen. I'll have a tall cafe latte please. And...hoping you could answer a couple of questions."

"Sure thing. But if it's about the police..."

"Sort of. I got filled in by them already. The missing professor."

"Yeah, some of us are pretty sure she's been here before. Sucks, man."

"Did she come in Friday night?"

"No. Campus cops already questioned all of us who worked that night. Austin PD, too." He pressed keys on his register. "Your latte'll take a minute." Owen leaned left to glance past me. There was still a short line of customers. "That'll be two eighty-five."

I paid. "I'll wait over there. Do me a big favor and ask your manager to come talk to me?"

"Yeah. No prob." Owen turned to whisper to a coworker, a girl younger than me. She hustled into a back office.

"Thanks, Owen." I moved to the waiting area.

"What is hip?"

Jeeze. I sighed.

"What is hip?"

I grabbed my phone. One text from Kat and another from Jaz. That was everybody, meaning everybody left in the band who would feel the need to gleefully text me. I'd celebrate later.

The manager came out of the back of Starbucks at the same time as the cute girl behind the counter pushed my latte at me. I grinned at her. She returned a blushing smile then scurried back to mixing coffees.

The manager, an average-sized, well-tanned Latino whose name tag read 'Roddy,' surprised me.

"Trip the Shark!" he said, grinning broadly and reaching over the counter to shake my hand. "I've seen your band a thousand times, Loch. *Awesome.*"

I probably looked happily shocked because I was. I shook Roddy's hand gratefully. "Yeah? That's a *lot*." I chuckled. "I've got some good news."

"Really? What?" Roddy seemed excited. This guy was a true fan, and I thanked God for it.

"We signed with LMG. Today."

"*No shit?* Wow! Holy shit, man, that's incredible! LMG? That's crazy. They're the biggest—"

"You're the very first fan to find out," I added.

"Hah! *Too cool!*" Roddy looked around and then back at me. "That's all cool as hell, but you needed something, right? It wasn't just that." We both laughed. "What can I do for you, Loch? Something wrong with your coffee?"

I looked down at my cafe latte and grinned. "No, no. Nothin' like that. I just need some info."

"Sure thing. Ask away."

"Were any of your people that're working tonight, here on *Friday* evening? The night that UT prof disappeared?" I leaned over closer to him then, lowered my voice a tick, and took a chance. "She's an old friend of mine, from the University of North Texas. The cops aren't taking volunteers yet for the search, but I can't wait, Roddy."

"Oh, man. I feel ya. Damn. Yeah, Vicki, Vicki. Sorry to hear about that. Vicki's good people. She's become a regular."

I shrugged. "Thanks. Yeah, she is. So..."

Roddy looked satisfied. "*I* worked Friday night. I'm here *a lot, too*. Too much sometimes." He looked over his shoulder at the cute girl I'd made blush a minute before. "And Suzie over there. She was here also."

"Great. Great," I replied. "Okay, so what I need to know is simple. Did any campus cops come in here that day? Say...late afternoon, early evening? Somewhere between five o'clock and eight p.m.?" That created a cover story. The cautious type. Remember? "I'm hoping if I track one down, who was in the neighborhood, I might find a new lead." And then some.

Another customer walked up near us to wait for her order. I looked uncomfortably at Roddy, who read my meaning right away and nodded his head to the right. I followed him.

"We can talk in my office, Loch," Roddy told me. "Suzie, my office please."

Suzie looked up from an espresso machine, then tapped on another girl's shoulder, gesturing to take over for her.

Once the three of us were in Roddy's office, he asked Suzie about police visiting the shop.

"There were a couple that day, sure. That night—" Suzie looked at me, tightened her lips, rubbed her hands and then looked up at the office ceiling as if it might have the answer written on it.

I waited patiently.

"That one woman with the platinum-blonde crop came in..."

"Officer Winter," Roddy finished.

"Yep, her," said Suzie. "She usually orders a Frappuccino."

"Yeah. I think I remember seeing her Friday. It wasn't dark yet, but it was late. Probably around seven," confirmed Roddy. "*Connie*. I think her first name is Connie."

"Officer Connie Winter," I said.

I smiled down at Suzie. "Thank you, Suzie. This is a huge help."

Suzie nodded happily. "Glad to help—"

"—Lochlan," I finished, before she could even think about calling me 'Sir.' I put out my hand.

Suzie smiled and shook my hand daintily. "Lochlan."

"Roddy, I owe you one. The band is at Emo's this weekend. If you come by, I'll take care of you and your guests. Like Suzie here, maybe."

"Hell, yes! I'll see you Saturday night." We shook hands.

"Great, man. I need to get over to the campus PD now. It's probably not far, right?"

"I'll show you. Hold on." Roddy grabbed a napkin off a shelf then scribbled a quick map. He gave me verbal directions once that was drawn.

"Gotcha," I said. "Okay, you two. Great meeting you. Again, big, *big* thanks. I better scram—see you at the gig!"

"Bye," Suzie said. "Nice meeting you, too."

"Later, Loch! Good luck, man," offered Roddy.

I left the office.

Through the front doors I could see that it had stopped raining, and it was close to sunset. I walked out of Starbucks then sipped my latte on the sidewalk for a minute. Cops and reporters were grouped up again in the center of the corner lot.

And I was starving.

But food could wait because Vicki couldn't.

I pulled my phone out and then made a call.

"Hey, Lochlan!"

"Hey, Lois. I promised I'd give you updates."

"You did."

"Well, we signed the contracts..."

"Yay!" Laughter. "You must be *so* excited!"

I chuckled. "Well, obviously," I snarked.

"*Obviously,*" retorted Lois.

We both paused.

Lois broke the silence first. "What about Victoria?"

I swallowed more of my latte. "I think I'm onto something."

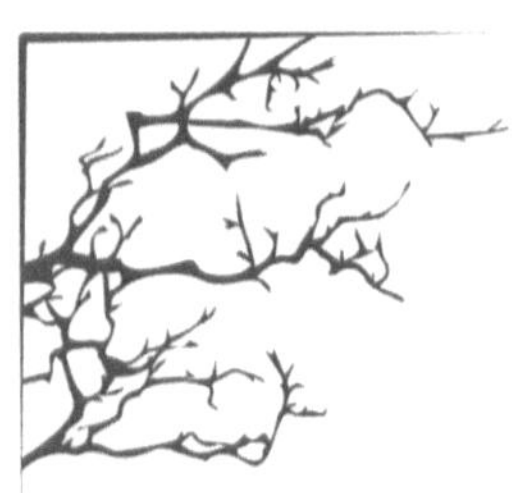

Chapter 5

"UT Police. Officer Carnley speaking."

"Hi. I'd like to speak to Officer Connie Winter. Is she available?

"One minute. I'll check."

I heard a rustling of papers and the tapping of something. Maybe a pen or pencil on a desk.

"Sorry, Officer Winter is off today. Can I take a message for her?"

"Ah. No, that's okay. I'll try back tomorrow—I wanted to thank her personally."

"I see. Is there anything else I can help you with?"

"No, thanks. Have a great evening."

"Thanks. You, too."

I hung up.

Okay, I needed to think. I snapped my earbuds into the jack on my phone and placed them in my ears. I reclined the Bomber's driver's seat far enough so I could stretch out, then swiped my phone's screen to shuffle Foo Fighters songs.

I was trying to not give in to a caffeine crash. Since nine in the morning I'd been going too hard on nothing but coffee and tea, and was damned hungry.

I was a moron who should have eaten more at lunch.

I was constantly imagining what might be happening to Vicki, while at the same time I was excited by the deal with LMG. A weird mix. I was a jumble of raw nerves and part of me wanted to crush the larynx of Vicki's kidnapper. Instead, I was having to be diplomatic, polite, and way too fucking sneaky.

So, music helped. Music always did.

"Learn to Fly" queued up in my ears.

If only I could.

I looked to the sky. The sun was setting. It was after 8 p.m. and getting humid.

By the time the song ended, I knew what to do next.

I let the music shuffle continue and pulled up a web browser again, pointed to a white-pages website, then found an Austin home address for a 'Constance Winter.'

Honestly. It was *that* easy. Privacy ain't what it used to be.

I examined some maps and then did a different search and pressed a listed phone number.

The music stopped automatically when the dialing started, so I left my earbuds in for the call.

"Yeah, I'd like to order a pizza... Carryout. One extra-large. Half pepperoni and mushroom, half plain cheese."

I PICKED UP THE PIZZA on my way to Winter's address. It lay on the floor of the Bomber's passenger side.

It smelled good. I thought about maybe having just one slice...

Somehow though, I resisted.

GPS on my phone was closing in on my destination pretty fast. The home address wasn't far from Austin's city center, just a few miles from UT campus. The pizza joint was around halfway between.

I've played a ton of places in East Austin, so the area felt familiar. The address wasn't *that* far east though.

If it turned out to be the Connie Winter I was looking for, she was doing okay for herself.

Any property close to Downtown Austin is big bucks.

Sitting at a stop sign, I noticed my left leg twitching nervously. Adrenaline. It figured. I'd no idea what I was getting myself into.

Maybe I should have gone back to the apartment to grab my concealable.

But it was too late for that. I was committed, and time was my enemy. However, I flipped open the Bomber's glove box. I always kept a multi-tool inside. I grabbed it and stretched in the driver's seat so I could slip it into a pocket.

It wasn't the greatest knife, but better than nothing.

I drove on neighborhood streets past many historic-looking houses (and some outright dumps). Soon, I was parked on a corner about twenty yards from the GPS destination.

After I exited the Bomber, I adjusted my phone's apps then pocketed it, stretched, cracked my neck twice, then walked around to the passenger's side to retrieve the pizza. It was still plenty warm in the cardboard box and, of course, smelled way too delicious.

There were lights on inside the house—a small, lightly painted single story that appeared to be made of wood and stucco, with no garage. Probably built before World War II. There was no fence in the front and hardly any driveway at all. A couple dozen paving stones formed two strips of the drive and one short walk to the front door. An ugly, sticky bayonet plant was next to the front walk and a blackish car was parked alongside.

As I approached the front stoop that was hardly a porch, I noted that a waist-high chain link fence enclosed the backyard. Thankfully, there didn't appear to be any vicious guard dog to go along with it. There were, however, some neighborhood mutts barking and not too far away.

Yeah, the pizza smelt good.

I heard music coming from inside the house as I got closer. It was "Lady Marmalade."

Connie's musical taste didn't suck.

That fact didn't put me at ease, but I reminded myself that, up to that point, I was still running on a hunch, with no hard evidence yet of any wrongdoing by Connie Winter.

I noticed the bulk of the multi-tool in my left pocket.

But just because I liked the song didn't mean the bitch wasn't guilty. I got my head back in the game.

I stepped onto the porch without even using the three shallow steps leading up to it. I had to duck to avoid clipping my skull on the roof's edge, but the ceiling of the porch was high enough that I could stand straight. Barely.

A storm door with a screened window on the top half protected the house's front entrance. I'd be talking through that. Inconvenient.

I took a deep breath and pressed the doorbell.

Game on.

The porch light snapped to life, forcing me to squint. The music from inside the house had changed tracks, and the volume increased as the front door opened inward.

I faced a butch-cut blonde a little less than a foot shorter than me. She had a curious smile on her plain face that grew bigger as her eyes roamed up from my waist to the pizza and finally ended at my head. Those eyes were having a difficult time focusing, and I noticed she had a red plastic cup in her hand. The scent of tequila was potent.

"Did I order a pizza or the pizza—" The woman evaluated me. "—man?" She laughed.

"A *pizza*, miss. Half pepperoni and mushroom. Half cheese."

Her head swiveled loosely, and she frowned. "I didn't order pizza. I'm pretty sure I didn't order a pizza, anyway." She stared at me, and her eyes narrowed as if she were trying to see through a smoke cloud. "You're the—the biggest, sexiest, damn pizza boy I've *ever seen*. Shouldn't you have a—a uniform or something?" She giggled. "They probably couldn't—*hiccup*—fit you in—right?"

I went with it. "It's embarrassing, but that's exactly the problem. Store had to special order my uniform. It's my first week, so still waiting." I held the pizza up a little higher and pretended to read off the back of the box. "I'm sorry, miss, but the address on this order says 'five-o-two Shelka Drive.' This *is* the address, right?"

"That's—my address, but I didn't order any—pizza." She inhaled through her nose. "*Smells yummy though.*" Her eyes locked on my face again. "You're—*yummier.*" She tried to strike a sexy stance in her doorway. It didn't work, and her empty hand slipped on the doorframe. She corrected herself quickly to avoid falling sideways and just barely kept from spilling her tequila.

"Oops!" She laughed and snorted.

"Careful, miss. Please be careful," I said, then conjured up a name. "So, no Jack *Hilfer* lives here? You don't know a Jack Hilfer?"

She scoffed at me. "Do I *look* like a *Jack* to you? No. No-no-no! No Jack—*Wilbur*—here!"

"I'm really sorry. Someone must have screwed up the order. It's my last one o' the night, too." I held the pizza out toward the storm door's window. "Here. You take it if you want. It's just gonna go to waste otherwise."

My stomach grumbled angrily at me.

"Free?" The blonde's eyes brightened. "Sure, I'll take it." She looked at me again. "It'll go good—*hiccup*—with my drink."

"Can I get your name? So I can prove to my boss that this was the wrong address."

"Sure." She opened the storm door. "Connie. Connie—Winter."

"Connie Winter," I repeated. "Thanks."

And there we were.

Connie took a step and reached for the extra-large pizza, but quickly realized, drunk or not, that she still had her drink in hand. She laughed.

"Mr. Pizza-man, can you bring that inside for me?"

Son-of-a-bitch, the pizza was like having a key.

"Um, yeah. Of course. It's a *big* pie. I'll just set it—on your coffee table *there*." I looked over her head to a small, wine-colored couch, and wooden coffee table, just a few feet from the front door.

"You're sweet." She stepped out of my way, but as I passed by, she squeezed my left bicep below my t-shirt sleeve. "And *big*. Fuck, you are—*hiccup—big!*"

"So everyone keeps telling me, Miss Winter."

"Connie. Just—Connie."

"Okay. *Connie.*" I placed the pizza on the coffee table then opened the box top. The smell wafted into the room. I thought I was going to snap and grab a slice, devour it right in front of Connie.

"Are you thirsty?" Connie looked at me, wondering.

"—Hugh. My name's Hugh."

"Do you want a *drink*, Hugh? I can't eat that...pizza...all by myself."

"Um." I faked hesitation. "Technically, I'm off. And I could go for a drink. Sure." I smiled. "Why not?"

Food is good.

Connie set her red cup on the table and scooped up a slice from the pepperoni side, stuffing half of it into her mouth. She made some happy sounds and wandered into the dining area that shared most of the floor with the living room.

The stereo changed songs again. "Photograph" by Nickelback.

"Tequila?" Connie clinked some bottles together. "I also have vodka and—Jim Beam."

"Jim Beam, thanks. Hey, do you have any paper plates?"

Connie had her back to me and dug inside some cupboards. I scanned the living room but saw no uniform, no police gear of any kind. There were no obvious weapons in the room either.

"Yes. Good idea, Pizza-man Hugh!"

I sat on the couch, feeling around it as I did for any possible secrets, but came up empty again. The coffee table in front of me had some magazines tossed onto it—a few women's magazines, a *Rolling Stone* and, surprisingly, a *Pilot & Plane.*

I picked up the piloting magazine and thumbed through it.

Connie came back with a red plastic cup and a few paper plates in hand. "Here you go, Huge." She laughed and staggered a half-step. "I mean, Hugh."

I accepted the cup and a plate and then mimicked swallowing some bourbon. "*Mmm*...good stuff," I said.

Connie must have wolfed down her first pizza slice while she was in the kitchen. She pulled another piece off the pie and slapped it on her plate, then sat at the other end of the couch.

"What's the occasion?" I asked.

"Huh?"

"The drinks. Did you get good news or bad news?"

Connie lost part of her smile then.

"I just needed a drink is all. To relax." She took a bite of her pepperoni slice.

"I can relate," I agreed.

I put a slice of pepperoni and mushroom on my plate then quickly ate half of it. Then I picked my drink back up and washed the pizza down with an actual sip. The whiskey was a welcome change from coffee and tea.

"You a student at UT?" Connie waited for my response with her red cup at her lips.

"Nope. Not a student anymore."

"Ah. You look familiar. I was just thinking maybe I'd run into you on campus." She drank.

"You're a student?"

"Ha. No! I'm a cop. A UT cop."

"Serious? I don't believe you. Where's your uniform?"

"I am!" Connie put her red cup on the coffee table. "Wait here, Huge."

Connie walked toward the far end of the small house, down a short hallway, then entered what I assumed was her bedroom. I finished my pizza slice then selected another. Plain cheese, since Connie obviously preferred meat.

A drunk, meat-eating cop, living alone, with no children or pets. Duly noted. Friendly enough on the surface, but maybe the tequila was speaking for her? I was about to find out.

"Okay, pizza-man. What do you think of these?"

Connie walked back into the living room with a police uniform on a hanger in one hand and a pair of handcuffs hanging from her index finger on the other.

"Nice 'cuffs," I teased. "Use those often?"

Connie's eyes twinkled. "Not often enough," she breathed.

"Well, now I believe you."

She tossed her uniform onto an arm of the couch and then walked past me to sit down again. She still held the handcuffs in her left hand and reached for her drink.

"Did you use those on Victoria?"

Connie's eyes went wide, and she spit tequila back into her red cup, then blinked at me like a startled, cornered animal.

"What did you say?" The drunken fogginess in her eyes receded a touch.

"Where is Victoria Lott!" I shouted at her in a sudden rage, shifted my weight and prepared to spring.

I have to give Connie credit. She was no coward. Connie Winter dropped her drink and thrust out her right fist at my throat.

But I was more than prepared for that. My left hand shot up and snapped closed on her forearm like a vice grip, and I stood, lifting Connie off the ground with both hands.

She'd intended to thrash the handcuffs across my face with her left hand but yanking her off her feet and holding her at arm's length meant she had no arc to connect with my head, and the cuffs weakly grazed my chest, just below my jaw.

Before Connie could yell out, my right hand gripped her throat, and I pushed her backward across the couch's armrest, until most of my weight crushed her chest and stomach with my right knee. Air whooshed from her lungs, and her eyes bulged. I took the handcuffs from her with a violent yank.

"Hold still and I won't hurt you again," I said. My voice was a snarl. My right hand crushed her throat enough to keep her silent. "Don't make a fucking sound. Understood?"

Connie's eyes watered. She nodded faintly. She wasn't stupid either.

I dropped the handcuffs on the coffee table.

"I'm gonna turn you over to handcuff you—that's all. Don't complicate it. I've had a long day, Connie."

She nodded again. I loosened my right grip enough so she could breathe.

Connie sucked in a breath, and when she did, I pulled her off the armrest across a throw pillow and flipped her onto her stomach. I thrust a knee into her spine, so it pressed her face into the pillow, and she let out a muffled groan in protest.

"Quiet."

I picked the handcuffs up, pulled Connie's arms behind her, and snapped the restraints closed. Then I removed my weight from Connie, flipped her over onto her back again and stood up.

She glared up at me but didn't make another sound.

"I'm gonna ask questions again. You're gonna answer. Right?"

"I don't know what—"

"You were with Vicki Lott on Friday night. Yes or no."

"No."

"You know who Victoria is?"

She hesitated. "Yes."

"How?"

"I read the report in my email."

"But you've never met her before?"

"*No.*"

I felt her fear shift to obstinance. And I mean literally felt it, like warm fingers stroking across my forehead and pushing the feeling into my brain, right between my eyes. I took half a step backward from the shock of it.

"No, I've never met her before," she protested again sharply. "What's wrong with you?"

I squared my jaw and peered straight into Connie's eyes, shaking off the stark realization. "You're lying."

Connie blinked and her eyes shifted. "No I'm not!"

"You were with Vicki the night she went missing."

"I told you—"

"I know what you said. I *know* you're lying!"

"What? How— You're crazy!"

Maybe I was. But I went with my gut right then. Like most of my life.

"Where is she?"

"How should I know?"

Her obstinance cleared away. Again, I felt her mind change—this time, like a light breeze on my face, and my skin tingled.

"You know who took her, but you don't know where."

"No! I don't know shit about—"

"Connie, if you lie to me again, I'm gonna hurt you." I retrieved the multi-tool from my jeans, then pulled open its longest steel blade.

Connie's eyes went wide. "You said you wouldn't!"

Fear again. Between my eyes.

"I guess I *lied*. Sound familiar?" I smiled. "How about this—if you're honest with me, I *swear* I won't hurt you."

Connie shifted her shoulders on the couch uneasily. "I can't say anything."

More fear returned to her. A lot of it.

"You mean you're *afraid* to say anything."

She glowered at me, but kept her mouth tightly shut.

"Someone's threatened you?" I grimaced. "I mean, besides me."

"You have no fucking idea who you're dealing with."

Fear.

"You're right, Connie, I don't. But these people, whoever they are, they've taken a friend of mine—a *precious* friend. And I'm pretty fucking upset about it, if you haven't noticed. So, your options are—cooperate with me now and I hand you over to the cops, who can protect you." I looked at the front door. "Or, I drag your ass outta here, toss you in my trunk, and decide what to do with you later."

I held my knife up and made every effort to admire it like I would a beautiful woman. I was convincing, believe me.

"*Fuck!* The police should be looking for *you!* Why would they think I had anything to do with Lott?"

"I'm willing to bet if I search this house, I'm gonna find a lot of cash. Am I right?"

"Now you're a thief?"

"No, I'll leave the stack of cash right next to you, all nice and tied up."

"That still isn't proof!"

"Oh—" I folded my multi-tool up and put it away. Next, I reached into my other pocket and pulled out my phone, opening the screen to the running digital recorder application. "Well, will you look at that? I've recorded our entire evening." I swiped the screen to *Camera.* "Say 'cheese,' " I quipped with a shark smile, and snapped a photo of handcuffed Connie Winter.

Anger overpowered Connie's terror. "*Fuck you!* I'll never tell anybody jack *shit!*"

"I get it. You're spooked. So, just tell me what you know, and I'll turn this off." I held up the phone to show her the digital recorder, clicked *stop,* then put it back in my pocket.

Connie's stereo was playing "Again" by Lenny Kravitz.

"I'm just one guy. What threat could I possibly pose to your scary employers?"

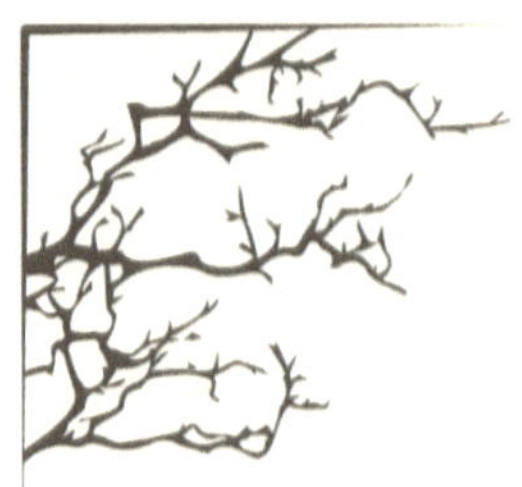

Chapter 6

Prostrate and handcuffed on her own couch, Connie stared at me like I was the Joker. Considering my state of mind at that moment, I *was* a crazy man, so again, it worked for me. Every second that ticked by was potentially Victoria's last. I wouldn't leave that house without a new lead.

I also had the new sensations in my brain to deal with. My earlier empathetic connection with Connie had all the earmarks of being real enough, but real or not, she had admitted guilt. I hadn't imagined that part. The rest of what I sensed had me off-balance.

Maybe that's what happens when I starve myself.

I walked around the living and dining rooms and made sure all the drapes in the place were pulled closed, then I shut any blinds.

When I'd closed the last drape, I asked, "You live here alone?"

"Yes."

I detected no lie. I walked over to the couch.

"They'll kill us both, you know," Connie said flatly.

"They. You keep saying *they*. I'm assuming you have no real idea who *they* are?"

"None."

Connie's naked fear of me had trailed off after I stashed my knife and especially after turning off the digital recorder on my phone. However, I still noted dread in her mind from elsewhere, as if she was focused on the air or the ceiling, or the emptiness in the room. Apparently, her bogeymen could be all around us.

I still stood between the coffee table and the couch to make sure Connie couldn't use her legs to kick me. The tiny living room didn't even have a chair. The couch, two end tables, a media center, flat screen television, lamps, and shelves all took up the majority of the space near the front door. I wanted to sit down on the couch and search the place later, so I decided to secure her legs.

"You have any rope or twine around here? Maybe a bungee? Extension cord?"

Connie glared at me.

"Look, if you do, I won't have to cut up one of your lamps."

Connie sniffed and shook her head. "*Fine*. In the kitchen."

I grinned. "Where in the kitchen exactly?" It was a nice try.

Connie rolled her eyes. "One of the top drawers should have an extension cord."

"Thanks. Stay still. Don't get any silly ideas."

I walked over to the kitchen and gave Connie a glance every so often while I rifled through the few drawers. Sure enough, I found a standard white extension cord in one drawer that stuck once before I yanked it open.

"This place is pretty old. I like it. Quaint."

Connie scoffed but made no other reply.

I walked back over to her. "Keep your legs together. If you even think about kicking me, I'll forget my promise."

"I have to pee," she said.

Of course she did.

I sighed and tossed the extension cord onto the coffee table. "I guess I should be happy you haven't thrown up." I looked down at Connie. "Okay, let's go..." I pulled her upright from the couch by her shoulders and then helped her stand. "March."

We walked into the hallway to the bathroom.

Connie twisted at the waist enough to look back at me. "Cuffs?"

I looked down at Connie's hands cuffed behind her back. "Uh-uh. You do your business with those on."

"In my shorts?"

"Oh, for Christ's sake..."

Connie was barefoot in a loose-fitting, off-the-shoulder, white cotton blouse and some cut-off jean shorts. I stretched her shirt down across her butt. It didn't quite reach all the way past her cheeks.

Her cut-offs looked loose. I put two fingers up under her blouse and in between her waist and her shorts. They were loose enough. There were no pantie strings beneath the cut-offs.

"Commando, eh?"

"Not exactly how I imagined this would go."

In one rough motion, I pulled Connie's shorts down to her knees. She let out a little yelp.

"Now go pee," I ordered. I watched her hobble into the bathroom. I turned away as she sat down on the toilet, but I left the bathroom door open.

"You're not going to watch?"

"Nope. I'm not wiping your ass either. Just get it over with."

Connie actually laughed.

I went back for more pizza and grabbed another slice, finished it off in three big chomps, and found lemonade in her fridge. I grabbed a paper towel off a counter dispenser to wrap around the bottle, chugged straight from it, put it back in the fridge, then wiped my fingerprints from the fridge's handle. I folded and stuck the paper towel in a back pocket.

Connie called out, "All done!"

I walked back to the bathroom doorway. Connie had managed to stand up off the throne without a problem. Her blouse just barely covered whatever modesty she might have had left. I reached past her and flushed the toilet.

"Okay, turn around," I told her.

Connie turned, and I quickly pulled her cut-offs back up.

"You could have just taken them off," she taunted.

"Back to the couch."

"But—"

"Not gonna happen. Move!"

Why was I not surprised?

I gave Connie a little shove out of the hallway toward the couch and sat her down. Next, I swung her legs up and around until she was lying down again, and I reached over and retrieved the extension cord from the coffee table.

She didn't move. I pressed the weight of my lower left leg across both of her thighs and quickly tied her ankles.

"You're good at that," Connie said.

"I was junior rodeo." I stood up and examined my handiwork. She wasn't going anywhere. "I'll let you sit up now."

I pulled Connie to a sitting position, then sat on the other end of the couch, reached over for my paper plate, and placed another slice of pizza on it. It was the last of the pepperoni.

Connie watched me closely. "You must really love her," she said.

I met Connie's eyes, but I didn't answer.

"You don't look like the ex-boyfriend."

"What ex-boyfriend?"

"She was with some guy for a long while. They told me to wait because of him. They broke up months ago. I'm warned about details like that, just in case. You don't match his description or photos."

"Damon?"

"That sounds right."

That was one hell of a revelation. Damon Smolik was with Vicki all through college. Their relationship was the main reason I never pursued her. I found it hard to believe they were over with.

I wanted to change the subject. I picked up the *Pilot & Plane* magazine off the coffee table and held it up. "You a pilot?"

"Learning."

"For your mysterious employers?"

"It's a hobby. That's all."

"Interesting hobby for a crooked cop."

Connie didn't respond right away. "How the hell did you figure out I had anything to do with Lott, anyway?"

"Ninja superpowers." I picked up my plate and eyed the pizza slice on it. "Who killed the battery in Vicki's Kia?"

"Not me."

"You were just the lure."

"Pretty much."

"Vicki trusted you."

"They always do."

The stereo switched music tracks again. Eddie Money.

I took a bite of pizza, swallowed, and continued my questioning. "Who did you bring her to?"

"Just one guy. A very scary guy."

That got my adrenaline pumping a little. "I assume he's the one that killed the car battery."

"Yeah."

"Tell me whatever you know about him."

Connie took a deep breath. "He's not as big as you, but he's well over six feet. Looks very strong. I never got close to him except on Friday night. And it was dark."

I grunted. "Go on."

"He's Asian. Chinese, I think. But way too big. Mixed maybe."

"Any distinguishing marks?"

"Yeah. It was hard to see, but he has some sort of tattoo on the side of his face. Something in China lettering, I think."

"*Which* side of his face?"

Connie closed her eyes. "Left. The left side."

That cop training of hers paid off.

"What was he wearing?"

No pause at all this time. "All black. Except for his head. Like a bodysuit. Might have been Kevlar."

Guy sounded like a professional.

I clenched my teeth. I didn't want to ask the next question: "Did he hurt her?"

Connie didn't want to answer either, but after a few seconds, and me lifting an eyebrow, she did. "He put a sack over her head and used a taser." Connie saw the dangerous glint in my eye and talked faster. "*But he didn't let her hit the ground.* He bound and gagged her so fast—he'd give you a run for your money, cowboy."

Connie was breathing quicker. Her anxiety had returned.

"Calm down. You're doing okay. What was this fucker driving?"

"A white Cadillac Escalade. Spotless. New-looking."

I leaned my head back and breathed deeply. That info was finally something concrete. Something it might be possible to trace to a limited number of people.

"That's a damn expensive SUV." I wasn't dealing with petty thieves. There was the possibility the car was jacked, but I doubted it somehow—the guy was a pro, busy trafficking a person. A stolen vehicle would draw police attention. "What about the license plates? Texas?"

"No. No, I don't think so."

"You don't think so? What then?"

"I didn't hang around!" Connie shut her eyes again. "I think the rear plate was blue and yellow."

"A designed plate? The colors were split evenly or what?"

"Yeah, like a strip across the top of one color and then a wider field below that. I don't remember which color was which."

I got my phone out and did a quick search on state tags and colors. Images appeared with all fifty state license plates setup in a grid. I scanned for yellow and blue tags with unevenly divided color schemes.

"Nevada," I said. I searched up a single Nevada plate then showed the image to Connie. "Nevada?"

"Yeah, that was it. I remember the wavy lines now. Those mountain tops."

"Okay. Good. That's something." I searched Google maps. "It's about nineteen hours from here to Vegas." That meant, assuming Nevada was the driver's destination, Vicki was held somewhere. For almost two days.

I snarled. "Where'd you make this trade with the Chinese?"

Connie looked anywhere but at me. "Behind a church."

"Seriously?"

"Yes. University Methodist. There's an alleyway. Usually empty on a Monday night."

"Jesus..." I almost growled. "*Why?*"

"I told you—" Connie's voice was as tense as piano wire.

"No! Why did they choose Vicki! What are they doing with her?"

Connie gazed at me with something approaching pity. "Oh, Sugar. I don't ask those kinds of questions. It's best I don't know and they don't tell me."

I reasoned out possibilities.

Victoria Lott was young and beautiful. So, the obvious, ugly motivations came to mind. But there are young and beautiful women all over the world. Why grab a college professor from a major Texas university, stage her car, try to disguise the kidnapping, and then transport her across state lines?

This wasn't some lone psychopath at work, looking to drench his fantasies in blood, sex—or both.

God, I hoped not.

Vicki was highly intelligent. Probably a genius. She spoke at least two languages fluently that I knew of. She was also very healthy. A gym rat. She used to run cross-country and had mad endurance.

All of it added up.

Because of all the many possible factors involved, traits that *might* make Vicki a special target, things I hadn't thought of or had no possible way of knowing yet, I came to one more stark realization.

"There's *another* accomplice. At least one more. Probably a local. Most likely another campus employee, like you, or even a student."

"What makes you say that?"

"They didn't have *you* select Vicki, right? You'd end up knowing too much." Connie nodded. "Classic double-blind. Gather a team. But each member only gets told what they need to know to get their job done."

Connie's jaw dropped and then she said, "Jesus. Who the fuck *are* you?" Connie was sitting stone-still on the couch, staring at me.

I let out a bitter laugh. "I thought I knew this morning."

Another thought came to mind.

"It's probably the scout that communicates with you—or *is* it the Chinese? How they do it? I'm betting they don't call."

Connie sighed. "Not the Chinaman. Dead drop. Encrypted thumb drive. I delete the messages after I read them. The drops change all the time."

Made sense. Untraceable.

At that point, I assessed Connie herself again. She didn't come off like a thug. She wasn't dumb. She wasn't a psychopath. Not full-blown anyway. She was cooperating. After all, she was a cop—a crooked one sure, but few police start out that way.

"What do they have on you?"

Connie's eyes flattened noticeably, then she glanced away. "You don't need to know that."

True enough.

I stood up and Connie snapped her eyes back onto me. "I'm gonna search the house now. Don't go anywhere."

"I felt like jogging, but okay." She gave me a smirk.

I smirked back at her, then walked down the hall to Connie's bedroom.

The room was sparsely furnished with two dressers, a queen-sized bed, and a single wooden chair nestled near a mirrored vanity. There was a closed laptop on the vanity. A Glock pistol in its holster was hanging from the chair. Keys were on top of one dresser.

I didn't touch the Glock, but I picked up the keys and examined them. Two smaller keys got my attention immediately.

I opened the bedroom's folding closet doors then started a search. A heavy fire safe was on the floor in a corner of the closet, under some low-hanging dresses. I tried both small keys and opened the safe with no trouble.

Inside the safe, I found jewelry, coins, and various personal items. What stood out most though was a zippered bank bag containing at least twenty grand in cash and a few loose thumb drives.

I wiped down the safe and keys with the paper towel from my back pocket, set the keys back on a dresser, and then brought the bank bag with me into the living room.

Connie took one look at the bag in my hands and didn't seem surprised. I wasn't getting any pokes between my eyes to tell me this—it was just the look of resignation on her long face.

"I'm guessing these thumb drives were used for the drops," I said.

"Wiped clean." Connie had erased the data.

"Figured." I was tempted to use one of the sticks to send a message of my own, but that kind of bravado would get Vicki killed. "I'm gonna contact the police now. The *Austin* police. But I have some advice for you first."

"Do tell," Connie said.

"They'll want a description of me." I fixed a hard gaze on Connie. "You're gonna lie."

This time Connie looked surprised. "Because..."

"Because, let's say, hypothetically, that I *do* find Vicki. Things get messy." I hefted the bank bag. "Your bogeymen are gonna put it together fast, it was *you* that gave me the leads." I looked at Connie sharply. "You wanna live longer? Don't make your vigilante story about me. Someone must have seen you walking Vicki to her car that night. There were thousands of students at

UT on Friday, any of them could have seen you two. If you don't connect the dots, your arrest looks random."

"They'll still get rid of me."

"Maybe. But since I'm gonna go gunk up the works, you should be rooting for the good guy. The longer I live, and the more I make them worry, the less time they'll have to worry about *you*."

"You could just let me go."

I thought about that. "I could, but I have no guarantee you won't try to warn someone. You might still warn them anyway after the cops take you in for questioning."

"I have no direct way to contact them. I told you. You'll have plenty of time."

I pulled the stack of cash out of the bank bag with my paper towel and then placed it in the middle of the coffee table. "I'd better. Because if I don't get to Vicki in time because of anything you say or do... I'll be back."

The now familiar poke between my eyes hummed with Connie's fear that time.

"You *are* fucking crazy."

I shook my head.

"No. It's way worse than that." I met Connie's terrified gaze. "You said it yourself. *I love her.*"

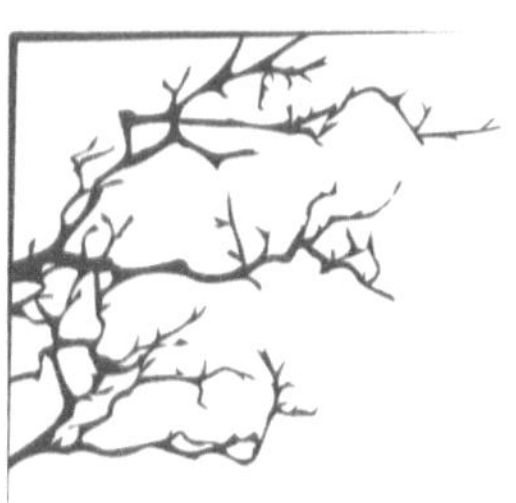

Chapter 7

Connie gave me all the passwords I needed, so I used her computer and her email account to construct a message to send to the Austin Police Department. It included details about the Chinese kidnapper Connie had described, along with his white Cadillac SUV in its Nevada plates. Last, I edited and then transferred the most damning parts of my surreptitious digital recording from my phone and onto Connie's laptop.

The sound bytes from Connie didn't amount to a whole lot, but they'd whet the appetite of detectives:

"I can't say anything."

"You have no fucking idea what you're dealing with."

"That still isn't proof!"

"Fuck you!* I'll never tell anybody jack *shit!"

I attached the audio files to Connie's email, addressed to Austin PD.

Signed, Your Friendly Neighborhood Samaritan.

Send.

I carefully wiped off the laptop and its keyboard. I gathered the pizza box and the remaining cheese pizza inside along with the paper plate I'd used, my red cup, the zippered bank bag, and the *Pilot and Plane* magazine.

From the front door of her house, I spoke coldly to Connie. "I expect the next time I see you, you'll be in jail."

"Doesn't matter. I'm a loose end now."

I opened the door with my handy paper towel covering the knob, pizza box under my right arm, and bank bag in hand. As I pushed my way through the exterior storm door, ready to close up behind me, Connie had something more to say.

"Thanks for not hurting me."

I nodded once and replied, "Sure," then tried to leave again.

But she continued, "Hey. Hugh—whatever your name really is—if you find her, do me a big favor." Her expression was grim. "*Kill the bastards.*"

Connie Winter sat there hog-tied on her own couch—tied *by me*—knowing police would be on the way to arrest her soon, and what did she want? For me to kill the very people who had been paying her, that got her into the whole horrible business in the first place.

I was walking into a world of fucking trouble.

"I'll consider it. Bye, Connie."

I closed the doors and left.

IT WAS ALMOST MIDNIGHT by the time I got home. There was no girl-friend to greet me when I walked in. No dog or cat. Not even a roach scut-tling across the floor when I flipped the lights on.

I was fine with all that. Silence was what I needed most. I was coming down from an insanely stressful day that had answered a lot of questions and replaced them with new ones, given rewards and threatened to take them all away in a flash.

My apartment is neat and spartan. I spend too much time touring—and money is always tight—so like most working musicians in Austin, I get by with just the basics and I could barely afford those.

But of course, the deal with LMG was bound to change some of that.

I tossed my keys, the LMG contract, and the bank bag onto the kitchen counter, then put the remnants of the pizza into the fridge. My red cup and paper plate I pulled out of the bag to toss into the trash can under the sink, grabbed that can, then headed outside to the dumpster.

While I dumped the garbage, the first quarter moon overhead tugged at me, and I stared up into the night sky. "So, have I gone completely nuts, Mr. Moon?"

There was no reply. Thankfully. I laughed quietly. I wasn't crazy then. Not completely anyway. Not yet.

Back inside my apartment, I took the bank bag into my bedroom and pulled the piloting magazine out of it and tossed it onto my bed. I carefully hid the bag—and the thumb drives inside it—under a milk crate in a corner of my closet.

"What is hip?"

The text was from Pack: **Dinner set for tomorrow 7 PM, will call in morn with directions**

I replied: **Thx, talk soon**

Pack: **K**

I set my phone on the nightstand, stripped naked, headed for the shower, flipped on the bathroom light, and started the water running. My face in the mirror was a sad sight. I looked stretched and tired but knew it was more from stress than fatigue. I needed a shave as usual. I ran one hand through my hair while rubbing at my bloodshot gray eyes with the other.

Showers can be transformational, and that evening I needed it. My mind kept lapsing to Vicki's face, and I pushed back tears as I scrubbed down and cleaned up.

The feeling of powerlessness. It's *shit*. Not having any idea where to strike next to help Vicki threatened to overwhelm me. I'd done what I could. I knew that. But the guilt remained.

My reasoning mind told me to sleep it off. It'd been a crazy day, and I had to stop thinking.

I put on some boxers, brushed my teeth, flipped off the bathroom light then crawled into bed—just a frame and mattress on the floor. I thumbed through the *Pilot and Plane* mag for a minute, but nothing stood out, and I tossed it onto the nightstand before turning off the lights.

Sleep came quickly.

I dreamed heavily, but when I awoke, I'd forgotten all of it. All except for *a flying red horse.*

Most people would think little of this—push it aside—but I'd learned over the years to not ignore my dreams, especially those that left me with a symbol intact in the morning. Given the strange psychic events at Connie's house the previous night, I desperately held onto Pegasus. I was sure it wasn't just some random image conjured out of my subconscious.

I was convinced it was another 'precognitive dream,' a snapshot of something from my future. I'd had them before. I know that's a lot to take in, to believe we might exist on a linear time stream that could allow us to sometimes view future events in stark clarity, but my déjà vu was often of a sort that felt more like I was looking at a photograph or a repeated segment from a video. So, I couldn't logically deny the possibility that such visions were, in fact, real.

The journal in my nightstand was for such dreams, and I quickly jotted that one down. *Sign of a flying red horse, on wooden wall (or fence?) Mobile gas?*

I stretched by the side of my bed, then walked into the bathroom to do my morning rituals. It was the search. Day number two.

I don't own a TV. I simply have no real interest in most of the crap on cable—and definitely nothing from the lying media. So when I do have the need, I point my computer to the right websites.

New information was hopefully coming to light about Vicki's disappearance, especially considering my gift to the police. I sat down at my computer desk in my bedroom, then searched up local Austin news feeds and visited all the major networks.

News sites all had headlines about Vicki's disappearance. The hottest report was about a suspect turned in by a vigilante, but identities were being withheld. Naturally, that part I'd expected.

What I'd forgotten to anticipate though was *family*.

Vicki's family had appeared in Austin, and YouTube footage of her parents delivering pleas to her kidnappers was on just about every front page. It was hard stuff to press play on, but I did it.

Vicki's mom was almost a mirror image of her daughter. Petite, redheaded, with an abundance of freckles, only the crow's feet at her eyes and a few wrinkles in her forehead the telling differences. Her mother held herself with courage when she spoke, while Vicki's taller, gray-haired dad stood stoically nearby. I'd never seen either of them before.

Memories of Vicki flooded into me. Her freckled nose. Her almost unnaturally perfect smile. Her laughter mingled with mine, us sitting on the grass outside a college library.

Firecrackers. That damned terrible day at Marquis Hall.

It turned out to be too much.

I looked away from the monitor, stood up from my computer, then went into the kitchen. I was out of milk and Cheerios, so I made do with some nuked oatmeal. While my cereal cooked, I put water and green tea into my one-shot brewer. If you haven't guessed yet, I drink a *lot* of caffeine.

Once breakfast was ready, I sat at the kitchen counter and contemplated my next move.

Perhaps I'd hit a dead end. I wasn't a police department. I didn't have the resources of a private investigator. I was simply a talented amateur. Smart and resourceful, with a penchant for improvisation, sure, but working miracles wasn't on my résumé.

None of that stopped me.

I recalled what Connie had told me about the Methodist Church being the trade-off spot to the kidnapper. It was a long shot—to guess there might be a clue there—but I had nothing else to go on without stopping by the police department or hiring somebody. And considering how little I trusted those options, especially after finding Connie—realizing that there had to be other conspirators at work—I knew if Vicki would have a chance in Hell of being found alive, I was her best shot. In fact, I felt that I was her *only* shot.

That's what I told myself, anyway. Call it naïve, call it love. When you're in the thick of it, you'll believe just about anything.

I grabbed my backpack and prepared, loading it up with my iPad, charger, a *real* paper notepad, pens, and whatever else useful I could fit inside. There was a traveler's first aid kit I'd brought with me on the road before. I pulled on blue jeans, a green t-shirt (plain—with no snarky remarks on the front or back), and my black sneakers, then grabbed my keys, Ray-bans, backpack, and finally my phone.

And I was almost out the door—when I stopped myself.

I walked back into the bedroom closet and with a press of my left index finger, opened my gun safe. I removed my 9mm Glock, checked the magazine, stashed two more mags inside pockets of my backpack, and strapped on a holster and gun belt under my t-shirt. I balanced the belt with two additional magazines because I could.

When walking into a world of shit, better walk in armed to the teeth.

I've got a concealed carry license good in Texas and most other states. States that don't honor the Texas carry aren't a big surprise. California, Illinois, New York, and a handful of others, but the most notable problem spot for me was Nevada. From the look of the way things were going, I'd have to be extra charming there, and soon.

Hopefully, I wouldn't need to even pull my Glock, but better safe than—well, yeah, you know. I didn't have time for 'sorry.'

Last, and to take my mind off the gun tucked into the small of my back, I slid one of my blues harps into a rear-end jeans pocket.

As I was about to exit, my phone sang out again.

It was a text from Lois: **Are you OK?**

I replied: **Y sorry I'm out the door again. But thanks for worrying :)**

Lois: **News reported some strange things. I don't want to know do I**

Me: **I have to go Lois. I'll be fine. Promise.**

Lois: **OK but u are crazy u know?**

I laughed.

Me: **So people keep telling me. Hey would you like to sound engineer our gig this weekend?**

Lois: **Really? Yes!**

Me: **Great. I'll make sure you get paid well. Get you more gigs later. I can do shit like that now**

Lois: **Yes I can tell people I know Lochlan Nohr! :p**

Me: **Hah. Bye, must jet**

Lois: **Kk Please be careful!**

Me: **Always**

I have to admit, even as independent as I am, it was a good feeling to have somebody watching out for me. I was getting in over my head and knew it.

I reached the front door, but got hit by that nagging *you're forgetting something* feeling. My LMG contract was still on the kitchen counter. *Nice one, idiot.* I grabbed the contract and stuffed the thick stack of papers into my backpack.

Finally, I shouldered my pack again, locked up the apartment, climbed into the Bomber, and aimed downtown—to Vicki's last known location.

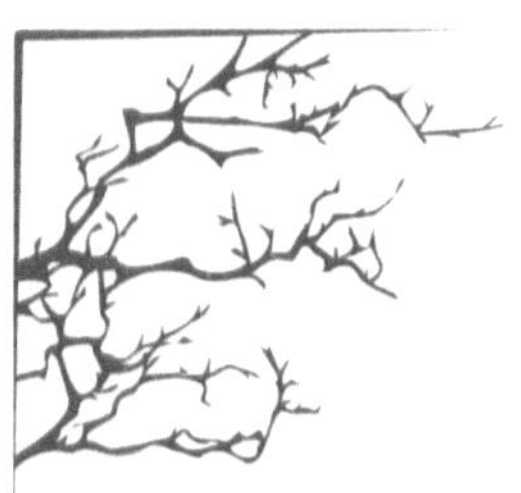

Chapter 8

The University Methodist Church was easy to find on a corner hardly three blocks away from the San Antonio Garage where I'd seen Vicki's Kia parked. Behind the church, I found an alley, just as Connie had described.

The alleyway was narrow, hardly wide enough for one car, and it stretched from one street to another, spanning the entire length behind the church. At night it would have been a perfect place to meet someone and not be seen from the nearby streets, blocked as it was by the church on one side and a wall and trees on the other. The red stucco wall was old but well maintained.

I realized I was driving between the church and some historic house. It scratched at my memory. *Little? Littleton?*

I opened my phone to a GPS map. *Littlefield!* I was standing next to the Littlefield House, built during the Civil War. God on one side, history on the other. There was something oddly fitting about that.

I parked the Bomber on the nearby street then got out to walk around. Didn't have a clue what I was looking for, but it was one of those 'I'll know it when I see it' sort of deals.

I half-expected to come across some police or the FBI in the alley, but it was empty on that Tuesday morning. There wasn't much at all along the narrow stretch of road. I'd passed a dumpster at one end, and there were several large air conditioning units behind the church. Old clothing and trash were sprinkled along the alley in the grass to either side of the concrete road and on a small adjacent stretch of sidewalk.

My best bet would be to march back and forth along the length of the alley with my eyes strafing the cracked cement under foot. The sky was bright and sunny, so that helped.

I'm naturally paranoid when I'm in any street. I kept looking up every so often and turned to check behind me. Years of parking in sketchy sections of cities and towns will do that to you.

I was counting on something, anything, that the kidnapper might have missed when he grabbed Vicki.

Vicki had locked her car before she left the parking garage with Connie Winter. That meant she had her keys with her, and probably her phone.

Her phone.

The kidnapper was a pro. He'd have searched her and gotten rid of the phone!

I ran toward the dumpster. Chinaman most likely tossed the phone—probably smashed it first to cut off the GPS tracking. Odds were high that Vicki still owned an iPhone like I remembered from college, so I was probably looking for one wrapped in a brightly colored cover. *Purple, I bet.*

As I ran, my phone buzzed again.

"What is hip?"

I didn't want to answer.

But I thought better of it by the time I stood next to the dumpster, and read the text. Surprisingly, the message was from Silana.

Please call me afterwards.

I had no idea what that meant. After what? Our upcoming dinner?

I got back to the business at hand.

The dumpster in front of me smelled as wonderful as you might imagine. I reflexively covered my nose and lifted the two lids open on their hinges.

I'd been worried the garbage men had been by to do their job, but no—the dumpster was almost half-full of garbage and debris.

I groaned.

I looked up and down the alley, and after seeing no one in either direction, I took a deep breath, swung myself over the edge of the dumpster then landed in its smelly interior. My right foot squashed something with a muffled pop. I frowned and looked down at my feet, now buried in garbage. It was impossible to tell what I'd crushed without lifting my leg. What appeared to be the remains of a watermelon rind dripped from my sneaker.

Oh, yeah. Good times.

I used both of my feet to shuffle cardboard boxes, a half-dozen, full garbage bags, and a variety of other odorous wonders out of my way.

My hopes leapt for an instant when I caught sight of something bright orange. But it was only a broken cookie jar.

I continued the dumpster dive for maybe five more minutes before giving up in frustration. If Chinaman had tossed Vicki's phone, he'd been smart enough to not do it in a giant garbage bin.

I grabbed the side of the dumpster and began to lift myself over the edge into the alleyway when I heard footsteps.

Two women with tattoos on their arms, chests, and legs walked up the alley in my direction. The pair reminded me of roller derby girls without the roller skates—somewhat androgynous and well-muscled but wearing miniskirts and v-necked ladies' t-shirts. Both wore matching denim vests, open and unbuttoned and covered in dozens of patches.

They probably *were* rollergirls.

The two saw me immediately—I'm not exactly a bunny rabbit—so I got out of the dumpster and then stood up straight to face them. I adopted a sheepish smile and awaited the inevitable reactions.

These were big girls if they were girls to begin with. I wasn't entirely sure. They were both over six feet tall.

One smiled, while her friend stared at me sharply and then looked over at the dumpster. In fact, she showed a mighty big interest in it. And I became extra aware of the gun holstered against my back.

"Hi," I said.

"Lose something? Or just waking up?" The smiling derby girl had a high-pitched voice, just short of whiny. So, just short of *annoying*. It didn't help my itchy back, lemme tell ya.

"The pastor... threw something out by accident, so I got sent to do the dirty work," I lied.

I know. *Bad* Lochlan.

The women kept walking past.

"Hope you found whatever it was you were looking for," said almost-whiny-voice over her shoulder. I couldn't tell if she was lying. That was interesting. Maybe I'd imagined my new 'superpowers' the previous night?

My eyes still worked. Watching their backs, I noted that the mute girl was examining the ground and no longer paid me any mind.

I ambled along behind the pair for two reasons. Number one, I wasn't sure they weren't searching for the same thing I was. And two, I had to keep looking for something myself—especially before they might stumble over it. *Finders, keepers.*

Something small and white caught my attention at the edge of the grass on my left, wedged into a crack of the cement pavement and shrouded by fresh weeds. The girls were still walking away, so I turned to take a closer look.

I'm not sure what I noticed first. That I wasn't hearing the clippity-clop of the Doc Martens that Miss Mute was wearing, or that the white square I was eyeing was a plastic-coated tag with a logo imprinted on it, but I whipped around to check on the derby girls again.

About twenty-five yards away, the hipster pair had reached the far end of the alley near the street then turned back around. Almost-whiny was standing still and watched me with her head cocked. It reminded me of something a dog would do.

Miss Mute stalked back in my direction.

I reached down for the white tag and quickly put it in my pocket.

Almost-whiny came my way, too, walking a few steps behind her silent, uglier partner.

I could have bolted, just run in the opposite direction, but those two were between me and the Bomber, and I don't like running that much. Beyond that, now the nosy pair were irritating me, and I wasn't in the mood.

I took the initiative when Miss Mute got within about ten yards.

"That's close enough, thanks," I called out. My left hand was almost behind my hip, poised to reach for my handgun.

Miss Mute halted and Almost-whiny walked up and stood about ten feet across from her pal.

They were both armed, too, I realized. Beneath the vests.

"Find something?" Almost-whiny talked creepily through her toothy smile. Like some cub-killing hyena from a cartoon.

"You seem awfully concerned about me," I said. "Not that I don't appreciate it, but don't you girls have a roller rink or something to get to?"

Miss Mute smiled for the first time.

Yeah, that wasn't good.

"You could just show us what's in your pockets," suggested Hyena-girl.

"You've lost something too? Wow, what a coincidence!"

Hyena-girl was still smiling. "Yes, amazing isn't it?"

Amazing. I said: "Okay, I know—how 'bout you tell me what *you're look-ing for*, and I'll tell you if I found it."

"How about you show us what you found, and we'll decide if it belongs to us or not," Hyena-girl said, and she punctuated her point with a contemp-tuous smirk.

Miss Mute hissed, "Why we even talkin' to this pretty boy? Look at him! Just anotha' arrogant male that needs puttin' down."

She could speak, if only barely. I'm not sure what surprised me more, hearing words coming out of her mouth or the Brooklyn accent. The man-hate? That was too common.

Now, you see, things were going from bad to worse and fast. I'd decided that these two 'ladies' were a genuine threat. They'd decided *I had something they wanted,* so I wasn't sure how they'd react to any moves I made, but odds were pretty good that they were going to go for their guns if I made them too nervous—or if they decided I'd be easier to frisk *dead*.

When you find yourself in a situation like that, what do you do? I know what I typically go with, and learned it from years on stage, playing my sax on city streets, and walking through crowds of unpredictable, often drunk and high people. I improvise. Distract. And then I look for an out.

"Okay, let's calm down, *sisters*. Obviously, you're here for a reason I don't fully comprehend, and I don't wanna be bothered. But, in the interest of world peace, I'll show you what I have in my pockets. Just gonna reach back here nice and slow. Nobody get twitchy. Okay?"

Hyena-girl nodded. Brooklyn continued to stare at me, even harder now that she saw my left hand was reaching into a back pocket.

I pulled out my blues harp and showed it to the derby girls, flipping it from back to front in my hand.

"See? Just a harmonica. That's all." I put the blues harp to my lips and played some breathy riffs that would have made Muddy Waters proud. After some of those, I improvised on a spontaneous melody and after a few mo-ments more I saw the eyes of my crowd of two soften. It was also right then that something astounding happened again. *I felt their emotions,* like a press between my eyes. Exactly like had happened the night before with Connie Winter. I sensed raw, hungry hatred cool down to a more tepid calmness, until I knew I had them listening to every single note in anticipation of the next. They emanated content—even a hint of happiness.

I had their rapt attention, but I stopped playing anyway. I kept the blues harp in hand and waggled my empty right palm at them. Both derby girls blinked as their eyes peeled off of my harmonica, and they stared at me hard.

"Okay, next item," I said, and reached into my right, front jeans pocket for my phone. "Well, would you look at that. A phone!" Again, I made the effort to twiddle it from front to back, making a display of just how ordinary an object the phone was.

"And what did I find on the ground?" I swapped my harmonica over to my right hand, leaning my weight to the side, and pointed a finger down at my left pocket. I dug inside slowly and withdrew my folded multi-tool. "This would have been a shame to lose."

The expressions on the derby girls waxed as both pairs of eyebrows pulled tight, and the uglier one frowned openly at me. Hyena-girl, on the other hand, still had the semblance of a toothy smile on her face. She unconsciously twirled the end of a long, braided ponytail that lazily dangled over one shoulder, the hair some unnatural, yellow tint. She said, "That's *not* what you picked up."

"Isn't it?" I shrugged. "Okay, when you're right, you're right. It isn't. But wanna see something cool?" I didn't wait for a reply. "Of-course-you-do…"

Brooklyn pulled a hand closer into her chest. I was betting there would be a lady-grip pistol hidden under her vest. Before she completed her move, I began juggling.

That's right. I can juggle.

I first tossed the multi-tool above my head from my left hand and quickly added my blues harp and phone into the midair mix. I'd done this hundreds of times since I was a kid, and three relatively small objects wasn't much of a challenge.

But what I make look easy, I can also make dazzling. I changed up the tosses from a circular rotation and into a piston-action, pumping in the air before me.

Hyena-girl let out a laugh, and Brooklyn dropped her hands back down to her hips. They moved closer together by inches while they focused on my act until the gap between them was only a body length.

"Now, I don't know how long I can keep this up, ladies. I'm a little rusty." As I spoke, I closed the distance between me and the derby girls, bit by little bit, keeping my foot movements from side to side, and forward, and juggling sometimes higher into the air to pull attentive eyes up and away from my body.

My phone soared to the apex of my juggle and the derby girls watched its arc.

And they both got struck hard in the face—when I hurled the harmonica and multi-tool simultaneously at their heads.

The two screamed out cries of pain and surprise and reflexively grabbed their foreheads. Though I'd hit my targets, both strikes scored above the eyes. Blinding throws would have been better for me. I needed to practice that move.

Just a second behind my throws, I snatched my phone out of the air and burst into a charge, extending my arms.

I spread my 'wings' well over six feet and clothes-lined the derby girls like something out of the WWE. They went flat on their backs, cracked their skulls good on the cement, and wind exploded from their lungs all at once. Hyena-girl got taken down by her chin and neck, so she was gagging. But Brooklyn got the worst of it with a bloody nose, and she groaned angrily.

What a messed-up week it had turned into. In just two days, I'd been forced to assault three women. But, hey, whoever enlisted these chicks was definitely an equal opportunity employer. Assuming these two were under the same banner as Connie.

Unfortunately, Brooklyn showed me some 'She can do it' attitude. Even knocked down and with a bloody nose, she got her pistol clear of its shoulder holster before I could stop her. It was a scary-looking, black Ruger with a silencer attached.

Things play out in slow-mo when your adrenaline races. The extra-long handgun oozed out from her armpit, until it got all the way loose and halfway pointed at me. Eventually, my brain determined that she was about to kill me.

But the advantage was still mine. My charge had taken me past the derby girls by a few feet, so I was behind them when Brooklyn went for her Ruger. This meant she had to turn over on her side and twist to get a bead on me. More bad news for Brooklyn was that she'd gotten blood from her nose in her left eye.

On the other side of things, I was still on my feet, pissed off, with adrenaline jack-hammering my heart. I didn't even want to try drawing my own gun. I'd have to shoot Brooklyn to stop her if I did, and she'd probably still get a shot off before me.

I did what I knew I could before Brooklyn corrected her aim...and kicked her in the back of the head with a super-sized leg—so hard the red ribbon tying her hair came loose. That also knocked her senseless, but she still pulled the damn trigger once. Whether consciously or by reflex, I'll never know.

The attached silencer did its job. The bullet sounded like someone pounded a large desk stapler on a stack of papers. In fact, the ricochet off the church buildings behind me was actually louder—loud enough to make me duck.

Hyena-girl barked a cough, pulled her own gun out and fired three shots wildly above her head. *Snick-snick-snick.*

Luckily for me she didn't have time to aim and was still on her back. All three rounds missed.

I did the most logical thing next. I ran. I moved under the covered walkway of the church's exterior, and used some surrounding trees as cover, then rushed in the Bomber's direction, hugging the wall and staying head-down behind a hedgerow.

Being a tall guy sucks when you're getting shot at, by the way. I felt as big as a barn.

Snick-snick-snick. Three more shots plunked into the surrounding terrain. They tempted me to roll on the ground, but I knew it was safer to keep moving.

I pulled my Glock, looked over my shoulder, then kept going in an awkward, ducking jog. Hyena-girl was kneeling next to Brooklyn, and took aim at me, but I popped off one quick shot at her before she could fire.

My Glock wasn't suppressed—it was loud and scary.

While I'm sure Hyena-girl was trying to hit me, I meant for my shot to miss. I wanted to make her face-plant on the concrete. So, loud-and-scary was what I was counting on.

Hyena-girl obliged and hit the ground flat. She still had her silenced pistol pointed in my direction though. She was no amateur, and I broke into a flat-out run.

By the time I was old enough to shoot, my father had already been gone for years, or Dad would have taught me guns, I'm sure. He'd been military.

My mother's brother Conor had been around, but he was a scientist and not into firearms. So, I'd picked up what I knew from friends and their parents. Going to the range or out onto someone's ranch, that sort of thing. *Texas, born-and-raised.* That's me.

Understand, I was more than prepared to shoot someone, if it meant my life, but I didn't want to. Not again.

Someone had sent these two killers. What's the mob term? *Cleaners.* They were searching for something to 'clean,' maybe anything, and I'd found *something.* They still had no idea what was in my pocket—I wasn't sure what the plastic tag was yet either, though I had a good idea. Unfortunately, this meant these two would be a problem for me again.

I needed to get out of Dodge, figure out what I'd found, and check if it would help me locate Vicki.

Oh, and not get shot.

A disturbance is exactly what these hit-girls were trying to avoid, thus the suppressed pistols. On the flip side, though I'd tried hard to *be the ninja* to begin with, a big, fucking disturbance was my best chance to stay alive and maybe get the pair off my tail.

I didn't turn to glance at my attackers. Instead, I fired three more booming shots over my head, and prayed for somebody to call the cops.

A bullet whizzed like a wasp past my left ear.

"Fuck!"

I finally reached the street near the corner of the church, ducked around it, and stopped. I planted my feet, turned hard, and poked around to look back up the alley.

Hyena-girl was running in my direction. Maybe thirty yards away. Behind her in the distance, I could make out Brooklyn crawling to her feet.

I breathed in, aimed my Glock at Hyena-girl, and fired two shots.

There was no smile on the tattooed girl's face when the first shot took her in the chest. My second shot missed.

Hyena-girl let out an ear-piercing shriek and stumbled a half-step backward, a hand clutched above her breasts near one shoulder.

Then, incredibly, the bitch managed to lift her gun and re-aimed.

I ducked around the corner and sprinted to the Bomber, keys in hand.

A few pedestrians were running in different directions. If anyone had seen me shooting, it couldn't be helped.

I holstered my Glock under the loose back of my t-shirt when I reached the Bomber. The driver's side allowed me to use the car as cover, and I inserted my key.

My hands were shaking.

Police sirens wailed, maybe a mile away at most. I clicked open the car door and risked one more look at the church and the alley, but there was no sign of Hyena-girl, although I half-expected her to do a female Terminator reveal and finish me in the street.

I jumped into my car, then started the engine on the first try. The old Volvo was nothing if not reliable.

As luck would have it, the intersection presented me with a green light, so I drove straight down the road, and tried my damnedest not to speed. A racing heart makes that difficult though. I'd just *shot* somebody.

I drove and drove, putting distance between me and the alley. An Austin police car sped past from the opposite direction, about a half-mile away from the shooting, but I resisted the urge to duck. To my utter relief, it kept going.

After what seemed like forever—but was probably only ten minutes—I pulled over into a grocery store parking lot where I could easily disappear the Bomber into a long row of cars.

I stayed in my car with the engine and air conditioner still running, sucking in deep breaths. And I kept telling myself I'd done what I'd had to do.

Eventually, I got myself under control. But my guts were tying in knots that seemed intent on reaching up and strangling my heart, too.

Amidst all those feelings of guilt and regret, at some point in the fight I'd shoved my phone back into my jeans. That was the good news. The bad? I'd left my multi-tool and a blues harp in the alley, after I'd thrown them at the derby girls—complete with my fingerprints.

Not my smoothest move. Had it been worth it?

I pulled the white plastic tag from my pocket. It was imprinted with a company logo. TraqThat.

My heart leapt. *Worth it.*

"Vicki, you absent-minded genius!" The prize I'd found in the alley was a GPS tracking tag. They're typically placed on phones, key chains—even people's kids. This was advanced tech—way beyond more standard Bluetooth tags. This sort could be found via satellite, just like most phones and larger mobile devices.

And Vicki being Vicki, she'd always had a knack for losing things. From the gummy sticker on the reverse of the TraqThat, it was easy to surmise that she'd pulled this off her phone before her abduction and then left it as a digital breadcrumb.

If I could somehow gain access to her TraqThat account, I might locate her. She might have stashed another tag on herself.

I dug into my pocket then unlocked my phone. The text message from Silana was still on the screen.

Please call me afterwards.

I dialed the contact number I'd input from Conrad's business card, and Silana answered on the second ring.

"Lochlan! Are you hurt?"

I was done being surprised. "I'm fine," I replied. "You were right. We need to talk."

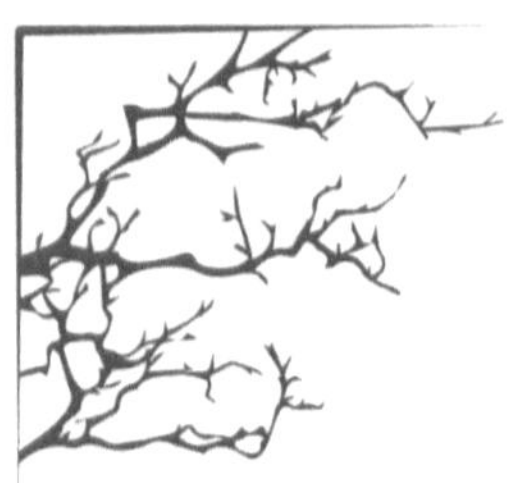

Chapter 9

"*Mais oui, bien sûr.* I gave my directions to Paz yesterday. Do you also want them?"

"Oh, dinner's at your place?" *Interesting.* "I'll get them. What time is best?"

"Yes, we wished to entertain you here at home, tonight. We will still, I hope." Silana's voice became adamant. "But come. You should come here *now*, Lochlan."

"All right, all right. I'll be there as soon as I can."

"Very good. *Please* be careful, *mon ami.*"

Be careful and don't be crazy. I sighed. "Always."

"*À tout de suite.*"

"*Ciao,*" I replied.

What the hell was happening? I'd had my doubts about the whole recording deal from the outset, but now? This had turned into another animal.

There was no reason to wait. I called Pack.

"Loch! How's it going?"

"It's going, Pack. It's going." I opened my backpack on the passenger's seat then removed my iPad from it. "Hey, I need those directions to dinner. Can you email me?"

"Yeah, man. Was about to send it. I got you. Give me a minute."

"Awesome. We're still on for tonight, then."

"As far as I know," Pack agreed.

"Great. I'll see you soon."

"Whoa, chief. You onto something? You find Vicki?"

"Haven't found her, but yeah, I'm on the trail. Best I don't talk about it, Pack. For your own good."

There was a brief silence. "Yeah. I see. Probably for the best."

"Yeah, it is. Sorry, Pack. I don't mean anything by it."

"No worries. But don't get yourself killed, man. We haven't even gotten to the tour yet!"

I laughed. "I'll try to stay alive. I swear."

"Okay, 'mano. See you soon!"

"Yep. Later." I hung up.

A minute after that, my tablet chimed and I was scrolling through my email, opening Pack's Google map to Silana's house. It was situated along the Colorado River, in the luxurious Lake Austin region. *Richie-Riches*. Hardly a surprise.

"A sunny day on the water. Could be worse," I said out loud.

The Bomber was still running, so I was back on Austin roads in no time.

THE SUN WAS NEARLY overhead when I reached Silana's estate. The drive would have been pleasant under other circumstances. Having just shot a woman in the chest though, my mind wasn't focused on clear, blue skies and the lush green of riverside forests.

Still, it was impossible to not be impressed by the estate. It was something. A riverside spread several acres in size, much of it easily viewable from the main road I'd just left.

I rolled the Bomber up to the closed iron gate at the entrance, and there was a curved, metal arm with keypad and speaker on the driver's side. I turned off the stereo before rolling down my window.

No obvious cameras, but I was sure they were there. Before I even pressed a button on the keypad, the speaker proved me right. The box squawked and a lady's voice that wasn't Silana's whispered at me through the intercom.

"Good morning, Mr. Nohr. Welcome."

"Uh, thanks. But no 'what's the password?' I'm a little disappointed."

"I was prepared in advance, Mr. Nohr. They told me it'd be hard to impersonate you."

"Ah, I see." *Cameras.* "Well, then you should know I don't want you to call me mister ever again. Lochlan. Or Loch, please."

A pretty laugh escaped the intercom. "As you wish, Lochlan. I'm opening the gate. Please park anywhere along the circle ahead."

"Thank you."

"You're quite welcome."

There was a barely audible beep, followed by a loud clack, as an automated lock disengaged. The arched, iron gate swung open wide in one long section. I noticed a coat of arms at its pinnacle. River waves surmounted by what looked like symbols of the four elements.

The driveway was long and wide, bordered by brick, and it branched in different directions off of a circle closest to the main house—like you'd expect at the entrance of a five-star hotel. There were no vehicles parked anywhere nearby, so I stopped directly under the outdoor archway that shaded the drive, in front of large double doors.

The compound was sandstone-colored brick and stucco, with terracotta roof, the grounds meticulously maintained and green—greener than I usually saw around Austin. Unless I was standing on a golf course. Yet, the whole place mingled modern with natural, in a charming way.

Honestly, it made me feel like an interloper.

As if on cue, two huge German Shepherds wandered around a corner of the house to my left and stood alert, staring at me. Amazingly neither of the dogs barked or rushed up to the side of the Bomber.

I didn't move.

I'm not afraid of dogs, but I knew better than to startle them.

That turned out a wise choice because things got more interesting. The two biggest dogs I'd ever seen in my life (up to that moment anyway) stalked up behind the Shepherds. I recognized the breed. They were Irish Wolfhounds, shaggy hair and all.

But there was still one more. Up sauntered the biggest Goddamn dog *period*. It walked—no, strode around the other four hounds and assessed me. And I mean literally. Its eyes had such keen intelligence behind them that the hairs on the back of my neck stood straight.

The alpha was another Wolfhound, but he was muscled, blue-gray, not mottled brown like the smaller pair, and I was sure if he stood on his hind legs, he'd be taller than me. Considering I'm six feet six inches, that's saying something.

I grabbed my backpack and slowly, carefully exited the Bomber, keeping my eyes on the dogs the entire time. I didn't bother locking my car. Someone would steal with the Jumbo Pack around? *Right.*

To my relief the ornate front doors opened inward, and Silana Michaux stepped out to greet me.

She was radiant in a forget-me-not flowered, yellow sun dress…barefoot, and her dark auburn locks flowed free across her back and shoulders. Quite the contrast from the business attire she'd worn when we first met.

I caught myself staring into Silana's deep blue eyes and abruptly shook my head.

She padded over, gripped my hands, and looked pointedly up at me, as if searching for a spectre.

"You *are* unhurt," she breathed.

I winced. "Yeah, I'm not bleeding, if that's what you mean…."

"Beautiful boy." Silana touched fingertips to my face and gently pushed my chin so she could closely examine me on both sides. I guess she didn't believe me. "I know. Questions. They can wait. Come inside and make yourself at home."

I shifted my eyes back over to the dogs and Silana followed my gaze.

"Oh, you've met my puppies." She laughed. "Don't worry. We keep them well fed."

I gave her a perturbed look. "Lucky me."

Silana let out another musical laugh, then spoke to her dogs, their leader in particular. "It's okay, Cu. Lochlan is a friend. Come say hello. *Come,* all of you."

Just like that, five dogs surrounded me, sniffing and chuffing happily.

"This big boy is Cú Chulainn," Silana said, scratching the alpha behind an ear (pronounced Coo-*cullen* in the old Irish). "He's smarter than some of the people who work for me, and as loyal as only a dog can be."

Cu's big, furry head reached easily past my waist, and I put a hand down for him to sniff. Or bite off. Once he was done with that, I pet him for good measure. "Hello, Cu."

Cu gave me a friendly bump of his head and then stepped back and gently nudged Silana. The rest of the pack circled around and took turns getting petted by her.

"Okay. You've met him now. *Go play*," Silana ordered.

Cu let out a short bark, low and happy, gave me one more look as if to say 'Mind your manners,' then led the four smaller dogs at a run, away and onto the grounds, quickly out of my line of sight.

Silana beamed a smile at me, tugged my arm once, then headed for the open doors.

I hefted my backpack and followed.

The foyer wasn't as fancy as part of me had expected—I guess I'd imagined Cinderella's castle. The large floor tiles were a brown, marbled granite. A carved-stone table stood just inside and a few feet in front of the French doors of the entrance, roses in expensive ceramic vases adorning its surface, those vases encircled by a wreath of entwined grasses, vines and flowers. Beyond that table was a very large room with a high ceiling, decorated in a tasteful combination of modern and antique.

Silana reached out and tugged lightly at one of my hands, guiding me toward a curved couch in front of a gigantic marble fireplace. I looked past the couch and out through tall, glass doors and windows that comprised most of the far wall of the great room and made out the shape of a pool beyond.

Absentmindedly, I dropped my backpack onto the couch and sat. My head was spinning when I noticed a silver tray on a glass-topped coffee table. The silver was lined with delicate slices of fruit of various kinds, and there were decanters of what I guessed were apple and orange juice. There was also a stack of freshly cooked bacon and sausage patties. The smell was incredible. After a moment I was salivating.

Silana smiled and stacked a choice of food onto a silver plate. She handed it to me and placed a fork in my left hand, poured me a tall glass of orange juice, and then set that on the coffee table too.

"Eat," she commanded.

In another minute, I wasn't thinking about gunshots and derby girl assassins. There was only bacon, sausage patties, and pulpy orange juice.

Unfortunately, I came back to reality too fast. "What the hell is going on, Silana?"

Silana sat on the couch next to me, watching me eat. A small smile never left her exquisite face as she watched my jaw grind, yet somehow it wasn't awkward. It was just who she was...like some great, unblinking cat, and I was eating her morning catch.

But eventually she huffed a tiny sigh. "I'm sorry. It was not my, nor Conrad's, intent to alarm you, but—I did not foresee this turn of events with Victoria. Things are happening too quickly..."

I set my plate down and wiped my mouth with a napkin. "You saw? You *knew* about the rollergirls?"

Silana's eyes glistened.

"Silana is a seer." Conrad entered from the long hallway. He was dressed in khaki shorts, leather sandals, and a loose, white button-down shirt, his mustache perfectly groomed. He extended a hand as he approached. "Welcome to our home. Good to see you're in one piece. You had Silana incredibly worried."

I shook Conrad's hand. "Yeah. Things have happened. But you seem to know that already."

"Some of it," Silana said. "I saw—*guns*."

I grimaced.

"Silana's precognition is...limited. A rare gift, but by no means predictable," Conrad said, squinting one eye. "I have to admit, you seem unusually accepting of what we're telling you. Though, I shouldn't be that surprised, I suppose...not after this morning."

Silana tilted her head at me, and her lips curled away from her perfect teeth.

"Yeah, well..." I looked across the pool. "She's not the only one." I let that statement hang in the air, then added, "You're married? I noticed the rings back at the Music Hall." I gestured around the room. "And now all of *this*."

Silana looked down at her wedding band. "Very observant. Yes, we have been married for ages."

"Forever," Conrad said.

His wife rolled her eyes but never lost her smile. "We have not been completely forthcoming. Finish eating, and we'll start by giving you a proper tour."

I gazed blindly at the food and the glistening silverware. "I shot someone," I said.

Conrad groaned and then barked. "I told you! The boy is too reckless!"

"*Conrad*," Silana warned.

Conrad still raged. "What possessed you, Lochlan? This missing girl means so much, that you're willing to risk imprisonment and *death?*"

"I think it's romantic," Silana said. "Surely you haven't forgotten the feeling, my love."

"As always, you're too easily swayed by idealism." Conrad reached for the silver serving tray, snatched up a piece of bacon then chewed it up angrily.

"I have a bad habit of doing what I want. And I want Victoria back, safe and sound," I growled. "This dirty cop I found spilled enough to lead me to that alleyway in the first place. I didn't know there were gonna be assassins! But I do know there's a big Chinese kidnapper involved. Maybe we worry more about him and Vicki and less about what a mess I'm making?"

"*Chinese?*" Conrad locked eyes with me. "I can't deny you've tracked down something before the entire Austin Police Department." His face softened into a grin. "You've got a set on you, boy, that's for sure. And brains to match. But you're going to need proper training if you plan to run around playing cowboy detective. I—"

"Unfortunately, there's no time for that," Silana interjected.

Conrad looked at her. There was complete silence, but then he nodded agreement, though it appeared grudgingly.

Silana closed her eyes. "Did your informant give details about this Chinese man? Did he, perhaps, have some distinguishing marks?"

She couldn't see, but my mouth was hanging open, so I closed it first before answering. "Yeah, she did. She said—he had facial tattoos down one side. Some Chinese script. Lettering."

Conrad chuckled softly and smiled at his wife.

Silana's perfect forehead wrinkled as her eyes caught mine again when she opened them. "Lochlan, do you know what a Blood Moon is?"

"Uh. Sure. A super moon. Earth casts a shadow over the Moon. And I suppose maybe scattered sun rays turn it red," I answered.

Silana pressed forward. "Exactly as you've been taught, though I've never seen a shadow change the color of something. But what is the significance of such a moon?"

I cocked an eyebrow. Silana's comment about the shadow had me think-ing, but I let it go and asked, "You're not gonna tell me a werewolf story, are you?"

"Bad stuff by bad people," Conrad said, and he reached for a piece of ba-con as if to emphasize his point.

Silana concluded. "Often Satanic ritual murder. The timing of this Blood Moon is not coincidental. Not to sound alarmist, but considering this week, it would be prudent to treat this lunar event as a clue."

"Great. So, maybe I'm up against a death cult of werewolves *and* Sa-tanists. Doesn't matter." I pulled the Glock from my back holster and placed it on the glass coffee table next to my now empty plate.

"You can't shoot your way out of everything," Conrad said. He chomped another piece of bacon.

"Not everything. Worked today though. Get me some bigger guns if you're worried." I frowned. "But...shit... I left evidence at the church. Univer-sity Methodist."

Conrad stared at me hard, then pulled his phone off a belt clip. It chirped. "Gloria."

Three seconds ticked by. "Yes, sir." It was the same voice I'd heard at the front gate.

"Send a covert team to University Methodist Church near UT. I want a sweep of the area for..." He gave me a querying look.

What the hell. I didn't have time to get my brain around it, so I answered him. "A multi-tool with a sharp blade. And a small harmonica. In the alley behind the church next to the Littlefield House."

"A multi-tool knife and—" Conrad laughed. "—a harmonica." He smiled at me. "In the alley between the church and the old Littlefield House."

Conrad's phone barked like a walkie-talkie. Gloria asked, "Sorry. What?"

"A harm-on-i-ca," Conrad stressed.

I motioned for Conrad to hand me his phone, which he did.

"There were two roller derby girls. I shot one...white girl with a rotten yellow dye-job. The uglier one's brunette and Hispanic. Jean vests on both...mini-skirts...body tattoos. Man-sized and hard-looking. Armed with Rugers," I said into Conrad's phone.

"Got it. Thank you, Lochlan," Gloria said.

"Thank *you*." I handed the phone back.

"Tell the team to clean up and sample any blood stains they find. Police are probably there already, but get it done," ordered Conrad.

Gloria responded, "We're on it. I'll inform you the minute we find anything."

"Thanks, Gloria." Conrad hooked his phone back onto his belt and said, "You'll have to tell us the whole story someday."

"It's a doozy," I replied.

"I bet," Conrad said.

Silana, still sitting next to me on the couch, gripped my left hand with both of hers. "Don't worry. We're used to problems like this."

Problems. Not exactly how I'd describe the mess I found myself in, but okay.

"Do you even work for LMG?" I asked.

"Yes and no," replied Silana.

"I knew it! Too good to be true! All of it!" I leapt to my feet.

Silana grabbed my hand hard before I could take a second step. "We *own* LMG."

"We own quite a few companies," Conrad added, casually.

I stared at the duo stupidly for a moment then sat back down on the couch with a heavy thump. It was enough to jostle Silana. She giggled and smoothed out her flowered sundress. Under other circumstances her curves would have further addled my brain.

"Wow." I have a gift for words sometimes, but this wasn't one of them.

Silana put both hands out, palms up. "We're real, Lochlan. We love music. It's perhaps my greatest single passion." She paused then gently pulled my face to look at her own. "We have never lied to you. We never will...if we can help it. We simply can't tell you everything overnight. We have to trust you. We have to trust one another. You do understand, don't you?"

I blinked. "Yeah. I get it. I get it."

Silana tugged gently at her dress where it only barely covered her knees. "The great irony is that if it weren't for LMG, we might never have found you. You're that special, Lochlan."

"Silana sensed something in you from the first. You aren't just an extraordinary musician. We want you to record with us, but we *need* to find out who the *real* Lochlan Nohr is. It was a logical step to sign you to the label, not on-ly for the music, but more importantly, to earn your faith in us," Conrad said.

"If I am right, we share a bond, as I do with my husband," Silana added. She stood. "Come. Let's walk, have a chat. You look, how do you say...shell-shocked. Best to get your blood flowing."

Sure, I was shocked. I wasn't so shocked, though, that I couldn't grab an-other piece of bacon as I stood. Silana laughed at that.

I also retrieved my Glock from the coffee table, then holstered it.

Silana joined Conrad, and I followed the two around on my tour of the compound.

"The kitchen is big enough to entertain large events. We sometimes host here on the property, but whenever you are here with us, consider it home. Nothing less. Take what you need from the fridge, whenever you want," Silana said. "There will always be more."

My entire apartment could fit into their pantry. There were two indoor bars, as well as outdoor grills and dining patios.

We kept walking.

Three elegant offices stacked one on top of the other, joined by a spiral staircase. The top office had a soundproof recording booth. There was a guest house with billiard and pool tables, built next to a grotto-style pool and gi-ant Jacuzzi.

There were six garages near the main house, but the highlight was the en-tertainment center. It contained workout rooms, a private home theater with a dozen leather recliners—and a *gymnasium.*

The gym had a very high roof like you'd find in any sports arena. The floors were polished wood marked for basketball. It all reminded me of high school PE and college pickup games.

"Wanted you to see this," Conrad said, and he pointed.

There, along one wall of the huge gymnasium-garage, was a touring bus. It was immaculately maintained—waxed and glistening in painted swirls of light brown and black.

It was beautiful. Beautiful enough to make my eyes water.

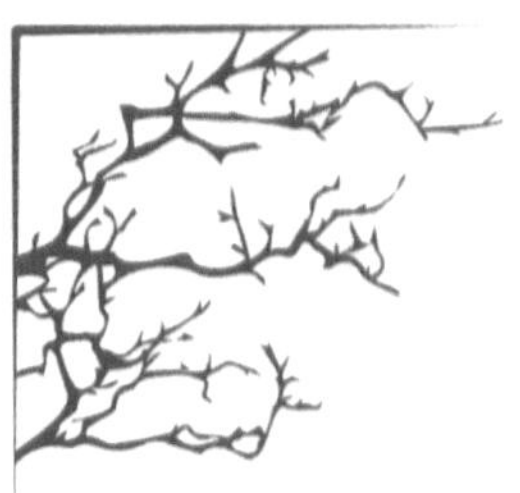

Chapter 10

Silana's tour of the grounds inevitably led us down to the river, a boathouse, and a thin strip of private beach.

Lake Austin is, in fact, not a lake. It's a section of the Colorado River, averaging perhaps a half-mile in width, and, in typically confusing Austin, Texas fashion, it's not even the Colorado River you're thinking of. It's the 'colored' river, and it begins and ends in Texas. Never even touches the state of Colorado.

The air near the water was so heavily oxygenated from the trees and flora, that it invigorated me. The temperature was near perfect and cooled by a steady breeze.

Silana picked up a pebble off the riverbank then skipped it across the water's surface. She was an expert—her first stone hopped a dozen times.

"One of your other hidden talents?" I asked.

Silana's laugh mixed with the light lapping of the tiny waves that crept up and back along the beach. She handed me a flat stone as large as her own palm, but in my hand, I could easily press it between finger and thumb. I cast it low and straight. The first skip off the river sprang the rock a good twenty feet before it hit hard for a second, third, fourth, and fifth skips, then machine-gunned into smaller splashes, and ultimately disappeared under the river.

Childlike, Silana clapped her hands happily. Her smile was even more beautiful there near the river, the sunshine beaming across her face and through her hair. She wore no sunglasses like I did, and yet she never squint-ed from the sun's watery reflection.

Conrad stood on the grassy rise behind us, just above the sand of the riverbank, and shaded his own eyes as he scanned the horizon. My backpack was on the ground near him. "No rain today," he said.

"Rained itself out last night," I agreed. "That's okay with me. It's beautiful here. In any weather, I'm sure."

"You should see the French chateau. Silana makes a habit of buying waterfront homes."

I'd already given up being surprised by the wealth of these two once we left the interior of the decked-out tour bus back in the gymnasium. Despite it all, the pair was grounded. This meant they were 'old money.'

Silana padded over. "We'll arrange a European tour for the band soon. Best to see the world while there's still a world left to see—and you must visit France! And..." Her voice trailed off.

I gave Silana a questioning tilt of my noggin.

"Many places. So many places. You'll see," she whispered.

"Sounds like you have people everywhere," I said then looked back at Conrad.

"Hundreds," Conrad acknowledged. "And those just our closest retainers."

"And the special teams? Like the one you called earlier. What's that about? Security company or something?"

"Something to that effect. But they're *my* employees, not subcontractors. We only keep security personnel we have a connection to. True loyalty can't be bought."

I nodded my approval. "You got that right." I gave Conrad a studied look. "You've had military experience. I know—my old man was Air Force."

"Yes, I served. The last time was in Germany. And your father. You remember him well?"

"I remember. I was seven years old." I glanced out across the river, and images of my father sprang to mind. His uniform. Me on his shoulders grasping my arms around his neck. A parade marching by.

His face wasn't clear, but the feelings were crystal. I swallowed back the familiar, hard tinge of regret—it had been awhile since I'd had such a clear memory of Dad invoked.

I came out of it to the touch of Silana's hand on my arm again. I smiled down at her.

"Losing people we love reminds us of why we are here, Lochlan," she said. "You have become the man you are in part because of loss. In part because of your father's love." She looked away from me. "Your parents sacrificed much for you. They have been blessed for it."

I didn't know how to respond. Should it have shocked me that Silana knew intimate details of my family? Perhaps. Perhaps not. These two had vast resources. I sensed I was going to use those resources to my advantage or get lost in unfounded resentment.

I adapt. I overcome. In that moment, I used them.

"You've done your homework. You'd better be prepared to share," I stated.

"Of course, *mon ami*," Silana replied.

"We intend to keep no secrets from you, Lochlan. Truth isn't our problem—the problem is knowing when and how to reveal it. Right now, you're clearly set on this road to rescue your friend. I suggest we focus on that first and come back to the history lessons."

Again, I agreed. Conrad was a logical guy. I admired that.

And Silana? Like spring sunshine on the river, she was naturally warm, inviting, and elemental. The chemistry wasn't sexual with her, not intentionally, despite her great beauty. She exuded a sensual yet motherly presence. It was an odd combo for a woman so youthful, yet her aura was undeniable.

I was already convinced of her friendship, and I'd known her for no more than a handful of hours. But then again, the best friendships tend to feel like old friendships right from the start, don't they?

I picked out a smooth stone for myself and a perfect pebble for Silana, which I handed over to her.

"Ready?" I asked.

"*Oui!*"

We both took up classic tossing stances, leaning low and back, with a foot extended in front—and we let fly!

My stone careened and bounced repeatedly, then skipped arrow-straight and far. It was a near flawless toss to make me proud and I was sure that Silana could never match it.

Silana's pebble flipped over across the path of my rock—and crisscrossed along the straight line of my toss, sometimes behind, other times in front. It should have been impossible. The two stones carried on like this for thirty yards before ending in a splash and vanishing in the same point in the river.

I stood up arrow-straight with my jaw hanging open. "What the—"

Silana went tight-lipped with a small smile and blinked her big, blue eyes at me.

Conrad was laughing. "She cheated," he said.

I cracked a slack-jawed smile and contemplated that statement, then stared accusingly at Silana. "You...did that?"

"I tossed the stone," Silana answered meekly.

My jaw was still open. "Uh-huh." I closed my mouth and glowered back at Conrad. "We'll come back to this. *Later.* I don't know how much more craziness I can handle right now."

"Smart," Conrad agreed. "Follow me, Loch. I think you'll appreciate my workshop."

Silana sighed. "Boys."

She wasn't wrong. I was instantly curious and jumped off the beach onto the nearby grassy knoll, deftly picked up my backpack, then lifted Silana to the grass next to me with my free hand. I caught up to Conrad in a few long strides. He headed toward the cement path that twisted its way from the boathouse back to the main compound.

The walkway banked around a large copse of trees for half the length of a football field—and then Conrad took a sharp right turn off the visible path and headed into the woods. He spoke a word in German I didn't quite catch and wouldn't know the meaning of, anyway.

Four loud metallic clanks went off from beneath the ground ahead of us, one after the other in quick succession.

A patch of ground the width of a freight elevator rose. Its top was cleverly camouflaged by netting and forest leaves and debris. It turned out to be a one-floor elevator, with double doors on opposite sides of a round chamber, wide enough for me to stand four times abreast.

The whole structure was approximately ten feet high once it completely surfaced. Two steps allowed us easy access to the elevator, and as we approached, lights automatically snapped on beneath the roof, though in the light of that morning we could see clearly, even under the shade of oak trees.

It entranced the geek in me. I'm sure I stared.

"Watch your step," Conrad warned, and he entered the elevator. I ignored the second step entirely and then turned to offer a hand to Silana, who took it and nimbly leapt inside with us.

The interior of the elevator was well lit. Conrad pressed a single large button and the doors on both sides of the chamber steadily closed. In another few seconds, a slight bang shook the metal floor beneath us, and the elevator descended.

Silana met my gaze, and I lifted both eyebrows. As usual, she just smiled, but I could tell my reaction amused her.

In mere seconds there was another series of metallic clanks that shook the elevator. I assumed it anchored below the earth somewhere.

Only one set of the elevator's doors opened, and a wide, lit hallway was revealed. Several doorways—some open, but most closed—branched off of the hall in every direction.

"Okay, Dr. No. I have to admit, I was expecting a garage with a wooden bench, buzz saws, and hammers, but you've got your own fucking fallout shelter," I said. "Oops. Sorry, Silana."

Silana only giggled. "Don't be silly. It's fine."

Conrad grinned widely. "In fact, it *does* double as a fallout shelter. Watch..."

I trailed behind Conrad with Silana by my side. Once again, her eyes never left me. She was intent on analyzing my every reaction.

"You're loving this," I whispered to her.

Silana's face crumpled like a four-year-old who'd just gotten caught with the last cookie from the jar.

"It is not often that we bring anyone new down here. So, *oui*—your face is priceless."

At the end of the hallway, Conrad pressed a hand onto a blue-lit pad on the wall and entered an additional code via a numeric keypad. Double doors hissed like an airlock unsealing, and there was a click. The doors opened automatically as Conrad approached them. I followed.

A series of bright, white LEDs sprang to life in links across the long span of the ceiling, one after another, after another. It was like something out of *Tron*.

My eyes took a moment to adjust.

The expanse of the room was enormous. At least a hundred feet across and just as long, there were workspaces of every kind imaginable within view. Mr. Science and Mr. Fantastic could both work there, so many gadgets, tools, computer consoles, test tubes, and workbenches filled every nook and cubicle.

"Welcome to the Workshop," Conrad proclaimed.

It reminded me of Air Force base hangars from my childhood.

"Holy shit," I said. "You run all of this? Alone?"

"Oh no, I have assistants that work on projects with me...and sometimes autonomously. But only those few I've screened personally get access. Tight security. It needs to be that way."

"Yeah, I saw that." I remembered the hidden elevator and the handprint lock. "So..."

"The Workshop is where I tinker away the hours. Some of it's my hobby, but most of what goes on down here is serious business. There're other sites like this one sprinkled around the world, and the work and research done at all of them is often coordinated."

"I'm gonna venture a guess that LMG is more like one of your hobbies. I mean...." I waved a hand at the room.

"Lucent Music Group is more mine than Conrad's."

"Silana is the arts expert. I'm science and industry. But we love to dabble in one another's sandboxes."

"We've become quite diversified over the years. Sometimes even forget what we are working on. If not for help, we'd often forget altogether," Silana added. "I'm too easily distracted by the rare and wondrous."

Silana poked me playfully in the ribs with an index finger, and I flinched then laughed. "I see. Which one of you has the hacking skills? I'm capable, but time isn't on Vicki's side, so any help with this would be awesome." I removed the small TraqThat module from my pocket and held it up.

"A prize from your search?" Conrad asked.

Silana walked up close and examined the module but didn't lay a finger on it. I lowered my hand to let her see.

"Hopefully. I shot a woman to keep this safe—so if it's just junk...well, that would suck."

"Let my wife hold it for a moment," Conrad suggested.

I placed the tracker into Silana's open palm. She flashed me a brief smile then closed her eyes, and her expression waxed serene.

After a minute she opened her eyes again.

"This belonged to a young...vibrant...intelligent woman," she said.

"Vicki," I breathed.

"I can't know for sure, since I've yet to meet her. But this is no coincidence." Silana handed me back the TraqThat.

I glanced at Conrad. "We'll need a cable for this thing. And a computer."

"Here." Conrad had already walked over to a long desk full of computer monitors, and he held up a selection of differently sized USB cables.

"Care to take a stab at the login?" Conrad asked.

I thought about it. "I can make a list of a few possibilities. Do you have any experience hacking? I could download some brute force software if—"

"One sec, Loch. *Sophie.* Wake up, my dear," Conrad said to the air in the room.

"I've been listening since the lights came on," a lovely female voice responded.

I scanned the room but saw nobody but the three of us. I lifted an eyebrow. "Um. Hi?" In a day full of surprises, what was one more?

"Hello, Mr. Nohr," the disembodied voice responded.

I raised my brows at Conrad. "One of your assistants?"

"In a manner of speaking," he replied. "Sophie, define yourself for our friend, please."

"I am an AI, Mr. Nohr. Artificial Intelligence. My name was inspired by Sappho, the Greek poetess born in the seventh century BCE."

That needed a few seconds to sink in. "Uh. Right. Um...nice to meet you," I said awkwardly.

"Nice to meet you, too, Mr. Nohr."

"Just Lochlan, please. My *father* was Mr. Nohr."

There was a pause. "Lochlan. Irish. A name often given to boys native to Ireland who were born from marriages between Norwegian Vikings and Irish women."

"That's...correct. My father was originally Norwegian. Mom is part Irish."

"Interesting that you have black hair," Sophie said.

I chuckled. "Yeah. The story goes...that I get it from a Black Irish ancestor, but that's just a bad joke."

Sophie's tone sounded oddly wistful. "Your hair contrasts extremely well with your light eyes."

"Fascinating," Conrad said.

"What?" I asked, trying to not appear creeped out.

"I've never heard Sophie take such an interest in a human's looks before. Duly noted, Sophie."

"Thank you," Sophie responded.

I wasn't sure what that little exchange meant. I lifted an eyebrow at Silana.

"Sophie has good taste." Silana laughed. "I think she likes you, Lochlan."

That was a relief. The last thing I needed was a fembot added to my growing list of disgruntled and murderous females.

"Sophie, we need to hack into this tracking device connected to station three. Lochlan will provide a list of potential logins. Create variations on those as needed and generate a brute force attack on the password," commanded Conrad.

"My pleasure," answered Sophie.

"Go ahead and use this computer. Just create a text file, add some of your guesses, and Sophie will do the rest," Conrad told me, and he had his hand on a massive computer tower.

I walked over to 'station three,' then sat in its comfortable swivel chair. "Luckily for us, it's hardware, so we won't have to hack firewalls," I said. I quickly had the tracker connected to a port, and a login and password window appeared on the main monitor. I typed in my guesses to a fresh text file on the computer desktop.

"Thank you. That will make my task easier," replied Sophie. "I'm having no luck with the login. Do you have any other suggestions?"

Vicki had standard email and social media contact info, already included in my list. I had to reach deeper into my memory.

"Yeah. Think I do." I added a few more words and phrases to the text file.

At once, Sophie said, "Pixie. Underscore. Dust."

Pixie_dust. I couldn't help but grin.

"Good. Very good," Conrad said.

"Ooh. I like Victoria," Silana said.

"Excellent guess, Lochlan," praised Sophie.

"Vicki always had a thing for Tinker Bell and Disney."

Sophie continued. "Please make some password guesses now. I will extrapolate from those while I also continue with random brute force attacks."

I did as the AI asked.

The goal was straightforward—crack the login and pass for the TraqThat device and then use those same login details online. Vicki had to have a matching web account, and I was fairly certain it would contain records of GPS ping times and locations from all of her working trackers.

What I was really hoping for was another TraqThat was still on or near her—and then the real search could begin.

Some luck was with us.

"I'm in," Sophie said.

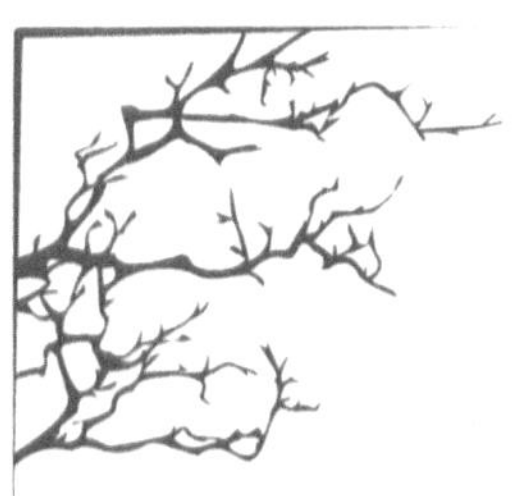

Chapter 11

"The last ping sent by Victoria Lott's key chain was on Saturday, May twenty-second, eight-sixteen p.m., originating from Harmony Smoke Shop, located on US-95 in the state of Nevada."

Sophie followed up her remark by flashing a detailed GPS map onto a large, wall-mounted monitor.

"Zoom into that, please," I requested.

At ground level, the image clearly showed that the cigar shop also sported two gas pumps.

I grunted. "So, the Chinaman took her to Nevada. I have to get there."

"See, Conrad? His risks paid off," said Silana. She patted my back. "*T'en fais pas.* We will take you."

Conrad nodded. "Indeed. Sophie, locate the airports closest to that spot."

Sophie replied lightning-quick. "The closest would be Yerington Municipal Airport." The map on the wall monitor transitioned to showing a route between the airport and Harmony Smoke Shop. "Approximate drive time from Yerington to Harmony Smoke Shop is twenty-three minutes."

"And flight time from here to Yerington?" Conrad asked.

Sophie again didn't hesitate. "Approximately two hours if you're using your G550."

I blinked. "Private jet?"

"*Ja,*" replied Conrad, in German, which was a first. "With the time change, we can have you there by lunch."

"Perhaps we should alert the FBI?" Silana mused.

Conrad shook his head. "I wouldn't advise that just yet. Could be alerting them will hasten some ill fate for Lochlan's friend. Let's get our own team on the ground and assess the situation. I suspect we're up against a capable organization that might very well have channels with the Feds."

"There's already been at least one bad cop involved in the kidnapping. After last night, the FBI's got plenty of reasons to get involved, but I still think I stand a better chance of finding Vicki on my own," I said.

"You won't be '*on your own*' this time," Conrad replied sternly. "I'm sending along two of my best. You have limited experience in this sort of thing, and while I admire your enthusiasm, you'd be better off following someone else's lead from this point."

I couldn't really argue with that logic, but I don't relinquish control so easily. "Just as long as your watchdogs follow *my lead* when I need them to, fine. I might surprise you."

Conrad sighed but a chuckle followed. "Just as strong as you are bull-headed, I bet." He grimaced. "Fine, fine. I'll explain things to the team, but you'll be best off reserving your opinions for things that don't include getting yourself killed. Am I clear?"

"Clear," I agreed.

"Sophie, contact Fan and Dante and have them come to the workshop ASAP. And tell them to be ready to roll," Conrad added.

"Calling now."

Conrad looked me up and down. "I wish we had the time to train you properly, Lochlan, but we don't. But I can equip you. Follow me."

Now, I have to admit something. Even though I was feeling emotional from that morning's shooting, I'm still a Texas boy. And every straight-shooting Texan loves gun metal. So, when Conrad Wiprut lead me to a vault door that looked like it belonged inside a bank, pressed his palm to yet another blue-lit pad on the wall, and the sound of released vacuum-sealed air whooshed into the workshop, it was like a welcome mind-wipe. My gut-wrenching guilt evaporated.

Inside the space beyond that foot-and-a-half thick, multi-layered steel door were rows and rows of racked rifles, pistols, shotguns, and varieties of fully automatic weaponry I was sure were illegal in the eyes of the Federal and Texas authorities and just about every other government on Earth.

I might as well have been ten-year-old me staring at the roller coasters at Six Flags for the first time.

A slow, steady whistle of approval escaped my lips as I walked into the armory behind Conrad. The walls were layered in hanging body armor and face-shielded helmets. There were closed lockers and open, tiered shelves, all of them containing metal ammo boxes by the dozens. There were even weapons that looked like recoilless rifles of a manufacture I wasn't familiar with, their missile and rocket ammo carefully stored in sturdy racks in a far corner of the long room.

"Welcome to the Armory," Conrad pronounced.

"This morning...is getting better," I breathed.

"Conrad lives to tinker," Silana said.

"What?" I was only half registering what was being said, I was so preoccupied with the bounty of weaponry.

"He crafted or modified much of what you see in here. He has natural gifts for engineering and transmutation," she replied.

"The Workshop isn't just a name. I have all the tools I need to gunsmith and manufacture ammo. Sophie makes that job even more efficient now, and I have a few human assistants too." Conrad walked over to an aisle rack and selected a large, black pistol. "I knew you'd appreciate my gun collection. Here. Try this one on for size."

Conrad checked the chamber on the gun before handing it over. From the side it appeared to be an ordinary M1911 pistol, but as I hefted the weapon in my left hand, I instantly noted the double barrel. "2011" was etched on the side of the thick handgun.

"I've seen videos of these before but never had the chance to shoot one. Thought someone was trolling me the first time I heard about a double-barreled .45," I said. "Holy shit. Look at this monster."

The black, semi-automatic pistol hefted perfectly in my over-sized hand, and the double trigger was no problem for my index finger. I removed and examined the empty magazine then reinserted it with a snap. The pistol was an impressive piece, no doubt.

"It's yours, Lochlan," Conrad said.

I looked down at Conrad and a stupid smile cracked open on my face.

"I could get used to surprises like this. Thank you. It's amazing." I held the 2011 up in my fist and pointed it toward the ceiling.

Conrad nodded, seemingly pleased with my assessment. "With that in your hand, you'll command anyone's attention. One well-aimed squeeze should stop anything on two legs—short of a grizzly bear."

I'm familiar with shooting .45's. I already had a prized 1911 Colt in my gun collection that had belonged to Dad. Still, I knew if I was going to use the 2011 in the field, I'd better practice first.

Conrad knew it, too. He handed me a box of bullets. "Test it out?"

"You know it."

Silana followed the two of us down to the far end of the armory, through a short hall, then into a private gun range complete with shooting stalls and automated targets attached to ceiling tracks. I shook my head in continued wonder.

"I don't suppose there's a DQ down here, too? I could go for a Blizzard," I joked.

"Heh. Not a bad idea. Sophie, put that on the to-do list," Conrad replied, and I wasn't sure he was joking.

Conrad's phone speaker barked. "Conrad." It was Gloria.

Conrad squeezed the trigger on his belt-clipped phone. "Go ahead."

"Sorry, our team didn't find the items you described. I'm assured the sweep was thorough. There *was* a police presence, both campus and Austin PD, but they mainly focused on interviewing potential witnesses, none of whom proved useful to the cops or to us. It must have been panic during the gunfire. The team sampled a blood stain before police forensics arrived. We've no reason to suspect they've found anything other than that blood. I'm concluding that Lochlan's assailants grabbed the harmonica and knife. If that's the case, we're definitely dealing with pros. But it's still possible somebody else grabbed the stuff. A transient or student. We're talking to more locals, but that's all we've got so far."

"Okay. Thanks, Gloria. Tell the team 'good work.' "

"Yes, sir. I'll inform you immediately of any changes. Anything else you need?"

Conrad thought about that. "*Ja.* Focus on finding those two assassins. One sounds like she's severely wounded. They'll have called in a pickup, but do a further sweep. Take no chances."

"Already sweeping. If they're around, we'll find them."

"Thanks. And Gloria..."

"Yes, sir?"

"I mean that. *No chances*. If they resist, the team is to kill and recover all possible evidence."

"Understood."

Conrad's phone went silent. His brow crinkled. "That's not good," he said.

"That's slick if they grabbed evidence, and still escaped with the one I wounded—all while avoiding the cops at the same time." I shook my head again. "What am I dealing with here?"

"Definitely not just some cartel running a human trafficking op. I don't like to jump to conclusions, but we can safely assume whatever group is running these criminals you've encountered, they have an agenda. The typical scum just isn't this thorough, this meticulous," Conrad replied.

Silana was silent. She was occupying herself by running a curious hand over various wall-racked weapons, but I could tell it was nervous energy being released.

"What d'you hope to gain from examining blood?" I wondered aloud.

Conrad took a breath, but Sophie was faster. "DNA," she answered. "To verify species, sex, race. Approximate eye color, hair color. For starters."

"Ah," I replied. Then I thought about what she—what *it* had said. "I'm sorry. Did you just say *'species'*?"

"Yes. Animal, human—"

"That's enough, Sophie," Conrad interjected.

"Of course," she responded.

I scoffed and rubbed my brow. "What a day. I don't wanna know, do I?"

Conrad hesitated. "I won't insult your intelligence, Lochlan. There's much to discuss. But it can wait. We have to stay on mission."

I stared at him, my left hand attempting to squeeze my temples together. I'm sure my face was like a stone for a few seconds. I wanted to dig, ask a flurry of questions—yell accusations at the same time—but he was right.

It wasn't the time. Stay on course.

Conrad handed out ear protection to Silana and me and placed a headband on himself. Silana followed suit.

"These are electronic, so we'll have no problem talking to one another," Conrad said.

I put mine on. "I can practice here?"

"Any time you like," Silana said.

Conrad was right. I could hear Silana perfectly.

He put a hand on my shoulder. "I wouldn't be showing you all of this if I didn't believe I could trust you. And I know you'll make excellent use of the facilities." He lifted his chin at me. "Show us what you can do with that cannon."

I checked the two magazines in the pistol, cocked back the slide along the barrels to chamber two rounds, stepped up to one of the half-dozen shooting stalls then aimed down range at a paper human silhouette.

"Twenty yards?"

"Yes," Conrad replied.

I took aim and fired one test shot. Two bullets ripped down the lane and impacted the target in the chest to either side of dead center. The recoil kicked my hand back just enough to get my attention. My M1911 doesn't budge me, but I expected this bang. The accuracy of the cannon shocked me, though, because double-barreled pistols are notoriously inaccurate.

I glanced over at Conrad, who nodded his approval.

Aiming down at the target again, I grouped-up double-taps for the remaining eight shots. *Bang-bang. Bang-bang. Bang-bang. Bang-bang.*

Paper went flying as if a buzz saw ripped across the mark when I emptied the 2011 in less than four seconds. By my last shot, the body of the silhouette fell down and hung by only a shred that clung to the head above.

Conrad howled with laughter. "By the Hells!" He pressed a button, and the target traveled to us via ceiling rails.

Silana clapped her hands.

I tore the target free, and the bottom finally separated completely. I handed both halves to Silana with a mock bow. "For you, m'lady."

Silana curtsied and accepted the mangled target.

"Sorry. Just showing off, I guess. Twenty yards is too easy." I gazed down at my new handgun. "This thing feels like it was made for me." I looked at Conrad. "Your work? I honestly didn't expect it to be on target, but... Thanks again."

"My pleasure. I see more and more what Silana has known all along," Conrad said. "I took six months to get that spec just right. You'll never put both rounds through the same hole. You wouldn't want to. But my design doesn't shoot wild like the old Italian models. I engineered the dual triggers to fire in tandem with ease, too. I'm sure you noticed."

I nodded. "Definitely."

Sophie spoke up again, from hidden speakers. "Sorry to interrupt, but agents Fan and Dante are on site."

"Let them in," Conrad ordered. He looked very serious. "Question for you..."

I lifted an eyebrow and removed my ear protectors. "Yeah?"

"The assassin you shot this morning. You let her live?"

"I did."

Conrad nodded. I couldn't read what he was thinking, but he wasn't frowning.

Silana smiled at me, but this time I noted something new in her eyes.

"He has a big heart," she said. "Despite his capacity for violence." She glanced at Conrad. "Are you not yet convinced?"

Conrad huffed, but grinned. "I know better than to argue with your hunches."

No sooner had Conrad conceded to Silana than two unfamiliar persons—to my surprise dressed in motorcycle leathers and carrying helmets and backpacks—walked into the armory chamber. I suppose part of me had been expecting SWAT uniforms.

The Chinese girl perked up and spoke first. "Hi! Silana!"

Silana exclaimed, "Fan!"

The two exchanged a hug.

Conrad stepped over to shake the hand of the man accompanying Fan, then pointed at me. "Dante Paccione, Fan Zhan. I'd like you to meet Lochlan Nohr."

"Hi, gang," I said.

"Hey," Dante replied and shook my hand. It was a good, strong grip.

Handshakes between men tell a tale. A good shake puts me at ease. This guy was confident and very fit, but also smart enough to not physically challenge me. Ex-military for sure.

Dante huffed. "Damn. You weren't kidding Conrad. I want him on my volleyball team."

I chuckled at that. I recalled the beach volleyball court I'd spotted during the earlier property tour. "Sounds fun."

Fan also shook my hand. "Lochlan. Cool name!" Her grip was firm, too, and matched her physique. The almond-eyed, black-haired girl was taut with hard muscle, not an ounce of fat on her. She had a smile to rival Silana's, but I was sure I'd just shaken hands with a weapon.

I'm not gonna lie. I was a little turned on.

"Gymnast?" I asked.

Fan threw me a sly look. "How'd you guess?"

"I see things. I know things."

"Oh, this one. This one is trouble." Fan smiled wide. "I like him already, Silana."

Silana twitched her nose as she gave me a matronly glare. "I'd say he's harmless...but I know better."

I suddenly remembered that morning's shootout—and the incident from college. "Um. Yeah."

Fan evidently knew about the shooting, too. "Don't sweat it. You did what you had to—what any of us would have."

"*Especially* Fan," Dante added, grinning.

Fan mimicked a look of pure innocence.

"I see," I said.

Her eyes snapped over and locked onto me.

"*Careful*, Lochlan. She can distract *anyone*," Conrad warned. "It's one of the main reasons I selected Fan for the mission."

She shifted her weight to one leg and seductively pointed the opposite hip in my direction. "I hope you can ride," Fan said, and she held up a motor-cycle helmet.

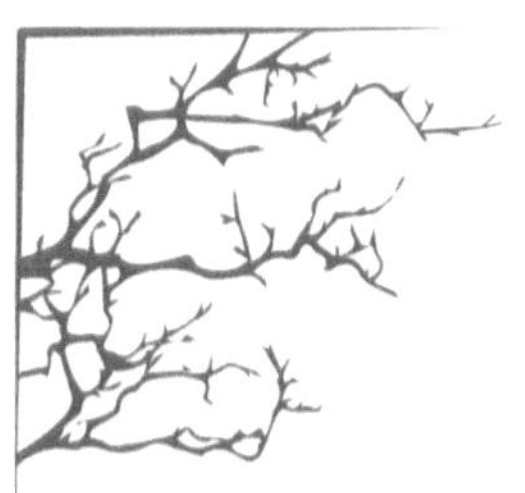

Chapter 12

I tapped Fan's helmet hanging by the jaw strap from her palm until it swayed gently back and forth.

"I know a thing or two," I said with a smirk. "In fact, I used to own a Shadow. Gift from my uncle. But I sold that years ago." I looked down at myself. "Was never really big enough anyhow."

Times had been tough since I left college and pursued music full-time. Hell, I was still sweating next month's rent until I got paid by LMG. Gigs in Austin barely pay if you're lucky enough to not have to work for the door or tips. Throw in all the expenses for parking, instruments, sax maintenance, practice space fees, reeds, car repairs, gas, and the rest, well, it's a testament to my band's success. I'd squeaked out a living without taking on too many side jobs, especially with no day job. That didn't leave room for luxuries.

Fan lowered the helmet to her side. "I'm sure. But don't be silly. A Honda? Big galoot like you belongs on a Harley. Whaddya think, Dante? Do we have a bike to fit him?"

Dante looked up at me. "I know just the bagger. How much you weigh?"

"Two fifty-five. Give or take," I replied.

"Goddamn, son! Your momma feed you steak three times a day?"

"Just twice."

That got a laugh from the room.

Dante continued. "Alrighty then. For you, I'm thinking a Road King with a tall boy seat. Won't take me too long to adjust it in the garage."

"Hell yeah," I said, and meant it. Any excuse to ride a Harley was cool in my book.

"And I'll find you some leathers, but that'll be tougher," Fan said. She looked at Conrad and Silana expectantly.

"Dig through the Armory. Should be a few pieces we can adjust to make work," Conrad advised.

Silana nodded. "*Oui*. We'll make do, but after this week we really need to tailor him some customs."

"I detest being this rushed. Decide what clothing you prefer, Lochlan, and let us know," Conrad said.

"We also need to consider new stage clothing for the band," Silana mused.

Conrad pushed a lock of Silana's auburn hair back from her face. "Silana and her fashionistas will work wonders."

I nodded. "I could use a new pair of cowboy boots. But let's talk...saxophones."

"Ah." Conrad smiled.

"Of course," Silana said. "Make another list. I love shopping."

I looked at the floor.

"What is wrong?" Silana asked.

I grimaced. "Nothing. It's nothing."

"Lochlan..." Conrad's voice wasn't harsh.

My honest streak kicked in. "It's just. Everything's been moving so damned fast. A day ago, you offered me the deal of a lifetime and this is the first minute I've taken to even seriously think about it." I sighed heavily. "These fucking people. The kidnappers. This just shouldn't be happening. Vicki should be enjoying her summer break. And I should be planning a party for Friday's gig—to tell fans the big news!" I looked around at every face. "But here we are instead."

I realized I'd formed two fists while I was bitching and squeezed them tight enough that my fingernails had dug into my palms.

"Sorry." I sucked in a deep breath then slowly let it back out.

Silana walked over and hugged me, just like that. "This life tosses us all into the storm. It's the price of free will. But do not despair. I have learned that quests are often unavoidable—and right now you have yours. It's healthy to let the anger out." She squeezed me tighter, and a weight lifted from my spirit. "We're with you."

"In fact, we're going on this plane ride," Conrad said. "Much to discuss."

Silana stepped back from me then patted my cheek gently with one hand. "*Oui*. And we will eat lunch in the skies, too. I'm sure brunch is wearing off by now."

"I can always eat," I agreed.

Silana's eyes glinted. She had that part of me figured out already.

Conrad stood up straighter then and spoke another series of commands. "Dante. Fan. I need to speak with you. Silana, please go with Lochlan to the armory and help outfit him properly. Sophie can help. And Fan too when I'm done with her."

Silana placed her ear protectors onto a nearby wall shelf, glanced at me, then led the way back to the armory. I gave a brief look to Fan and Dante. Fan smiled, but I trailed behind Silana without another word.

I brought my new double-barreled pistol with me though. It needed a holster.

IN THE ARMORY I FOUND a proper shoulder holster and harness to fit me and the 2011. Finding biker leather and body armor—or a combination of either—well, that proved to be more challenging. The armory wasn't exactly the Big and Tall shop.

But I had the duo of Silana and Sophie working on my wardrobe.

By the time Fan hurried into the armory to help out, I was already in a leather jacket that Sophie had created in the workshop from two smaller versions. It was brown leather, and despite the retrofit, I have to say it looked good. It made hiding my sidearm a snap, too.

I wasn't shy, but I entered a dressing room anyway.

"At least come out of there one time with your shirt off, or I'll feel cheated forever," Fan quipped through the closed door.

"Oh, that's professional. Aren't you supposed to be busy finding me shoes?"

"As if anything around here will fit those paddles!"

"You should have more respect. These 'paddles' could meet your caboose."

Fan laughed, and I envisioned Silana's feigned look of disapproval.

Silana came up with a pair of jeans I thought would be too small, but they fit me perfectly, felt comfortable, and were armor-stitched in all the strategic places. Perfect for motorcycling.

I tucked my old jeans into my backpack, along with my sneakers.

Despite her teasing, Fan found boots in the armory storage lockers. They weren't cowboy style, but I didn't complain. Black leather and rugged, with steel toes, they were perfect for a biker. Best of all, they were in my size fourteen.

"Conrad must have gotten a sale price on hard to sell shoes," Fan said, which made Silana laugh loudly.

Gloves were the last item. My gorilla mitts are stupidly huge, so none of the full leather gloves fit me, but a pair of extra-large fingerless riding gloves did the job. I prefer having fingerless—it makes it easier to shoot and type on handheld devices.

Once they had me outfitted, the ladies assessed their work.

"Well, when you're ready to form your own biker gang, you've definitely got the look down," Fan said.

"Very handsome," said Silana.

"You should be able to withstand most motorcycle accidents without serious injury," Sophie noted.

"What about a helmet?" I asked.

Conrad walked into the Armory. "Dante will find one. He's busy readying your Harley." He moved around me in a circle. "Everything fitting okay?"

"Yeah, feels fine. I had all the helpers needed."

"Superb. Only a couple more items I'd like to take care of before we head to the jet." Conrad walked over to a rack of martial weapons I'd assumed were for practice or decoration, but when I looked closer, I realized that many of the swords, in both Western and Asian styles, were razor-sharp. "How are your hand-to-hand skills?"

"I've barely had any martial arts, to be honest, but I've seen my share of bar brawls. That's how I got this..." I rubbed at a small scar that ran down my right cheek, just in front of the ear. "Guy thought he had a right to slash me with a broken bottle."

"Lesson learned? Small scar for a bottle gash," Conrad observed.

I shrugged. "I guess I heal well."

"And the guy with the bottle?" asked Fan. "Did he live to tell the tale?"

"I tossed him into a crowd of my friends and bandmates. Didn't even know he'd cut me... I was too busy with two *other* idiots." I grimaced. "The crowd kicked the crap out of him, and then the bouncers got involved. I backed off at that point. I know security wherever I work and like to keep things legit."

"What was the fight about?" Fan asked again.

I tilted my head. "What are bar fights always about?"

Conrad chuckled knowingly, but Fan gave us both a blank stare. Silana pursed her lips into half a grin.

I offered my hand to Fan, and she took it. Then I looked deeply into her light brown eyes, put on my best angsty face, and said in a low, breathy voice, "A woman."

Fan slapped my hand away. "Oh, fuck you!" But she laughed along with the rest of us.

I didn't protest. "Hey, I'm no saint, okay?"

"I knew you were trouble," Fan replied.

"No more taken women, honest." Vicki popped into my mind again. Funny how that works. "Vicki Lott, for instance."

"The kidnapping victim? Our objective? You two were never a thing?" Fan looked genuinely surprised.

"I'd developed a code of conduct by the time I met Vicki. I still kick myself for it."

"Chivalry," said Silana.

"Commendable," Conrad added. "Worthy of a sword, if I trusted you with one, yet, but for now—here." Conrad handed me a nylon baton holster. "You should always carry a close quarters weapon."

I inspected the case and removed what, at first glance, appeared to be just what I expected—a baton—but once it was in my hand, and I hefted it, I knew it was a more complex weapon.

"It's a sentry baton. Flick your wrist and it extends. Not typically lethal, but it could be if you strike the head," Conrad continued.

I snapped the baton out into an extended piece of steel almost as long as my arm. It felt light and dangerous in my grip.

"You'll want to strike in the high-water areas of the body to stop someone. The thighs for instance. Strikes in the arms and chest can more seriously disable. And like I said, strike the head if you need to kill." Conrad's voice became ominous. "But with your size and strength you already know this can kill."

"Yeah, I get it," I agreed. "Good to have, just-in-case." I half-removed my leather belt and added the baton holster to it.

When I looked up, Conrad was pulling something out of a wall locker he'd just unlocked with a thumb scan. He walked over with a black t-shirt on a hanger.

"I made this in the workshop last night. With you in mind." Conrad handed me the clothes hanger and short-sleeved shirt.

Only it wasn't just a t-shirt—when I reached to pull it off the hanger, the feel was all wrong.

"What's this?" I asked. I pulled on the bottom of the cloth. It stretched only a fraction and snapped back into perfect shape.

"The finest body armor on Earth. My design too. Lighter, thinner, and tougher than Kevlar. You can wear it under just about anything that isn't a v-neck and nobody will be the wiser."

I held the armor up in front of me, then handed it and the loose hanger to Fan. I stripped off the newly crafted leather jacket and my green t-shirt.

"Oh my," Fan sighed.

I laughed.

"Agent Zhan," Conrad scolded, but only half-heartedly.

"Now I see why you should stay away from 'taken' women, Lochlan," said Silana.

Fan was biting her bottom lip when I reached over to take the armored shirt from her.

"Oh, brother. Hurry up and get into that armor, boy, before they rush you. It's like I'm watching an AXE commercial," Conrad said, but through his own chuckling. "Honestly, Silana. You've sculpted nude athletes and behaved less like a schoolgirl."

"You're not being fair to those models, my love," Silana replied. I met eyes with her as I got the armor over my head, and she looked away, grinning.

"Sorry. I should've used a dressing room."

"Don't be ridiculous," Conrad scoffed. "How does that feel on you?"

I finished pulling my t-shirt back on and was amazed by how smoothly and easily it went over the thin armor.

"I can hardly tell I'm wearing it. Incredible." I extended my arms and twisted at the waist in both directions.

Conrad thumped a hand on my chest and his workmanship. "I haven't had time to test that shirt as extensively as I'd like, but the materials I used are definitely not standard grade. You won't be *Superman* in it, but bullets *will* bounce. Usually."

"I need the underwear next," I half-joked.

"The equivalent is on my list." Conrad grimaced. "I'm sorry this tech isn't ready for the whole team, Fan. It's a slow process."

"No worries," she replied. Fan opened a flap of her dark green, white-striped racing jacket, and revealed what I assumed was a Kevlar lining. I also noticed a shoulder holster.

"Nice," I said. "Okay, so we seem to be set. I'd like to check out that Harley now, if you don't mind."

"I'm sure," Conrad agreed. "Fan, take him to Dante please. Silana and I will make sure we're prepared for the plane ride. We'll call when we're ready to go to the airport."

"Yes, sir." Fan tugged my right arm. "Come on, you."

Silana gave me a reassuring smile. "Burgers for lunch?"

"Yes, please," I answered over my shoulder, and let Fan lead me out of the Armory.

WE LEFT THE WOODS THAT hid the workshop then returned to the main part of the compound, where I'd parked the Bomber in the visitor's circle. Dante was holed up in a horseshoe of three double-doored garages with my Harley and two BMW sport bikes.

He was wiping grease off his hands with a rag when Fan and I entered his open garage. "So, how d'ya like it?" Dante pointed a wrench at the Harley Road King parked in the garage's center.

The Harley was yet another beautiful machine being gift-wrapped for my use. It was painted in a high-gloss black, with chrome details across the wide-bodied frame. The twin exhaust tailpipes were customized in black, too, and had a look that reminded me of 50-caliber machine guns. They weren't though, I checked. Can you blame me?

"Get on. That seat should give you a good three inches of extra leg and arm room," Dante said. "It's been used by some of my security crew, but none of them are your size. She's practically brand new. As if somebody knew you were coming."

Silana again? I climbed on the Road King and it fit like the new gloves I had on. "She's outstanding, Dante. Fit is sweet."

Dante tapped the bike behind my seat. "Great. Hard saddlebag containers are big enough for that backpack of yours, and I've already stashed some basic camping gear: rations, canteen, tent, mylar blankets, et cetera. Just in case we have to rough it in the wilds."

"You're taking those Beemers?" I asked.

"Yep. Fan and I ride these a ton."

"Never ridden them in Nevada though," Fan said. She patted the leather seat of her cycle.

Dante's phone barked. He pulled it loose from his belt and clicked speaker mode. "Dante. Go ahead."

It was Sophie. "Conrad wants you to bring the motorcycles via covered trailer, to avoid prying eyes. A trailer *and* escort vehicle will arrive shortly. Please prep and be ready to leave for the airport by 12:30."

"Roger," Dante replied.

"How long did it take to get used to that?" I asked.

"What? Oh—Sophie? Not long really," Dante said. "She's more human than most humans. And a shitload more trustworthy."

"She's saved our fat several times. And Conrad intends to give her legs, eventually," chimed in Fan.

"Legs? Like robot legs?" I arched an eyebrow.

"No. Nothing that simple. There's already a robot shell for her now, but she rarely needs to use it on the grounds...and it's too clumsy for urban use." Dante grabbed Fan by an arm for emphasis. "Android. Humanoid robot."

"No shit?"

"*No shit*," said Dante and Fan in unison.

"Okay, I should believe it after today, but so help me, if any of you turn out to be aliens, have the decency to not show me a tentacle."

They both laughed.

Dante's eyes grew wide. "Oh, damn. Almost forgot. Here's a helmet. It's equipped with communications gear. Satellite-rigged, so we'll be good to go if we get separated."

My helmet was reminiscent of a classic military guard—flat black and gray coloring—with a visorless eye space and removable muzzle piece that gave it an ominous appearance. I dug it.

I tried it on for size and sported my Ray-Bans with it. Again, either by luck or design, the helmet fit my big noggin perfectly.

"Just when I thought you couldn't get any sexier," Fan said.

"Hey, the day ain't over," I replied, and waggled my helmeted head at her like drunk Darth Vader.

"Jesus, you two. Help me get these rides outside. Trailer'll be here any minute." Dante held up a hand. "Here's your key, Loch. It'll automatically engage and disengage the security system on your bike, depending how far away you get."

I removed my helmet, accepted the key then pulled my backpack off my shoulder. I was about to store the pack in a saddlebag when I remembered that I'd stuck my contract inside before I left my apartment. I pulled the LMG paperwork out, then tucked the pages into a jacket pocket. Then I stuffed my gear safely into a saddlebag, locked it, and shoved my helmet onto the back of the bike

"All right. Let's roll 'em out," I said.

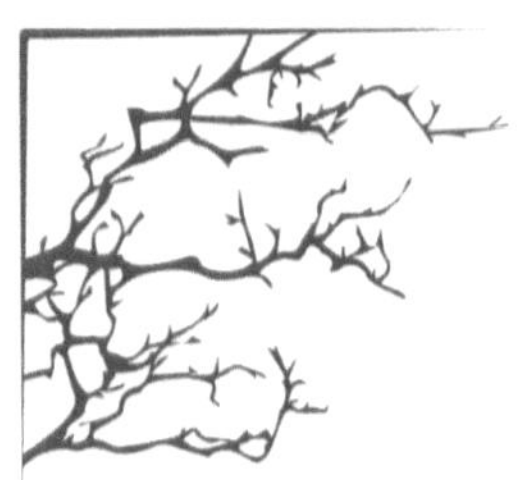

Chapter 13

After Fan, Dante, and I loaded the covered trailer, we piled into an unassuming, dark green SUV driven by a bearded guy named Grant. Grant drove us from the garages to the visitor's circle and up alongside the Bomber.

Silana and Conrad exited their house to join us. They'd changed into more road-ready clothes and shoes, and both carried small travel kits.

Conrad sat shotgun. Silana climbed into the backseat next to me, and patted the bag she tucked onto the floorboard in front of her. "For lunch."

"I've never flown on a private jet," I replied.

"It's the *only* way to travel," Fan said from the seat behind me.

"Since TSA got booted out of Texas airports, I don't mind flying coach," Dante said. "But yeah, the Gulfstream kicks ass."

"One of many LMG benefits...you will eventually bore of," Silana said.

I rubbed the back of my neck. "If I ever get bored living this way, someone slap me."

"With pleasure," said Fan.

I huffed. "You can't reach this high."

"I'll use Dante as a stepladder."

"You've bonded quickly," Silana noted, a loose smile on her lips.

I didn't have a response, but Fan couldn't resist. "The *Yang Guizi*...is not so bad."

Yang-gway-zi? That wrinkled my forehead a notch. "The *what?*"

Conrad spoke up before Fan could answer. "She speaks fluent Mandarin. I believe she called you...a 'foreign devil.'"

"'White devil.' But I meant it in the best possible way," Fan said. "Honest Asian."

I chuckled. "Been called worse."

"Another reason to have Fan along—if the kidnapper does turn out to be Chinese, she could use it to our advantage," Conrad revealed.

"I was born in Seattle, you know," Fan said. "My father was just old-fashioned."

Grant laughed gruffly and started the SUV. "And not a racist or anything."

Fan sighed. "My old man isn't crazy about Westerners—but he hates Red Chinese more."

Grant drove around the driveway and headed toward one of the property's two gates. "Yeah, well, he might have to get friendly with the Reds if things keep going the way they have been," he said.

"It's not that bad yet," I replied. But I hardly convinced myself. The world had been on the brink of world war for so long, nobody believed peace could hold out much longer.

"No, not yet," Conrad said. "But my European agents have been on high alert ever since the cathedral bombing."

"So horrible," whispered Silana. Her face was uncharacteristically stern.

"Paris? I guess I've become numb to the shit going on," I said. "I just keep playing music."

"Compartmentalization," Dante said.

"Yeah, guess so," I agreed.

"A useful skill, but don't become too jaded, Loch. That's when things sneak up and bite you in the ass," Conrad warned.

"Well, this is a happy conversation," Fan noted somberly.

"Yes. Please change it," Silana pleaded.

Silence set in. Grant exited the compound grounds behind a diesel pickup truck that zoomed by, and we began our trip to the airport.

I remembered something and nudged Fan. "My bass player is from Spokane."

Fan grinned and nodded. "I've been there a few times. Is he Tribe?"

"Yeah. He's called Running Bear. He moved to Austin a few years ago."

"That's a good name," Grant said unexpectedly.

Fan agreed. "Very cool," she said. "The river through the reservation is great fishing. And I've hung out at the casino."

Then Silana took the initiative herself: "Have you been to Nevada before, Lochlan?"

"Sure, plenty of times. Vegas still has good venues. If you don't mind playing at 3 a.m."

"Ouch!" Fan exclaimed

I shrugged. "No biggie. I'm a creature of the night."

"I guess you'd have to be, in your business," Dante noted.

"We're night owls sometimes, but I prefer the early mornings," Fan said.

"Yeah, and I've finally gotta ask. What *is* it y'all do? This whole—secret agent thing."

The silence made it clear nobody was ready to answer my heavily loaded question, but I waited patiently.

"We fix problems," Conrad said finally, without a hint of sarcasm.

"*Problems.*" I studied him. He watched the road ahead, his face blank. "Please. Feel free to elucidate."

Again, Conrad didn't respond right away. I'm sure he was deliberating on how much to disclose to me, the rookie.

"We obviously agree there are too many awful people in this world. The terrorists in Paris. Victoria's kidnappers. *Worse* skulking in the shadows." Conrad turned his head my way. "We're on the other side of all that. We're the *good guys*." He smiled. "But...we don't answer to any government...any corporation. I'm free to decide when and where to fix things. No interference from lobbies, judges or presidents."

"So...you do the 'right things,' but answer to *no one*," I said. My obvious point hung in the air like a balloon ready to burst.

"I didn't say that exactly," Conrad said.

I scrunched up my brow and glanced at Silana. "You don't look like the Mob."

"Our battle goes beyond what you see in this world, Lochlan," she said.

That made me lean back until I touched the headrest. "*Okay.*"

"The rabbit hole is deep, son," Conrad paused. "Once you go in, there's nothing for it but to hit bottom. Be sure you want to jump before you do."

I nodded silently, but Conrad was watching the road again, not me.

Was I ready?

"How can it hurt to know the truth?" I asked.

Fan, Dante and Grant laughed at once.

Silana touched my right hand resting on the car seat. "Most humans cannot handle reality, *mon ami*," she said.

I met Silana's gaze. There was sympathy there, which calmed me down a notch.

"I wanna know all of it, but can it wait until lunch?" I asked.

A hand popped me in the back of my skull. "Stomach rules *that* brain," Fan jibed.

Laughter filled the SUV, and I couldn't help but join in. That was as good a time as any to shut up for a change.

Over the next few quiet moments, I lost myself in the drone of the car's engine, and thoughts of Vicki returned to fill my mind again. Was she alive? If she was, was she hurt? How badly? I was flooded with doubt.

But gradually, I removed each worry, pushed every negative thought way, way back to the recesses of my brain, where maybe they didn't belong, but where I could hope to starve them out.

The power of positive thinking: I had to believe Vicki was alive. That we'd rescue her. And life would get back to normal.

Funny thing though? I didn't believe that last part. Not even for a minute.

THE DRIVE TO AUSTIN International took close to an hour. During that time there was a lot more friendly banter between me, Fan, Dante and Silana. In contrast, Conrad and Grant united in a taciturn bond while watching the highway.

I also took time to check my phone, but there were no new messages, and my email was the usual mash-up of spam, app-related updates, and calendar reminders. When I saw two old, opened emails from Pack, it dawned on me he was still expecting to join me for the LMG dinner.

The SUV stopped and everyone gathered their personal items and bags, then exited the vehicle. Everyone except for me. I poked Silana's side gently to get her attention just before she could open her door and completely drown us in the white noise from the surrounding airliners. "I nearly forgot about

Pack." I stressed each word with motions from my hands as if that might help beat the noise. "He's expecting to come to dinner tonight. What d'ya think? Not likely, right?"

Silana frowned. "I will contact him from the plane. Let us see how our trip plays out, then I will reschedule your friend."

I nodded.

Silana patted Grant on a shoulder. "*Merci,* Grant. *Nous devrions être de retour quelque temps ce soir ou demain.*"

She thanked Grant, that much I understood. And to my further surprise and confusion, our brooding—and evidently multilingual—driver turned to smile at Silana and responded in fluent French: "*Je serai là. Bonne chance, madame.*"

Silana returned Grant's smile and opened her door.

We were the last to exit the SUV, except for Grant, who stayed in the driver's seat with the engine running.

A couple of dozen yards away was Conrad's every-kind-of-sexy Gulfstream G550. A sleek, metal bird of prey, in white with navy blue trim. I was still pumped from checking the tour bus, getting fit for a Harley-Davidson—and now I was about to take my first flight on a multimillion-dollar private jet.

"Let's get the bikes unloaded," Dante said, pulling out a ring of keys.

"Right," I replied.

Dante unlocked the trailer doors, and we rolled our bikes out onto the tarmac. Fan walked past to get her BMW.

"I'll go lower ramp. Mind giving Fan a hand?" Dante pointed.

"Sure thing." I went back in to help Fan unlatch her cycle's tires from the trailer.

"Thanks," Fan said.

I nodded and pulled open a metal wheel brace.

Fan eased her BMW out of the trailer and down its low ramp until it rested on the tarmac next to my Harley.

"Haven't loaded these on a plane in ages. Come on...you'll love the jet," Fan said.

Fan led the way to the rear of the Gulfstream where a long, wide ramp had lowered to contact tarmac. Dante's riderless bike was within arm's reach of the incline, and he appeared from the bowels of the plane and walked down to us. He had to shout over the din of the jet's idling engines.

"Okay, it'll be easier to just drive these on board. But be careful. There's not much cargo space, so don't crash through into the cabin!"

I nodded and the three of us rode our bikes up the ramp in single file. The space was cramped, but I had headroom, and we weren't packing much in the way of luggage.

We got the bikes quickly locked into place and hung our helmets on handlebars.

Dante leading the way, our trio walked through a single door from the aft storage compartment and into the plane's crew area and galley. A lone, very lovely flight attendant in black and white skirted uniform stood inside. She was preparing what appeared to be Silana's burger patties. Her long hair was dark as jet, blacker even than my own mop, her skin light olive and sparsely freckled. She was unusually buxom for such a small-waisted woman, but her hips were broad. I could tell she was not store-bought.

She turned to greet us with patented airline cheer, smiled at me and said, "Welcome aboard." Then she and Dante exchanged a quick smack on the lips.

Well, hello. Very friendly service.

"Glad you're along, Court," said Dante.

"Hey, Courtney," Fan said.

"Hi, hi. I wouldn't miss the chance to bounce out of state with you two. Can't go hungry, can you?" Courtney replied. I detected the hint of an Irish brogue.

"Nice to meet you," I said.

"Very nice to meet *you!* The *infamous* Lochlan Nohr." Courtney winked at me as if to put a period on her remark.

I chuckled. "That's me."

"Silana speaks incredibly highly of you. And that's all I need to know." Courtney glanced at the unwrapped burger patties on the galley counter, then measured me up and down. "Will two burgers be enough?"

"Sure, that should get me by."

Courtney smirked. "I'm not believin' you. I'll make three. Who knows how long you'll be on empty Nevada highways, with not a diner in sight?"

She brushed fingertips with Dante's, hands low at their hips. "I'll make extra for everyone. For the road."

"You're awesome," Dante said.

"Thanks, girl," said Fan.

"Definitely, thanks," and I patted my stomach for emphasis.

Courtney grinned, and her eyes twinkled under the kitchenette lighting. "Find a seat. The captain said we'll be in the air—in less than fifteen minutes." She turned back to her work and sprinkled herbs onto the burger patties.

The luxurious seats and couches in the main cabin didn't surprise me by that point. Flowered vases adorned a pair of shiny, laminated tables along the walls of the jet. A handful of flat-screen televisions were placed strategically throughout the length of the aircraft, too, and I noticed that the couches could be extended into beds as needed. The plane reminded me of a tour bus, but with even more economy of space designed into it.

Conrad and Silana were already sitting near the front of the plane, close to the closed cockpit, and talking quietly together.

I walked up, took over a nearby couch by stretching my arms out along its back, then peered through the nearest portal. Teams were scrambling around the tarmac, prepping the plane for takeoff. Hydraulics whirred for a full minute from the plane's rear, followed by some low, metallic clangs. They'd raised the ramp.

An overhead PA speaker barked: "This is your captain speaking. The tower tells me we'll be ready for departure in five minutes, so please strap in. If you need anything before takeoff, tell Courtney. And as always, glad to have you on board."

Dante and Fan got situated near the galley and far enough away from me that we couldn't talk without shouting. While twiddling some air-sax riffs with one hand, I cocked my head at Fan when we made eye contact, to which she pointed a finger at Silana and Conrad.

I got the message and nodded gratefully at Fan. "Y'all have something you wanna talk to me about?"

"*Oui*, there *are* a few things," Silana answered.

"As good a place as any," Conrad said. "But let's wait until we're in the air."

I shrugged.

Courtney walked past with a smile, then secured the cabin's side door. Stairs-on-wheels outside got pushed down the tarmac, out of my line of sight. Courtney returned, still smiling, her eyes wandering to our waists. But I'd already snapped my seatbelt into place, so I mugged at her victoriously, to which she grinned that much wider and walked down the cabin to take a seat near Dante and Fan.

A minute later our jet began to taxi toward the runway.

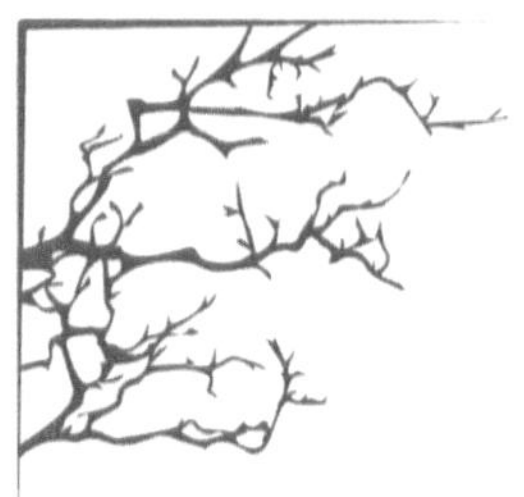

Chapter 14

The takeoff went without a hitch and once the fasten seatbelt signs blinked off, a lot of tension left the passengers' cabin.

The PA speakers chirped again, and the captain spoke. "Weather is nice and clear, straight-all-the-way to Nevada. Estimated arrival time is 12:54 Pacific. So, please kick back and enjoy the ride."

I watched the clouds slowly trail past our plane, then I turned to Silana and Conrad.

The man with the mustache spoke first. "How about you fill us in on exactly how you found that tracking gadget?"

I nodded. "I checked out the parking garage where Vicki was last seen. The security cameras were positioned all wrong—so wrong it *had* to be intentional. I followed up with some interviews in the nearest shops. And that's how I ended up with a trail to a UT cop. Constance Winter."

"Quick work," Conrad said. Silana nodded, a thin smile on her face. She was watching me more intently than ever.

"I guess. Didn't think about it much. Just a dog with a bone. So, I followed my hunch to Connie's house and got her to give up the goods."

"Got her to talk? How did you do that...exactly?" Conrad asked.

I paused and smirked at Silana. "I delivered a pizza."

She laughed merrily. Silana has a beautiful and contagious laugh, mind you, so I couldn't help but join right along with her. The whole scenario *had* been absurd.

And yet it worked.

Conrad had a skeptical look, so I continued quickly: "She was drunk, so that helped. I worked my way into her house, with the pizza...and...let's just say, she was interested in more than just the pie." I flexed my left hand as I recalled that night's events. "And so, I questioned her." I paused and rolled my eyes toward the ceiling. "After I restrained her."

Conrad and Silana stared at me sharply but didn't interrupt.

I told them the rest of the story, then recalled the elevators. "She'd also tampered with the surveillance cameras."

"And traded Vicki off to this big Chinese fellow," Conrad concluded.

"Yeah. I sent an anonymous tip to Austin PD before I split. The cops picked Connie up after, and I don't know anymore about it than that."

A now familiar voice manifested out of the air—actually the plane's PA speakers. "I have been monitoring police scanners and news channels. Constance Winter is still in custody and has been criminally charged. I'll alert you when I know more."

"Thank you, Sophie," Conrad replied.

"You are welcome."

Conrad noticed the questioning eyebrow I raised. "Sophie's in the Cloud," he said simply.

"Cool." I leaned back on my couch and continued with my storytelling. "So, Connie, her bosses—*she doesn't know who*—pay her well, but obviously they've got her on a short leash. Must have some dirt on her. There's no love lost there, that's for Goddamn sure. I doubt she'll give me up, unless something else changes, but she's still convinced she won't live long. I'm not sure what to make of that, but we're dealing with some shitty-bad people, so she's probably right."

The rest of it they already knew.

"People who send pros to clean up after them. Which reminds me..." Conrad's voice trailed off.

Sophie responded. "Still no sign of the assassins. Our team in the field will give the search another hour, but it's not looking likely that the outcome will change for the positive." Quite the multi-tasker, that Sophie.

Conrad frowned. "That could come back to haunt us. Those items you left in the street. Are your fingerprints on record?"

I grimaced. "Fuck." I put a hand to the bridge of my nose and squeezed. "I had to give up fingerprints when I got my concealed carry."

Conrad nodded. "I figured. I'd half-hoped you were carrying illegally, but it's better that you aren't."

"They'll figure out it was me. Assuming the Fugsley Twins grabbed my harmonica...."

Conrad aimed his voice with a lift of his square jaw. "We can take care of that. Sophie, alter Lochlan's Texas CHL records please. Replace his fingerprints with some suitable variation."

"One minute," Sophie droned, for once sounding more automaton than human.

I didn't believe she'd be able to do something like that.

"Alteration complete."

Much to my relief for once, I was flat wrong.

"Good work, Sophie." Conrad smiled. "There's always a tiny risk when she hacks into a computer system, so we like to avoid it."

"Thanks." I corrected myself and awkwardly talked at the ceiling of the plane. "Thanks, Sophie."

"My pleasure, Lochlan."

I remembered something else. "There's one more thing. I figured out that Connie had to've had somebody else on campus. Picking her targets and delivering orders. That's what the thumb drives were for. So, we've got at least one more bad guy running around UT."

"That's *definitely* worth checking into. Pass that info along to Gloria's team, Sophie," Conrad ordered.

"Right away."

Conrad nodded at Silana, and they both reached into separate carry-on bags they'd stashed next to them, then removed tablets, powered them on and finger-swiped the screens a few times before looking up at me again.

"Now, I don't want you to consider this an interrogation, Loch, because it isn't. But it is necessary we ask you some questions...about *you*...and your parents." He paused. "But first, let me ask you this. Are you really prepared to deal in secrets? *Big* secrets? You've gotten an eyeful, that much is obvious." He shifted in his seat. "We need to trust one another, or this won't work. In exchange for your commitment, Silana and I are prepared to lead you down the path and make you an integral part of our team. But only if that's something you really want."

I shifted my eyes nervously, something I wasn't used to doing. Then I remembered the contract tucked inside my new jacket. "Well, I've already committed to *this* much," I said, pulling the heavy contract out and offering it to Silana.

She took the contract from me then held it up for Conrad to view. My signature was impossible to miss. He nodded and smiled.

"I'm glad *that* legality is out of the way," he said.

"As am I," Silana agreed. "Your music is so important. We know how loyal you are to your band. So this was necessary, more for them, than for the three of us."

I leaned back. "Was it?" I sighed. "I'm not really sure what it is, but I trust you two." I took a deep breath. "I'm in. Go ahead and give me your nightmares."

Silana and Conrad glanced at each other and then Silana smiled so warmly at me I thought my heart would stop. "In a way, we are family, Lochlan. You can sense more than most. Do you not feel it, too?" she asked.

I recalled my recent empathetic flashes with Connie and the Derby Girls. "Yeah, about that…"

"*Oui?*" Silana's smile faded a notch, and I could think clearly again.

"I know I'm the sensitive artist and all that, but…the past night and day… I've had several odd sensations. And another one of my *dreams.*"

"You can sometimes read the emotions of others. *Explicitly*," Silana said. "And you have premonitions while asleep?"

"Yeah. Exactly. Like…so e*xtreme,* I'm inside their heads. And I've had my weird dreams forever, but it's usually just mundane shit that I see." I tossed my hands in the air. "I'm just goin' crazy."

"No, I do not believe so." Silana was still smiling, but something else now tempered it. "When you felt these sensations, was there something different going on? What were you doing?"

"What was going on in your environment?" Conrad asked.

"Ever the scientist." Silana pursed her lips, to which Conrad only shrugged.

I hadn't taken a breath to consider any of that before. I stroked my hair back and went through the scenes burned into my brain. Connie's apartment and the church alleyway. I'd been pumped full of adrenaline. Dangerously aggressive. But, when I'd sensed an emotional connection in that alley, it had happened—*after I played my harmonica?*

And when I was in Connie's apartment, I'd noticed the songs in her playlist. It's just second nature.

I had a holy shit moment because it all suddenly came together.

"*Music*," I blurted.

Silana settled back in her seat with a contented smile I didn't need to be an empath to read. "Music," she echoed. "*Mais bien sûr.*"

"There was music playing?" Conrad asked.

"Yeah. Either playing...or me playing it." I huffed. "Wow. I've always felt the exchange with a crowd. The *vibe*. But I've never really thought of it as anything more than energy. You know—just a feeling. Not—*the feelings*."

Silana giggled. "This is wonderful."

I wasn't so sure.

"Fascinating," Conrad breathed.

"It is exceedingly rare...this gift. And we shall help you harness it," Silana said. Her eyes were wet and might have changed colors. I was sure I was just seeing things though.

"But what the hell is it? Am I psychic?" I fidgeted on my couch like I was eight years old again and being convinced by Mom that not everyone could memorize songs after only one listen.

"Yes, you're a true empath. And evidently exposure to music heightens your power. But I'm sure there is more to it. I believe you are like one of the great, ancient poets. You know. A bard. Like *the* Bard." Silana was talking fast, excitedly now. "But much, much more. Much more."

Conrad sat forward in his seat with his fingers intertwined. "Think of it almost like...a recessive gene that's been awakened, after many generations. Somehow, you've been *unlocked*."

"*Exactement!*" Silana peered at me as if for the first time again. She smiled very wide and steepled her perfect hands before clapping them together. "Let us put your powers to a test."

That request raised my eyebrows, but I figured what the hell. "All right."

Silana peered down the length of the jet toward Fan and Dante. Courtney was nowhere in sight. "Fan, Dante, please get Courtney. Lunch can wait a few minutes. And bring me a cloth napkin, *s'il vous plaît*." Dante nodded and walked to the back of the plane, through curtains and into the galley. Silana then turned to gaze at me again. "This will be fun!"

I chuckled. "Uh-huh. I'm on pins and needles. Can't you tell?"

"I'm afraid you're her new pet project, my boy. Better get used to it," Conrad said.

"Oh, *taire!* He needs to learn—and *we* need to see what else lies beneath."

The other trio approached us. The naked curiosity on their faces was obvious, no empathy required. Fan held a beige cloth napkin out to Silana. Courtney was wiping her hands on an apron she'd put on during the flight.

"*Merci.*" Silana took the napkin and folded it over once, then stood and walked over to where I still sat. "This will help you concentrate. And then we will see...*pardonnez.*"

She blindfolded me.

Silana tugged at my arm with both of her hands. "Stand up, *s'il vous plaît.* The rest of you. Please change places—and *no talking!*"

I stood. Silana, I assumed, squeezed my hand once and then moved away from me. I kept my eyes closed to be sure I was blind for all intents and purposes. I wanted to learn more about my new superpowers, too—perhaps just as badly as Silana did.

"Conrad and I will not take part in this test," Silana said. "Lochlan, I want you to try to sense the emotions of all persons near you. Then point at Dante, Fan, and Courtney, if you can."

The interior of the plane grew quiet until all that was left was the low growl of the jet's engines. But my nose itched, and I could smell faint hints of perfume. "I can smell the girls. Their perfume, or whatever," I said.

"Ah! *Attendez un momento!*" There was a rustling of what sounded like fabric. *"Je suis désolé,* Dante." Something made a spritzing noise and the cabin blossomed with the fruity sent of fresh, even more pungent perfume.

I laughed. "Okay. *Woof.* That's enough."

"Please concentrate. Tell us if you sense anyone." Silana's voice was farther away than before.

I concentrated. I wasn't sure if I was sensing anything other than my own doubt though. My old fear of failure. That went on for a good minute or more before I got exasperated.

"It's not working. I'm not feeling *anything,*" I said angrily.

"You're inside your own thoughts too much," Silana said. "Let's try with some music. Sophie, give us some music please."

Sophie didn't respond, but classical music played throughout the cabin. I recognized it right off. Mahler's Eighth Symphony: "Symphony of a Thousand." I scrunched my brow at the *perfect* selection. I found it hard to believe it was just random.

Mahler's Eighth is full of huge choral flourishes and power. Beautiful and dynamic, with intense vocals and *emotion*. Lots of it. It requires a large array of talented instrumentalists and a choir to achieve the composer's desired effect.

The symphony washed through the cabin, and over me, and then I *felt* things. Not just the presence of Mahler's genius, but again, I was reading other people's emotions. And this time I was doing it blind.

It was an odd, intense epiphany, to fully own that I possessed such a gift. Up till then I'd thought I was going a little crazy, that I'd only been rationalizing through my own delusions. But I noticed individuals, not just a range of emotions. I could pick out points in the dark space around me. Curiosity, amusement, admiration—*and even a hint of desire.*

Fan. That was Fan. I was sure.

I pointed at her, or where I believed Fan was standing, anyway. "Fan," I said.

"Quiet, quiet," Silana warned. "Say nothing until he is done!"

Of course, I'd a good idea where Silana and Conrad were. I believed I could sense them too—the concern and anticipation—but I brushed those sensations aside as I searched for Dante and Courtney in the opposite direction.

Unexpectedly, I picked up on some boredom and good humor emanating from my right side, in the direction of the plane's cockpit. The pilots. I'd forgotten about them. The only faces on the plane I hadn't seen yet. But there they were. Their emotional auras anyway.

It was fucking crazy.

I reached out with my mind again and sensed a tinge of fear, but mostly intense curiosity, waxing to a sense of—*awe?* But the emotions were all laced together by a masculine assertiveness and hyper-attentiveness, as if this person were on guard. There was no doubt who that was.

"Dante," I said, and pointed.

That left only Courtney, but I wasn't sure where she was standing yet. I turned back and forth in place until I was positive. There was a strong sense of amusement, curiosity and—*approval.*

I knew. I pointed again. "Courtney. That's Courtney right there."

There was a breath of silence, and then Silana's beautiful laugh mixed with the "Symphony of a Thousand." "Stop the music!"

Mahler's music ceased, and again someone's hand clenched my right. "You may take off your blindfold now, Lochlan," Silana told me in a gentle tone.

There was a titter from nearby as I removed my blindfold.

In front of me stood Dante and Courtney—exactly where I remembered pointing. But Fan was nowhere in sight. That made me blink.

"*Bien!* You did it!" Silana could hardly contain herself, smiled brightly, and bounced up and down on her toes.

"Huh. I guess I *did*," I replied. There really was no denying it.

"Yeah, that was really something," Dante agreed. "How'd he pull that off?"

"He's an empath, silly," poked Courtney, and she gave me a smile as if she'd already heard the punchline to some joke that was on me.

"Huh," Dante grunted.

"Fan, you can come out now," Conrad called, and, much to my surprise, Fan emerged through the galley curtains and walked up the cabin aisle.

"Wait a minute. She was out here when I put on the blindfold—"

"Yes, I waved her away. I needed to test your strength," said Silana.

And I thought I was a ninja? Fan clearly had me beat in that department.

"And? Did I point at her?"

"You did," said Conrad, grinning.

"Whoa." I never even imagined that I could sense emotions yards away, let alone through walls. Hell, a few days before I wouldn't have believed any of it!

"Neat trick, Boy Scout," Fan said, and she winked.

I gave her a smirk—and some simmer. Fan's fair skin couldn't hide the blush rising to her cheeks.

"Much more than a trick," Courtney said.

"Yeah, a little more maybe," I agreed. It wasn't fair of me to tease perhaps, but I couldn't pretend I didn't know either. That would have been uncool to Fan.

Luckily, the feeling was mutual. I always appreciate exotic, beautiful things. Who doesn't? And they trained Fan to attract. Conrad had said so himself. Well, it worked.

But it wasn't the time or the place.

"Knocked it out of the park, boy," Conrad said. "You really are full of surprises."

"Yes, you are," Silana agreed. "But there was never any doubt, really. Not for me."

"So, my tel—tel-empathy. Empathy. Whatever we're gonna call this shit. Do you think it relies solely on music?" I was already figuring out ways to work around that.

"I don't, actually. I think music *enhances* your empathic power, as it is now. That much is clear. But like a muscle, the more you use it, the stronger it will become. We will have to wait and see. And practice, of course," Silana said.

Practice I could do. I'm a musician.

Conrad scanned the group and said, "Okay. Thank you, folks, but we need to chat with Loch privately again."

"*Aw,*" Fan whined and gave me a little frown.

"Okay," Dante agreed.

"I'll have burgers ready for lunch in a few minutes." Courtney caught my eye. "You're sure you're not a vegan?"

I scoffed and smiled at her wolfishly.

Courtney giggled. "No. Definitely not. Cheeseburger then? I have provolone and American."

"Provolone sounds great."

"Show me a grizzly bear that's a vegan," Dante said over his shoulder as he walked away. Courtney laughed and playfully smacked him once across the back as she followed. I winked reassuringly at Fan, which got me a grin in return, and she walked after the others.

Silana lightly jabbed a hand into Conrad's ribcage. "So. Tell him the rest."

A lump formed in my gut. "*The rest?*"

"Let's sit and relax. We have a lot to discuss," Conrad advised.

I flopped heavily on my couch and glanced out at the slow-moving clouds and blue sky beyond the nearest window. Silana and Conrad got situated then used their handheld tablets for reference again.

"Your mother Tressa. You probably know she attended the University of Texas," Conrad said.

"Yep."

"Did you know Victoria Lott's mother did too?"

That set me back. "No, I don't think Vicki ever mentioned it."

"Well, it turns out they attended UT at the same time, though they didn't appear to know one another."

"Huh." Vicki and I were the same age, so... "UT's a huge college. We're both twenty-six. Not really a shocker."

"I agree. That fact by itself, not much of a coincidence. But we did more digging and found that your mother and Reagan Shiels—Vicki's mom—both took part in the same two-week study...supposedly on *sleep deprivation*. It paid very well, offsetting most of their student loans. Marketed on UT campus by a private company. However, we've reason to believe that this 'study' was actually a front for a CIA Monarch operation."

"The CIA?" My brow furrowed. "Monarch? I'm not following you. What the hell is that?"

Conrad leaned in his seat. "Monarch is another code name for a long series of *illegal* CIA tests that originated way back in the Fifties, under another, more widely known code name: *MKULTRA*."

That name rang a bell. "Okay, wait a minute... That I've heard of."

"Probably. The CIA was prosecuted for its MKULTRA operations when it was proven many of the victims died. No such tests were ever again supposed to be carried out. But of course, they have been. Conspiracy pages all over the Net discuss MKULTRA, Monarch and the long series of rumored testing and torture involved. Conveniently, the CIA destroyed all their associated records before Congress could get their hands on them. More than a few members of Congress knew the real details, I'm sure, but corruption in that house is nothing new."

My mother was sitting in a mental health institution as we were debating. The ramifications of that weren't lost on me.

"So, hold the fuck on. Are you telling me that the government of the United States of America did something to *my mother*? The PTSD she's been diagnosed with—This shit is related?" My breathing got heavier as my heartbeat thumped in my ears.

"Unfortunately—and I'm very sorry—yes, that's what we're telling you," Conrad replied. "Though to be fair, the Federal Government rarely knows what one hand is doing while it's using the other."

"We've seen this before," Silana added.

I closed my eyes, took a deep breath, and held it for a few seconds. My skin was on fire, but I pushed my rage back down. Barely.

Conrad went on. "We don't know the full details. Yet. These operations are well guarded. The people running them do so beyond the scope and knowledge of their own organizations. And beyond that, the CIA is just another front for more nefarious groups that usually push these vile agendas. And that's when things get interesting." Conrad paused. "I know this is a lot to absorb. You've already been through so much in the past twenty-four hours. But we promised you the truth...and there it is."

I opened my eyes and met Conrad's concerned gaze. I clenched my lips together but nodded. "No, it's good. I mean, it's *good* that you're telling me all this. My family's been stressed out for years worrying about Mom. This explains a lot. But why didn't she say something...?"

"There's more," Silana whispered, and her uncharacteristic foreboding made me uneasy.

"It's most likely your mother just doesn't remember," Conrad said. "If she was part of Monarch testing, her memory was manipulated. Wiped—or at least repressed."

My mouth dropped open. "They can actually do that? Like in the movies? Men in Black?"

"Yes. They can. Well, not like the movies but, yes," Conrad answered. "In fact, it's possible to go much deeper. People can be controlled. Set up as sleeper agents. Assassins. Even slaves."

I rubbed my face and eyes with both hands. It was like something out of James Bond, but I'd read the war stories and some related science before. Stockholm Syndrome—that was definitely real. Manipulating the human mind was possible under the right conditions. Hell, just about everyone has witnessed a hypnotist do his thing with a room—and probably wondered who was faking it and who wasn't.

But *this*—what Conrad and Silana told me—this was terrifying. We were talking about *my mom, for Christ's sake!* Under other circumstances, I'd have been outraged by such an invasion of my own and my family's private medical history—but I'm not an idiot. This went along with the territory when you find yourself down the proverbial Rabbit Hole, as Conrad had warned.

Truth be told, I was damn impressed by Conrad's deductive reasoning and attention to detail. "You've put a lot together in a short time, Conrad," I said.

"Oh, it's not just me. Silana and Sophie are just as guilty," he replied.

Sophie spoke up from an overhead speaker. "I'm actively searching for records. The lack of any clear trail is proof in-and-of itself that something important is being guarded. It's also possible that the study results are being held in only physical form. But it's just as likely that they have destroyed all records."

"I would like to visit your mother. With your permission, of course," Silana said gently. "We must be delicate though. If she has had her memories tampered with, we don't want to recover them without taking proper precautions first."

Tinkering around with my mother's brain was something her doctors had been doing for years. For all the good it had done. She hadn't had night terrors in a long time, so that was a success. But if Conrad and Silana had methods that could find the root of Mom's supposed insanity, I wanted their help.

"If you think you can help her..."

"I believe we can. We'll tread carefully. Don't worry," Conrad said.

Silana consulted her tablet. "May seventh."

My worried mind snapped back to focus. "My birthday," I said.

"March twentieth," she said next.

I wasn't sure what that date meant, but if I were following a pattern... "Someone else's birthday," I said smugly.

"Victoria Lott's," Silana replied.

"Huh. We weren't dating you know."

Silana laughed. "This isn't a test."

"Your mothers both got pregnant just a little over a month apart, according to records. Both in their early twenties. Both while finishing up their degrees at UT," Conrad said.

A vein in my left temple twitched. "Where're you going with this?"

"When you met Vicki for the first time...how did it feel?" Silana asked.

I winced. "Honestly?"

"Please," Silana implored.

I sighed. "It was like...a lightning bolt hit me." I grinned weakly. "I know how that sounds...."

"Considering what we have learned, it sounds right," she replied.

Conrad turned his tablet off then put it down on his lap. "Love at first sight. Like you'd known her your entire life," he said. "Does that about sum it up?"

"Yeah. Cliché—but yeah it does," I admitted.

"June ninth," Silana said.

My brow wrinkled. "I have no idea." I'd tired of the guessing games.

"That was the starting date of the sleep deprivation study. Just over *nine months* before the birth of Victoria Lott."

"What. What?" The implication hit me like a battering ram. "Vicki's mom. She got—*pregnant* during the test?"

"Not just her," Conrad said. "I think your father covered up the actual date of your mother's pregnancy. You were conceived close to the same hour as Victoria."

Was that crazy? My father wasn't just an officer in the Air Force. He was an M.D. That's how my parents met, during Mom's nursing studies. What Conrad said was plausible.

It dumbfounded me until my adrenaline kicked in.

"What? Get the fuck out" —I stood. I couldn't help it— "There's no fucking way!" I did the math. "This is nuts! Even if that happened to Vicki's mom, I was born more than a month after Vicki! There's no damn way you can say—"

Silana caught my eyes with her dark blue gaze. "Lochlan. Please...please sit back down. You need to stay calm."

To Hell with that! I wanted to pick up furniture and hurl shit around the air-locked cabin. I wanted to find doctors and scientists I imagined in their bleach-white coats, poking needles into Mom—into Vicki's mother—I wanted to find these people and break them into tiny little pieces.

"Lochlan," Silana pleaded.

The rage flew out from me, almost like a living creature. I shook my head and sat down again on the couch. "Goddammit!"

"Give him a minute," Silana said to Conrad, I assumed, but by that point my eyes were watering, and I couldn't see clearly.

After what seemed like an hour of silence, I spoke up again. Slowly. "You think I'm...connected with Vicki...from that Monarch test. That's what you're getting at."

"Yes." Conrad's voice was as serious as I'd ever heard it. "Think about it. Your empathic ability. It has remained dormant, just out of reach of your conscious understanding. But it's always been there. So, what if you somehow, were aware at conception? And if that were the case—you might have bonded with your mother, and quite probably Vicki's mother, too. Even with Vicki herself."

"That's insane," I breathed. "What you're saying...isn't possible."

Silana whispered at me. "Just as impossible as *you*. Just as impossible as your powers. Powers that are proven—that we have witnessed here for ourselves, just a few minutes ago—are very, *very* real."

My vision cleared enough for me to make out the worried faces of the couple across the aisle. "But how do you explain a ten-plus-month gestation period? That blows gaping holes in your theory."

"No, Lochlan. It only makes me believe even more," Silana said.

Conrad lowered his brow and locked my gaze. "Lochlan." He hesitated but didn't blink. "We believe you are only *half* human."

Okay. Up to that point I'd swallowed a lot. Secret agent men running around? Sure. I could roll with that. NSA is up our asses. Artificial Intelligence? I'd seen the Terminator movies. Musical-psychic powers? Been there, done that. Mom part of some super-secret test, then having her brains scrambled in the process? Would help explain *my* scrambled brains.

But *me*—being only half-human? I couldn't help myself.

I laughed hysterically.

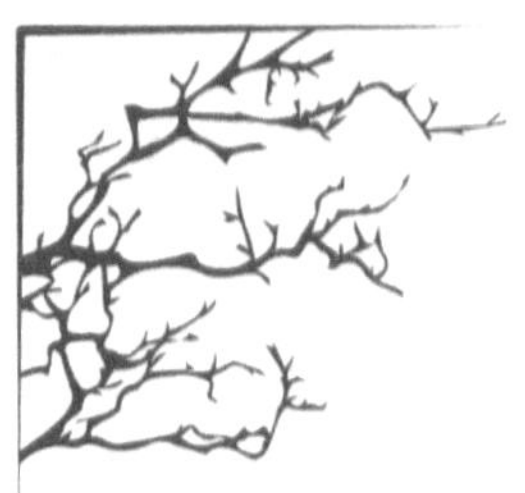

Chapter 15

"Okay, man." I could barely speak through my own laughter. "Seriously. You guys are killing me." I swallowed a deep breath. "You just had to go there, right?" And then I finally managed to stifle a laugh. "Oh, fuck..." Another deep breath. "Whew!" I exhaled loudly. "Good one. Really...." When my vision cleared (after I wiped a tear from my left eye), I saw Silana sporting a tiny smirk. Not the big, toothy smile I'd expected. In contrast, Conrad had a look halfway between fatherly patience and amused uncle.

You've got to be kidding me.

Conrad looked down at his tablet and finger-scrolled on it again. "How many broken bones have you had?"

"Um..." I wiped my eyes then sat up straight on the couch. "*None.*"

"How many times have you had the flu? Or a cold?"

"Zero."

"Chickenpox?"

"Nope."

"Cavities?"

"None."

"STDs?"

"*Seriously?*"

Conrad chuckled, and Silana covered her mouth.

"Have you *ever* been sick?" Conrad asked.

I had to consider that. "I get headaches occasionally." That came out more defensive than I intended. "I've had a stomachache before."

"But you've never, to the best of your knowledge, ever contracted a virus or bacteria-born illness." Conrad wasn't asking a question that time.

"You've got some of my medical records?" I asked.

"Yes. You have no medical history past the age of thirteen. And up to that point it's all just routine pediatric exams." He paused. "A very interesting side note. Your parents refused *all* vaccinations for you. I'm not sure if that really has anything to do with your...*origins*...or if it was just unusually informed parenting. But either way, I'm willing to bet it wouldn't have mattered. We could inject you right now, with a dose of the Ebola virus, and it would affect you no more than orange juice."

I shrugged. "Okay, so—I'll play along, assuming what you're telling me is true—even if I'm some *mutant* immune to disease, that hardly means I'm part *alien*."

Conrad grinned at me but with a serious glint in his eye. "Assuming we are to believe you are the first human in recorded history to be immune to all disease, you mean?"

"We don't know that! I just—haven't gotten cancer yet! I'm *young*!" I realized I was yelling then, and I looked back over my left shoulder to see Fan, Dante, and Courtney staring at me, perplexed. I shook my head, gave them a half-smile, then a waved hand.

Silana spoke up. "We know this is a lot to take in." She reached over and placed one hand on my knee.

And I calmed down. *Just like that.*

Two plus two equals... "What did you do?" I asked her. And not too gently.

Silana bit her lower lip, but her fingers remained lightly on my knee. "It's a talent. A transference of energy," she said.

It filled me with another sudden realization, and my knee jerked reflexively away from Silana's touch. Her face waxed from a smile to shock and sadness all in a fraction of a second.

"I'm sorry. I am only trying to help you," Silana said. "It is not harmful, I swear."

But her touch wasn't what had unnerved me— "You're... *You're not human.*"

A tiny grimace froze Silana's face as she stared into my eyes from across the aisle. "Conrad. We should show him now."

I was listening to my heartbeat in my ears by that point, but I'd said I was ready for the whole truth, hadn't I? I took a deep breath, nodded at Silana and turned to Conrad. "What about you?"

"I'm like you. In *some* ways," he said.

"Like me? Are we related?" The other ramification of 'half-human' hit me then, and I'm sure my face was a sight to see. "*You're not...*" I couldn't bring myself to finish the question.

Thankfully, Conrad didn't leave me hanging. He laughed instead and told me, "No—I'm not your *father*, Lochlan. Whether or not we are related, that is a much more complex question, and I'm simply not sure. Not yet. However..."

"Oh, here we go," I said sharply, and sat back on my couch.

"We do share the same rare blood type."

Not an interrogation? "Blood type. Do you always dig this deeply into people?"

Conrad flinched. "Only when we come across someone like you. Like *us*."

"I'm aware I'm AB negative. So it's rare. That doesn't mean I'm from Mars."

"You're definitely not from Mars. None of us are—if that's what you're really worried about. We aren't going to turn into bug-eyed monsters or little green men. Everyone on this plane was born here on Earth."

"What a relief," I grumbled.

Silana was almost frowning now. "*Conrad...*"

"Right, right. Lochlan. Let's go talk to the captain," he offered.

I wasn't sure who Conrad was talking about at first, but he moved toward the cockpit door. "If the pilot is crazy too, we could be in big trouble," I quipped.

Conrad chuckled then knocked on the door. "Captain. Open up please. I'd like to introduce you to Lochlan Nohr."

The door unlatched, and I saw one pilot as he opened the portal. To my relief he was an ordinary-looking guy. No horns, antenna, or bat wings!

"Thanks, Gabriel. How are you?" Conrad asked.

"Yes, sir. Good, sir." Gabriel smiled up at me. He was blue-eyed, bald and in a familiar pilot uniform. "Hello."

"Lochlan Nohr, meet Gabriel Perrault, our copilot."

"Howdy," I said, somewhat weakly. My mind was still whirling.

We shook hands, then Gabriel moved out of my way.

Silana followed us in last and greeted Gabriel. "*Bonjour!*"

"*Bonjour, madame!*" Evidently another French agent. As was so often the case, Silana hugged Gabriel briefly, and then he shuffled back into his copilot seat.

Silana turned toward the only other person on the plane I hadn't met yet. The captain himself. "*Salut, mon ami!*" Silana patted the captain's shoulder, and he stood when Gabriel took control of the jet.

The captain was a tall, handsome man—taller and outwardly older-looking than Conrad, if I were to judge by his graying hair. Despite his age, his skin was deeply suntanned, and I sensed he worked and played outdoors a lot when he wasn't piloting the plane. "*Bonjour à nouveau, madame,*" he replied to Silana. His French was as native and perfect as hers.

Conrad shook the captain's hand. "Captain Jean-Pierre Chomette, this is Lochlan Nohr."

The captain's English was fluent. "Ah, the man for whom we are piloting this bird today. A pleasure to finally meet you."

"Ditto," I replied, shaking his hand. "*Captain Comet.*" I couldn't help but grin. "How much shit have you taken about that?"

He laughed, and Gabriel snickered. "Get in line," the captain told me.

All the gadgets and lights around us caught my eye. "It's been a long time since I've stood in a cockpit." I distantly recalled visiting Air Force museums with my parents and standing inside a huge, old B-17 Flying Fortress. "A lot to keep track of."

Captain Chomette shrugged. "It might look like that, but I have a good copilot. *Usually.*" Gabriel snorted. "And Sophie is often along for the ride. Though, admittedly, I'm still getting used to her."

Conrad scoffed. "The captain is being humble. His flight hours are so high, I doubt he even keeps track anymore. Am I right?"

The captain grinned. "It's only that I'm getting so old—I can't remember."

Silana and Conrad laughed together. I smiled crookedly. Conrad continued: "Lochlan and I are having a discussion I believe you could shine some wisdom upon, my friend. Especially from this vantage point."

"From the skies," the captain said. "Clearer thinking on a clear day?"

Outside the wide, high windows of the cockpit's windshield, the sky was bright, light blue and layered with wispy clouds that our jet pushed its way through.

"It's gorgeous outside," I agreed.

The four of us stood behind the pilot chairs and I moved forward a little to get the best look I could through the windshield.

"Notice anything unusual about the clouds on the horizon?" Conrad asked.

I concentrated on the sky ahead, on the layers of clouds and the layered lines of varying shades of blue and white. "I'm not sure what I'm supposed to be looking for," I admitted.

"Find the curvature of the Earth," Conrad urged.

I glanced at him and then Captain Chomette and Silana. They all had expectant expressions. That irritated me enough to make me concentrate harder on the horizon the second time. I almost slapped myself when the obvious answer finally hit me.

"There *is no curvature*. The horizon is flat as Kansas," I said.

Conrad prodded me. "As far as you can see?"

"To each extreme, as far as I can see. Yes."

"Is he missing anything, Captain?" There was a tone of irony in Conrad's voice.

"No. It does appear flat out there. These windows aren't convex," the captain replied.

"Why am I getting the impression there's about to be some lesson here?" I asked.

"You're having a difficult time accepting the truth of your heritage. So, I thought it would be easier for you to understand if we opened your eyes to a tremendous *lie*—one they have conditioned you your whole life to accept as truth," Conrad replied. "If we can convince you of this, then we may convince you more easily about yourself."

"Like a veil being pulled away," Silana said.

I stared out at the flat horizon. "We should see curvature." I looked intensely, almost straining my vision—better than twenty-twenty, by the way. "You probably know how good my eyes are, you seem to know everything else about me." Though they hadn't mentioned Marquis Hall. Some secrets were too secret. Even for these people.

"*Oui*," Silana replied at the same time as Conrad said, "Yes."

"This is a lesson about something else impossible," I said, my mind galvanizing.

"*Oui, oui*," Silana emphatically agreed again, her voice breathy and trembling.

Flat as Kansas. I leaned back when the realization of the lesson finally dawned on me.

"*The world is flat*," I said. "The Goddamned world is *flat!* That's what you're saying?"

"What I—what *we're* trying to tell you—is that the Earth is special. That it isn't the random glob of mud spun into a ball." Conrad reached out and gripped me firmly by the nape of my neck. "And like you, my boy, it's no accident. You exist as part of a grander design, just as the Earth *is* the center of the Universe."

My mouth hung slack as Conrad's words slowly sunk into my havocked brain. But I wasn't so easy to turn. "Why should I believe any of this?"

"You shouldn't," said Captain Chomette. "You should always question. But if you get answers..."

"You might awaken," Silana said, which pulled my eyes to her deep-blue wells. She reached out a hand, but hesitated. "The world you know isn't changing. You simply haven't been allowed to see it."

I stood up straight, and Conrad and Silana pulled their hands away from me, cautiously, probably expecting me to scream at them. But I'm not stupid. All of this effort forced me to rethink, to reevaluate just about everything I thought I knew.

"Next, you're gonna tell me we never landed on the Moon...?"

"NASA was a Cold War construct. What do you think?" Conrad asked.

I grimaced. "You just ruined a lot of good sci-fi movies." I nodded to myself. "I'm the only one on this fucking plane that doesn't know what the fuck is going on, right?"

"Pretty much," Conrad replied.

"Mm-hmm," Captain Chomette hummed in the affirmative.

"And *you* two," I said, as I waved a hand at Conrad and Silana, "I'm done dancing around." I pushed out a snap of breath through my nose. "*What the hell are you?*"

Conrad deadpanned. "Besides being married for a very, *very* long time?"

Silana rolled her eyes then shook her head in mock disgust. "Forgive my husband, Lochlan. He enjoys these moments a little too much."

"I'm not allowed to have fun?" Conrad protested.

Silana glared at him and Conrad relinquished. "Fine, fine. My boy, just know whether you're married one year—or a *thousand*—it never pays to argue with the wife."

I braced myself. But they disappointed me.

Conrad shook hands with our pilot. "Thank you, Captain."

"Of course."

Silana waved at Gabriel and Captain Chomette and walked out of the cockpit first. Conrad motioned for me to follow her. I took his cue, nodded at the pilots and proceeded back into the passenger's cabin.

I was numb by that point. The past seventy-two hours had been a theme park ride full of ups and downs, twists and turns. I was believing I must be more than human—or less than—to even have the endurance to deal with it all.

And why *did* I care so much? A romance had never bloomed with Vicki back at North Texas. I'd reconciled that years ago—*I thought*—yet the moment I heard she was in danger, I mounted a Harley on my chivalrous crusade, Lochlan-to-the rescue, delivering pizza, bullets, and ready to burn a scorched path across the Nevada badlands.

Yeah. The Earth is flat? Why not? In a world that rarely made sense anyway, that somehow sounded reasonable.

Then a buried teenage memory weeviled its way back to consciousness, and I had a pang of guilt all over again.

Silana stared at me hard like she knew what I was about to say.

"I got a tattoo once," I admitted.

"*Oui?*"

"Drunk for the first time. One of the only times. Sixteen. But looked older—tall and all that already, so nobody stopped me. I'd been missing Dad on his birthday and..." I gulped. "I sobered up quick while the artist did her thing. Got home with a Celtic cross, Dad's name underneath it. Rory." I breathed deeply through my nose and exhaled the painful memory. "Next morning it was gone."

Silana's eyes caught mine and her brow wrinkled as she tilted her head at me, the tiniest of frowns on her mouth. "Another sign."

Opposite Silana, her husband smiled and nodded. "Not as unusual you might believe, Lochlan."

I plopped myself on my couch and gave a surrendered shrug to everyone. I noticed the delicious smell of grilling meat wafting down the length of the plane from the galley. Lunch was on the way.

So, I sighed loudly. "I give the fuck up. Tell me if I need to drive a stake through my own heart—*but can I get some lunch first?* Those burgers are already killing me."

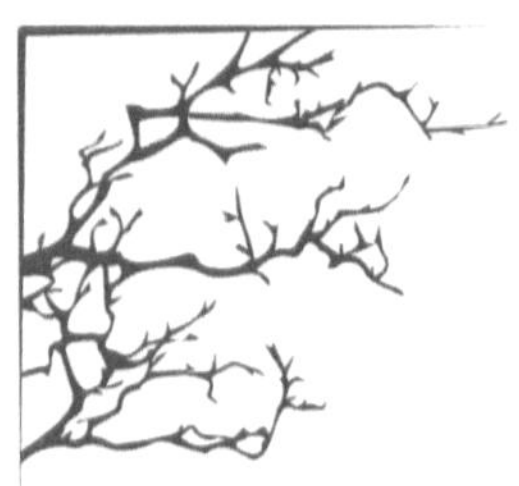

Chapter 16

Flight attendant Courtney served up our hamburgers with exuberance. But I was in no mood for bouncy—or company—so I took my lunch tray to a far corner of the cabin, flipped on a nearby television and sat with the remote in one hand and my food in the other. If any of my fellow passengers noted me stomping away, I didn't care. My body language had to be plain enough. *Fuck off. I've got to think.*

Flat Earth and all its ramifications swirled around in my brain, and as I hungrily eyed the round, beef patty sandwiched between the two hamburger buns, the trope wasn't lost on me. I coughed a stifled laugh, then mercilessly chomped into lunch.

After a couple of bites, I thumbed the TV remote to CNN.

"...more Muslims than Christians now in Europe? London's Muslim mayor continued to insist the recent series of terrorist attacks aren't the work of groups seeking to overturn the British government. Our resident expert on Political Islam disagrees..."

Just another peaceful day on Pancake Earth.

The burger hit the spot. It didn't kill my hunger, but Courtney had promised extras. I stoically awaited her second delivery.

"...controversy over 9/11 has risen to an all-time high with the recent release of even more damning evidence, claims by a New York state grand jury linking both Saudi Arabia and Israel to the event. Hal, you've got some strong opinions on these antisemitic..."

Just one day without hearing about terrorism. It seemed too much to hope for. Europe was on fire—literally in some parts—and it was spreading.

I finished off the last of the french fries on my tray.

Courtney read my mood perfectly and came by with a fresh plate, complete with a sizzling burger and more fries. She grabbed my dirty dish away from under my nose. "Ready for another, I see. I've a third one set to go on the grill, love. I'll check back in a few."

"Thanks, Courtney."

She smiled then whooshed away back to her kitchenette.

"...record numbers of earthquakes. Scientists warn that California is due for a massive quake. Could it be the Big One this time? Let's look at the stats on this graph..."

Fan appeared in my peripheral vision. She wiggled close while I ate, and I pretended to only watch the news.

I turned to acknowledge her though. Fan had her own burger cut diagonally. She gave me a wry little smile then nibbled delicately at a half. It was just enough coaxing to make me lose interest in my food. Not entirely, mind you—I love to eat—but there was no denying Fan's allure. Pouty lips, butterfly eyes and satin skin all played games with my inner animal. She smelled great, too, despite the charred meat nearby. Or maybe better because of it?

Just goes to show you, a man will be a man, day or night, rain or shine. Some things we have limited control over, or no control of whatsoever. And my passions win out a lot more often than I should probably admit.

I lifted an eyebrow at Fan, but with some effort, looked away, giving thorough attention—or trying to anyway—to the rest of my second burger.

"They gave you the flat Earth speech," Fan said matter-of-factly.

I was chewing. "Mm-hmm."

"Crazy right?"

"Mmm." More chewing.

Fan devoured a fry. "It's true."

I set the remaining half of my second burger back on its plate then scooped up one of my own fries. "Is it?"

"Yep."

"No offense, but I'm gonna need more than that." I ended the french fry.

"Of course. Of course, you do."

"Fuck." I'm eloquent all the time like that.

"Yeah."

I picked my burger back up. "Did they show you? Something *real*, I mean."

"Yes. They have their ways. They'll show you, too, I'm sure. Just a matter of time."

Time. She was right. Time wasn't exactly an expendable commodity right then.

Vicki's face appeared in my mind's eye.

I shook my head bitterly, blinked, then took another bite of my burger.

Fan placed a hand on my shoulder. "The more you understand, the easier everything else will get. If you're as smart as they say, that won't take long."

I scoffed. "I'm not much for hard thoughts right now." I paused then breathed in deeply. "You smell too damn good, you know that?" I locked eyes with Fan, wrinkling my nose.

Fan scrunched her nose right back at me, and her eyes twinkled.

"Yep. I knew it," I said. "You have no fucking idea what you're getting into."

Fan moved her hand off my shoulder then picked up the remaining wedge of her burger with both hands. "I'm a big girl. I know *exactly* what I'm getting into."

I sighed.

Finally, I laughed and relented. "I'll admit, I'm intrigued. We'll see."

"We'll see," Fan agreed.

We finished our burgers in silence after that. Eventually Courtney returned with thirds, and I devoured that too. All the tension of the past forty-eight hours, in all its myriad forms, had evidently built up quite a need for bovine fuel.

Fan watched me in plain fascination as I killed off the last burger.

"Scared yet?" I asked.

Fan crinkled her brow. "Maybe a little bit. Where does it all go?" She poked my ribs gently with an index finger.

"For me to know..."

Fan laughed.

THE REST OF THE FLIGHT to Nevada was uneventful. I talked quietly with Fan while Dante helped Courtney clean up the plates and trays. Conrad and Silana lingered together in the jet's front cabin, and our pilots did their thing hidden away in the cockpit.

And Sophie? She stayed silent most of the way. Until she piped up as we got within striking distance of our destination.

"We will be on approach to Yerington Municipal Airport in approximately ten minutes. Everyone should get safely seated for landing," she said.

We complied.

I couldn't wait to get off the plane, so the closing of my seatbelt across my waist felt more like a step toward freedom than security. Fuck all revelations, all the questions from the day. I wanted to get ground underfoot again, rubber on the road— and off on the hunt. The farther I could ride away from my growing insanity on the plane and toward some real damn answers—and whatever conclusion Fate had in store for me—the better.

Fan strapped in across the aisle. I couldn't help but analyze her profile as Captain Chomette rambled on again over the PA. I don't think she noticed, but she *was* a spy, right? What could I really know—without whistling into one of my emotional reads anyway. And that wasn't something I wanted to get comfortable doing, not on a whim.

At least not yet.

Our jet circled the airport once and landed. Once Captain Chomette taxied to a halt, I was out of my seat before anyone else. Dante appeared behind me as I went back to unhook the motorcycles.

One by one, we rolled the bikes down the ramp and onto the tarmac. I checked my pack was still safely in a compartment on my Harley before everyone from the flight, including our plane's crew, had gathered round.

The skies in Nevada were clear, the air crisp. A sharp difference from the weather in Austin, and the leathers I wore were keeping me nice and warm. I noticed Silana and Conrad were also well-prepared. They'd put on windbreakers from somewhere.

The airport itself was relatively small and far quieter than your standard international operation, so we could converse without shouting. Handshakes or hugs were exchanged with Captain Chomette, Copilot Perrault and

Courtney. The only exception was a quick lip-smack between Courtney and Dante. Ultimately, the three crew members marched over to a nearby hangar.

The rest of us moved away by motorcycle, Conrad partnering up with Dante, and Silana hitching a ride with me. She hugged my waist and spoke into my ear.

"We'll continue our conversation soon. Don't worry," she said.

I nodded.

And all shall be revealed, said the sorceress.

"I called your friend Paz and canceled. Another night."

"Cool." I revved up the bike. "Hang on."

We rode past a series of towers and low buildings closer to the airport's main exit. It was a short trip. Nobody even bothered to put on a helmet.

Two vehicles were waiting for us. One unimposing, black sedan, driven by a car rental agency rep, while the other was provided for Conrad. He'd selected a tank. Well, the next best thing anyway. A hulking, luxury Land Rover SUV in gun metal gray.

Go, Conrad.

Which reminded me of my shoulder-holstered hand-cannon, which then further reminded me that nobody had questioned me at the Austin airport or in Nevada about what sort of luggage I had, or what sorts of terrorist activities I might be conspiring to unleash upon the world.

Chalk up another point to the growing respect I had for team Conrad and Silana. They had pull. A lot of it.

I knew to not get too used to private planes.

But I wasn't complaining.

"We're finally ready to go." Conrad scanned his eyes across all of us. "Let's understand something. We're on a search mission. You're not to engage any potential enemies unless they force you. The element of surprise being key here, people. All anyone needs to know about us is that we're a bunch of motorcycle enthusiasts, out for a good time, touring the countryside. No need to be coy about it. If anyone asks where you're from, just tell them the truth. You're from Texas. It's a big place and anybody could check flight logs, anyway."

Conrad glanced at Silana as if the two were exchanging a thought. He continued. "We're looking for clues. Signs of the Escalade we know they used to transport Victoria." He faced me and then Fan. "And we're really looking for a giant Chinese with a face tattoo. The rest...you'll just have to trust your instincts." Conrad opened the back of the Land Rover then tossed his travel bag inside. Silana did the same. Conrad still had a medium-sized, hard, black suitcase at his side. "Silana and I'll monitor the three of you from a safe distance." He lifted his phone. "GPS positioning on each of your bikes and also your cells."

Dante nudged me then handed over a new phone. I swiped the screen and found a short contact list for everyone in our little party.

Conrad continued: "We'll stay in contact via phone and the detachable comm units inside your helmets. Acting as two groups. The car—and bikes. Can cover more ground that way. We'll also draw a lot less attention, and in the event of something unexpected, we can keep the element of surprise."

The man had done this before. But he trumped everything he'd said up to that point with one more move.

"And *this*...will be our eye in the sky." With that statement, Conrad eased his black suitcase over on its side, unlatched the top, and then removed it completely. Inside was a drone: white, light blue, and gray. About the size of two bread boxes.

Conrad gently placed the drone on the tarmac then stepped back. Instantly, the thing beeped—a subtle digital tone—and it popped open wings in four places, each with tiny turbines mounted upon them. A second later the flying robot was a yard overhead.

From a speaker inside the recesses of the drone, a voice spoke out. "Hello again," Sophie said.

FOR MOST OF OUR JAUNT along the alternate highway, housing and traffic were sparse. Dante and Fan rode their cycles side-by-side in front, with me close behind, and the Land Rover, a few car-lengths farther back. Sophie was somewhere overhead, but I never spotted her, despite trying several times.

My helmet's earpiece chirped to life. It was Conrad. "Silana and I'll be making a detour. There're some shops and grocery stores where we want to ask questions. Catch up with you at Harmony soon. All right?"

"Roger," replied Dante.

"This thing's working?" I asked.

"It is," said Conrad.

"We'll see you soon then," I said.

A few minutes later, Harmony Smoke Shop appeared on our right.

The convenience store-slash-smoke shop had a large sign looming outside its flat landscape. One word painted in neon green.

GAS.

Two gas pumps were shaded by a tall roof. The store itself was a single story, ramshackle joint that had definitely seen better days. But I guessed it was the only game in town for buying tobacco, because in addition to one car at the gas pumps, there were several other vehicles surrounding the place.

None of them were a white Cadillac Escalade.

We rumbled our bikes in near an empty pump and shut our engines off. I dismounted and briefly eyed a middle-aged woman who was filling the tank of a small, dark pickup truck nearby, but her appearance didn't cry 'kidnapper.' Surprise, surprise.

We removed our helmets then I hung mine off my Harley's handlebar.

"I'll top off the tanks," Dante said.

Fan unzipped her jacket. "I need to use the ladies' room."

"Yeah," I said. "Same. Well, not the same, but you know..."

Fan snickered then bee-lined for Harmony's double glass doors.

On the inside, the shop held rows of snacks, toilet paper, and aspirin bottles, along with racks of cigars, cigarettes, pipe and chewing tobacco and yes, medicinal marijuana.

A pot dispensary. Which explained the steady supply of customers in the lonely spot.

The shop was cleaner on the inside. And it smelled great. A mix of leafy aromas filled the long room, and you could be sure that pipes had been sparked in the place recently.

Two nondescript customers were browsing the wares. A single store clerk, an elderly fella, lounged behind the counter and was watching a wall-mounted television with its sound muted.

"The restrooms are outside, I think," Fan said with a light brush of her hand across my forearm. She wandered up to the old store clerk, who blinked a couple of times when he noted Fan's approach and peeled his eyes away from a rerun of Barney Miller. He had a warm smile.

"Yes, miss. What can I do for you?"

Fan glanced around the shop. "Your restrooms?"

"Keys are right there..." The clerk pointed at a small turnstile display on the counter. From two hooks dangled keys with his and hers fobs. "They're outside to the left as you exit. Just please bring them back when you're through."

Fan flashed the old man a big smile— "Thanks."—and she pulled off both keys from the stand then handed me one.

I exchanged nods with the clerk, and followed Fan outside.

I hadn't emptied my bladder since early morning, I'd been so caught up in the conversations with Conrad and Silana, and it was letting me know its growing disapproval.

"Give it a quick once-over while you're in there. I doubt there'll be clues, but you never know. Be right back," Fan said, then vanished into the ladies' room.

I walked into the men's room, flipped on some old, cranky, fluorescent lights, and locked the door behind me with a button press on the doorknob. It definitely didn't smell like inside the shop, but it wasn't as horrible as I'd expected.

There wasn't graffiti on the walls or the single stall's exterior. All-in-all there was really nothing out of the ordinary. A toilet tells no tales.

Didn't take me long to complete my business at the urinal. A quick wash of the hands and I was outside before Fan.

I stood with my back to the ladies' room and gazed out past the corner of the store toward the highway, but I couldn't see our motorcycles or the pumps from where I was.

Which turned out to be lucky, because the next thing I knew the door opened behind me and Fan tugged on my hand, gently at first, but then she yanked me forcefully toward herself. It surprised me enough that I half fell at her, and before I could counter it, my weight combined with her strength had pulled me into the ladies' room.

Fan closed the door behind us and locked it.

"Hurry," she breathed, and her hands were on my belt.

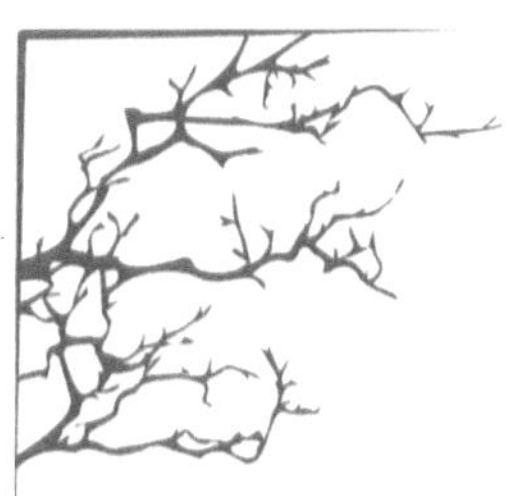

Chapter 17

I didn't fight her. It was a culmination is all. Inevitable and magnetic.

In my experience, attraction can be visceral, carnal and lightning fast, and I'd already known what Fan was feeling. She knew what she wanted. She sensed what I needed.

Those two forces crashed one against the other like waves against a shore, and the first contact of my fingertips on her smooth skin turned me into a maelstrom.

We were still almost fully clothed by the time I was spent. Somehow, we'd kept quiet, which had taken no small effort, believe me. It left us both sweating and breathing heavily. My cheeks were hot to the touch.

Fan peered up at me with heavy eyelids, her two hands outstretched and flat against my stomach. "*Mmm,*" she moaned.

"What are we doing?" I asked. I know it was a stupid question.

Fan laughed gently, her soft face fluttering, pressed against my thigh.

I huffed out a relieved breath. "That was incredible. But—" I lifted Fan to her feet with one hand as I pulled up my jeans with the other. "—we've got business."

Fan gave me a sly smirk, then turned her back to me. I zipped up her leather racing pants, then helped her into the matching jacket, one sleeve at a time.

She helped me buckle my belt and then stood tip-toe, offering up her mouth, so I kissed those full lips, and Fan flicked her tongue against mine just as we separated, to tease me again.

I smiled down at her. "Trouble. With a capital T." I stood from my resting position against the sinks. "Turns out to be *you.*"

Fan just pursed her lips at me, turned to the mirror, adjusted her hair, and wiped her mouth with a wet paper towel.

I reviewed myself in the mirror, too, and decided I didn't look too worse for wear. Leather doesn't wrinkle.

"Ready?" I asked.

"Mm-hmm."

I moved to the restroom door and popped it open.

"*Fuck!*"

Hovering right outside was Sophie's drone.

"Jesus Christ, Sophie! You scared the shit out of me."

The drone bobbed up in the air maybe half a foot higher than my head. "Apologies. I was concerned...until..." Sophie searched for words. That unnerved me even more than her unexpected presence outside the restroom.

"Yeah. Um, Fan and I were just—"

"I'm well aware of what you were doing."

I blinked. Of course, she was.

"Okay, well, let's not make an issue out of it. I expect your discretion, Sophie. You understand me?"

"I do. I will not pretend to understand the timing for this, but human behavior...is not always predictable."

I glanced sideways and half-accusingly at Fan. "No. No, it is not."

Fan's cheeks flushed, and she covered her mouth.

"Do you feel better?" Sophie's question didn't hold even a tinge of irony, and the drone moved up and away from me. Just slightly.

I straightened and tried not to glower at the machine. "As a matter of fact, I do." I scanned the sky overhead. "Shouldn't you be keeping watch from out of sight?"

Sophie didn't respond immediately, her drone still hovering steadily a few feet above us.

"Yes. I apologize again for—"

"It's *fine*, Sophie. If you have more questions about this sort of...'human behavior'...we can discuss it later." I hoped that would put an end to it.

"I look forward to it, Lochlan." And with that, Sophie soared away, until I could barely discern the drone. I guessed I was in for an even longer conversation later.

"Son of a bitch." I put out my hand. "I'll take your key back inside," I said to Fan.

By then, Fan was grinning ear to ear. She plunked the ladies' room fob into my palm. "I'll go see if Dante is done." She turned on a heel but halted. "Don't sweat Sophie, Loch. She's like a child. Overly curious, but she'll be discreet."

Fan walked around the corner toward the gas pumps. I grumbled and followed her, but changed directions to the shop.

Harmony still had a few customers browsing the tobacco products and paraphernalia. And someone had joined the old clerk behind the counter. A younger woman.

"Thanks," I said, and placed the keys back on their rotating rack. To my relief, I didn't get any strange looks from either clerk.

Ninja sex had been ninja enough.

I grabbed two Dr Peppers and a Coke from the refrigerated displays, then went back up to the counter. It was time to investigate.

"I'm lookin' for someone. Think he might've stopped by here. Can't miss him. Big fella. 'Bout my size. But Asian." I swirled an index finger pointed at one cheek. "With a face tattoo."

I hoped I hadn't gone too far, too fast, but it was worth the risk. Even if the pair of clerks were secretly allied with the Chinese, I'd just question them that much harder.

In those first few seconds awaiting a reply, I realized I was humming softly to myself. The old subconscious had taken the wheel for a few. So, I reached out with my empathy as the elderly clerk looked up from the register with my change in-hand.

I detected nothing from him, or at least, detected nothing that set off any of my alarms.

"Nope. Doesn't ring a bell, kid," said the old clerk. He handed over my change.

I frowned.

"Oh, I remember *him*. You weren't here, Ed." The female clerk wandered over and stood next to the old man. Again, my Spidey-sense didn't do flip-flops, but I wasn't exactly sure if it was working either. "He special ordered some Red Pagoda last week and came in again yesterday."

I was legitimately curious. "Red Pagoda?"

"Red Pagoda Mountain. A top brand cig from China. We don't normally carry them."

"Ah, so he picked them up."

"Not yet." She patted a cardboard box close to the cash register. A yellow sticky note clung to the side. "They weren't in, but the shipment got here this morning."

My heart jumped, but I tried to keep a straight face. The sticky note had a single name scribbled on it. Chiang.

"You have any more of those packs on display?" I asked.

"Sure do. Right behind you." The lady clerk pointed me toward a long row of cigarettes. "The *gold* packs and cartons."

I walked over to the cartons and cigarettes, gold with red pagodas on them and picked up a single pack. "You expect him back soon?"

"He was adamant about getting them. Paid in advance, in cash. So, yeah I'm pretty sure he'll be back sometime today."

I waggled the pack in my hand at her. "Nicotine is a serious drug," I said.

The woman laughed. "Hey, don't knock it. It keeps me in a job." She tilted her head at me. "Why all the questions? He a friend of yours?"

I wasn't sure where to take the conversation. Honesty could fuck things up in several ways. If someone at the store was closer to the Chinese than I was registering, he'd get a warning, and we might never find him. If I told them about his criminal behavior, they might panic and *that* could tip him off when he came for the cigs.

I walked the single pack of Red Pagodas over to the counter and then plopped it down. "Yeah, that..."

The bells on the front doors jingled. It was Fan. Wonderful, *Chinese* Fan. *Saved by the...*

I turned toward her. "Hey, just in time. I was about to explain why we're looking for—" I waved a finger up and down the right side of my face. "—*Chiang*."

Fan processed the situation like the professional I was counting on.

"My *phone* died. I lost all my contact info—I know! *Stupid!* I should have had a backup," she said.

"He's coming back here," I said, resisting the urge to wink.

"Oh? Great!" Fan gazed expectantly at the clerks. "Soon?"

"I think so," replied the lady clerk, smiling.

Fan walked up and tucked herself under my right arm, playing the good girlfriend. "You don't mind if we wait, do you, baby?"

I rolled with the routine. "No problem." I picked up a Dr Pepper off the counter and handed it to Fan. "Here."

"Ooh. Perfect!" Not missing a beat, Fan grabbed the bottle, met the lady clerk's eyes, and said, "Chiang and I met the other day and he mentioned your shop. I was just hoping by some stroke of luck..."

Before either clerk could respond, I pushed the cigs forward on the counter and reached in my back pocket for my wallet. "I'll take this pack, too."

"Ten forty-three," he said.

"Yikes," I almost gasped.

"Taxes and import fees. It'd be three times that in New York," said the lady clerk.

"I'll take a receipt, thanks," and I grinned down at Fan. "Road expenses."

Fan just smiled back up at me and wiggled a little tighter against my side. She was enjoying our little charade.

Which was fortunate, because I had an idea she might not like.

"Thanks for the help," I said sincerely to the two clerks.

"You're welcome," said the lady cashier, and she handed me my change. The old man just nodded and turned back to watch his television set again.

I gently separated from Fan, grabbed the Red Pagoda pack, then handed it to her. That got a perplexed eyebrow. I one-handed the remaining Coke and Dr Pepper and led the way to the shop exit, pushing open the door for Fan. Dante was on his way inside, I assumed to pay for gas.

I held out the two bottles. "Take your pick," I urged.

"Coke all day," Dante said, and took the bottle from me. "*Grazie*. Any news?"

"Yeah, we might have incoming," Fan said.

"The Chinese," I added.

"No shit?" Dante was grinning.

"A little luck never hurt. At least, I hope not," I said.

"I'll be right back. Gotta pay. Fan, go give Sophie the heads-up. Loch, you'll probably wanna stay out of sight."

"Yup," Fan agreed.

I thought about that for only a second. "Yeah, you're right. Nobody should recognize you two."

"Exactly," Dante said, and then pushed past us to enter the shop.

I followed Fan toward our motorcycles. "I hope you smoke," I said.

Fan stopped mid-stride and turned toward me. "Socially. And since we're expecting a guest..." She raised up the pack of cigs I'd given her. "You're awfully big for such a sneaky sneak."

"Nobody expects..."

"...the Spanish Inquisition," Fan finished with a laugh.

We continued walking side by side, and she reached for her helmet. "I figured if your tight Chinese butt is smoking one of those things near the shop, you'll be like Chiang catnip."

"So, you like my butt, do you?"

I guffawed. "Wasn't it obvious?"

"It sort of was...but a girl likes to hear these things."

"On mission, *soldier*." But I couldn't fake much militarism through my stupid grin.

Fan stood up straight anyway, and pushed out her chest, her small breasts hovering. "Yes, sir!" She smiled wickedly at me, relaxed, then put her motorcycle helmet back on. "Sophie, you there?"

I grabbed my helmet.

"Hello, Fan," the AI responded.

"We might have inbound, Sophie. The Chinese," Fan said.

"Immediate?"

"No way to know for sure," I replied.

"I see. I will inform the others."

"Good," I said.

"Let us know if you spot a white Cadillac Escalade approaching," Fan added.

"I will. Anything else?" Sophie sounded excited, which was a weird thing to sense in the voice of a machine.

Fan didn't think so. "That'll do for now."

"You might want to keep your helmets handy to avoid me chirping your phones."

"Right." Fan tapped my phone. "Make sure your walkie-talkie is muted, Loch."

I unclipped the phone from my belt and switched it to silent. "Done."

"That's it, Sophie," Fan said.

"Good luck," Sophie replied, and then our helmet comms went silent.

We pulled our helmets off. Dante was walking back from the shop, a Snickers bar in his mouth and his sunglasses on.

"Sophie's playing eye-in-the-sky for that Caddy," Fan said.

"Hmm? Mm-hmm," he mumbled around his candy bar.

"I'm gonna make myself scarce. Hang out by that warehouse, all casual-like," I said, nodding toward a long, lonely building less than a hundred yards south of the Harmony shop. I stabbed a thumb at Fan and smirked. "You should get acquainted with those commie cigs."

"I'm going to have a smoke near the entrance," Fan replied, thumbing casually over at the double-doors to Harmony. "*All casual-like.*" Her attempt at a Texas twang was comically bad.

I snorted approvingly.

Dante had swallowed half his Snickers bar by that point. "I'll be over near the air...compressor. Might as well check tire pressure...while we wait. Roll your bike over there for me, Fan."

She nodded.

I tucked my Dr Pepper into a saddle compartment on my Harley, revved her up, then rode south via a short dirt road parallel to the two-lane highway we'd arrived by. There was barely a tree on the barren landscape along that stretch, and the warehouse stuck out like a matchbox on a pool table.

Luckily for me, there was shade on the north side of the building, allowing me a straight shot to Harmony, so I rolled my bike into that long stretch of shadow, then shut off the engine, and hung my helmet from the bars.

I popped open my Dr Pepper, took a long chug, and watched Dante, as he put air into four tires. And Fan, who stepped back into the smoke shop for a couple of minutes. She exited again, leaned up against the shop wall next to the doors, and lit up a cigarette. No doubt she'd gotten a lighter from the clerks.

I got comfortable. There was no telling how long of a wait we were in for.

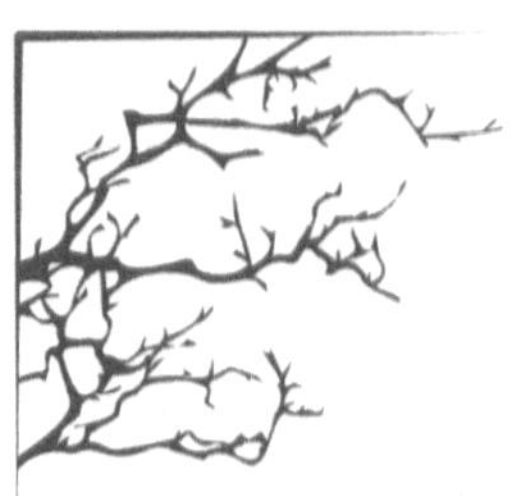

Chapter 18

More than an hour passed.

I'd gotten so bored, I was playing a game on my iPad. Fan had wandered in and out of the Harmony Smoke Shop between smokes, and Dante finished pumping air into the BMWs. He was detailing the bikes with a soft cloth and what I presumed was cleaning solution.

I put my tablet down and lifted my helmet near my mouth, holding the chin guard. "Dante, you hear me?"

I saw him flinch, and he looked at his helmet hanging from the handles of his cycle. He moved over and grabbed it. "Yeah, what's up? The excitement getting to you?"

"Positively giddy," I replied. "You're gonna chip away the chrome if you keep that up."

Dante's head tilted down to examine his work.

"I can see myself though. What's not to like?"

I chuckled. "Yeah, it's like I can hardly tell the difference between you and Fan."

"I know, right?"

I huffed as I switched to something serious. "I'm startin' to think he's gonna no-show."

Silence for two heartbeats and then, "No. He'll show up. Cigs are just short of crack. He *special-ordered* the fuckin' things."

"Yeah, I know. I'm just bitch—"

Someone coughed behind me, around the corner alongside my warehouse.

"Hold on. I've got company."

"Roger. Shout if you need me."

"Will do." I hung my helmet from the Harley's bars again.

The stranger hacked, then spit. That loosened me up. I had an inkling of what I was in for.

A tall, grizzled white dude with a green kerchief tied under his chin, a floppy, gray, fisherman's hat and an overstuffed backpack peaking up over his shoulders, came shambling around the west corner of the warehouse. The hobo straightened up at the sight of me, but his face broke into a smile.

"Oh, hey there, chief! I was just lookin' for a spot to eat my lunch. Didn't mean to bother ya."

I shrugged. "It's no bother, man. You're more than welcome to crash here. Not my place."

The old fella smiled broader. "Well. Well, then. I appreciate that. I do. My feet are killin' me."

"Have a seat. Plenty of shade to go 'round."

The hobo removed a backpack strap from one shoulder and quickly had his burden on the ground next to him. "Appears so." He half-carried, half-dragged his big pack into the shadow of the warehouse and placed it against the aluminum-paneled wall, which complained with a metallic screech.

He removed a hand-knit Mexican blanket and spread it on the ground, its thick edge made snug against the warehouse. Once that was set, he sat atop it, cross-legged.

"Name's Wayne," the old hobo said.

I hesitated but saw no reason to lie to the old man. "I'm Lochlan. You can just call me Loch."

"Ah, well, in that case, you can call me Lucky." That seemed to amuse the old guy to no end as he chuckled a long time to himself. "Loch and Lucky. Sounds like a strip in the funny pages."

I smiled then nodded. "Yeah, it does, doesn't it?"

Lucky removed a water bottle and a paper bag from his pack. He popped open the bottle and downed a few gulps. "Ah! Whew! I'd built up a thirst!" His smile remained.

My Dr Pepper was already long gone by that point. "I see that," I said. "You headin' anywhere in particular? Or just out for a stroll?"

Lucky opened his paper bag and pulled out a sandwich. If I'd had to guess, I'd have said egg salad. "Me? Oh, I'm just movin' north. Nowhere in particular." He lifted his sandwich and waved it at me and the sky. "Perfectly good walkin' weather, not to be missed." He bit into his sandwich, still smiling.

"Not bad for riding either." I tucked my iPad back into my backpack. Lucky had a questioning expression as he swallowed more of his egg salad.

"You aren't flying colors. You're not from around here, are you?"

"Colors?" The term took a sec to sink in. "Oh—*gangs*." I snorted. "No, no colors for me. I'm just a tourist, passin' through."

"Thought so. You sound like a Texan."

"I should. I am one."

Lucky laughed. "I've always liked Texas. Used to be the friendliest folks. 'Course things change."

I nodded. "Whole damn country has... West coasters, Sharia, and too many Mexicans. Taking its toll."

"You don't approve of our President's immigration policies?"

"Heh. Um, *no*. Texas can't afford any more."

"It'll all come to a head, soon enough. Mark my words."

"Good thing I've got spare ammo then."

"Good thing..." Silence set in for a minute as Lucky finished off his egg salad. Then he asked, "You looking for someone?"

My head almost snapped up, but I let his observation roll off. "How'd you guess?"

"Oh, not too hard to figure out. You've been staring over at those two motorcycles since I dropped my blanket."

"Yeah, they're with me. We're hunting." *Now, why the hell did I just say that?*

"Hunting. Without rifles. You bounty hunters?"

"Not strictly speaking. But there *is* a bad guy. Unfortunately."

Lucky grunted. "Well, I'll be damned. What's the crime?"

I grimaced. "*Kidnapping.*"

Lucky let out a long, low whistle. "That's some *shit*."

"Yeah."

"Who's he got?"

I huffed out a breath. "A friend. A girl I used to know, from college. Not sure why her —why he took her—but I've tracked him this far. Not going home without her."

I was staring back across the way to Harmony. Lucky said, in a quieter voice: "I believe you."

"Can I ask you a question?" I turned to face the old guy.

He wiped his mouth with a paper napkin. I have to admit, I was surprised he had napkins.

"Sure, kid. Fire away."

I looked up at the sparsely clouded sky. "The world is round, right?"

Lucky barked out a single laugh. "Earth? Sure. Well, NASA says so, anyway. All the globes in school libraries pretty much say so." Lucky rolled up his paper bag then tucked it into his backpack with a brief torrent of loud crinkling. "*But...*" I aimed an ear at the hobo, suddenly keen on the conversation. "... if we consider spiritual belief systems, we get very different definitions of Earth."

I couldn't help but give Lucky my most perplexed face.

"Teacher before wanderer," he said, matter-of-factly, half a wry grin creasing one corner of his mouth.

"Huh," I said. "Go on. Please."

"The Hindu, for instance, sometimes claim Earth to be spherical, while at other times, that it can be rolled up like this blanket here." Lucky tugged a corner of the blanket he was sitting on. "If you look long enough, you could probably find any manner of explanation for the shape of the earth you're after, depending on the ideology." I half expected Lucky to call me grasshopper then, but he continued: "But since you're askin' me about *round* earth, I'm guessing what you're really asking me is, 'Is the earth flat?' Yeah?"

"Yeah, that's pretty much it. Some friends are fucking with my head. I think." I knew that wasn't true. Deep down. "Anyway. I just figured I'd get a fresh perspective."

My eyes were back on the sky, but Lucky exhaled and continued: "Christian belief talks about 'the four corners of the earth,' and such. Plenty of people will try to tell you that's flowery language, not meant to be taken literally. Others will insist the Bible *is* literal, always and forever.

"But the 'circle of the earth,' that might mean either globe *or* flat, nobody can say for sure, really— not even the scholars."

I grimaced. "Pancake Earth."

"You got it. But you asked me my opinion, so I'll give you *my* opinion." Lucky cleared his throat then half-shouted, half-sang, " '... for the pillars of the earth are the Lord's, and he hath set the world upon them.' " His voice boomed across the flat plains spreading wide beyond the shade of our warehouse. Its resonance jolted me. "Sort of implies something that language, don't you think? You wouldn't typically set a globe on pillars... Sounds more like a floor, or a rooftop. So, in my opinion—and being a good Christian and all—I'm inclined to believe the world is *flat*.

"Not much you or me can do about it, either way. Live long enough, you realize the world is *full* o' lies. That's just the way it is. It's up to each of us to find what truth we can. Find our own truth."

"That doesn't exactly put me at ease, Lucky," I said.

He laughed, but not bitterly. "I'm sorry about that. Really. Take anything I say with a grain o' salt." There was a pause and then, "Gonna be a full moon tonight, looks like."

I glanced over at Lucky to see him pointing an index finger skyward. I followed that pointing digit until I was staring at a blue-gray moon in the clear afternoon sky. I don't think it had been there a minute before. A shudder escaped with my next breath.

A blood moon for Vicki. Time was running out.

"Don't suppose that thing is made of cheese, do you? Or hollow maybe?" Lucky teased.

I shook my head and glowered. "Hell, honestly? That'd be a relief, compared to what I *do* know it is."

Lucky went quiet, probably trying to decipher my last comment. I didn't look in his direction. Instead, I gazed back across to the smoke shop.

Fan had rolled her BMW over to the side of the store, and she was sitting astride it, while still smoking. I had a stupid thought that I'd end up responsible for getting her addicted to cigarettes, but that idea didn't linger for long.

There was a beep from my helmet. I lifted it to my ear. "Excuse me. There is a white Cadillac Escalade inbound on Veteran's Highway. Heading south." Again, there was a hint of excitement in Sophie's voice. If it was artificial emotion, it was scarily convincing. "I estimate its possible arrival in less than one minute."

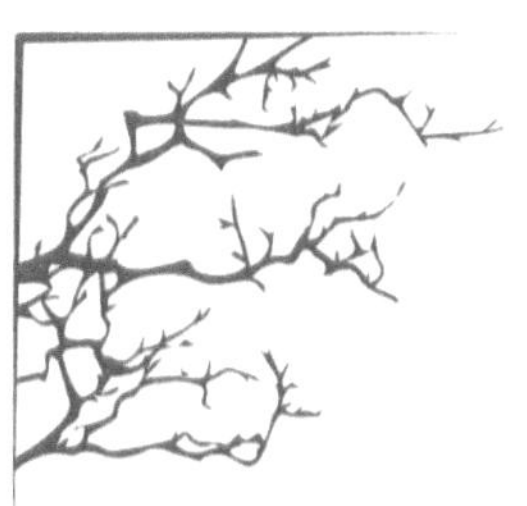

Chapter 19

Another voice spoke up through my helmet's comm unit. It was Conrad. "We're parked off the highway. *Close.* Fan, I'm sure you're prepared to engage. The rest of you, keep your heads down."

Engage?

"Roger. I'll 'Betty Boop' our new friend," Fan said.

Fan shook out a fresh cigarette from her pack then lit up. Then she struck a pose on her motorcycle that, even from where I stood, could not be ignored by any straight man with a pair of eyes. Unless the Chinese turned out to be some 'going his own way' type. Then we'd need a fresh approach.

I knew of a few 'approaches' *I* wanted to use.

Fan's green and white racing jacket was unzipped, and her matching striped leather pants fit her like spray paint. The smoke she puffed out into the cool air only enhanced her exotic beauty that much more.

Asian Betty Boop was sexy-dangerous all right. I had to steer my mind back to business after it wandered off to the earlier restroom rendezvous.

A few seconds was all I was going to get, regardless.

Sophie alerted us through the helmet comm: "The Escalade is here! It's pulling in. I believe the driver is alone."

"Sorry, Lucky. Looks like I gotta cut our convo short." I kept my eyes on the gas pumps, and a white SUV pulled off the two-lane highway and wheeled around toward a parking spot alongside the smoke shop.

"Don't worry about me, kid. Do what you gotta do. I'm gonna pack up. Sounds like things getting a little too interesting for my taste..."

A rustling of fabrics and paper came from behind me, and I knew Lucky was folding his blanket and cleaning up his lunch. "Probably smart," I replied.

The Escalade parked a few meters from Fan, who was side-straddling her motorcycle near the double-door entrance to Harmony. The muscles in my back tensed up as the scene unfolded, so I cracked my neck with a head tilt to the side and then stretched to loosen up some more.

Come on out, motherfucker.

I couldn't see the driver's side of the SUV from my angle, but I saw a head peek above the car's roof as he exited. If it was the Chinese, he was just as big as Connie Winter had described him. Not quite my height, but easily over six feet.

I wished hard for a pair of binoculars right then, so I did the next best thing and grabbed my iPad, and used its camera zoom to take a better look. By the time I'd done that, the driver stood close by Fan and the two were talking.

The Chinese was tall, with jet black hair—and the right side of his face, that profile facing me as it so happened, had an obvious tattoo. He wasn't all in black though. Instead, he dressed more like a character out of an anime, flamboyantly attired in a light blue suit and tie, with a pink shirt.

Chiang. The sharp-dressed son of a bitch. I reached for my helmet's microphone again. "It's *him.*"

"Good. Don't move! Let it play out. Fan will try to get a read on him. We need to track him to Vicki, that's all," Conrad replied. "We'll be there shortly."

Chiang was still chatting with Fan, pretty casually it seemed. She was off her bike and she showed the Chinese her pack of Red Pagoda cigs, which he took from her, then examined. He nodded approvingly, even appeared to laugh, and then handed the pack back.

Damn, the girl is good.

After another minute, Chiang strolled into the shop. Fan stayed outside and half-sat back on her motorcycle.

I was sweating as I watched her.

She'll be fine. Dante's close. Sophie. Hell, who knows what Sophie can do? Fan'll be fine.

Chiang exited the shop with his shipment under his arm. He stopped again near Fan, who'd finished her latest cigarette, pried open his cardboard box with ease, pulled out a golden pack, and then handed it to her. Then he took out another pack for himself.

Fan was smiling. She said a few words and then knocked another cigarette into her fingers. This time she reached up and popped the cigarette into Chiang's mouth. He accepted it with no apparent care in the world, then bent down to let Fan light it for him.

Chiang stood tall, puffed out some smoke, then conversed some more with Fan—I had no way to know for sure, but I was guessing the talk was in Mandarin. Fan's helmet was hanging from her cycle, so probably couldn't pick up the conversation from that distance, even if the microphone were active.

"Sophie, can you hear what's being said down there?" I asked.

"I can. My directional microphone's capture is not one hundred percent clear from this height, but they are speaking in Mandarin about the tobacco product. Fan seems to be gaining his trust."

Go, Fan.

"There is something else though. I'm receiving sporadic cell and Wi-Fi interference. Actively adjusting for static. I—I'm scanning the source."

I'm not sure what concerned me more, that Sophie was complaining about comm interference—or that she'd just stuttered. I held my tablet's camera up with my right hand, keeping Fan and Chiang in focus, and reached inside my leather jacket to make sure my 2011 was loose in its shoulder holster.

Chiang and Fan walked toward the white Escalade, Chiang moving around to the driver's side, almost entirely obscured from view again, as Fan moved to the passenger door. *What the fuck?*

"What the fuck is she doing? She's not getting into the *car*, is she?"

"*What?*" Conrad's voice was as strained as I felt.

I jumped onto the seat of my Harley.

The passenger door popped open as Fan reached for it.

"She won't. Hold on," whispered Dante over the comm. Despite his words, Dante had put on his motorcycle helmet and was astride his BMW, looking very ready to bolt in pursuit.

Sophie interrupted, loudly. "I'm being scanned! The scan is coming from—Chiang!"

I almost dropped my tablet but shoved it into the open saddlebag. As I pulled my helmet on, I barely had time to register that Lucky wasn't on his blanket next to the warehouse.

"Protect Fan!" I shouted, no longer caring who might hear me.

I gunned my Harley without thinking. My calling card in life really—muscle memory and instinct, binding actions to my mind—and I took full advantage, for Fan's sake. I crossed the roughly one hundred and fifty yards between the warehouse and Chiang's parked Escalade like a harpoon fired from a cannon.

Still, even as fast as my charge was, I wouldn't reach her in time. The entire world slowed around me as my brain raced to calculate my next move, and I simultaneously cursed time itself and the uncaring Universe.

That's when I saw Sophie's drone drop like a piece of the sky, a blue and white turbine-controlled comet. My gut wrenched tight as I watched helplessly, and swung my cycle left into a forced brake, my intent being to stop close to Fan without ramming her, Sophie, or Chiang's SUV.

When I was twenty feet from Fan, Dante came to my left, no helmet on now, running full out at the Cadillac.

But Sophie hit Fan first.

A silenced gunshot snapped. Blood sprayed from Fan's head, and she cried out as Sophie forced her sideways, then down to the cement.

I pushed off my cycle and used my feet as wedges on either side of the Harley, forcing a complete halt, while I strained briefly with my upper body to flatten the bike quickly to the ground. There was an unavoidable scrape of the paint job, and then I leapt beyond the machine to get to Fan.

Dante was ahead of me by a second, pulling Fan up into his left arm while freeing his sidearm with his right. I flanked him, grabbed Fan from the opposite side and aimed my double-barreled .45 at the Escalade. But the tinted windows made it tough to see Chiang. I'd expected him to be aiming at the three of us, but he wasn't.

Instead, Sophie took a second gunshot into the side of her drone as she righted her frame and hovered a mere two feet from the ground. Sparks flew out from the chassis, but I couldn't tell if the bullet had punctured or ricocheted off.

The drone didn't wait for a third bullet. It spewed out a blast of gray chaff and smoke into the open interior of the Escalade, while simultaneously flying above the vehicle, to a second story height.

Chiang let out a curse I didn't understand, then his Cadillac lurched hard left, barely missing the side of the shop as it turned. Sophie's countermeasure cloud expanded quickly, obscuring Chiang's car just enough that I couldn't get a clear shot at the driver's seat, so I examined Fan instead.

Blood streamed down from her right ear and across her cheek, her right eye closed in a pool of red, but she was still breathing and alert. Her good eye was looking right at me.

Sophie, the miracle of Conrad's science, had saved Fan's life by mere inches and milliseconds.

This wasn't going according to plan at all. We were supposed to trail the bad guy back to his hideout. Simple, right?

Instead, what we had was a cluster-fuck!

"You'll be okay," I said to Fan. I pushed her into Dante's grasp and moved between them and the Escalade.

I collected myself, realized what a damn fool I'd been for almost shooting Chiang—our only link to Vicki—a moment before, and aimed my pistol again, this time at the right rear tire. It was angled away from me but presented plenty of rubber, and, though Chiang was gunning his engine, my reflexes were fast enough. I hit the tire with both rounds. Thankfully, the loud burst of the 2011, amplified by blacktop and cement, was deadened by my helmet.

Startled Harmony customers shouted and screamed near the gas pumps.

But there was no explosive bang from the tire.

Chiang's tires were *solid*. Sure, I took a chunk or two out of the one I'd hit, but that didn't slowdown the Escalade.

"We see him!" It was Silana's shout this time in the comm.

"Help Fan! She's hurt. I'll follow Chiang!" I half-ran to where my Harley lay on the ground. "Sophie, can you jam his cell?" I quickly mounted my motorcycle.

"Done! He has a proprietary device he used to scan us. And he may have overheard us *talking*," Sophie said. "That won't happen again." She sounded genuinely pissed off.

"Get him, Loch!" Dante shouted from behind me.

"Fuck!" The Escalade screeched its tires and sped straight out of the lot, roaring north onto US-95. I revved my bike, then took off after it, the rear tire of my Harley burning rubber and spitting dirt and gravel in all directions. I rocketed onto the highway, my torso and head aimed forward and down like an arrow ready to fire out between the handlebars.

I didn't even realize I was yelling until I was firmly on the blacktop of the highway and needed to take a breath. My first ever car chase—motorcycle chase—had begun.

"We'll take care of Fan. Dante, go assist Loch," said Conrad.

"I will alert you if I detect any more potential hostiles," Sophie said.

Chiang was speeding, but there was no way in Hell he could outrun my Harley, and I'm sure he knew it. I closed the gap between us in under a minute, then I followed him from six car lengths back. Traffic on Veteran's was fairly light, and so far, nobody had gotten hurt besides Fan. I wanted to keep it that way.

But cops showing up was only a matter of time at the speeds Chiang was hitting. We were already at one hundred and six miles per hour. He could push it even harder on the straight highway if he wanted to.

Will he? He knows he can't shake me by racing.

And then Chiang slowed down.

Tell me you're not a mind-reader. Scratch that. Don't tell me.

"I'm coming, Loch! You okay?" It was Dante.

"Yeah. I'm all right. He's slowing down a little. How's Fan doing?"

"She'll live. Ear took a hit. She said if you don't catch this joker, she'll bite *your* ear off."

Yep, she was fine. "Working on it."

Expensive SUVs and tinted windows are like peanut butter and jelly, and I couldn't see Chiang through the Escalade's rear. I debated whether to just shoot out the window.

That debate didn't last long. The rear door of the Escalade popped open and rose on its own.

"Um, guys. The rear door is opening up."

"I see. Be careful," replied Sophie.

I was somewhat reassured that Sophie was still with me, but as I watched the rear door open, I sensed a flash of amusement from up ahead. It had to be Chiang.

"Yeah. Careful."

I tapped my brakes once and let off the gas. Just as I did, the Escalade's rear door stopped rising at about a forty-five degree angle, and a mini beer keg, like one of those cute things you see Heineken selling in the grocery store, rolled out from under the door, then onto the highway in front of me!

I barely had time to react but swerved my Harley hard left. The keg rolled a few feet, clipped some cracked surface of the highway, then popped into the air in a wobbly spin, barely missing me. I could feel a disturbance of air as it sailed past.

"Heads-up, Dante! Incoming!" I yelled and opened up the throttle to speed forward.

"What? What's—" Dante's voice cut off, then a second later there was an explosion behind me. I righted my cycle again, then chanced a glance over my shoulder. A cloud of smoke and a burst of billowing fire rose straight into the sky, a dozen feet or more.

"Dante!"

"Okay! I'm Okay! Goddamn mine! Don't get too close," he advised.

Exploding beer kegs. You've got to be fucking kidding me.

I'd had enough. I pulled out my 2011 and put two bursts through the rear window at an angle, meaning to take it out without harming Chiang. They impacted but didn't break the glass.

You have got *to be kidding me!*

Chiang swerved his vehicle left then right, but I shot again once, hitting close to my first four bullet marks. The glass cracked, but still didn't break.

"The thing is a tank. Bulletproof glass. He's probably got another one of those mines too…"

Of course, he did. Chiang gunned the Escalade, then another keg popped out from beneath the open hatch the second I was in his rearview mirror.

"Another one!" I shouted.

"I see it, I've got it," said Dante. I saw him behind me, helmet on now, speeding up fast on my right side. His pistol was out and pointed forward.

"Wait—" I dodged the rolling keg—before it could spin into the air off the highway this time—then I swerved into Chiang's blind spot on his right rear. I only breathed in once before there was another explosion and fireball. Dante's motorcycle plowed straight through the dark and fiery cloud but appeared undamaged.

"Got it! *Got it!*"

"Nice!" I slowed again to avoid Chiang trying to clip me with the Escalade. I let up until I was riding farther back, next to Dante. On our left, a car, then a truck, passed us by in quick succession in the southbound lane, honking their horns.

Yeah, it's all fun and fireworks, right?

"Ideas?" I asked, snapping a quick glance over at Dante.

"He's gonna kill someone if we hit more traffic," Dante said. "We need to stop him."

"Cops maybe?"

"No! Fuck no. Cops'll probably kill him. Then we'll never find your girl..." Dante made a good point. "We need to let off him."

"Let him go? Are you nuts?"

"No, not let him go. Just don't follow him." I cocked my helmet at him, and Dante looked back at me. "Sophie! Can you put a bug on the Chinese?"

"Yes—" Sophie replied.

"We can't do that," I said.

"*What?* Why the hell not?" Dante yelled.

"Because eventually he's gonna figure out a way to get a message to his people. We're not sure how far he's gonna drive, how long Sophie can keep squelching his comms. Where or what he's even driving *to.*"

"Actually, I can keep up with Chiang at these speeds for well over a day, without recharging—" Sophie said.

"Right. Great. Well, we—"

"But I know where he is going."

"Excuse me?" I blurted.

"I've hacked into the Escalade's onboard mapping system. I've also scanned and photographed Chiang's GPS through the sunroof."

Our robot masters have arrived.

"I can also do *this.*"

"Wait—what?" I barely got the words out before the white SUV racing ahead of us suddenly slowed—and kept on slowing. I hurriedly pressed my brakes.

"She's cut his engines," Dante said through a laugh.

"Please steer clear, gentlemen," Sophie requested.

Dante went off the highway right while I veered left. I couldn't see Chiang's face through the sides of the Escalade as we passed him, but I tried to reach out with my empathy—and a clear mixture of surprise and anger came in reply.

Chiang turned his car enough to drive off the highway west, toward a convergence of two dirt roads. The Escalade soon came to a halt on the Nevada barrens, and we rode back toward it.

"You're something else, Sophie," I said.

"Yes. I suppose I am."

I corrected my mistake. "I meant—*good work*, Sophie. You did good."

There was a brief pause and then, "Thank you, Lochlan."

I parked my Harley a few car lengths behind Chiang's vehicle. "Let's have a little chat with this fuck."

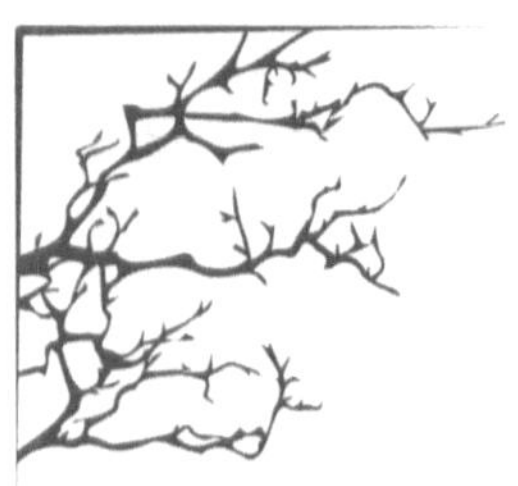

Chapter 20

My pistol was in hand and so was Dante's. We knew this asshole could rage out of his car any second—guns blazing—but I'll be honest, I didn't expect it. Chiang had been a cool customer so far. That scared me even more.

"Sophie, can I get a little music in my helmet please? I need to get a feel for this guy."

"Okay. What are you in the mood for?" Sophie asked.

I laughed bitterly but kept my eyes locked on the immobilized Escalade. "Some Coltrane would be great."

"Ah, I enjoy jazz. Here you go."

The dulcet tones of a piano struck the intro into "A Sentimental Mood," followed closely by the unmistakable tenor sax of John Coltrane. The somber tone of the music contrasted wildly with the tension of our situation—but my inner irony approved.

"Be careful with that one, guys." *Fan.* It surprised me to hear her voice again so soon.

"Wasn't planning on askin' him for a ride." I let that sentence linger. "Good to hear your voice. You okay?"

"I think so. Silana bandaged what's left of my ear. Pain's gone, at least. Don't worry about me—'cause I wanted to tell you. *Chiang.* I didn't catch any tells from him. Was going to give him my number—but then shit went south. Something definitely triggered him."

"I gotcha. We'll be extra careful." Coltrane was still playing behind the cell conversation, and I reached out at Chiang with my feelings—at least I hoped I was. "Maybe this clown has some of *my* ability? Hold that thought."

Calm focus met my mind. No fear. No anxiety. Just calm.

"Crisp as a cucumber, this fucker. He's hardly breathing, I think."

Sophie spoke up. "I am still jamming all cell signals—other than our own. Activity from Chiang remains evident. He's closed the sunroof now. I've never seen him use a handheld. No phone. That has me considering..."

"Transhuman," said Conrad.

"Possibly," said Sophie.

"You mean a *cyborg?*" I asked, and wasn't happy about it.

"Shit, shit, shit," muttered Dante.

"It would make sense—for Chiang to be enhanced with implants," Sophie said.

"Yes, it would," Conrad agreed. "Especially considering our current location, the direction he's heading."

"What's that supposed to mean?" I asked.

Silana responded, "Lake Tahoe is close, maybe an hour away. I was hoping that was only a coincidence, but now..." Her hallmark merry vibe was all gone. I arched an eyebrow reflexively. "We may know the group we are dealing with, Lochlan. My sister..."

"Your *sister?*" A slight breeze crossed my neck below my helmet and chills ran down my spine. "There's another *story* coming, isn't there?"

"For later," Conrad injected. "We'll be at your location in a few minutes. You shouldn't do anything—"

The driver's door popped open an inch, and Chiang said, "I come out. Do not shoot. *Right?*" I was just barely able to understand him over the combined music and voice in my helmet's headphones.

Conrad finished, "Until we arrive."

"Keep your hands where we can see them, asshole! Move slowly!" shouted Dante, both hands pointing his Glock at the SUV's ajar door.

"Chiang is exiting the car," I said. I still detected absolute calm from him, but despite that and what Chiang had just said, my trigger finger still itched.

The Chinese pushed his car door most of the way open, enough for us to see him fully.

"Just take my smokes. *Right?*" For the first time I had a good look at Vicki's kidnapper. He appeared Eurasian, about my age, with cut cheekbones, piercing dark eyes, and three Chinese characters tattooed on the right side of his face. These symbols stacked from just below his eyebrow, one next to his eye, another on his cheek and the bottom one along his jawline. He wore his pastel blue suit well, despite the pink shirt, jacket casually unbuttoned. He held up his delivery box from Harmony Smoke Shop.

"Toss your weapons first, motherfucker. Then toss the box on the ground and step out of the vehicle," Dante commanded. "*Slowly.*"

He didn't understand English too well because Chiang turned sideways and gently tossed the brown cardboard box onto the dirt road first. Then he lifted a silver pistol off the passenger's seat next to him, using just index finger and thumb on the end of the grip, dangled it outside the car door and dropped it.

"Fan, call me curious, but what exactly does this scribble on Chiang's face say?"

The Chinese exited the white SUV with his hands up at his shoulders. The bastard actually had a small grin on his lips. *Yeah, you and your precious cigarettes. Smug prick.*

"*Ba shyr wu.* It's a number. Eighty-five," Fan replied.

What the fuck? "Eighty-five?"

"I know. Fucking weird."

Chiang placed his feet on the ground, then stood straight, just outside the Escalade. He was thick in the neck and broad-shouldered. Definitely lifted weights in his spare time.

"Open up your jacket, nice and wide," Dante ordered.

Chiang had an empty shoulder holster but no other obvious weapons.

"Now your pockets," Dante continued.

Chiang complied, the silly grin still on his face, and he pulled out the pockets of his trousers. I assumed he'd left his keys in the ignition, because all that he dropped on the ground was a pack of cigarettes from a jacket pocket, along with a lighter, a USB thumb drive, and wallet.

The last item he pulled was what appeared to be a compass that he seemed reluctant to drop. He bent at the knees to let it land lightly in the dirt.

"I'm going to take this jacket off, if you don't mind?" This time Chiang spoke with a distinctly British accent. At least, I thought he did.

I blinked. I was just hearing things maybe?

But I caught Dante's helmet in my peripheral vision, turning in my direction.

Dante whispered, enhanced by our helmet comms. "Tell me his voice just changed..."

I nodded. "Yeah, his English just went Oxford or something."

Chiang had now dropped to his knees and placed the jacket on top of the cardboard box, neat as you please. "I assume you want me on my stomach, so you can cuff me. That's usually how this goes, correct?"

My mind raced as adrenaline kicked in. *The folded, blue suit jacket. Sitting atop the box of cigarettes. And Chiang gently placing himself face-down in the dirt road....*

Sophie spoke up. "Gentlemen, I don't like the readings I'm getting—" *The compass shining in the dirt....*

I ducked down behind my motorcycle as if someone had my skull targeted in a sniper's reticule.

"Dante! Dante get dow—"

An explosion ripped the air in front and above me, sending forth a smashing force that knocked me on my ass. The Harley crashed sideways on top of me, and I let out a painful grunt.

"Lochlan? What the hell was that?" It was Fan's voice that squawked dimly through my comm unit. Or it only *seemed* dim. The overwhelming boom of the explosion seconds before had left me equal parts stunned and near deaf.

"The Escalade has exploded. Chiang is running!" Sophie sounded as close to panic as I'd yet heard. Distant and my ears were ringing, but I still made out every word. "Dante is...*Dante is down. No.* No, no, no!"

"We're almost there!" Conrad yelled. I *think* he yelled.

"Hang on! Hang on, you guys!" Fan again.

When I came back to my senses—which could have been instantly, or minutes later for all I knew—my eyes were closed. I snapped them open. My helmet was still on, and my Ray-Bans too.

"I'm pursuing Chiang," said Sophie. "Lochlan might require assistance, but he appears to not be seriously injured. I can't let Chiang escape."

"I'm okay!" I shoved the Harley Road King off me then pushed hard to my feet, hard enough that I sent the motorcycle toppling over onto its opposite side. "I'm all right. I'm okay..."

I patted my chest and arms, satisfied that they were in one piece, and looked around.

What was left of the Cadillac Escalade burned steadily, black smoke churning up into the early evening sky. The SUV was less than half of what it had been, the top portion all but gone, including all the windows. Glass shards surrounded me in the dirt. If I hadn't been shielded by my Harley and wearing a helmet...

Dante's body was crumpled on the ground behind his motorcycle that, somehow, was still standing. His arms and legs were sprawled at odd, horrific angles, like someone had dropped him from a tall building.

He wasn't moving.

Blood splatter was in the dirt of the road, on all parts of Dante's body in view from where I stood. Even on his BMW Sport.

I rushed around the motorcycle, then jerked to a halt.

John Coltrane's music still eerily played through the comm, and I couldn't blink, couldn't look away. My lungs felt frozen over as I stared hard at Dante's corpse.

There wasn't any emotion or energy coming from that body. Just cold, uncaring reality. And as that reality sank in, something of my own stirred inside me, like a burning in my lungs to melt the frost.

Slowly, without moving my feet an inch, I scanned the junction of the two dirt roads forming the highway exit behind our motorcycles. Then I spotted Dante's helmet, facing me, tinted visor glinting in the waning sunlight. Blood pooled darkly next to it. Even at that distance, a chunk of glass was plainly wedged into the helmet's face shield.

Dante had been decapitated.

I hadn't known him for even a day, but the sting of salty tears welled up in the corners of my eyes. I should have been faster!

Guilt is a bitter thing. But there was nothing I could have done. Not really. But I knew what to do next.

"Dante's dead," I said. "I'm sorry."

There was silence except for the jazz inside my helmet.

"Don't pursue Chiang alone, Lochlan." Conrad. The grim voice of experience.

But I didn't care.

"This ends," I replied.

"Lochlan, you don't know what—"

"*I don't give a shit!* I'm not letting him get away!" I was already walking to my Harley and examining it. It appeared to be functional enough if not undamaged. The tires weren't blown.

Conrad persisted. "You don't understand what might be waiting for you, where he's running to!"

I mounted my motorcycle then throttled the engine. "Sophie, give me directions. I'll catch up."

"Sophie, *do not*—"

Sophie cut Conrad off. "I'm sorry Conrad, but I cannot catch this man alone. And he must answer for killing Dante."

Three cars had pulled over off the highway now, and there was a siren far in the distance.

"Ride west, south of the highway. Chiang is running farther southwest. I will fly lower so you can spot me more easily."

Dust sprayed from my back tire as I sped in that direction. "People have stopped at the wreckage. I'm sure police are coming. You'll have to deal with them, Conrad."

"I'll handle it," he said, and surprisingly he didn't continue arguing with me—*or Sophie*. Instead, he added, "Be *merciless*, Lochlan. If you pursue this man...do not waver. Do not give him *another chance*."

The anger was so hot in me by that point, I could barely speak. "He's done," I growled, though I realized even as I said the words, despite the blood lust, I could still benefit from squeezing answers out of Chiang.

Vicki remained the mission, and the blood moon was rising.

I aimed my Harley west across the flat Nevada desert.

"I'm coming."

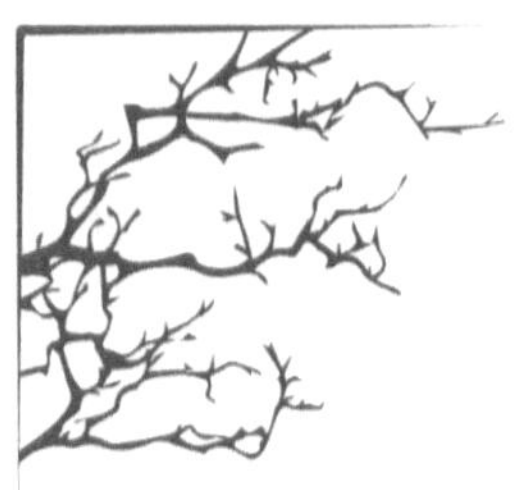

Chapter 21

I'm a musician. I make music, not war. Making audiences happy, sharing my art with people. It's the foundation of my world. That rare, wonderful, mutual feeling that few music outsiders fully understand.

Given a fair set of choices then, I'd have been perfectly happy just dodging groupies and composing, playing my saxes, and leading a band. For the rest of my life.

Or so I thought.

Funny thing about life, it doesn't give a *fuck* what you want or what you *think* you want.

Riding my Harley across that shrub-dotted landscape, I realized my life had changed forever. I'd just seen another corpse, up close, and not a stranger. Not *this* time. Dante's blood might as well have been painted across my eyes for all the red I still saw.

Chiang, whoever—*whatever* he was, had almost murdered Fan back at Harmony. Now Dante was dead. By all rights, I should have been, too. It wasn't my time, I guess.

As for the kidnapper himself? I intended to kill him. I didn't know if I could, but I'd certainly try. Hopefully, he'd tell me what he did with Vicki first, but I wasn't counting on it.

"He's remarkably fast," Sophie said.

"Running?"

"Yes, he's at near full sprint, and he's been doing it for several hundred yards now. *Burdened.* I calculate his current speed at twenty-two miles per hour. If he keeps this pace up, we are witnessing a shattering of all known cross-country records."

"*Transhuman*," I grumbled.

"Undoubtedly," Sophie agreed. "I'm continuously jamming cell signals emanating from him. He's implanted with a computer chip, at the minimum."

"He'll never run fast enough to out-distance this motorcycle."

"Definitely not. But he's aiming for terrain that will make it difficult for you."

"Like?"

"A cattle fence."

Shit.

Ahead of me, I made out a flying, blue-gray, oblong shape that grew quickly as I continued racing west and angled away from the highway to the north.

It was Sophie's drone. "He's already at the fence."

"Is there a road through it? Anywhere close?"

"Yes, farther ahead. Not too far, but Chiang will gain ground heading south."

"What choice do I have?"

"None really. Keep riding west then take the first left turn. I'll guide you again to my position."

I traveled until I came to a narrow dirt road that split the barbed wire fence, and then I aimed south again. There was a long metal gate across the road, but to my relief it wasn't padlocked. I parked, leapt off my Harley, then opened the fence just enough for me to squeeze through. Back on my motorcycle, I revved through the gap and followed the road beyond.

"I'm past the fence. Lost sight of you, Sophie."

"I see you. Stay on that road. You're aimed in our general direction. Unfortunately, Chiang is nearing some ranch houses."

I started breathing even harder. "Can you get to those houses ahead of him? Go warn the people there! Make a racket if you have to!"

"I can. You'll need to veer off to your right now and angle about forty degrees. Stay on that straight course, and you should see these houses. Less than a quarter mile."

At that short of a distance, and the speed I was going, I knew I'd see the houses in just a few seconds.

Before any buildings came into view though, a blaring horn blasted, repeated several times, like one of those annoyingly loud air horns you'd use at college football games—or to prank a sleeping dorm mate.

Not that I'd ever done anything so horrible. Well, not sober anyway.

It had to be Sophie.

It was. "There are several adults and children here. Isn't much time. I'm telling them to lock their doors or flee." I pushed my Harley even faster, risking my neck, but I was determined to reach Chiang before he got to the ranch. "They do not seem willing to leave."

"Tell them to call the sheriff," I told her, no longer only concerned for myself and Conrad's agents. There were *kids*.

Sophie's voice displaced the music in my helmet comm again. "That won't be possible. I'm sorry."

"*What?* Why?"

"If I'm jamming Chiang's cell transmissions, I have to jam all foreign ones in the vicinity. He is cycling channels. The only reason we can converse without interruption is because I know and control our line. I am not actively blocking ours or having to alter it. Though that's—"

"I get it! *I get it.* I wasn't thinking..."

The ranch came into view. It had no outlying fence and looked to be comprised of a corral, main house, guest house, and at least one shed. The whole area was dusty soil, devoid of all but a handful of shrubs and one or two trees.

A man was running to the main house.

"Chiang is heading for this home," Sophie warned.

"I see him!" I rode out from the barrens and into the ranch's flattened perimeter, a mere hundred yards from Chiang. But I wouldn't get to him before he reached the house ahead.

A shot barked. Sounded like a shotgun, quickly followed by a second bang. Chiang changed directions and ran toward the next closest buildings. The corral.

"I believe that was the *father* firing," Sophie said.

Goddamn right! "Good!" I kept heading straight for the main house. There wasn't time to do much else. If I went straight at Chiang, I'd probably take a bullet before I even dismounted.

I might take a slug from the rancher instead, but I had an idea.

As I rode at the home, I concentrated my mind onto, well, what else would you call them? Happy thoughts. Nothing but Christmas and puppy dogs!

"Don't shoot!" I yelled. "I'm with the drone! I'm here to help!" The crying of children came from inside the one-story house, and a large dog barked crazily.

I'd never intentionally projected my emotions before, like I did then, envisioning some ocean waves in my mind, a serene beach scene, anything calming. I had no clue what I was doing, honestly. But the kids inside the house, I'll be damned if they didn't quiet down, followed by the silencing of the rancher's mutt.

Most importantly though—I didn't get *shot*.

Taking a chance I had to take, I hard-braked my Harley in front of the rancher's yard, and a cloud of sandy dirt burped into the air surrounding me.

"You don't look like the highway patrol!" The agitated voice of a man came from a window with no screen attached. A shotgun stuck out of the window, the barrel pointed straight at my chest.

"I'm *not*." I had to think fast. "I'm a bounty hunter. Please stay inside...and *call the cops*." He didn't need to know that would be pointless. Maybe he had a land line though, however unlikely that would be. I swung off my bike, then parked it close to the house and out of sight of the nearby corral. "I'll deal with this bastard."

"Where'd he go?" I sensed the rancher's fear.

"Toward your corral. Horses?" I didn't imagine this would turn into a Wild West stunt show, but I didn't want to shoot any animals by accident.

"No. No horses." That was a relief. "Nothin' over there but my tool sheds."

"All right. I won't be long. Don't come outside!" I wasn't so sure it was working, but I was trying like hell to keep those people calm.

Sophie's drone whirred down from above the house then hovered close. "He's inside that shed," she said.

I pulled my double-barrel from its shoulder holster. "You saw him go in?"

"Yes, and I can nearly gauge his exact distance because of that implant in his skull. He's trying desperately to make a call."

"I bet he is."

"Lochlan, are you there?" It was Silana.

I activated my helmet comm. "Yes, I've got Chiang cornered."

"We are tied up with the police and cannot get to you. Perhaps you should wait for help?"

I considered the suggestion. "No. I'm sure more cops'll be here soon. I need to end this...before more people get killed." For reasons I couldn't really explain, I felt I had what it took to stop Chiang by myself. "I'll update you soon. Gotta go."

"Loch—*Lochlan*. If it is possible, Conrad would like you to *recover* Chiang. Dead or alive. We wish to examine him. And...it would be bad if the police acquired him. They would not understand what they are dealing with. And that would cause...even *more trouble*."

I frowned at the ground beneath my boots. "You know more than you're telling me. *Again*."

"*Oui*."

I sighed. "What makes you believe I can handle this by myself then?" I could, but I wanted to hear her say it.

"We don't know that you can."

That admission straightened my back. "How am I supposed to take that, Silana?"

"We don't *know* you can, but this is *your test*, Lochlan Nohr. No one else's." I stared past the corner of the ranch house at the corral fence then stepped over enough to peek at the small cluster of shacks in the corral's center where I knew Chiang was waiting for me.

"*Bon courage! I believe* in you. Do your best, and you shall prevail."

Do my best. I might prevail. Well, wasn't that all kinds of cheery and heroic?

More like do my best and try not to get my fucking head blown off!

"I'll get back to you," I grumbled at Silana. "Sophie, turn the music down, please. Maybe give me something *else*... I dunno..."

I don't know if it was the anger still pumping adrenaline into my veins, but I was fearless. I was, if anything, getting impatient. I wanted this over with. I wanted to find Vicki, go home—pretend none of this insanity had ever happened.

So, I wasn't really that surprised at Sophie's next music selection. It had just been that kind of week.

War drums pounded in my headphones, followed by low, brassy horn blares, and long, bold tones thundering over the syncopated hammering of timpani.

It was unmistakable.

"*Conan the Barbarian.*" The original, not that half-baked remake. "You're funny, Sophie."

"I have my moments."

Fine. I'm sure I struck the figure of a modern barbarian, in my leather riding garb and helmet, muscles flexing, feet planted, waiting for my brain to order legs into action.

The music worked. My rage built up steadily as I prepared for inevitable conflict.

I walked around the ranch house and into full view of the not-very-distant corral.

"Chiang!" I stalked forward, my eyes alert behind my Ray-Bans, searching for any sign of my enemy. Any sign of another gun, grenade—*a nuclear bomb.*

"*Chiang!* Come out! Surrender!" I continued forward, steadily. "It's the only chance I'll give you. You aren't murdering anyone else. I know you took Vicki."

A window opened in the corral's front shed closest to me, but I resisted the urge to run for cover.

I couldn't spot Chiang in the window. I presumed he was standing to the side or crouched below it. "You are one persistent fellow...really. I'm beginning to admire you." Chiang's voice was distinctly British. No doubt about it. "You probably shouldn't come any closer though, um—what *do* I call you?"

I stopped then knelt down with the hand cannon pointed up from my hip toward the open window. "Call me *Hugh.*"

Chiang guffawed uproariously. "So, it *is* you then. You fit the description." I squinted, guessing what that meant. "Connie never has had much self-control, the poor dear."

"Pizza's hard to resist."

More laughter rolled out from the window. "So it wasn't just *you*, it was *pizza!* I have come to enjoy that very much."

That admission rang oddly in my mind. *Have come to enjoy?*

I stood and prepared to rush the shed. "I'm sorry, I'm feeling kinda naked out here, and this James Bond villain routine of yours is skeeving me out. How 'bout we cut to the fucking point! You surrender—and I don't end you." I thought back to the wreckage of Dante's corpse and what was left of the Cadillac. "Start by tossing that pistol of yours out the window."

"I guess I *could* do that," Chiang replied. "But honestly, Hugh, you will be hard to miss, don't you think?"

I ran.

Chiang's chrome pistol appeared in the open shed window and fired twice in quick succession.

Both shots hit me in the side, just below my right armpit. And let me tell you, they hurt. Hurt like motherfucking *hell*. But I didn't stop running. I broke into a full sprint and Chiang shot at me once more.

And missed.

I prepared to hurdle the low wooden fence ahead of me, to veer out of Chiang's line of sight, and was stunned to see a flying red horse cut from a flat piece of lumber nailed to the fence as a decoration. *The red horse from my dream.*

I leapt over the pegasus and the fence in one bound, then dashed for the side of the white-walled shed Chiang had just shot me from, making damn sure to avoid the window opened at me from *that* direction. The ribs on my right side were stinging painfully.

I gingerly touched where I was hit, fearing to look down, and my fingers reflexively flinched away from hot metal. I did look down then and it amazed me to find no blood. Instead, two flattened bullets had torn through my t-shirt, stopped by Conrad's black armor.

I scraped the metal blobs off my vest with a flick of my wrist then watched them drop into the dirt.

I cannot understate the relief of not dying. I knelt next to the window and sucked in some searing breaths as pain emanated from my ribs.

"Are you *dead*? You really *should* be." Annoyingly, Chiang sounded like he was enjoying himself.

I closed my eyes then concentrated, reaching my mind out toward the interior of the shed, and sensed Chiang easily. There was amusement, but I also detected a note of...*confusion*. Not the fear I'd hoped for, but I'd take what I could get. He was on a diagonal from me, next to my window.

"Very alive, thanks!" I winced. Talking stretched my ribs, and the pain was excruciating. I pressed the talk button on the side of my helmet comm then whispered, "Cut the music, Sophie."

"Done," she responded.

"How extraordinary. You're not another niggling robot, are you? That flying one has been quite the annoyance."

I grimaced, then spoke deliberately. "One hundred percent organic. You though, not so much." The pain from my ribs had subsided by half.

"Ah, just so, just so. Well, then. I must admit, I'm not used to this level of complication. I suppose I still have much to learn..."

My forehead wrinkled. *Learn?*

"So, you give up then?" My ribs still protested, but again, the pain was less than before.

Chiang laughed.

Grudgingly, I grinned. "Yeah, didn't think so."

"Only one of us can walk away from this, Hugh. It would have been so much easier if you had just *died* along with your friend." That remark wiped the grin off my face. "Excuse me..."

A distinct scratching like sandpaper on metal sounded, followed by the unmistakable chewing of air by fire. I stood flat against the shed, making sure not even the point of my helmet's mouth guard could be seen from the building's interior.

"Just having another smoke, if you don't mind. I do love these bloody things."

My eyes rolled reflexively. "*They* won't kill you today."

Chiang coughed and laughed loudly. "Ah, very good, Hugh. Yes, very good. You may be *right*."

That was enough chit-chat.

I took a breath and the prior stabbing pain was almost entirely gone. "I guess you're *not* going to tell me where Vicki is."

"Can't do that. Against the *rules*."

"Is she alive?"

"Alive? Oh, surely. Didn't go to all the trouble of transporting her this far...only to *bury* her." I let out a sigh of relief. So, she was in Nevada at least. "But...how long will she live? I'd guess not too terribly long. No, not much longer at all, really. The moon keeps rising."

The fucking moon. "What d'you want for her? Money? What?"

"Money?" Chiang paused. "This is not about *money*, boy."

The moon climbed above the sunset. The blood moon was coming all right. The sight made my guts harden, and my teeth grit.

Instead of being filled with despair though, I got angrier. "I'll rip your arms off, I think. You can die slower that way."

"Oh, now! That's not very civilized. And here I thought we were getting to know one another."

I ignored him. In a whisper, I asked, "Sophie, you think you can lead me to Vicki?"

"I have a clear log of Chiang's recent travels. It's not impossible," Sophie replied.

"That'll have to do," I admitted. *It has to.*

My nose suddenly itched. On the inside. The pungent taint of gasoline was in the air.

"What are you doing, Chiang?"

"As much as I've enjoyed our little repartee, I must be off. More of you will soon show up, I'm sure. And that will just not *do*."

By then I sensed where Chiang stood inside the shed. His initiative glimmered like a beacon in my mind's eye.

I pointed my pistol at the wall—what I hoped was nothing more than aluminum, wood beams, and plaster board—then emptied half my clip, rapid firing both triggers. Dust and wood splinters erupted from the tight grouping of holes in the shed close to the window, and small debris peppered my face, but my sunglasses and mouth protector shielded me.

"*Argh!*" No more Mr. Fun Chiang. I felt him move, and the very next second a crash and bang came from the south side of the shed.

I readied myself and aimed at what I guessed was a shed door. No sooner had I pointed my gun then Chiang came charging into view, his chrome pistol out and ready. I barely had time to recognize that he held a hatchet in his other hand.

Chiang was in terrible shape. He was bleeding from his face and his right leg and maybe the groin, too. He'd even put his suit jacket back on, and his suit and hair appeared soaking wet. The whole spectacle made my lips draw back from my teeth in horror.

I fired both barrels once, then backpedaled north around the shed, toward the ranch house.

Unfortunately, my shots missed.

In a quick return, Chiang fired at least *four* shots at me, but by some miracle two missed, one grazed my helmet, and the last caught me low on the left shoulder—just below the armored t-shirt—before I sprang behind the corner.

"*Fuck!*" My shoulder burned horribly, but it was only a flesh-wound. I'd gotten lucky.

Though out of sight again, Chiang's feet were crunching dirt. He was still coming.

I'd almost forgotten about the baton Conrad had given me, but my survival instinct awakened—the next thing I realized, I'd swapped my gun to my right hand and pulled the baton out of its belt case, then fully extended it into three feet of skull-crushing steel.

When he appeared, Chiang snarled at me like an animal. He wielded his pistol, a chrome Desert Eagle, and I was in no hurry to get shot by the damn thing *again*.

I came down hard with an overhand chop that cracked into Chiang's forearm.

Incredibly, he didn't drop his pistol, but I knocked his aim off, to the ground at our feet—*instead of at my big, stupid head*. The Deagle barked, followed by the satisfying *click-click-click* of its empty magazine.

The pungent stench of gasoline was so bitter now I nearly gagged. Chiang was soaked in fuel. So distracted was I by the stink, I almost got my head taken off by Chiang's left-handed hatchet swipe.

I dodged backward and the small axe sliced the air where my neck had been.

Chiang attacked and moved like an experienced martial artist. He dropped his empty pistol to the dirt then assumed a sideways stance, his hatchet swapped to his right hand and ready for a stronger swing.

His eyes were alive with hatred. Hatred of me, hatred of *everything*. Hate seethed off of him like the fumes of gasoline that stung my nose. It was a stark contrast to the polite, mocking words that had been coming out of his mouth earlier.

In that moment, I might have questioned my resolve. Such a desperate, inhuman opponent could end me. He didn't care about my heroics, my quest for Victoria. He had to escape—and murdering me was his only way out.

But never underestimate the power of adrenaline and fear, especially in a frame *my* size.

I planted my feet like a sprinter, then—

Barbarian timpani beats filled my ears even louder than before.

I smiled. Feral and vicious.

And then I charged.

The whites of Chiang's eyes widened as he understood that I was on the attack again. He swung his hatchet with both hands in a wild overhead chop at my skull, but I stopped his blow with the steel baton in my right hand, pushed his strong arm up and away, and shoved my double-barreled pistol into his gut as we collided. The last two rounds left in the twin magazines of my 2011 roared into Chiang, and his blood—and some of his intestines—sprayed across the spotty grass and dirt of the yard, followed quickly by the tumult of our two bodies falling together.

Chiang shouted in a language I'd never heard before, a combination of sharp consonants and guttural syllables. The body crushed beneath my own went instantly *cold*. Cold as a bathtub full of ice. I pushed off him and rolled away to put distance between us—and *especially* his hatchet—because I wasn't sure what had caused the icy chill.

Chiang laughed, half choking, between splutters of blood that bubbled from his mouth and nose. But his legs didn't move.

I knew it was over. "You're dying." I lifted up on an elbow. "Tell me where she is! Chiang! Tell me what you did with Victoria!"

I rose to my knees, and as I did, Chiang's empty hand removed a lighter from the left pocket of his jacket

He sparked the lighter into flame before I could form a word, and then Chiang turned to glower at me. He spit out one last glob of blood. "I'll see you again," he said, then dropped the lighter onto his chest. His gasoline-soaked suit, tie, and shirt caught fire, and, in seconds, his entire body was engulfed in flames.

At first Chiang only laughed. It was surreal and horrible, his limbs not even twitching, simply burning up like one of those suicide videos of Tibetan monks. But not long after the laughing ended, he screamed, shouted out and cursed—in Mandarin, I believe.

Eventually, horribly, Chiang was finally silent.

Seared bone and flesh popped and snapped, as smoke from his burning remains churned up at the rising moon.

The smell was disturbing. Thick and nauseatingly sweet.

I turned away and holstered my gun.

"Chiang has been eliminated," Sophie said.

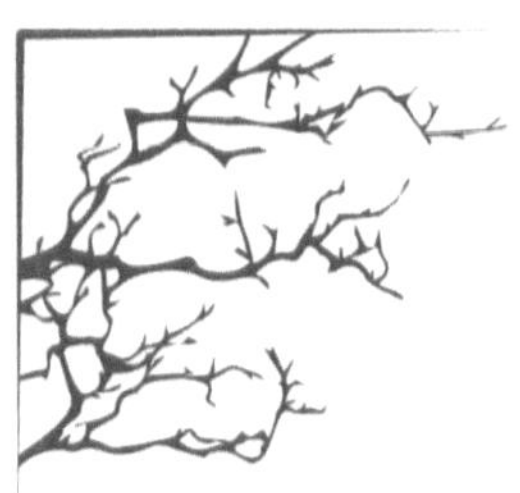

Chapter 22

"Jesus H. *Christ.*" The rancher's name was Alejandro. "Jesus, Jesus." He looked like he was about to be sick as he stared at Chiang's charred remains.

"Don't look at it." Silana took Alejandro by the hand and directed him back to the main ranch house where I'd first seen him aiming a shotgun at me from his kitchen window. "Come, let's talk to your wife. I want to meet these sweet children of yours, too." The rancher met Silana's eyes, nodded weakly, then allowed himself to be led away.

Alejandro's family was huddled in the doorway where Fan talked to them in hushed tones.

My helmet was off and hanging back on my Harley, and Conrad stood next to me, a somber look on his face. "She's done this before," I said.

Conrad glanced up with a pained grimace. "*Too* many times." Silana and Alejandro reached the house. "Soon they'll hardly remember any of this."

"*What?*"

Conrad watched his wife. "There's no sense in keeping you in the dark anymore—you've guessed plenty already." Conrad turned away from Alejandro's family to face me squarely. "She'll *spellbind* them. They'll sleep for a few hours. By the time they awaken, this trauma will be little more than a fading dream."

My mouth hung open.

Conrad chuckled. "It'll take time to process...but you'll have *plenty* of time..."

I shook my head and blinked. I misunderstood him. "Time. *Time?* No time, Conrad. I need to get moving. Sophie's got a GPS location and can get me to Vicki, *hopefully.*" Chiang's corpse had stopped smoking. "We need to clean this mess up and get back to it."

Conrad nodded. "I wouldn't dream of stopping you. Let's find something to cover that," he said, pointing at Chiang.

Conrad walked toward the nearest shed, the one Chiang had used as his last refuge. My bullet holes were near one window—each about the size of an orange—and there was some blood spray on the outside panels.

"No dreams will erase *this*," I mused as I pointed a finger at the damage.

"Fair point," Conrad said. "I'll leave cash on the kitchen table to cover repairs—*and some extra*."

We entered the shed. Conrad eyed the damage from the rounds that didn't end up in Chiang. He raised a hand, closed his eyes for a few seconds, then walked over into a corner of the room. "Is there a toolbox in here? I could use some pliers."

No surprise, there *was* a toolbox, and every good toolbox has a set of pliers. I handed a pair to Conrad, who deftly jammed them into several holes in the wood and cement board of the walls. One by one, the pliers came back out of the holes with the squashed remains of my .45 slugs, puffs of dust spewing into the air.

"We can't cover our presence here completely, but we won't leave a mess," Conrad said, seemingly satisfied with his handiwork.

I took back the pliers from him then replaced them in the toolbox. "You explained things to the cops somehow? Dante?"

"Captain Chomette's retrieving Dante's body." Conrad frowned, a pinched, painful wince on his face. "I wanted to be there to console Courtney, but..." He waved a helpless hand around the shed.

I tried to envision how the police at the site of Dante's murder had been handled by Silana and Conrad. I imagined uniformed officers asleep on the side of the highway or slumped behind the wheels of their patrol cars. "The cops? How'd—?"

I spotted a familiar cardboard box on the floor, tucked into a corner.

"Favors," Conrad said before I could go on. "I called in some *favors*." Conrad shook his head back and forth then half-grinned at me. "And Silana and Fan helped. The police didn't have much to go on—the explosion of Chiang's vehicle was *expertly* planned. Plates, tags, onboard computer. *All destroyed*." Conrad clapped his hands together when he located a folded tarp on a shelf. "Ah, here we are..." He removed the tarp and motioned for me to follow him back outside. I picked Chiang's open box of cigarettes off the ground and followed.

Conrad unfolded the tarp and dropped it over Chiang's burnt remains. "There'll be a connection in the police reports, between here and Austin. But nobody will easily figure out Chiang's identity, and that's what matters. We can't have humans getting too deeply involved."

I opened the back of Conrad's Land Rover to place the cigarette box inside.

"What about Vicki? Her parents? They deserve to know...*something*."

Conrad rolled Chiang up in the tarp. I helped. "Yes, of course. *Of course.* We'll cross that bridge..."

"I've got it," I said, and gently nudged Conrad out of the way. I knelt down low, then lifted Chiang's tarp-wrapped body up in both arms. He was heavy, but I'd squatted far heavier at the gym.

I placed the body inside the Rover's trunk. The smell—like barbecue—might never rub off.

Conrad moved to slam the Rover's back door closed, but I put up a hand to stop him. "Wait a sec."

I turned Chiang's box out next to his wrapped corpse. Nothing but cigarette cartons, all but one unopened. "Well, shit. You really did die for a smoke." I put the cartons back in the box, tossed it in next to the tarp, and then Conrad closed the trunk.

"I need to get going," I said, pointing at the moon in the darkening sky.

Conrad kicked dirt and sand over the dried blood where Chiang had bled out. "Fan wants to go with you," he said. He looked over in the ranch's direction.

"It's too dangerous. You know that, Conrad."

"I *do* know that. Which is exactly why she's going with you."

"To do what? It's not like we'll be able to walk through a front door. I've got Sophie to over-watch—"

"Sophie will feed us intel, sure, but Fan is a sniper. She got caught flat-footed by Chiang. She's pissed off about that, messed up about Dante...but she's a pro. She'll get you back in one piece." Conrad brushed dirt off his shoes. "You're *taking* her. *Period.*"

Fan stood in the ranch house doorway. She made eye contact with me. Her face was grim. I nodded, then waved her over. "You're right. I'm the rookie here. I have no right to leave her out. Not after Dante..."

Fan walked up. I put a hand out, and she took it in both of hers.

I spoke softly. "I'm really sorry. I didn't know Dante long but... I'm sorry. I wasn't fast enough..."

She met my eyes, and I could see she was fighting back tears. "Not your fault, Lochlan. He knew the risks. And he didn't die for nothing. We finish the mission."

I grit my teeth. "Conrad and I were just talking about it." I resisted my sudden urge to scoop Fan up into a hug. Like it or not, we had to suck up our loss and move on. She would grieve more later, and I could sense her resolve. "Sophie will track us to Chiang's destination and act as over-watch. You cover me. I go in deep." I frowned. "I know this is probably the dumbest fucking thing I've ever done—running around all G.I. Joe—but it's Vicki's only shot."

Conrad walked closer to where Fan and I stood. "The map Sophie sent. It's almost one hundred percent an enemy compound. Considering the kidnapping, the lunar eclipse approaching. An out-of-the-way forest on the water. It *stinks* of Silana's sister." Conrad huffed. "I shouldn't let either of you go. You'll be in way over your heads. And outnumbered."

"Can we contact the police? The FBI?" I asked.

"*Fuck* no."

That was bad. I hadn't heard Conrad cuss before. It made me lift an eyebrow.

Conrad continued. "We can't trust police, especially government agencies. The corruption is too severe. I presume you've heard of the Illuminati, but the branch we're facing...we'll call them the *Round Table*, for simplicity's sake. They own many of the cops, the FBI, CIA, NSA, you name it. We have to stay in the shadows to avoid their eyes. But, truth is, they know of us, they just haven't had the strength to destroy my order. Not yet anyway. Especially since some of them *are* us."

I wasn't about to argue the point. I'd already learned to trust Conrad's judgment where so-called authorities were concerned. The man had built upon a foundation of bizarre connections. That he had double agents within the alphabet soup agencies? I believed it. I'd met some good FBI agents once who'd saved my fat. Could they have been part of his organization, too?

"The Illuminati. *Real?* Not just hocus pocus out of the music industry?"

Conrad shifted uneasily on his feet and crossed his arms. "Real. A *collective* of evil...rather than one, cohesive group. Conspiratorial families and inhuman lines. A few one and the same. Sometimes—dating back beyond written legends. Pushing monstrous agendas in plain sight while most of mankind goes about the daily chores of living, too busy to notice or too stupid to comprehend. Societies, both public and secret, most of which I'm sure you've already heard whispers of or read about on Wikipedia."

I gnawed on those revelations. "So what does that make *your group? Our* group? Do we have a fancy title? An order of knights to answer our call?" The dark spot of dirt and Chiang's blood was a grim reminder. "We could use a few."

"*We...*" Conrad smiled, his teeth showing under his mustache. "*We* are the Ordo Severinus."

"Severinus?" It was an unusual name.

"The Order of Saint Severinus. Named after a very old friend. One of the Godliest men to ever walk this plane."

Silana joined us from the house, alone. Sophie was still off somewhere on the property, perhaps recharging her batteries.

I gave Silana a half-smile. "The family going to be okay?"

She smiled in return, but tight-lipped. "They'll be fine. When they awake, the worst thing they'll feel is thirsty."

I didn't want to know. "Uh. Good." I paused. "Look, there's something that's still bothering me about Chiang." Silana, Conrad, and Fan all looked at me, waiting. "The creep spoke English and Mandarin. That, not a big deal by itself. But it wasn't just him being bilingual that surprised me, how fluent his English was...but more like, I got the sense he wasn't Chiang all the time. He felt...out of place somehow." I tossed my hands up. "Does that make sense to any of you?"

"He only spoke Mandarin with *me*. But no surprise since that's how I started it off," Fan recalled.

"Possession," Silana said.

"That's what I was thinking," agreed Conrad. "Would help explain his unusual tattoo. 'Eighty-five.' "

"Wait...what?" My curiosity ramped up, despite the foreboding that went along with it.

"Chiang was probably a vessel. *Possessed.* Maybe willingly so," Silana explained. She faced her husband. "Another clone?"

"I'll know more after I do my autopsy—but yes, it has all the earmarks of bio-engineering. Another *supersoldier*." Conrad considered his next words carefully. "Stronger, faster—probably smarter—than most human beings. At least one cybernetic brain implant. Chiang would most certainly be—have been—considered a prime body for possession by a powerful entity." Conrad grimaced. "Only rumors until now, rumors from allies across the oceans. But there he rests." He pointed a thumb back at the Land Rover containing the burnt remains of Chiang. "Willing to burn himself alive? Not as willing as the demon that possessed him was."

"Mother of God." I wasn't given to acting the devout Catholic—but this was beyond me.

As it turns out, I wasn't the only bad Catholic in our little circle. Fan crossed herself with her right hand and gave me a guilty frown.

"Don't even say it," she warned me, but there wasn't the usual fire in her words.

I put on the face of innocence. "What? I figured you for a Buddhist."

Fan hadn't secretly inherited the mystical power to kill me with the stink-eye, or surely I would have died right there on that spot.

Taking no chances, I quickly turned the subject back to Chiang. "Possessed supersoldier—kidnaps Vicki—just happens to run into us while grabbing cigarettes." I grimly clenched my teeth.

"Welcome to *our* world," Conrad offered. Then he looked deliberately at Fan. "Go grab your rifle. Behind the front passenger's seat. You'll be aiming" —he poked a thumb *my* way— "over *his* shoulders tonight."

Fan bit her bottom lip briefly, nodded, then strode with renewed purpose to the side of the Land Rover.

I was in a foul mood by that point. "Fucking *demons* now! So, what's it all mean?"

"It *means*...that somebody is breaking the *rules*," Conrad answered.

"Something's very *wrong*," Silana added.

The Rules.

I tossed my hands up in frustration. "The rules? *What* rules? *Whose* rules?" Then a sobering thought hit me. "You don't mean..."

"Yes. I *do* mean." Conrad pointed an index finger up at the darkening sky. "The *Creator. God. Numero Uno*," he said. "There are *rules*, Lochlan. Rules immortals do not break...unless they want to get their asses kicked."

"Immor—*oh my...*" I didn't say it. I squeezed my temples so hard with my left hand it's a wonder I didn't pop a blood vessel. "This week. This week..."

"I know," Conrad agreed. "I'm sorry. Not how we wanted this to go, but under the circumstances..."

"I did not have visions of this," Silana half whispered, maybe to herself.

Fan returned to our huddle with a large, black briefcase in hand, but she said nothing. Her eyes were distant.

A shadow swept over us as Sophie hovered down into view. "Sorry to interrupt, but we need to move on, Lochlan. The lunar eclipse—"

"Begins at one forty-seven a.m." I had the adjusted Nevada time already burned into my brain. "Do you think exact times will matter to these nutjobs?

Conrad?"

Conrad breathed out a heavy sigh. "Times matter, but the eclipse will run for several hours. If they're using ritual magic, they'll intend to start at the first sign of blood—the eclipse—and they won't stop until they're done. Holding their conclusion until the maximum eclipse."

"Four eighteen in the morning then," said Sophie.

Conrad nodded.

"How long of a trip from here?" I asked.

"Less than two hours," Sophie replied. "We'll get to the vicinity of Chiang's destination after nine p.m. I expect it will take us at least an hour to push through the wilderness on foot. But probably even longer because we must assume they have security measures in place."

"Yeah. I would," I agreed. I pointed at Fan. "Your bike is back at the smoke shop. What about" —I choked up suddenly— "what about...Dante's?"

Fan stared at me hard. "The tires weren't punctured…but the engine took shrapnel."

"Dammit," I muttered.

"I'll see what I can do," Conrad said. "The police should be done with their accident report by now."

I turned to face Conrad. "You have enough tools?"

Conrad smiled, close-mouthed. "I'll borrow the rancher's. Give me a few minutes. Get in the car, Fan. Be right back." He walked into the nearby shed.

Fan held out the briefcase. "Hold this or load it onto your bike. He won't take long." She walked to the Land Rover then jumped into the passenger's seat.

Conrad exited the shed with a toolbox, put it next to Chiang's body in the Rover's rear, and then sat in the driver's seat.

Fan and Conrad drove back east toward the destroyed Escalade.

My eyes followed the dust trail kicking into the air as they left, distantly aware of a hum from Sophie as she lifted higher into the air again. Then Silana caught my attention.

"May I, Lochlan?" she asked quietly.

"I…uh…"

"Trust me." Silana reached out a delicate hand.

I wonder how I looked in that moment, the sun slowly dropping down to the horizon, shadows bouncing around us from the nearby buildings. Probably not friendly. But I made an extra effort. I'd never sensed evil in the woman.

I nodded my assent.

She came to me, took up my right hand, smiled, then turned my palm up. She used both of her hands to gently spread my fingers, then ran a middle finger along the lifelines of my palm.

It felt amazing. My eyes closed, and I listened to my breathing.

"This will rejuvenate you. You will need all your strength for what lies ahead…"

I felt a calm in my mind despite her words. Because I knew she was right.

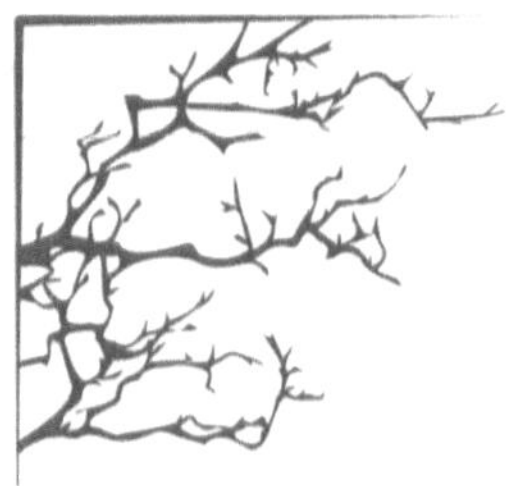

Chapter 23

Conrad took nine minutes to repair Dante's motorcycle. I clocked him. Another hour later we were down the highway and across a mountain range to the west, heading parallel with the peaks on the Nevada side of Lake Tahoe. The scrubland we'd been running across to the east, past the airport, was no more. Fir trees marked every ridge line. It was a beautiful sight to behold as the sunset and the shadows grew longer and melded into darkness.

Now there was only the moon and stars in the sky and the crisp evening air whipping past.

"We're going radio silent once we reach the mountains surrounding the basin," Conrad said through our comm. "We don't want a repeat of what went down at the smoke shop."

"Roger," Fan and I replied.

The long trip west gave me time to contemplate things. For instance, the mouth covering on my helmet pressed uncomfortably against my nose, which caused an awful itch that I couldn't scratch. I made a mental note to get a new helmet. If I lived.

I thought a lot about Vicki, too. Every so often I'd look up at the full moon and imagine horrible things happening to her. I couldn't avoid it. Visions of demons dancing around. Stupid shit like that, but yet...not so stupid, really. Not after what I'd experienced with Chiang.

I prepared myself for anything. The week had taught me that much.

The comm in my helmet clicked. "I will not be of much help either, past a point," Sophie said. "The moment I detect electronic surveillance systems, I will be forced to ground. Given what we have seen so far—Chiang's implant and his rigged vehicle—it is safe to assume that all manner of drone detection will be in play."

She was right.

"Gonna miss your eyes, but—we'll make do. Fan and I'll go on foot, closer to the compound. A few miles across 395," I said. The highway kept going north, but the bad guys were west, down roads that cut through the mountains circling the east side of the basin. "It'll be a trek...but if we keep along the roadside, doable. Whaddya say, Fan?"

"I have night vision gear. Just follow me, and I'll keep you from breaking your neck."

I grinned behind my itchy helmet and glanced at Fan's BMW Sport. She returned a peek, but I couldn't make out eyes behind her face shield. "You'd better. You don't wanna have to carry me."

Fan shook her head. "Just a hunting trip. Get in, bag your doe, get out."

I wasn't big on hunting, but I had my share of experience trudging around woods with my uncle. The low mountains surrounding Lake Tahoe would be new, rough terrain. But I figured my long legs could handle things all right.

"Lochlan." It was Silana. "If you find yourself in dire need, run to the lake. Conrad and I will drive northward to a village on the water and rent a boat."

"Have you had another one of your visions?" I asked.

There was a pause in the comm. "No. No, I have not. I *wish* I had. But I sense something. Some*one*." I listened more intently, ignored the cool air that buffeted me as I rode the Harley. "My sister loves this sea. It is a deep, ancient fresh water. If cults are holding dark rites along its shores, she will know of them and most likely conspire along with them for her own twisted amusement. Do not underestimate her, Lochlan. Her power is equal to my own."

Her power... "Uh. Aside from my growing *laundry list* of questions, how am I going to know your sister? Less *cryptic* please."

"You will know her as you know *me*," Silana answered, not at all cryptically.

"*Right.*" Despite the lack of details, I figured I'd have no problem spotting another woman like Silana. Her sister might walk like her. Sound like her. *Mesmerize* like her. "I'll know her. I can work with that." But what else could she do like Silana? "Any advice? If I *do* run into her?"

"Yes," Silana said, followed by another uncomfortably long pause. "Do not let her *touch* you."

Well, that's not terrifying or anything.

At the next intersection, Fan and I split from the Land Rover trailing us. We headed west into the mountains, along a well-maintained alternate highway.

Almost immediately, I caught sight of a police vehicle in our lane. A small truck. "Slow down, Fan," I warned.

Fan nodded, then slowed to match my speed. We were still many car lengths behind the cop wagon, but I could make out one set of markings.

K-9. "There's a K-9 unit driving ahead of us," I said. "What the hell?" My gut instinct didn't like it. Not one bit.

"Not unexpected," Conrad replied into the comm. "What do you think it means?"

A test. And it wasn't the first time from Conrad. "You said these people we're up against...that they're connected. Assuming worst-case scenario, these cops could be doing guard duty." I grimaced. "I don't like it. People we can dodge, but dogs?" It was time for a change of plans. "I'm playing this all wrong. Pull over, Conrad. We're coming to you."

"You have something new in mind then?"

"The *lake*. We'll go to the lake. Together."

"Smart lad," Conrad said. "Sophie, make calls ahead to Incline Village and inquire about boats. We'll need something large enough for all of us, but also big enough to carry an inflatable. With an outboard engine."

"On it," Sophie said.

"That isn't really necessary," Silana said.

"It is...and you know it. We must restrain ourselves, my love. Until time for restraint is over," Conrad replied, not too gruffly.

Silana didn't respond to that little exchange, but instead said, "It will be nice to see the water." It was easy to imagine Silana by the waterside, feet bare again, skipping more of her magic stones.

Fan and I turned left at Highway 395, then went north. We caught up to Conrad and Silana, who'd parked just off the road on a hill bordered by evergreens. Sophie was already there and had landed her drone on top of the Land Rover, looking like some HD radio antenna attachment if you didn't notice the folded arms of her turbines. In the growing gloom of night, few would.

Regrouped, we rode through Carson City—*Bonanza*—then onward to Lake Tahoe via Incline Village, a well-known tourist spot. It took us off the direct path toward the GPS location Sophie had hacked from Chiang, but, when I factored in the ground security we were almost sure to run into back the way we'd just come—including those possibly very inconvenient police dogs—there would be no loss of time. In fact, once on a boat, I calculated we'd actually *save* a few minutes.

How well secured could Lake Tahoe be, compared to the grounds surrounding our target? The lake was public. Then again, we were dealing with fucking Illuminati. The bogeymen of bogeymen and conspiracy theorists. So, what did I know?

I was improvising again. I knew it. But honestly, on a short list of things I'm great at, improvisation is near the top. Right below eating contests.

INCLINE VILLAGE IS appropriately named. From the outskirts of the large village, we literally drove down a massive, slow incline to the Lake Tahoe harbor where Sophie had located us a suitable boat rental.

Lake Tahoe stretched out before us in all her majesty. Even in the moonlight, I could see boulders below the waves near the shore, that's how clear the waters were.

We parked the Land Rover, BMW cycle, and my Harley, and Conrad and Silana went inside the rental office to complete arrangements for the boat. Fan and I removed our helmets, sucked in the fresh night air, and waited.

Sophie was still resting on the Land Rover, but a light clanking sound rang out after a moment, and I watched in fascination as she extended her turbine arms from her drone chassis, then took flight, zooming straight up into the night sky.

"There she goes," I said, to nobody in particular. Fan didn't respond, but I saw her looking up, and we both followed Sophie's ascent until she disappeared over some tall trees near the lake's edge.

I've never breathed air purer than the air around Lake Tahoe. It created some primal yearning deep inside me I hadn't known until that moment, sitting on my motorcycle, under the night's stars and full moon. Texas was the home I loved, but it didn't have mountains like the ones forming the lip of Lake Tahoe's basin.

The Moon itself tugged at my spirit, too. That's always been a thing with me. I'm not sure why. As a kid I'd imagine the Moon to be a magical being, staring down at the world. On this night the Moon wasn't just staring. It was on watch.

For a short time, I almost forgot about the pain of those past few days, but Dante's sacrifice was still fresh. I looked over at Fan and recognized my pain on her face, only amplified. She mustered a weak smile for me. We stood silently, taking deep breaths, looking out across Lake Tahoe.

A van and trailer hauling a large motorboat pulled into the parking lot behind us. Five people exited. They all appeared Japanese, three men and two bikini-clad women. The group set about cleaning up their boat by removing plastic trash bags then dumping silver Coors cans into a recycling container near the rental office. Two of the men were handling scuba gear.

Fan's expression changed. Suddenly she looked like the Fan I'd first met. She casually approached the men. "Hi! How cold was the water?"

Both male divers were shorter by an inch or two than Fan. One turned toward her. He had smooth, tanned features and dark, alert eyes. He smiled and replied in perfect English, "*Cold*. Tahoe's *always* cold, but it doesn't get too bad until you get deep. It's around fifty-five degrees near the surface right now. You going in?"

"Thinking about it," Fan answered. "We just got here." She pointed at one of the scuba tanks. "Gear for rent?"

"Yep, they've all kinds in the office, though I'm not sure they'll want you diving at night. If you're certified though..."

"I am. Think I'll go ask. Good to meet you. And thanks for the info," Fan said and waved.

"Welcome! Have a great time," the Japanese man replied, and he and the other diver both waved back then nodded at me.

I followed Fan into the rental office.

"You going for it?" I asked.

"Sure, why not? I can get in clean under water, take up position anywhere I want without being seen. My rifle case is waterproof."

"Damn." I nodded. "All right then." Fan's eyes were iron.

We entered the office, and sure enough, there were rows of gear. Fishing, scuba, suntan oils. You name it.

"I won't be long," Fan said, then she walked straight toward hanging racks of rubber suits in various colors. Good to her word, she was up at the counter with her gear in mere seconds, and I watched Conrad pay for the additional goods. Fan entered a changing room before the transaction was completed.

You might've wondered why I didn't jump at the chance to don scuba gear myself. That's simple enough. I've never scuba dived. Not much call for that sort of thing in Texas. But it's on my bucket list.

Our rental needs taken care of, the manager, a pristinely manicured old gentlemen in khaki shorts and a white polo shirt, led us outside then took us directly to our boat, which turned out to be a sleek, dual-engined beast-of-a-thing. Not quite a catch-air speedboat from a Redbull commercial, but it would get us across the water at a respectable clip. I estimated the vessel to be over twenty-five feet long. Once we got closer, I counted seating for ten.

Nestled on the very back of the boat, tied down with bungee cables and rope, was a three-man inflatable raft, complete with a small outboard motor. My ticket to the shores of the Illuminati.

CONRAD PILOTED AS IF he'd been a naval captain his entire life. He put us on a southerly course about a mile off the beach. The air was cool, and the bite of the wind might have been uncomfortable, but the boat had excellent aerodynamics and most of the breeze flowed over and around us.

We could have lowered the extended top to keep us snug and warm, but Silana wouldn't hear of it. She stood in front of the passenger's seat next to the captain's chair, smiling like a child, her arms raised into the air and her auburn hair streaming behind her like dark fire.

Silana was oblivious to the cold winds.

Fan sat across from me in the row of seats toward the middle of the craft, and she grinned as she watched Silana. "This is her element. Now you'll see," she mused.

I stared, not entirely sure what she meant, then looked back at Silana. She was gracefully waving her arms now, from side to side.

Conrad had the boat going fast, but it certainly was not near its top speed, so when he leaned toward Silana and spoke, I wasn't entirely surprised to hear, "I don't want to gun the engines. Too loud. Give us a boost?"

Silana glanced at her husband, laughed merrily, and put out her arms to either side, palms downward at the lake surface.

There was a rough bump from the rear of the boat that pushed me forward in my seat, giving me that feeling as if I'd swallow my Adam's apple. Our vessel lifted higher off the water and the rush of foaming currents on my starboard side grew in intensity. I turned to face the stern.

Our wake had doubled in size, water blowing backward as if we had a third engine. Yet, the twin engines powering our speedboat hummed evenly and low, hardly louder than a truck idling at a stoplight.

I was slack-jawed again. Pure, girlish giggling broke out next to me. Fan.

"I told you," Fan said. She'd turned one-eighty in her seat to watch the churning wake of our boat. One hand gripped the headrest while her other gently rubbed my shoulder.

"Wow," I breathed. It was magic. Real magic.

What else could you call it? Though we were zipping across the lake faster than ever, the ride was smooth, with barely a jolt to the hull beneath us.

A shadow caught my attention as it passed over Fan, and I spun around instinctively. Happily though, it was only Sophie, come home to roost on one of the boat's empty seats.

"I've got a solution to our communications problem," Sophie said.

"Really?" I replied.

"*Encryption.* I may not be able to safely follow you to the mainland from here—I have detected multiple layers of laser, cellular, and radar countermeasures blanketing the area—a *mansion* that appears to have been Chiang's base of operations. But I can act as a local hot spot and encrypt our communications in real time. Even if it is possible for the enemy to decode these, it would take them a very long time, and we will be far away by then. It is more likely they will not realize our communications are encrypted at all, and write them off as bouncing, broken signals originating from halfway across the world."

I held up my motorcycle helmet. "Great. So, we can use the comm. But this helmet's just gonna get in my way in the dark. Can I detach the unit?" I tried to get a look inside my helm, but even my eyes don't adjust that easily to the darkness.

"Yes, they are portable." A dull, red beam appeared from a port on Sophie's side, and she aimed it at my helmet. I turned the helmet so that the light illuminated the ear and microphone attachment inside.

Fan stuck her fingers into my helm then deftly removed the comm unit and handed it over. She repeated the operation to her own helmet, again with the help of Sophie's red spotlight.

"Those are waterproof, but not designed for speaking underwater, Fan," Conrad advised. "You'll be out of contact when diving."

Fan shrugged. "No problem. I won't be in the lake for long... Can you find me an over-watch point near the coast, Sophie?"

"Southwest of the mansion, south of the entry road, there is a gap in security. I will update your handheld," Sophie replied. "Doing the same for you, Lochlan. Everyone should now have a satellite map of the region."

I unhitched the phone from my belt then clicked the incoming message to examine Sophie's GPS map. A house that looked more like a castle appeared in the center. Expanding the grid showed our current position to the west-northwest.

"Holy shit, that's big," I said, being careful to keep my voice down. "Does it have a name?"

"Serenity Mere," Sophie answered. "Note the compound west of the private lake. That is *bustling* with activity right now. While I flew along the coast and monitored the road leading to the mansion itself, I counted police cars, private security guards and dozens of visitors. It appears to be a party."

"Why not a funeral or a wedding?" I asked.

"I've never heard of a wedding where people attended wearing cloaks and masks," Sophie said.

"Then no Star Wars costumes, I guess."

Fan muffled a laugh.

Sophie didn't get the joke. "No. No such pop-culture disguises. The masks appear ornate. Renaissance. Dark cloaks and hoods. Black. Maroon perhaps. It was difficult to make out in the current light through these limited optic scanners."

I looked beyond the prow. Silana sang softly to herself in a language I didn't understand, her arms still outstretched, foaming water to either side of her and our craft.

Conrad kept his eyes on the lake ahead and steered steadily. He asked, "A plan coming to mind?"

I looked up into the dark sky. Few clouds crossed the full moon. The air was moist and cool. "A good night for a party. And I know parties. What fun is a bash without *music?*" I stood and balanced myself with a firm grip on the boat's guardrail. "The tricky part's gonna be me getting to shore unseen. After that, I can blend in. If I can get a mask and cape and follow the crowd. If anybody asks—*I'm just with the band.*" My friends in Trip the Shark flashed through my mind, and I closed my eyes.

Conrad asked, "That actually works?" For once, it wasn't *me* being mystified.

"You'd be shocked," I answered, and opened my eyes again.

Sophie stirred on her seat, turbine arms snapping outward then whirring to life again. "Boats! Boats are approaching!"

"*Silana,*" Conrad implored, but I had no clue for what.

I couldn't hear any other engines over the hum of our own. Fan and I both scanned the horizon on all sides, but without the eyes of a cat, I saw nothing but dark water. Conrad had been running our boat without headlights the entire time, so the only strong illumination beamed down from the moon above and from the blue and red LEDs glowing in the boat's dashboard.

While I stared hard across the stern, something got in my eyes. I shook my head back and forth before rubbing a hand over my face, but the lake only grew darker.

It was fog. Deep, impenetrable fog. Mist had swept up from the lake waters and clung to our boat like a shifting gray wreath.

I looked again at Silana standing like a goddess, channeling water and air. It was her doing.

"Let's stop for a minute," Conrad said, pulling down on the boat throttle until the engines fell silent.

Silana turned her palms up, then stepped back until she was sitting in her seat. She faced me and opened her eyes, smiling, and I smiled back.

Our boat slowed, and gradually the prow lowered into the lake.

All was quiet.

Nobody breathed a word. Then came the not-too-distant roar of boats to the west. A glimmer of headlights played across our pocket of fog for just a second.

"They will pass," Sophie said softly. "Heading straight toward Serenity."

I consciously breathed out and back in. "Should have expected boats. We really need to get out of the direct path."

"Agreed," Conrad said.

The roar of the passing boats eventually faded to nothing.

"It should be safe to continue now," Sophie said.

Silana stood again and assumed her eagle pose, then Conrad pressed the throttle.

Waves and mist swirled from the bow of the boat all the way to the stern, and we pushed onward.

Under other circumstances, it would have been fun. I'd have had a beer in my hand, with Fan on my lap. Someone would go skinny-dipping or fire up a joint.

But out there, across Lake Tahoe—I thought I could feel Vicki, closer than she'd been in years. She was scared and confused. Near hopeless.

For the second time, I was her best chance to live.

"I'm going to skirt around farther south. Out of the way. We'll be within a mile of shore in roughly ten minutes. Get your gear ready." Conrad removed his hands from the boat's controls and reached into his backpack that lay near his feet. "And take these. Don't lose them."

Conrad held out two calculator-sized GPS units. One for Fan, one for me.

"Sophie will direct and locate you with those." I looked at Conrad and was about to ask, but he preempted me, "Don't worry. They're secure."

"Right on," I said. I watched Fan slip her GPS into the open front of her wetsuit, then zip it closed again. "Ready?"

When she looked at me, Fan's eyes were still hard and determined. But she smiled. "Absolutely."

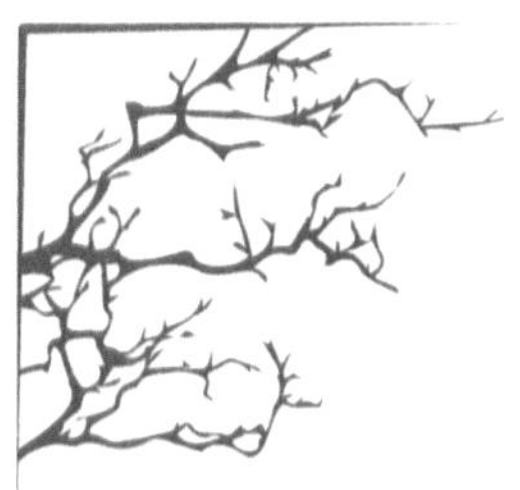

Chapter 24

Fan sat facing me as she double-checked all her scuba gear. I was in the rear of our raft manning the amazingly quiet, electric outboard motor. We wouldn't break any speed records, but lights on the shore ahead grew at a respectable pace.

I still ground my teeth in anxiety—I just didn't grind them into *pulpy* anxiety. That's a win, right?

"Thanks," I said.

Fan looked up from a gauge on one of her wrists. In the moonlight, there was stark wonder in her brown eyes. "For?"

"You know. For doing *this*. For helping me get this far...for helping *Vicki*." I realized I sounded sappy as the words left my mouth, but it was too late.

Fan's eyebrows lifted. She looked pleased. "You're welcome."

I had a sudden pang. (Or a stomachache.) I looked across the low blanket of gray mist that surrounded our raft. A parting gift from Silana.

"Ouch!" I almost shouted but caught myself in time. Fan had not so gently kicked me in my shin. I looked back at her, then shrugged a big shrug.

"Don't get soft on me *now*, hero." Fan smiled. "We'll get this done." She adjusted her scuba tank harness and weight belt. "You've got a gig on Friday night, right? I plan on bringing a date."

"You..." Hey, of course she had a life. "All right. I get your point. Don't sweat me." I waited for proper impact. "What's her name?"

Fan's mouth dropped open.

"Oh, I see. You think just because a girl likes to play with guns..." She put a hand on the knife on her belt. "Be very careful what you say next, *Yang Guizi*," she said, but—to my relief—she was still smiling.

"Yeah. That must be it. I can't read people at all."

I received another kick in the shin, but not as hard as the first.

"I haven't decided who to ask...but maybe now it'll be a dude. I don't need you hitting on my date," Fan whispered.

Chuckling, I pushed Fan's two feet with one of my own. I sighed, looked down at my GPS, and whispered back, "We're getting close. Under a kilometer." It was ten forty-four in the evening.

Fan adjusted one of her wrist gauges, the one I assumed monitored her own GPS tracker, kept safe inside her wetsuit. "Close enough for me." She reached up for her diving mask but stopped and looked at me again. "Break a leg," she said and then slid her goggles over her eyes.

"Break a leg," I replied. I shut off the motor, then we waited a minute for the raft to slow down. I stuck an oar in the water to halt forward progress, first on the left side of the raft, then the right.

Fan pushed her buttocks up onto the nose of the raft, placed her oxygen regulator in her mouth then gave me a thumbs up. She dropped backward, leaving nothing more than a light splash to mark her entry point.

I compensated for the loss in weight from the raft by leaning forward, and while I did, I stretched my neck and looked for any sign of Fan.

Her head popped up out of the lake to my left and made me jump. She waved, then disappeared again under the water. I checked my GPS. Her dot blinked northeast toward shore. I didn't need to be an expert to see she was a strong swimmer.

I watched, waited another minute, just in case, then I started up the outboard again. I tapped the comm on my left ear. "I'm heading to shore."

"Affirmative," Sophie replied.

BEACHES AND SHALLOWS around Lake Tahoe are covered with boulders, rocks, and millions of pebbles. In the dark, using no artificial light to guide me, I might have had serious trouble maneuvering safely to shore. I could have gotten hung up on a dead tree or punctured the raft on a rocky outcrop jutting from the lake bottom. But the bright, full moon in the sky, combined with clear weather, made my approach uneventful.

That didn't keep a small splash from snapping my head around as I came within a hundred yards of shore. I caught sight of a trout breaking the crystal-clear surface before diving back under.

"Damn fish. Has to eat. And scare the fuck outta me," I grumbled.

Tall trees loomed beyond the dark beach, rising steadily in rows, up, up the low mountainside. It was beautiful.

I cut the outboard and paddled at the destination Sophie had set for me. There were no docks, buildings, or people anywhere ahead. As far as I could tell, anyway. Lights on the shoreline freckled the beach for a mile in both directions, but where I was rowing, there was only unadulterated forest and rocks. Sophie had assured me—and she had the telescopic night vision.

Sophie was waiting on Conrad and Silana's hidden speedboat. She said it would be safer for her to avoid flying until absolutely necessary, and it would conserve her battery power. She'd fully recharged on the boat and would be good for half a day in the air according to Conrad, but Sophie had learned her caution from her father.

I didn't know Dad long enough to learn much caution. Or much else. Shit, if it wasn't for photographs, I'd hardly remember what he looked like.

Funny the thoughts that go through your mind when you're putting yourself in mortal danger.

I paddled quietly as I neared the beach. Crabs along the shore scuttled for cover, their shadows dancing across pebbles and rocks. Then the bottom of my raft struck lakebed. I stood, waded into inches of water, and stepped out onto the soft sand, quickly towing my raft up and out of the moonlight.

I lifted the raft up onto a rise of forest beyond the sand, tucked it beneath a fir tree, and covered it with leaves and fallen branches. After a minute of listening to make sure I was still alone, I marked the GPS location and crept up the slope of the mountain until it enveloped me in darkness.

"I'm...in position," I said. I was still getting used to military lingo.

"Roger," Sophie replied.

The plan was to wait for confirmation from Fan before I headed toward Serenity Mere. So, I waited.

For what seemed like forever.

I let out a sigh of relief when Fan's voice finally broke the silence. "I'm ready," she said. "It's all clear."

"Excellent," Sophie said. "All clear here, too. No more boat traffic, and I see only a handful of people near the docks between you." Sophie paused. "Good luck."

"Thanks. Moving," I replied.

"Same," Fan said.

Our plan was simple on the surface of it. I'd climb up the mountain and avoid detection until I could get eye contact on the party attendees. At that point, I would have to figure out a way to infiltrate the event. In my mind that meant any avenue that could make me invisible in plain sight.

I'd become one of the help. Preferably a musician. Otherwise, I'd improvise.

Fan was my watcher...my guardian angel. She had to get to a high point undetected, then cover me, while keeping eyes on the exterior of the Serenity Mere compound. If things got hot, she'd clear a safe path for me and Vicki. A *deadly* one.

I recalled the iron look in Fan's eyes and pitied any enemies who might get in my way.

MOVING THROUGH TREES in the dark is dirty business. I wasn't used to it, and I'm not built for stealth, but my sharp eyes helped. Sometimes my other senses too, but I still tripped more than once as I followed the path marked on my GPS. I got a good scratch on the forehead from a dead tree branch, what could have easily meant an eyeball lost. That slowed me down—and I wished there had been an extra pair of night vision goggles in Conrad's bag of tricks.

Ultimately though, it didn't matter. I kept going. Up and over the Tahoe basin toward the acres of Serenity Mere—and, God willing, Victoria.

"I've found a good line of sight to the objective," Fan said. She meant the mansion. "Taking up position. Copy?"

"I copy. Still moving. Getting close." I'd had no big problems so far. So far.

My destination was a long drive up to the front of the mansion where Sophie had recorded the costumed guests arriving. I could see the lights ahead through the tree branches, distant and blinking from the gentle bobbing and swaying of a multitude of leaves and pine needles in between.

I grimaced and pushed on. Things were getting interesting.

I sensed people ahead of me. No music in my ears, nobody in sight, and yet I definitely knew—*for sure*—that there were human beings near those distant lights.

There was a tingling and the hair on the back of my neck stood up. I froze, stopped breathing and listened, but nobody jumped out of the woods. I looked down...up, expecting something, someone to be there, to explain my sudden awareness. But only the Moon was with me, shining over me, as if saying, *Yes, it's me. Your only friend now.*

That odd thought became a revelation. I had the unquenchable understanding that in some way I couldn't explain, it *was* the Moon boosting my empathic ability.

Son of a bitch.

I didn't dwell on it for long, attributing it instead to a mixture of adrenaline, fatigue, and good old-fashioned worry. It wasn't as if I could control the Moon.

And that kept me from believing I was going crazy.

I grabbed a handful of tree roots growing through the dirt slope in front of me, then pulled myself up the mountainside with greater intensity.

I wasn't rock climbing on the inside of the basin, but it was difficult going in some spots. My size and strength—and my leather half-gloves—made my trek across the terrain manageable, but slow.

Next time, bring a grapnel. And take mountain-climbing lessons.

Some chattering critters hidden in the trees kept me company. Probably raccoons laughing at my awkward climbing technique. I didn't know if there were raccoons around Lake Tahoe, but this Texas boy wanted to assume so. What would be the alternatives? Gibbering demons fat on the bone marrow of some tourists and fishermen?

I kept following my GPS path, every so often checking my tracker to make sure I wasn't veering off course again. And I veered often. At night. In the woods. *In the dark.*

Up ahead I saw brighter lights. And a big shadow of…a spooky mansion…
I tabbed the comm. "Hey. I see Serenity, I think."

"Good," Sophie replied. "Now be *very* careful. They've been sloppy with ground security so far. Not even a single laser trip…or wire fence. So, I expect the compound will be walled and too high to scale without gear."

I peered at the giant silhouette up the long rise ahead of me, and a series of angular rooftops poked above flat walls.

"You nailed it. Walled. Looks like it's cresting a big hill," I said.

"Yes, too big. Even for *you*," Fan injected, in typical Fan fashion. "I see movement on roofs and balconies. There's flat space on the tops, men with rifles…architect did his job."

"How many heat signatures?" Sophie asked.

"Count ten outside the mansion. Two on the roofs. Probable snipers. The rest…could be anyone. I see masks on a few, but this vantage point is not ideal." Fan paused. "I'm estimating a half-dozen guards around the place, with an equal amount inside."

"Just a dozen? Is that all?"

"Keep going, Songbird." That was my handle for the mission. Fan was Hawk. She chose the names. Sky was Sophie's. "I've got you covered."

"I've placed a new waypoint, Songbird," Sophie said. "Make your way around to the southeast of the compound. There's a small house and some docks on the private lake. You should be able to make your way to the mansion from there, but move quickly to the water's edge first. Use any embankment along the beach to give you defilade."

"Defi-*what?*" I added French lessons to my bucket list.

"*Cover*," Fan said.

"Roger." Of course. "I'm moving."

I trudged through fir trees on my right and tried my best to walk flat-footed like an Apache. I'd heard that somewhere before and, I'll be damned, it works. No heel-toe and your enemies will never hear you coming.

And evergreen trees don't drop crunchy leaves, so that helped.

The ground leveled gradually, and the muscles in my legs rejoiced. A few more long steps and I reached a gap in some trees that showed me a downhill, tree-cleared path toward the boathouse Sophie had marked.

The house was a well-lit, rectangular building sitting on top of docks. Serenity Lake glimmered beyond it. I couldn't see any movement outside, but undoubtedly someone was in there.

I sat down behind a tree to catch my breath, rest my sore legs, and assess the situation.

"Eyes on the boathouse," I said.

Strobing lights caught my attention to the north and east of the mansion's hill. Headlights moving toward the main compound. I checked the map and noted that was the direction of the main driveway. "There are cars arriving at the mansion."

"Confirmed," Fan said. "I counted two cars that came down the northwest road a minute ago."

"Roger," Sophie replied.

"Party in full swing," I said. "Nobody seems much interested in this boathouse."

"Be careful. I'll lose sight of you if you go down to that lake," Fan warned.

"It's okay. I'll move around through cover and hit the beach. Maybe I should check the docks?"

"Do you sense anyone?" The voice was Silana's.

I was tempted to smack my forehead. "Um. Good point. Hold on." *I'll get used to this, eventually.*

I closed my eyes. Not that I needed to, maybe, but I'd been blindfolded on the plane, so my initial instinct was to recreate that first test.

A point toward the center of my forehead warmed up. I reached out. My mind's eye held the fresh image of the boathouse.

Two people. A couple.

"Two. There's at least two people inside," I said, breath short. I was giddy at my quick and unexpected success.

There was silence on the comm.

"Hello?" *Dammit!* "Did we lose comm?"

Silana's light laugh burst through, just loud enough to make my heart skip. "You do not realize," she said through the comm channel.

"Realize? Sorry. Realize what? I told you—there's a *couple* in the house."

"*Oui.* And is there a symphony playing nearby? A *band* at the party?"

I sat there for a minute dumbfounded.

"No music," I replied.

"No music," Silana echoed.

"Significant," Sophie said.

"Your powers are growing," Silana said. "Do you feel stronger?"

I couldn't help it. I glanced up at the Moon. "Yes. I've sensed it for a while...but...but I..."

"The night and the wilds agree with you, I think," Silana said. "Yes, quite the puzzle—"

"The *mission*." It was Conrad's voice. Ever to the point.

"Right, right," I said. "I'm heading for the docks now." I pushed to my feet, surveyed the vicinity, and, seeing no one, worked my way on the edge of the grassy hill, keeping to the trees for cover. "Going radio silent."

"*Bonne chance*," Silana said.

I kept the eerily pristine waters of Serenity Mere in sight the entire way down to its beach. It was glowing like a mirror from the full moon overhead. The weather remained clear and cool.

Hunched down between some bushes just above the sand, I peered northward up the beach. Still not a soul but me—and the couple above me in the boathouse.

Something from the conversation a minute before popped back into my brain.

No band playing. No band playing? No music at all from what I could hear. What kind of party doesn't have music? And it was late. Late enough that any shindig should have beeen in full swing.

There wasn't a party in that mansion. It was what they'd warned me of, Silana and Conrad. It was a *gathering*.

I grimaced and dropped from my shrub line to a narrow strand of stony beach. The only sounds were the light crunch of sand beneath my boots, and the singing of frogs and crickets around the lake.

It was time to crash the 'party.' Starting with lucky couple number one.

Serenity's boathouse was a relatively simple, angle-roofed cottage atop twin docks. Light streamed out both windows on the south side facing me, and a much larger window on its east side opened out onto the water. There was a single, flat-bottomed fishing boat resting in the lake, protected below the boathouse itself. A good hiding spot.

Slowly, I worked my way up along the lakeside, the water on my right and boulders, rocks, and sparse tracts of sandy beach all along. It was tricky going in the dark of night, and I was very careful to not twist an ankle, but tall shrubs covered me most of the way to the boathouse.

Once I was safely in the boathouse's shadow, I stopped again to take a survey of my surroundings. At that angle, I couldn't see inside the boathouse, but I could make out some distortions in the light. *Movement.* My empathic sense also told me—with my eyes open this time—that the boathouse was heating up.

I decided. Whoever was up in that cottage was not likely to see me coming, and they might have clothing I could use.

I rose to my feet and headed straight to the dock. In one pull of my arms, I was up and kneeling on the boards. A man's moaning emanated from the floor of the boathouse above. I scowled. There was nothing else to do but get up there and scout it.

Up a short flight of wooden steps I went, as quietly as I could manage, keeping hunched down and out of the light of the windows. There were partially open shutters on both windows on the long side of the cottage. I moved into the shadow to the right side of one, on the east corner where I could scout the private lake.

A peek around that corner showed me plenty of light streaming out of the large French doors—what I'd mistaken for one big window—on that side, so I hesitated. There was still no sign of any guards. I slunk around on my hands and knees to reach below the surrounding balcony wall and crept quietly to the edge of the windowed doors.

The doors had flimsy curtains.

I knelt and readied myself. *Add Peeping Tom to my list of awkward adventures.*

Inside were two figures dressed in black-tie tuxedos, cloaked and masked, one sitting on a couch that was angled away from me and the other one on knees in front of the first. The man facing the southern pair of windows had a wolf or jackal mask on, all white with silver and blue filigree. It covered his face to just above his open mouth. He was the moaner.

Awkward or not, this was luck playing in my favor. Two tuxedos, so probably two men. Masks. The whole nine yards. All I had to do was figure out how to get a costume without causing a hailstorm of shit.

The pair weren't concerned about being missed at the mansion, that much was clear. Bonus points.

I had to try my powers again.

At the ranch when I'd chased down Chiang, I knew I'd channeled emotions to Alejandro's family. Even to his dogs. I shut my eyes this time and concentrated.

Work. Work, dammit.

I conjured images of paranoia. The sort of crap that goes on in your head after taking one too many bong hits. Hell, I even tossed in hunger pangs while I was at it.

I needed these two to straighten up, clean up, and get to the party.

There was no music. I wasn't high on adrenaline. I had no serious faith I'd succeed. But the Moon was beaming down on me. I opened my eyes and risked another peek into the cottage.

Mr. Moaner, close-mouthed and quiet, gently pushed the other person's head back—another man. A bearded guy. His mask was red and carved like half a devil's face.

Mr. Moaner was breathing hard. "We need to stop. I don't want to but..."

The devil on his knees laughed and replied, "No, you're right. We're acting like fools. As long as I get to finish you later..."

"*Yes!*" Mr. Moaner adjusted his mask. "You've made me so *hungry.*"

"There'll be lots to eat," said the devil.

They laughed together.

I winced. I'd done it again, but...*holy Creepsville.* Their twisted cackling and the lurid feelings that lingered around them. They disgusted me.

I shook off the negative energy and focused on being the ninja again.

Across the cottage's interior was the main exit. I needed to be quick.

I crept underneath the windows on the side of the boathouse where I'd first approached, slid around the corner, and hunched down near the door. Again, I searched for signs of a guard or more wandering, masked revelers.

It was still all clear.

I breathed a steady breath in and back out. This would have to be fast and brutal, but most of all it would have to be stealthy. I almost felt sorry for the two horny bastards. Almost.

Without warning, someone hit me with a wave—or wind—of emotions. Hard to describe. Like getting pummeled by a rogue, fast incoming tide. Raw terror and loathing washed over me. *From the mansion?*

My eyes shut reflexively, and I found myself frozen in a flashback to my college senior year, back at Marquis Hall. The day terror came to North Texas.

The details of that event had been covered up so well by Texas sheriffs and the Feds that even Silana and Conrad didn't know of my involvement.

The first human being in my unasked-for vision from that day was Victoria Ann Lott, sitting near me on the grass and waiting for a class as we'd done dozens of times.

Vicki bit her lower lip and turned away from me, looking across the green expanse of our North Texas campus, then said, "I knew you were an amazing musician, Lochlan, but I..." She hesitated, using both hands to pull a tiny, broken leaf out of her red hair, freshly fallen from the oak we sat under. Then she huffed and glared at me. "You never said you could sing like that!"

"Like what?"

"That!"

I couldn't help myself. "What that?"

"Oh, Lord. You—just stop!"

I laughed gently. "I sing okay, I guess."

"Hon, you sing like... Just never mind. It was beautiful. Thank you for inviting me."

"Thanks for coming. It meant a lot," I admitted.

Vicki had attended my senior vocal recital the night before. I'd sung for her more than for me, but I would never tell her that.

I broke the tension first. "I could definitely eat. Don't suppose you've got any goodies in your bag?" It was close to lunchtime, but on Tuesdays our International course was at noon, so I wasn't above scavenging. And she always had something stashed in that canvas backpack of hers.

Vicki smirked "—You know I do, dork—" and pulled her pack over. She rummaged inside, and the crumpling of a candy wrapper made my stomach clench.

She opened her palm, so I could see what had poured into it: M&M's. Red, blue, yellow, green, orange. A smattering of browns. Plain, not peanut.

"You've saved me," I breathed. "I'll even eat the brown ones for you."

Vicki laughed, and as I picked out the browns from her palm, she flipped over her phone to check the clock. "Here, just take them. It's time." She turned her small palm over, so the candies fell into my hand.

I smiled, popped more M&M's into my mouth, and reached for my backpack.

Vicki slung her own pack across one shoulder, and her blouse stretched tightly across her breasts.

I diverted my eyes. It wasn't easy—she made my blood rush hot—but Mom had raised me a Texas gentleman.

When I looked back, she was ready to go but had that familiar expression on her face. I hadn't been fast enough.

She has to know, *I thought.*

We'd been meeting before class outside Marquis Hall for the better half of the Spring semester. It had started innocently enough. We'd discuss books we were reading or music we liked. But I always kept in mind that Vicki was a taken woman. Pre-med boyfriend. Stiff competition for a change, though I'd never met the guy. Still, it was just enough to keep me at bay.

I hated myself for it. The whole ruse. I wanted to just admit what I felt, but I had my silly sense of honor. Where had I gotten that honor? I couldn't even tell you for sure. My father? Maybe. But he'd died when I was little. More likely, it came from books I'd read growing up, and somewhere along the line, chivalry had rubbed off on me.

I pretended not to notice the mischief in Vicki's eyes. "Inward and onward," I said and took a step toward the pillars of Marquis Hall.

We made our way up the short flight of stairs, and I held open one of the double doors for Vicki. She liked me doing that.

Our class was on the first floor. Room 111. Just halfway down the long, checkered hallway where our classmates straggled in from all directions. I nodded greetings at many of them.

"Sup, Jabari," I said to the lanky guy who walked toward us.

"Mornin', y'all." He reached the door to Room 111 first and pushed it open.

Everybody in the classroom settled at their desks. We had an unspoken seating order by then. Vicki sat on my left side and Jabari on my right, in the middle of the rows.

Normally I'd have been in the back, but Vicki did the choosing at the start of the semester and, yeah, you know.

Vicki searched inside her backpack for a pen and her book. Me, I rarely cared for taking notes, but Vicki was meticulous about it.

The door opened again, and old Professor Langton entered the room. He had on his tweed jacket with the brown elbow patches. A classic.

"Morning, everyone," he said.

"Morning, Professor," most of us responded.

Vicki tapped her pen on the top of her desk and grinned at me. The patch of freckles on the bridge of her nose crinkled up when she did that.

I'm sure I stared at that nose too often. It was perfect. At least to me.

I was staring at her nose when firecrackers started exploding outside our closed classroom.

Crazy what love does.

But I came out of my love-sodden stupor when Vicki's eyes went wide. Classmates yammered all around us, and one girl behind me screamed so loudly after a burst of gunshots from outside our door, I stood out of my desk. In the next moment my hands were on my backpack, unzipping it, and I pulled my Glock from the holster I'd Velcroed inside.

I had to protect Vicki.

My vision leapt ahead a few minutes.

I was standing in that hallway again, facing the back of a medium-built, dark-skinned man, dressed in body armor, blue jeans, and tennis shoes, his head covered by a checkered scarf. He turned toward me, and I recognized the AK-47 in his hands. Our eyes met as he raised his rifle.

I shot him in the face. Twice.

Outside of this scene in my trapped mind, out in the actual world, back at the boathouse, two voices rose in the distance. No, not in the distance. Close. They were the joking voices of men. I knew these men. From just minutes before.

I couldn't break out of my walking dream. There was another presence I remembered as clearly as I remember the face of my own mother. It was Vicki. She'd been behind me with several other students in our classroom, barricaded off the hallway. It was her fear that had inspired me then. It was this same fear staggering me again. From the mansion.

My rage stormed.

I knew I had to snap to, had to be ready. The Devil and the Wolf were coming to the door.

The door handle clicked.

My eyes snapped open, and a leg appeared just inches from my face as one of the two men exited the boathouse. I sprung up and punched him in the stomach with a heavy swing of my left fist. He choked and sputtered as he crashed back inside. The other man exclaimed in surprise.

I bolted through the doorway. Wolf was crumpled on his back, on top of Devil, and Devil was about to cry out.

I still had a vivid picture of Vicki in my mind. Her red hair and the checkered, red and white scarf of the terrorist all blended into one.

Into blood...

My fists landed in the devil's face. One. Two. Three. Four times.

The devil didn't make a sound then. Didn't make a move. His bearded mouth hung open, slack and dripping more blood.

The wolf had caught his breath, rolled, and tried to get to his feet. But he was staggered from my gut blow and wasn't quick enough. I didn't want to smash furniture. Too much noise. So, I grabbed him by the throat with both hands to crush his voice. I wanted to choke him to death—but I resisted. I didn't know this man. I couldn't know what he was guilty of.

I hadn't become an executioner. Not yet.

It's difficult to knock someone out. The movies and TV are full of illusions. However, a blow to the back of the skull or to the temple is effective. I did both to the wolf, first slamming him onto the throw rug, then repeating the move, but this time on the wood floor where I roughly dragged him, all the while my hands squeezing his larynx shut. His eyes practically bulged through the holes of his mask.

To finish it, I removed my hand from his throat and smashed him once more, with my fist, hard in the left temple.

Wolf fell limp.

For a few seconds, I feared I'd killed him, but I touched his chest and it rose under my palm. I glanced over at Devil. He remained unconscious.

I knelt on the wooden floor of the boathouse, very still, and listened, using both ears *and* my empathy.

Vicki was in the mansion's direction, but her flood of terror was gone. I couldn't focus on her and didn't know why.

But then other fear hit me, from other terrorized…

Kids?

Children. There was no doubt. Someone had kids here.

What in the actual fuck?

"Songbird? Songbird what's your status?" It was Conrad's voice in my earpiece.

I assessed my surroundings. Glitzy furnishings fit for a showroom. Shuttered windows partially closed. The exit door wide open. I quickly shut it, crawled over to the north windows, and pulled the shutters, too. I could only pray nobody had witnessed my attack. For the moment, I sensed nobody else around the boathouse.

"I—I'm okay. Dealt…with some problems," I replied. I removed a golden tablecloth from a glass breakfast table and tore it into wide strips. "Tying things up."

"There's no new movement on the hill. You're still safe, Songbird," Fan said.

"Good to know," I replied. The two unconscious, masked forms at my feet had what I needed. "I've got some party garb. Mask, the whole bit. Will have to move the bodies though. Too risky to leave them."

"Right," Conrad said. "Suggest you use the forest."

"Yep."

I sized up Wolf and Devil. Both were in shape, but neither was exceptionally tall. That was a problem. However, the cloaks they wore would help cover my leather. I could put a tux shirt and tie on even if I had to rip the arms off. Pants. Same deal. Tearing wouldn't matter. I was just looking to create camouflage so I could move across the compound without drawing attention.

I gagged both men with a wad of cloth in each mouth and tightly bound strips to keep everything in place. I also blindfolded them because I didn't want either getting a clean look at my face if they woke up. Then I bound Wolf, the smaller of the two.

Devil I stripped down to his Calvin Klein's. Wolf woke up during that and groaned and complained through his gag, tried to roll on the floor, but I'd hogtied him too well. He could only squirm a few feet away from me, so I ignored him.

I worried that Devil might awaken before I got him tied up, and he *did*, just as I got a cloth strip around his ankles. He kicked at me, so I punched him where it hurts the most. Just once is all it took. His face went tomato red. If I hadn't gagged him, he would have howled, and I saw Wolf's head jerk blindly at his partner's agony.

"Struggle again and I'll make you both regret it, you got me?" I instantly regretted not killing them. I'm sure that came across in my voice. "Nod if you understand me."

Both blindfolded men nodded furiously.

I lifted Wolf up over a shoulder in a fireman's carry and hoisted Devil under my right arm, half carrying, half dragging him toward the exit door. I balanced Wolf on my shoulder and pulled the door open, but before I exited, I flipped the outdoor lamp off. Under the cover of darkness, I went down the stairs to the docks below, Devil's feet dragging, thumping lightly on each step as I went.

I moved onto the beach, then crept into the closest bushes I could find. In a line of evergreens past the brush, I dumped both men on the ground—not gently—each far from the other. Neither were Harry Houdini, but why risk making it an easy escape?

They groaned, but only briefly, remembering my promise. I could sense their terror.

Without another word, I left Wolf and Devil and made my way back to the boathouse.

I crept up the walkway to the cottage and neared the gloomy spot I'd created by dousing the porch light. I felt good about my progress.

That should have been my first warning.

"All guests should be gathering in the mansion, sir." The man spoke from behind me. From the walkway. "Did that light burn out?"

I froze in place but didn't turn around.

Fuck.

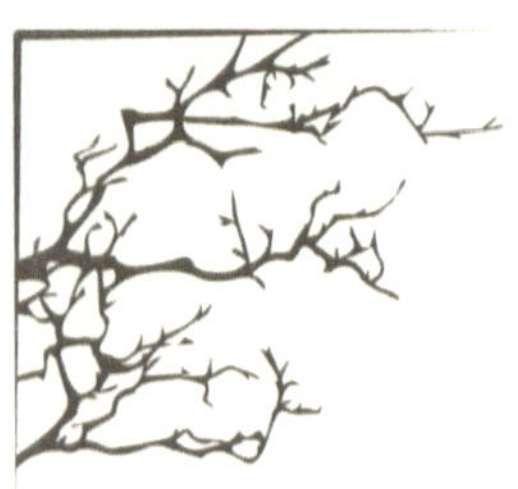

Chapter 25

"I think the light *did* burn out," I said. "Could you check it, please? I need to get changed." I pushed open the cottage door.

Just inside, I nervously noted the pile of stripped clothing I'd made minutes earlier. The two white masks were close by. I walked in and hurriedly kicked the devil mask under the couch, then bent over to retrieve the clothes and the wolf mask.

Anyone paying attention up to this point should be wondering how this guard snuck up on me. Believe me, I wondered, as I anticipated hearing his footsteps on the stairs leading up to the deck behind me. But there wasn't so much as a whisper from him, a squeak or a squawk from the wood decking itself. Still, I felt his movement, sensed his presence through my gift, as he came toward the house. But I deliberately closed the cottage door without a glance in the guard's direction and pretended to not notice anything unusual.

This was something new, and I'll admit, it excited me. I knew I'd figure out the cause in short order, but I had to set the stage first, and do it quickly.

I hoped to buy myself time, and to my relief the guard didn't knock on the door or call out. I risked a glance through the small window at the top of the door and could make him out as he reached for the exterior light's glass enclosure. He'd soon discover the bulb *wasn't* burnt out, assuming he bothered to unscrew it and give things a shake.

A small screech of metal-on-metal, and I knew this was it—unless I somehow altered things and fast. I also noted the noise he made. Whatever his ninja aspect was, evidently it didn't apply to his hands.

Beyond that first nervous appraisal, and all my efforts to avoid eye contact, my brain ultimately registered one more critical point about this guy.

He was wearing a tux.

I turned on the shower, then went back into the living area and closed the bathroom door behind me.

Then there was the wolf mask. I wore it and swung the front door open again. The guard quit twisting the light bulb and gave me a surprised glance.

"I bet there are bulbs in here somewhere," I said. It was easy to talk below the half-mask of the wolf.

The guard smiled crookedly. "You're right, sir." Light from inside streamed past me enough to glint off the man's blue eyes. He wasn't quite my height, but he *was* big.

Big enough, I decided. I needed pants.

He took two steps into the guest house and then, just as I'd feared, looked around and said, "Excuse me for having to ask, sir, but isn't there another VIP here?"

I responded with as much calm and pomposity as I could muster and thumbed my hand at the bathroom. "No, that's quite all right. He's taking a shower."

The guard gave me a sheepish half-grin then nodded. "Ah. Yes, sir. I'll just find those bulbs and be on my way." He moved to the kitchenette in the corner and then opened cupboard doors below the countertop.

I could have taken my chances then, clobbered him from behind with a table lamp or something, but I opted against more unnecessary violence. There was no telling how wired this guy was, how many alarms he could set off. Not to mention there was still the peculiar way he moved that needed figuring out.

I was curious. It was like watching a video with the sound off every time the man took a step. Surely those he worked for would have noted this amazing ability.

Then I knew.

This was innate. It had to be an artifice controlled by some object, or some natural or, yes, I'd gotten used to the idea, a *supernatural* condition.

I really *was* intrigued. I couldn't help myself, I had to ask. "How do you move so silently? I mean, I'm not imagining that, right?"

The blue-eyed guard chuckled, closed a cupboard door then turned. He held a fresh light bulb in one hand.

"You're not crazy, sir. Only, I'm not at liberty to discuss it. Security protocols. You understand?"

I understood perfectly, but I wasn't satisfied. I focused my mind on the man and looked straight into his eyes from about eight feet away.

Again, I had no real idea what I was doing. No control yet. I simply went with it and let my feelings flow. In seconds, I was rewarded with an awareness that the air in the room had changed—like a crackle that might snap if it were a taught string. But this 'string' was the energy that moved between my mind and the guard's.

I risked a command with a deliberate tone. "You can tell me. I'm sure I'm important enough that nobody will mind."

To my amazement—and relief—the guard responded to my Jedi mind trick like my newest, best friend in the whole, wide world. "I'm not sure why, but you're right," he said, then his face relaxed. The guard swapped the light bulb to his left hand and then placed his right inside his collar and fished out a silver chain necklace. Hooked onto the chain was a silver icon in the shape of an old weather vane. A bird perched on its top, but it wasn't a rooster. It resembled a crow or possibly a raven.

I pressed my luck. It's what I do.

"I'm confused. That? It's a shiny necklace, sure, but..."

The guard puffed up and for a millisecond I thought I'd blown it, but then he replied, "It's a gift. From the *Lady*." He emphasized 'lady' as if that answer cleared up the entire affair.

Obviously, I didn't get it, but I wasn't about to tell him that.

Silana had warned me for a reason about her sister. Not a coincidence. The reverence with which this man held his silver bauble. The occult nature of it. The elemental symbolism.

"Ah, the *Lady*. Say no more," I said and smiled.

Then I did something *really* dumb. Well, dumber than normal. I asked, "Can I hold it, please?"

The guard's eyes shifted away from the necklace and straight to mine. The 'string' between our minds gave a tug as his brows dropped into a glower. "No," he answered.

I wasn't done. "I'll give it straight back. I just want a closer look at the craftsmanship," I lied and pleaded.

The blue-eyed guard carefully placed his necklace back inside the collar of his tux, shifted his stance, then dropped his right hand under his left shoulder.

Our 'string' snapped, and I sensed nothing at all from the guard after that. Not that I didn't know what would happen next with plain old eyes and ears.

There wasn't time to consider. I rushed the guard and brought up my fist into the air like a mallet. He looked surprised. I'm not sure why. Perhaps it was that he didn't expect me to anticipate his move. Didn't think I'd attack. Or it was just how fast I moved for a big man. Maybe it was the pop the light bulb made on the floor when he let it slip.

Once more, I was full of energy, overflowing with a fresh jolt of adrenaline. My fist swung down.

And missed.

The guard rolled to his right and came up deftly to his feet.

I was impressed. And a tad humbled.

The big man went for his shoulder holster again. If he got his gun free and fired off a shot, I was as good as dead. Either from him or from the horde of security that would surely descend onto the lake house.

I didn't fully lose my balance when my punch failed to connect, but it left me in an awkward position that ensured another charge would be too slow. I had to stop him from getting his weapon free.

To my right, I pulled what I presumed was an obscenely expensive stainless-steel espresso machine off of the kitchenette countertop. It wasn't crafted to be wielded in such a manner—just imagine—and there was a ripping of metal and loud snaps from the wall as I tore the appliance away from the counter and hurled it.

The poor bastard got a machine pistol out of his shoulder holster and was swinging it in my direction when I watched his eyes go wide as a combination of stainless steel, spilling coffee grounds, and water smashed into his chest.

The impact landed with a sickening crunch.

The guard's muscled body flew past the entrance door, crashed through a wooden chair and ended up propped into the corner of the room. There was blood on the wall from where his head had impacted. His stunned face looked at the ceiling briefly before his eyes rolled closed, and he collapsed in a heap toward the floor, pulling a long brush of red along with him.

It left the wall cracked and dented.

I blinked a few times in awe and horror at what I'd just done.

My senses returned, and I ran over to examine the mess. The guard's machine pistol had dropped quietly out of his hand without firing a shot. He wasn't breathing. I'd crushed his sternum, the espresso machine lodged in the cavity it formed on impact. I could make out a bulletproof vest beneath his tux shirt where buttons had popped open or torn away. There was almost no blood except for where his skull smashed.

I knew I was strong, but this—this was otherworldly power. I struggled for a few moments with the concept. I almost triggered my hidden comm unit to ask Silana and Conrad what had happened, but thought better of it, and instead pushed the guard flat on the floor to remove his tux coat, pants and necklace.

He had a cell phone in a pocket. I didn't dare turn it off. Odds were someone would call, and just as likely it was being tracked via GPS. I didn't have his security code to get into the phone, but I could set it to silent mode.

I risked another look out the entrance's peep window. All still appeared clear. I opened the door then stepped outside onto the wooden deck, took a deep breath, and closed my eyes. I sensed no one nearby and didn't feel eyes on me. That would have to do.

I got dressed, including Devil's cloak, turned off the shower, made damned sure I wasn't sporting any blood on myself and then wrapped the guard's body in a blanket I'd found in a closet. I straightened up the kitchenette, replacing the espresso machine but was unable to reconnect it to the mangled wall from where I'd ripped it. I kicked the shards of the broken bulb into an alcove to the side of the stove. I also checked the machine-pistol's full magazine before shoving the gun into the small of my back.

The blood smeared on the wall was another problem, but I dragged a bookshelf over that. I knew any security worth a damn would figure out something was wrong, but all I needed was enough time to get to Vicki and get the hell out.

Once more, I checked the guest house exit, and with the exterior light still off, I slunk down the deck stairs with the guard's body and his phone.

The phone I tossed into the rowboat moored to the docks beneath the house. I shoved the body under a tarp that was meant for firewood, out of the way and in no immediate line of sight. Damned near made to order.

Then I untied the rowboat and shoved it out onto the big pond. It scooted with a rippling wake, taking the guard's phone toward the center of the water.

I'd wasted too much time. I brushed off the sleeves of my stolen tux, walked calmly back to the house, and switched the exterior light back on.

The roll I'd made from my leathers still lay on the floor of the boathouse. Not only did I not want to throw them away, I also knew it would be stupid to leave my DNA at the scene of my growing list of crimes. So, I scooped up the roll, made sure the house was closed tight, then went down to the edge of the woods.

"Sky, you there?"

"I am," Sophie replied.

I tucked my GPS into the roll. "I've got a package for you. I'm putting my tracker inside and will try to make it easy for you to find, but in this dark...well, no guarantees. Can you grab it?"

"I can carry up to a twenty-five-pound load in this current unit and fly, but are you sure your GPS would not be better kept on your person?"

"Y'all know where I'm at. I'm taking a big chance walking into this place armed. I'd rather leave as little behind as possible and doubt you'd be able to find this stuff without the electronics, am I wrong?"

There was a few seconds pause. "No, you are not wrong. There is still the possibility I could trigger radar or laser trips, but considering you apparently have not—"

"Means that this little valley and pond should be safe for you to reach. Just fly low and I'll try to throw this package as far as I can to the south. Hold on." I placed a suitably large rock from the pond's beach into the 'package.' My boots I still wore.

Making like a quarterback, I moved up onto solid ground, planted my right foot, brought my left hand down to my hip and heaved.

The roll soared up and out over the nearest treetops until I lost sight of it.

Some seconds later I heard snapping branches, the rattle of leaves, then a distant thump.

Guards wouldn't find that bundle anytime soon, even *if* Sophie didn't retrieve it.

I thumbed the comm again. "It's away."

"I see the signal. Won't take me long," Sophie replied.

"Good. Thanks."

My wolf mask had remained on through the entire ordeal. I looked up at the Moon, tinged in red, then I huffed out a low chuckle.

Pure insanity.

I adjusted my mask. "I'm heading to the party. Wish me luck."

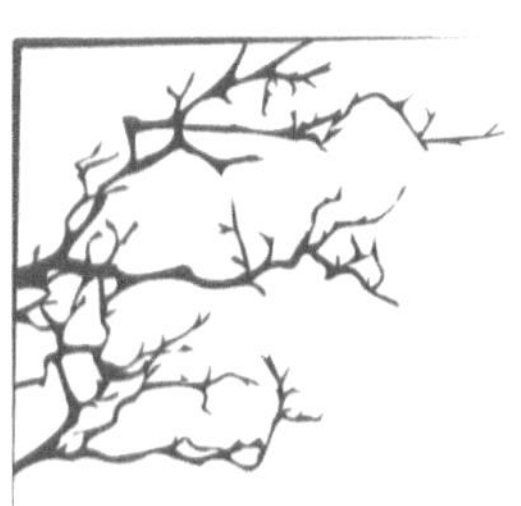

Chapter 26

Whatever time I lost at the boathouse, I more than made up for, thanks to the tuxedo and costume pieces I'd ended up with. Because of these, I risked a brisk walk in plain sight, right up the hilly pathway leading to the mansion.

I was alone on my walk north until I first made out the lighted stone railing that surrounded a sculpted plateau outside the easternmost wing of the compound. I could distinguish the silhouette of a man. He paced deliberately behind the low pillars of the railing, looking like a sentry.

This realization didn't slow me down. Best to keep up appearances. I was a guest of the estate and had somewhere to be.

A stairway came into view around the left bend in the path, leading up to where the sentry was.

"Hawk. I'll be at the mansion in a minute," I whispered. "One guard in sight."

"Roger," Fan replied.

"Not the mansion yet, Songbird," Sophie put in. "It appears to be a pool veranda with a separate building in support."

I was close enough by that point to make out the dark beard on the guard. He stood still beneath a lamp that brightened the stairs.

He looked at me.

My skin tingled, from what I'm not sure. Adrenaline. The Moon perhaps. But it wasn't fear. Not my fear anyway. I took a deep breath and kept going.

The guard peered down. He was probably an excellent poker player because his face revealed nothing from behind his heavy beard. He looked Arabic, well-dressed in a suit and tie. I sensed no aggression. He was just a man on duty that was all.

I waved at him, then marched up the stone stairway. The Arab nodded once and made a crappy attempt at a smile.

The stairs were of a Renaissance design, but in exceptional shape, so I assumed much of everything about Serenity Mere would feel old *and* new. Opulence in. Riches flaunted. All of it meant to disguise the rot beneath.

Light laughter echoed as I reached the veranda, and, exactly as Sophie had foretold, there was a large pool, but it wasn't outside on the spacious balcony. It was inside the adjoining building. The pool complex was topped off by a massive series of windows formed into a skylight. This glass structure stretched for yards, not mere feet.

It represented money. Buckets—no, wheelbarrows full of money.

The gleeful chattering was a mixture of men and women. A small crowd of masked party attendees caroused around the pool, many of them lounging on stone benches and heavily pillowed chairs and couches. Several sets of wide glass and metal doors were swung open along the eastern side of the building facing me. Masked couples moved out onto the terrace where I now stood, almost all of them sipping champagne or wine.

Milling in and out of the rich were the obligatory servants, similarly masked and garbed in maid and butler uniforms. Their costumes were colored in black and maroon. All of them were handsome people, the shapely legs of the waitresses especially enhanced by fishnet stockings.

On a different night, I might have counted myself fortunate to be there, especially if my band was getting paid, but the knot that formed in my gut as a waiter approached me reminded me what time it was. His tray, laden with champagne glasses, left me with only a sick sense of dread.

"Champagne, sir?" the waiter asked cheerfully. He wore a mask shaped like a jackrabbit.

I didn't hesitate, just nodded and took a tall glass of bubbly from his silver tray. I smelled the champagne and got a tickle to my nose for my trouble. Nothing poisonous knocked me dead though. *Joy.* I took a sip and then began a slow, steady walk toward the pool, like the good guest I was playing.

My intent was to get inside, near the pool, and find my way to Vicki. I could make out people from the other side moving out onto the terrace where I stood sipping my champagne. The indoor pool was attached to the greater compound, so that was my next logical step.

I walked away to the northwest then leaned up against a section of ornate stone railing, glass in hand. I knew Fan was hiding over my shoulder, somewhere in the trees.

"I think I *see you*, Songbird," Fan said, obviously amused. "The big, bad..."

"That's me," I told her. "Should I huff and puff?" I was reassured by her eyes on me. Crazy manhunters need friends, too, especially when surrounded by a crowd that looked like the extras from a Kubrick film. "The pool's gotta lead to the compound, but I see a flood wall past the skylight. Place seems snug up against a hill. Is that right, Sky?"

"That's correct," Sophie affirmed. "It is most likely a tunnel complex beneath that hill that will lead you deeper toward the mansion."

"Monsters underground," I grumbled.

"I found the package," Sophie said, meaning the roll of clothes I'd hurtled into the forest.

"You're the best."

"I do what I can," Sophie answered.

I took another sip of my champagne, and as bad luck would have it, a tall couple exited the pool house and walked in my direction. The man wore a tuxedo, too, with a purple cloak and a white peacock mask edged in a rainbow of glitter and sequins. His lady companion was adorned in an owl's mask.

I turned away to look out across the woods below. "I've got company. Going silent."

"Roger," Sophie and Fan replied.

"...and fresh air feels good," the peacock finished as the couple came nearer.

I hoped I might just walk away unnoticed. I sipped champagne, watched, and waited for my opportunity.

The owl nodded and said in a sing-song voice, "The red moon approaches." She giggled. "I can hardly believe it!"

Was time to move. I walked toward the pool, but the owl's eyes caught mine before I could glance away and she said, "And there's even a *wolf* out here." She giggled again then saluted me with the champagne glass she held in a delicate hand. "And the *size* of him!"

The peacock chuckled and said to me, "You must forgive her. It's her first blooding. She's had a bit too much to drink already, I'm afraid."

But the owl protested. "I am quite in control of myself, thank you! Allow me to admire the wildlife, Adam."

Blooding? I stopped and politely tipped my glass. "It's fine. Enjoy your-selves."

The peacock grinned, and the owl continued, "It's still early. I hate wait-ing!"

I tilted my head, and the peacock laughed at the owl. "Do you have to pee again?"

The owl giggled. "Hush!"

My exit presented itself. "Actually, *I* do. Forgive me," and I aimed myself at the pool.

"See you later, Mister Wolf," the owl whispered, tittered, then clutched the peacock by his elbow and swung around hard enough to make her long skirt swirl lightly in the breeze.

In fact, I *did* need to use the facilities. I walked away double-time and entered huge double doors that were rolled open on rails. The pool's sur-roundings were bathed in a blue-white light mixed from beneath the waters of the pool and the moon beaming through the multi-faceted skylight above. Groups of masked revelers gathered in clumps throughout the hall, laughing and cavorting. The hall and pool were as big as you might imagine, to contain the Olympic waters, and there were at least three dozen people about. All the stonework was white and light gray, very expensive, high-end marble.

A bar, two bartenders, and another dozen attendees filled one corner over to the northwest side of the conservatory.

My gut clenched again. A feeling of evil. Black corruption. Pure, potent psychopathy in its most hateful, gleeful form—struck my mind.

The emotions came at me with no conscious effort of my own, and that damn near unnerved me.

Outwardly, they looked normal enough, these people, despite their cos-tumes and the surrounding opulence.

But inside they were *rotten*. Tainted. They gave off a hunger and blood-lust that was growing. I almost retched onto the floor from it all, but I moved fast, past the pool then through the next set of doors that opened into a long hallway, wide enough to march in a small army.

To my relief, there were two LED signs marking his and her bathrooms. Guests steadily entered and exited both, so I walked to the men's room, doing my best to not lurch or stumble.

So, this is when super-empathy is not so cool, I thought as I pressed past a gorilla-masked man and entered. Another guest stood drying his hands at a sink, but I ignored him, swung open one of the empty stalls, shut the door and bolted the latch.

I sat on the closed toilet to gather myself and gulp down the nausea. The sickness receded quickly, whether from me having put distance between myself and the pool or by my force of will. I shut my eyes and sucked in a series of deep, steady breaths.

I heard the man at the sink leave.

Then came a fresh, stabbing pang in my gut, but this one carried something familiar. Like my blindfold test on the jet. I squeezed my eyes shut again. And thankfully, my nausea had completely vanished, so it was easier to concentrate. I reached out, trying to sense the surrounding space, past the walls, repelled here and there by the vileness bleeding from the attendees. In my mind, I sped past them all out into the giant hall—

Vicki.

Victoria Lott was close! She wasn't fearful, or excited, no. She was unnaturally calm.

Drugged? Considering I was no longer feeling terror from the kids I'd sensed only thirty minutes earlier, perhaps. I prayed that was the reason, because other possibilities were far too grim. I couldn't locate the kids no matter how hard I tried to sense them.

I opened my eyes. With my resolve renewed, I took care of business in the toilet. My bladder was happier for it, believe me. Some measure of reassurance and calm returned.

The restroom was deathly quiet, but I exited to the sinks and checked all the stalls to ensure I was really alone. I also checked for any security along the ceiling edges but saw nothing obvious. I suppose even the rich and Satanic sometimes afford people their privacy.

Satisfied that I could speak without being overheard, I triggered my comm unit.

"I'm inside. And Vicki's super close, I can feel her," I whispered.

Fan answered first. "Great. There's still a crowd outside where you left. But nobody seems to have paid you any mind. Are you free to talk?"

"Yeah, for now. I'm alone in a bathroom."

Sophie chimed in. "This channel is still secure. I'm actively scrambling transmissions, but there appears to be an increase in network activity closer to the mansion."

"What time is it?" I asked.

"Eight minutes to midnight," Sophie replied. "Might I assume that is ominous?"

I stifled a laugh. "You could."

Suddenly remembering, I reached into an inside pocket of my 'borrowed' tux jacket and touched the cool silver of the pendant.

"Skipper, I've got something. A silver necklace with an unusual pendant attached. Its former owner said it was a gift—" I felt the pendant's chain against my skin. "—from the *Lady*."

Silana sighed. "I was hoping it would not involve her but, *oui*, that sounds like my sister. Describe the pendant for me, please."

"It's a weather vane. With a crow perched on top. Silver. Spotless. Looks new but...feels old," I answered.

There was hardly a second's hesitation before Silana said, "Wear it."

I blinked. Unsatisfied, and now even more on edge, I re-entered a stall and whispered back, "Seriously?"

"Did the wearer give it up willingly?" Silana asked.

"No, he didn't."

"Did it confer him with any...*gifts*?"

"Yeah. He moved like a Goddamn ninja. Totally silent."

A brief pause and then, "There is some danger. There always is with this sister, but it is a boon of air—elemental magic. She sometimes gives up amulets to her favorite pets. You should find that while wearing it, your feet are sure and silent. In fact, you will not be touching the ground at all. Which can be both boon and curse, depending? I will have to instruct you in this some other time...."

This sister. "Huh. Okay. If you say to wear it, I'll wear it. You've seen some—"

Silana interrupted me. "*Oui*, I have."

I easily slid the over-sized necklace around my head and the pendant dangled low on my chest beneath my tux shirt.

Conrad spoke up next. "Sky, leave Songbird's comm open from this point until I say otherwise."

"Roger," Sophie replied.

"Songbird, you're about to enter the hyena's den. Above all else, *you* are to come out of there alive, do you understand me? No risks are worth losing you tonight. *None*. Understood?"

I gritted my teeth. "Vicki—"

"You do what you can, but this situation... We'll do anything we can to aid you, but this will be a tough nut. Find the girl and then get the hell out."

I was silent for a time.

"Songbird?" Conrad's voice was brittle.

"Yeah. Yeah, I hear you. Understood." The realization of the shitstorm I was in finally, fully settled into my stubborn brain.

I heard steps outside the restroom.

"Gotta go," I whispered.

I exited the stall just as two men entered. I nodded to one's glance, but neither of them said a word as I exited back into the carpeted hall, all low-lit by multiple, crystal chandeliers hanging one after another.

At least two dozen people milled about in the hallway. The length of the way measured about half a football field. From where I stood just outside the restrooms, a brightly lit northern archway opened into what had to be a main wing of the Serenity mansion itself. But that wasn't where Vicki was. She was beyond the hallway wall directly ahead of me to the west. I counted three doors on that side, each separated by long bookshelves and podiums surmounted by statuary. More of these displays decorated the grand hall along the center, here and there. There was a wine cellar, too.

I counted at least three unmasked men in suits and tuxedos standing casually yet attentively along points on the west wall. Two of them were closest to bookshelves.

More guards.

A low gong reverberated from somewhere beyond that west wall, and the hair on the back of my neck tingled. I half-expected a cultist out of an Indiana Jones movie to run at me with a dagger.

Instead, the gonging resounded a second time. Guests stopped in their tracks then looked around expectantly. People crowded into the long room from the pool and bar, so I moved along with them, tried to become just one more mask amongst the many.

A third, low gong rang out, still half-deadened by distance and walls, but this time the guard closest to the nearest bookshelf stepped away from the wall—and the tall cabinets moved on hidden tracks and separated to reveal a huge, black door.

To my eyes, the door appeared constructed of heavy metal. I could make out rivets along its borders. It might as well have been the entrance to a government bunker or Swiss safety deposit boxes.

It opened inwardly as a fourth gonging reverberated, this time clear and loud from the recesses beyond the doorway then out into the grand hall where I stood. The growing crowd of masked patrons stirred and tittered all around me, swelled in numbers as more and more bodies walked toward me from the mansion, and I saw more silhouettes in the distance. The padding and shuffling of all their feet on the maroon and gold carpet became a buzz.

It all took on the appearance of some macabre version of a Hollywood movie premiere. Nobody looked at me though. There were no paparazzi. All eyes stared at the open, black door.

The gong sounded a fifth time, and then a tuxedo-garbed man, pale-skinned with a brush cut and no mask, exited the black door. He spoke in a loud voice, not quite a shout, not quite a command.

"Ladies and gentlemen, it is time to assemble for the ceremony. Please enter this way." The master of ceremonies waved an arm toward the black doorway behind him.

The gong sounded again for a sixth time. It wouldn't stop until the twelfth.

The masked throng filed into the portal.

At this point, a reasonable man would have fled.

So, of course, I followed the black-souled lunatics right into the darkness.

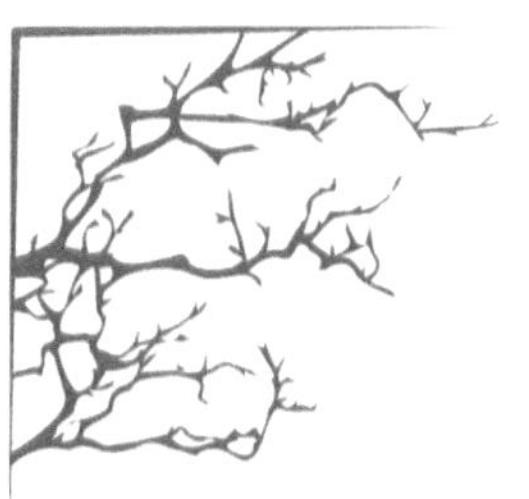

Chapter 27

On the other side of the black door was an ordinary square room with ornate antique couches along the walls, two large red doors opposite the dark entrance we'd just come through, and some old paintings depicting scenes from what appeared to be eighteenth and nineteenth century Europe. One especially large artwork caught my eye, centered on the right wall as it was. A macabre scene of winged devils skewering many naked and pale people upon spears and tridents—men, women, even children—kicking them to the ground, strangling them, and otherwise murdering, in a wide variety of creative ways. I turned my sight back to the twin doors, doing my best to not let my uncovered mouth twist into a scowl.

I was committed. Deep in it. Yet, despite it all, I wasn't frightened. Because I wasn't thinking about myself. I wanted to learn more, and this kept me hyper-focused if anything. I needed to know what the fuck was going on and find Vicki as fast as possible.

The nausea from earlier didn't return, but growing spiritual revulsion and disgust took its place. I'd get Vicki and pound an exit with my head on brick if I had to, to get away from Serenity Mere.

I gritted my teeth and walked forward into a new line that had formed to the left.

The costumed masses politely and patiently filed through the two doors ahead of me into an oddly angular room with a cathedral ceiling. In the low light of dozens of candles and candelabras around the tiled floor and ensconced in the walls, I could barely discern the height of it. Easily a good thirty feet up or more.

Along the north wall was a huge archway. A baseball team could have walked out side-by-side from behind the wine-colored curtains that covered it. It reminded me of a warehouse entrance on the backside of a concert hall, meant for the movement of large gear and equipment by forklifts.

All of this was the ordinary part of the huge, scary room.

Along the walls were unmistakable buffet tables, long, white, rectangular, and waist high. I'd seen plenty in my music career. My *starving* musician career. Weddings, bar mitzvahs, Austin city council gatherings, you name it. I'd eaten free food off more than my share.

If only these tables were catered like those events.

Instead, there were humanoid shapes on some of them. I couldn't tell if they were actual bodies, living, breathing, dead, or mannequins, but they made my stomach twist into a fresh knot.

Notably, many of the tables remained nearly empty.

Each body on display was naked, but covered in various foodstuffs and ornamental decorations. Plant life, dark roses, pineapple rings, and more.

I couldn't make out more from that close to the center of the...

A spotlight snapped on, aimed at the far northwest corner of the room, and a small cheer broke out from the crowd. There, cross-legged, fat-bellied and grotesque, sat a massive statue, some twenty-feet high, of a creature with the chimeric features of man, goat, bird, and reptile. The eyes had slit pupils, the chin, a goatee below a round owl-like visage. The ears and legs were of a satyr, and there were countless scales along the edges of its protruding, human stomach.

In front of the statue, now illuminated by lighting from above and from ambient light shed by the statue's spot, there was an immense Jacuzzi. No, actually, it looked more like an adult-sized kiddie pool that you'd find at a high-end hotel. Immaculate white ceramic formed the edges of the empty pool, but its bottom was out of sight from where I stood.

It was only after the initial shock of the spectacle had worn off that I heard the music now softly filling the large room. Some kind of Gothic-industrial hybrid meant for ambiance.

The effect on *me* was clear. I breathed heavier.

This wasn't a simple banquet room or giant hall.

It was a temple.

The gong rumbled one more time, only once, and upon hearing it, the majority of the crowd turned to face the curtained archway.

The curtains split in the middle and rolled back, foot by foot. The rumbling of rollers reminded me of my high school days, sitting in the pit orchestra for the latest school musical. If only this would have been just another performance of *Damn Yankees,* my heart would not have beaten so heavily in my chest, pulsing blood so fast through my arteries that my neck quivered.

A single Devil did not appear from behind those curtains. Instead, there were five. Five people, dressed in fine clothing adorned with dark cloaks, some black, some crimson. Four men and one woman. They wore masks of a kind I hadn't seen all night. *Human* masks. White, expressionless, but sculpted uniquely and adorned with varying degrees of filigree, lace, and more sparkling things. Light from behind the figures, where they'd been convening, spilled into the temple hall where I stood. It forced me to turn away as my eyes adjusted.

The medium-height man in the center bore a nondescript, black staff as tall as he was. Ceremonial robes surrounded his own tuxedo, opened in the front to reveal the black-tie, layered in shimmering dark green and crimson. Silk would be my guess. His cape was midnight black. His fingers bore several rings, but I was too far away to make out the designs.

Behind these menacing ringmasters, through the archway, a helicopter parked on a wide metal floor. Like the sort that the President of the United States is shuttled around in. There was no Presidential Seal evident on the dark blue machine, though, at least not from where I was. The copter was angled with its gray nose pointed straight at the arch.

I resisted the urge to walk around to try to get a view of the helicopter's tail.

It didn't matter anyway. The curtains closed on the hangar, and in short order, the temple hall was wreathed in low light again.

Then the staff-bearer spoke.

"Welcome, ladies and gentlemen. It is an honor once again to be surrounded by such esteemed houses and representatives." He raised his arms into the air, spread them wide then angled his staff down before him in the crowd's direction. "The blood moon approaches above, as you are all well aware. What transpires here tonight under this boon shall empower all of us with the vitality to carry forward. Thus, our table is once again united." He smiled. "And as you can see, our *tables* are set." The staff-bearer gestured around the room toward the banquets.

There was laughter from the crowd on all sides of me. A confused part of my brain wanted to laugh along with them because the creep with the staff had a British accent. The aristocratic kind. The same kind as Chiang's demon.

Staff-bearer continued. "Most of you have partaken of the Blooding before. However, a few of you are new. So again, welcome." He dropped his arms, and his staff banged against a tile. "The clarity you shall attain after the feast will hold the answers to everything you are undoubtedly wondering right now. Throw care away then. There is no room for guilt in this space." The Ringmaster surveyed the temple, his white mask a muddle of shadows and light. "We are on the brink of ultimate victory, after so many centuries of planning and preparation. Mastery over this world and the ushering in of the Messiah and his heralds. It is the grandest of times to be alive, my friends!"

Cheers, shouts, and clapping erupted throughout the temple.

The only woman amongst the five ringmasters caught my eye as she demurely shifted her stance with the staff-bearer's last sentence, her mouth opened softly into a half-smile, just enough to show a few of her perfect teeth. She was adorned in a form-fitting, silver and white gossamer gown. A spectacular form if I'm being honest. Slender yet curvy. Her hair was loose and long, platinum and glistening. Her very pale skin flushed pink at the nape of her long neck, and she wore no obvious jewelry, except for a silver and diamonds necklace.

If I'd run into her at a cosplay convention, I would have assumed her for a vampiress. A convincing look, whether she was going for it or not.

Silana's sister.

Despite her almost perfect presentation, I was instantly repulsed. I shouldn't have been. Meeting her on the streets of Austin days before that madness, I would've struck up a conversation, and invited her to the next gig. But a taint was on her. Not a rotting *smell*, but it might as well have been.

I risked muttering to myself and to my crew listening in. "*The Lady...*"

Silana spoke up immediately in my earpiece. "She'll appear fair. Lithe but strong."

I didn't respond.

The Ringmaster continued his welcome speech. "Overhead, the Moon. Not yet the perfect time for our sacrifice, but as it is now past midnight, we're prepared to offer all of you an appetizer—"

A cruel murmur of approval rose from the surrounding crowd. I couldn't help but shift my eyes every which way behind my mask to scan the mass of costumed people on both sides of me and in front. My jaw tightened, and I shifted my weight back and forth on my feet, like a great, trapped animal.

The Ringmaster lifted his head and peered past the crowd before him. He rapped his staff two times on the tiled floor. "For your approval…"

The creak and clacking of a metal door sounded from the rear of the temple, then some extra light swept across the huge room in a single strobe. Everyone in the place turned to see.

Two large men in suits and human masks exited the opened door, pushing a petite form before them.

As she came out of shadow and into the temple candlelight, I recognized Victoria by her walk first, then her face. Her red hair was shorter than I remembered, but the freckles across the bridge of her nose were unmistakable.

Vicki wore little more than a white shift. Her face was blanched, her steps short and stuttered, but she walked straight enough and kept her head high and defiant.

When she came another ten feet closer, I could see her eyes clearly. Agonized, confused. Her neck remained stiff, but her haunted expression assessed the temple chamber in sweeps up, down then side to side.

At one point, she even made eye contact with me for a second, and it felt like my heart would explode.

The ringmaster's booming voice interrupted. "I present to you our guest of honor. I trust she meets with your satisfaction."

The crowd responded with a round of clapping and thirsty affirmations.

Vicki stumbled briefly and her mouth dropped open, but she didn't utter a word. One man behind prodded her roughly forward with his hand. She recovered and moved past the empty pool in the temple's center, then was ultimately pulled to a halt not too far from the four men and the Lady. Another of her handlers turned her to face the audience.

"She's exquisite," the Lady said in a velvety soprano. "Where's my pet? Where's Aaron? He should indulge himself with this one."

"We'll all taste of her before the sun rises, Katrina. She's quite special. Quite special, yes." The Ringmaster with his staff rapped it once more upon the floor for emphasis. "She's of my own seed."

The audience went into a fluster of gasps, laughs, shouts, and applause. Victoria's head turned and locked in horror upon the Ringmaster. She opened her mouth again, as if to speak this time, but after a few seconds, evidently thought better of it and remained mute.

The Ringmaster noticed. "I can see that comes as quite a shock to our guest. I assure you it's true, Victoria, though your mother has no recollection of me, I'm also sure. A long story, I'm afraid. One too long for tonight, but I felt you deserved some explanation of 'Why you.' You are my daughter after all. And so, there it is."

I wasn't breathing and gasped to compensate for the lapse caused by the Ringmaster's revelation. Silana and Conrad had told me my mother and Victoria's were raped around the same time, in the same facility. So, I wondered if this monster was my mother's attacker. And my father.

My upper lip curled reflexively into a snarl beneath my wolf mask.

I evaluated the mad situation I found myself in, surrounded by a cult of psychopaths—criminals, murderers, and rapists. It was a bad spot. As sure of myself as I am, I'm not crazy. I recognized that this was an encounter I wasn't likely to escape.

But it wasn't time to escape. It surely wasn't the moment to mount a rescue of Vicki either. Instead, I made calculations that would matter when the time was right.

First, I knew we were all standing underground. In fact, we were beneath the private golf course outside the mansions of Serenity Mere. The maps of the property Sophie had shared were fresh in my memory.

Second, the helicopter in the hangar next door was only a curtain away. Logically there had to be a way to the surface from there. Whether it was a massive elevator or only an opening ceiling, that was one option for escape. That it was a slim option didn't matter.

Next, there was the unknown route deeper down the nearby hall that led north to the heart of Serenity Mere itself. A longer way to potential freedom and a far more dangerous one.

And lastly, there was back the way I'd come, out into the hall, south past the pool's conservatory then out into the woods and west to the beach of Lake Tahoe.

I glanced at Vicki. She still stood straight, but her head was bowed forward, her eyes closed.

They hadn't broken her, whatever she'd been through up to that point, but Vicki seemed on the verge of despair.

The machine gun tucked into the small of my back was cool and uncomfortable. I also had my double-barrel still in its shoulder holster. Nobody had bothered to stop and search me, and that was reason for hope.

But slim hope grew slimmer by the second.

A completely bald, unmasked security goon with an obvious earpiece appeared from out of the shadows behind the five ringmasters. Scarred and hard-faced, he looked remarkably like many Secret Service agents. I'd even seen a few up close during a pickup gig for a Congressional candidate on her campaign trail.

Baldy whispered into the Ringmaster's ear.

Despite the Ringmaster's blank, human mask, his body language spoke volumes. I focused on him in those seconds, and that's when another uncomfortable truth manifested—I couldn't read this man.

I couldn't read the Ringmaster's emotions at all. I concentrated, closed my eyes, and focused. I drew in some power from the ambient music in the chamber then actively, forcefully reached out with my mind as I had a dozen times or more since the plane ride to Nevada.

There was nothing. The fucker was a blank page.

The Ringmaster spoke again, at first quietly directed to the guard, but then to the rest of us. "That is unfortunate. Activate the appropriate response." Baldy nodded, turned, pressed a hand to his earpiece and mumbled words I couldn't make out. A pair of suited, burly figures joined him as he hurriedly exited the temple.

"Yes, sorry, my friends. It appears the wreckage of one of our agent's vehicles has been found on a nearby highway. It's probably just an unfortunate accident, but the timing being what it is, I'm choosing to increase security. I'm sure you understand." He smiled toothily beneath his human mask. "Not to worry. Let us continue on..."

The Ringmaster pointed his staff in my general direction...and, I have to admit, for a second I stiffened and clenched certain parts of my body I normally pay little attention to. But he pointed past me at the only temple door that still remained closed.

"Bring them in," the Ringmaster commanded.

The crowd turned, this time to my right. I followed suit and saw another well-dressed, but mask-less security grunt open a plain-looking door. It snapped open with a distinctive metallic clack. Plain to the eye or not, the door was metal with a heavy, slide-bolt lock.

Yet another large goon appeared through that door, followed by a dark-haired woman in a pantsuit. She was talking softly to someone.

Then the first child appeared in the temple's light. A little girl, only five or six years of age, blonde-haired and innocent. She held a hand of the dark-haired woman.

The little blue-eyed girl wore only a simple white t-shirt and white shorts. She was barefoot, and her skin nearly as white as her clothing.

I stood up straighter as the scene unfolded. All around me the audience fussed again, evidently pleased with what they were seeing. Ravenous hunger came off them in a wave so hard and so vile that my eyes snapped shut as I fought back the urge to vomit.

Two more children appeared through the doorway, one after the other. A boy of perhaps ten, and a girl of maybe thirteen. Again, both white and light-eyed, barefoot and dressed in bleached white like the first little girl. The boy had brown hair, but the girl was another blonde.

All three kids were beautiful. All three felt not so much scared as they did curious and confused. Whatever fear I'd sensed from them earlier had been quelled by someone, or some *thing*. Perhaps they'd been drugged.

I turned and stared at the ringmasters. All five watched the children's approach, like snakes about to strike a pack of field mice. I still couldn't read the Ringmaster himself, or another of the men to his right, but the three others were no problem, especially the Lady. Of all the scum in that room who I could sense, she was the most fair *and* the most vile.

You know the fairy tale of *Hansel and Gretel*, right? It's a warning. But don't be fooled. Not all witches look like bag ladies.

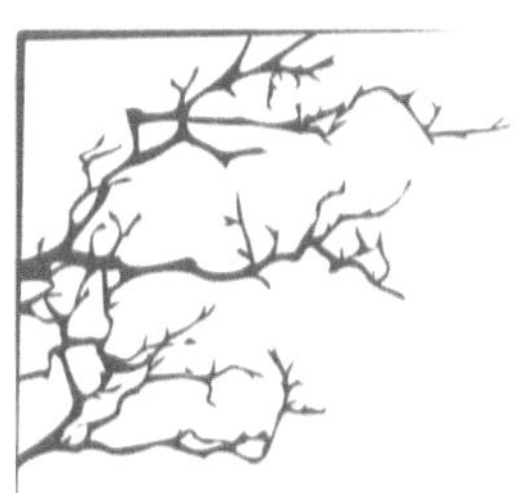

Chapter 28

"**A**re you ready for some fast food then?" the Ringmaster asked glibly. Laughter rose from the gathering once more.

An inside joke maybe. Some forgotten memory itched at the back of my mind.

And something still droned in the background of the dark temple.

I'd forgotten it for a while but became cognizant of the house music again as the kids were herded to the cabal's leaders. The Ringmaster himself diverted the woman leading the children with a point of his staff at the white ceramic pool in the temple's center. The entire crowd formed a circle around the children and, ultimately, that empty, shallow pool.

Once at the edge of the basin, the three children were led down small steps onto the ceramic bottom. But Vicki wasn't. I saw her standing stone-still. She watched the kids, and her horror was as obvious as my own.

My nausea was building again.

It turns out that my empathic abilities have a massive negative side effect. The more people I read in a relatively short time, the more imprinted those feelings become upon me. I didn't know it then, explicitly, but that's what was happening. The vile monsters all around me were bringing me along for the ride. Into their darkness.

You can probably imagine that that gets to you. You'd be right. It sure as fuck does.

Luckily, there's a remedy. A palate cleanser you might call it.

Anger.

Every single time I was repulsed, depressed, horrified by the level of the evil that surrounded me, I rebounded with a level of anger I always knew was deep inside but was terrified to let loose.

Ever since I lost my father when his plane crashed, I've harbored pain and resentment. A natural response from any kid, I guess. But then I saw the tortures my mother endured in her mind after losing her husband, and that tore me up, too. Eventually, she ended up where she is today, spending time with professionals, often for weeks in a row, to get the psych help she needs.

Combine all this with the pressures of growing up, getting through college, pursuing a life in music, then leading a band to some measure of success in a world that doesn't give much of a shit about artists anymore—and you build up quite a reservoir of anger.

I needed it—*all* of it, because I never could have predicted I'd find myself in the dark light of a demonic statue, overlooking a trio of kids who should have been tucked safely in bed, not trapped barefoot in a white Jacuzzi big enough for a Hollywood pervert party.

"Bind the two eldest. In Moloch's name," the Ringmaster stated calmly. I got the impression he'd done this more than a few times before.

The crowd responded in low voices, heavy with breath, almost a whisper, "In Moloch's name."

"Let all care be cast away tonight. Let us partake in the sacrifice and move one step closer to the return of the Messiah. In Moloch's name, we serve."

"In Moloch's name." The crowd sounded more urgent which each successive utterance of that creepy B-movie line. I gritted my teeth and didn't utter a word. Considering none of the masks turned in my direction, I was sure nobody noticed. The crowd focused on the ringmasters, and the ringmasters focused on the children.

I jumped a little when Sophie's voice came over the comm piece still hidden in my ear. "Bad news in, a disturbing police report out of Austin. Connie Winter is dead. Found hanged in her holding cell."

I didn't respond. I couldn't. I was elbow to elbow with creepy cultists.

"Suspected suicide but unconfirmed at this point. I remain suspicious. Keep your guard up, Songbird."

Keep my guard up? If I got any more up, someone was going to have to scrape me off the ceiling.

Connie had been murdered, almost certainly. Always assume worst-case scenario. One of my rules to live by.

I looked from side to side, but again, as far as I could tell, nobody so much as gave me a second glance. I shouldered a little closer to the lip of the empty pool where the kids were dragged. Not for the last time, being tall is its own reward because I didn't have to go very far, or annoy too many cultists, to get a better view.

The two older kids whimpered in protest. The boy and teenage girl were being tied by their wrists with heavy rope fastened to large steel rings built into the side of the empty pool. The pool itself was deeper than I'd expected. Less than five feet, but not by much. At the center of the white ceramic basin was a huge drain with a collapsing cap lifted open.

The actual design appeared more like a massive bathtub, really. Built to drain and drain easily and often.

But what freaked me out even more than the plumbing was the massive circle-encased pentacle surrounding the bindings and the kids. It was formed in unmarred gold, surely poured into place, not simply painted over white ceramic. All along its golden border were strange sigils I'd never seen before, but intertwined with these was lettering I *did* recognize as an ancient He-brew alphabet. Within it all, eight lines originating as points on a compass converged on the tub's ominous drain.

The youngest girl wasn't really sure what was going on so she giggled ner-vously. The woman guiding her talked to the girl sweetly in a voice so soft that I couldn't make out the words as she laid the girl onto her back near the center of the basin, but not too close to the drain, so still on a level surface. There were four cuffs, manacles—whatever you might call them—installed in the pool's floor, and the woman observed as two men snapped one after the other over the girl's wrists and ankles.

I held my breath. Not only were these cuffs designed to restrain children, but the restraints formed a spread-eagle.

I'd seen enough.

What the fuck could I do? I was absolutely outnumbered. Forty, maybe fifty to one. But then I looked at the kids. Vicki's face was a white sheet of growing horror. The original plan had been to get in, find her, and get out. Nobody had factored in other victims, least of all little kids!

Why hadn't Conrad or Silana warned me that this might be what was up?

A flash of steel caught my attention.

The little girl saw it too, yelped sharply, then started crying. The woman handling her wielded the knife and began to deftly cut, but not the girl herself. Instead, the cultist, who at any other time I could have believed was a schoolteacher or librarian, slashed off the girl's tiny white shorts.

Something burned. My neck. My cheeks. Blood flushed to my forehead in a rage as the spectacle manifested before me.

Sophie spoke—shouted—again. "Songbird! My sensors just detected a wireless jam—" But she was cut off before she finished her outburst. A sharp bleep screamed from the comm—then nothing.

Dead air.

The ringmasters weren't speaking either. The room was filled with the droning, humming music piped in from hidden speakers. The soft cries of the children. The outraged protests from Vicki. And the ghastly amusement of the surrounding crowd.

I processed the whole situation as my mind went into full gear. It's part of my makeup, my natural gifts. Improvisation. Analysis. Action.

If only I'd had my saxophone.

With the comm dead, I didn't even have Sophie and her piped-in symphonies to call upon for power.

I had a *song* though. A piece of music that had been resurfacing for the past two days, brewing away, half-conscious and organically.

I didn't pull out my guns. I didn't strike down the perverts next to me that had unzipped their pants, even when they fondled themselves. That took a grim measure of my resolve—to not smash their skulls in right then and there, believe me.

Instead, I drank in a huge breath and sang:

Ave Maria
Gratia plena
Maria, gratia plena

Masks don't reveal much about the emotional state of the people wearing them. The five ringmasters no longer looked at the children in the pool though, and that was what I wanted. All around, I noted the body language of the cultists shifting. Several of the closest perverts turned to face me.

Maria, gratia plena

Ave, ave Dominus
Tecum

I can only imagine what they were all thinking. *'Has he lost his mind?'* It was my intent to sow as much confusion as possible, so I stood in defiance and continued to belt out. A microphone would have been nice, but the acoustics inside the temple chamber worked to my advantage.

With my powerful lungs, the low hum of the ambient house music couldn't match me, and I easily drowned it out.

Benedicta tu in mulieribus
Et benedictus
Benedictus fructus ventris tuae

I don't know if I'd ever been as teeming with emotions as I was in that moment. I was moved by the little girl bound in the empty pool's basin. Her shining face, wet with tears and red with strain and terror, looked me straight in the eyes. Fear had frozen her like that.

"Obviously the excitement has overcome our brother's better senses. Someone please escort him outside so he may get some fresh air," the Ringmaster shouted.

I looked up from the little blonde girl, and the Ringmaster was pointing his staff at me. A redundant gesture.

As I kept singing in spite of his orders, I scanned the masks of the other ringmasters, and the faces of the children. And of Vicki, of course.

Ventris tuae, Jesus
Ave Maria

I had no way of understanding what I detected then, but this is the way it rolled out.

Vicki and the kids, even the little girl strapped down and half-naked from the knife work of her evil nanny, all watched me intently. None of them cried, screamed, or whispered a word.

Vicki's mouth was open a notch. She recognized something in my voice. I knew—because I felt her shock.

Just a few feet to Vicki's left, past the Ringmaster himself, the Lady let out a blood-curdling wail and pointed a long, pale finger at me, then she shrieked one unfamiliar word:

"Abaddon!"

Her emotions were as raw as a severed nerve. I flinched, not knowing whether she'd just cursed me with some evil hex or uttered a command in a foreign tongue. Her prime emotion though was clear. Katrina—the Lady—was *terrified*.

Terrified of *me*.

Across the rift of the basin, one of the other ringmasters laughed. I paused for a breath, and he spoke in a steely tone. "Impossible."

I continued on unabated:

Et in hora mortis nostrae
Mortis nostrae
Ave Maria

Two of the remaining ringmasters who had not said a word, suddenly doubled over as if in pain, followed by cries of dismay all around me in the temple chamber. I stared in disbelief as the room turned into chaos. Men and women ran for the exits or crawled over the floor like wounded animals.

The only people in the room who held their ground—weren't retreating or writhing about in pain—were the children, Vicki, the Ringmaster, the Lady, and the one other man who did not believe in whatever *Abaddon* was.

"Do you believe *now*, Bathory?" Katrina spat.

Bathory, tall and gaunt, glanced in Katrina's direction for a second, then looked back at me. His eyes glinted oddly, but maybe it was just a trick of the candlelight.

Four unmasked men interrupted, entering from the direction of the black door.

The Ringmaster frowned at me and yelled at the quartet of guards, and again he pointed his staff in my direction. "Silence him! Now! Shoot him if you must!"

I glared at these new arrivals but continued singing. I was all in.

Hail Mary
Now and at the hour of our death
Our death
Hail Mary

The guards drew a variety of pistols and small automatic weapons from beneath their jackets, but before any of them could even aim at me, they, too, stumbled around, fell to the floor, or retreated back the way they'd come.

Bathory snarled, raised his chin up high and hissed, "I smell blood—like any other mortal."

I took a breath for the next verse and wondered if I should try to gather the children while I sang, but before I finished the thought, Bathory leapt over the pool basin like a great cat. I was so surprised by the jump, I didn't dodge.

Bathory landed on me not with his feet but with his front hands, displayed like great bony talons. His nails were disturbingly long and sharp.

And his flesh. His flesh was just *wrong*. Not human. The skin on his hands had a chilling, purple sheen.

Vampire, I thought.

That's the first thing that popped into my head. No shit. Why wouldn't it. I'd watched Buffy. I knew about vampires. *Everybody* knows about *vampires*.

Not everyone gets to meet one. Lucky you.

He scratched my neck with his nails before I could get a hand up to block him, and we tumbled backward together. Air flew from my lungs when I hit the floor and, finally, my song was over. The machine gun tucked into the back of my belt came loose when we landed—which hurt like hell—and it scuttled and scraped across the tile for a few feet to my right.

But I had bigger problems

The vampire clenched one white fist in the lapel of my tuxedo and pulled back his other hand for another swipe. His sharp nails dripped with my blood, glistening wet in the low, wispy light of the temple.

"Son of a—," I shouted, but had to catch another quick breath.

Katrina screamed encouragement. "Kill him!"

Bathory laughed as his bloody claw came down at my face again.

This time I was ready. I blocked his swiping wrist with my left forearm, aimed the flat of my right hand at his chin, and lashed out with every ounce of strength I could muster while on my back.

I struck him under the jaw with a *thunk*, and my tux jacket ripped as he flew off of me.

I rolled sideways and jumped to my feet.

Bathory was already standing. He glared at me and held his jaw with one hand while he flexed his mandible back and forth. "He's strong," he said.

Katrina wailed something unintelligible, but hate and fear emanated off of her. "This is our time, not yours! Who sent you?" She pointed a hand at me, and a blast of ice-cold air struck me in the face and chest like a block of concrete.

The bolt staggered me, but nothing broke, and I didn't lose my footing.

"Fuck!" I got angrier and still needed to get to the kids.

One snap survey of the room and I saw that most of the cultists who'd fallen to the ground were still writhing in some kind of agony or mental battle. Any others who had regained their feet—after my song was so abruptly cut off—ran for the exits. Some stumbled toward the giant curtains that blocked off the helicopter hangar.

The children cowered in the pool basin, the older boy and girl clutching one another. The youngest, still bound and half-naked, cried out, "Mommy! Momma!"

Next to the child, her evil nanny was on her back, eyes wide open, stone-still and staring at everything and nothing overhead. Her dagger had dropped out of her grasp and glinted off the white ceramic basin, just inches from the drain cap.

Past the far rim of the pool, Vicki stood and stared at me. Her escorts had retreated out of sight, but the Ringmaster was approaching her.

I shouted at her. "Vicki!" My Big Bad Wolf mask was still on somehow, despite all the battering I'd taken. Vicki stared at me mutely for a split second before she turned her attention to the approaching spectre. The Ringmaster hesitated.

Whether she recognized my voice or not, Vicki responded by plunging a knee into the groin of the Ringmaster as he reached out to grab her. My yell had distracted him, and that was that. The rapist bastard huffed out a loud groan of pain and fell to one knee.

I smiled and wanted to bark at Vicki to run, but, out of the corner of one eye, I saw Bathory was about to spring at me again, and from only a quarter of the distance of his first lunge.

My hand was already on my 2011. "Get *down*," I yelled in Vicki's direction, then pulled the double-barrel free of its holster and snap-shot two rounds as Bathory dashed toward me.

The vampire was inhumanly fast. No sooner had I pointed my pistol in his direction than he strafed hard to his right—and then again to his left to avoid my second shot. He rolled along the ground on that second shuffle, and my compensation for his movement was just enough to blow two large chunks out of the satin cape that flowed out behind him.

I didn't wait—*because I learn.* I dove to the ground where the small machine gun had settled, snatched it up in my right hand and dropped my pistol.

Bathory was on his feet so fast it was as if he'd never dived to the floor in the first place.

I was sprawled on my side but still cocked the machine gun's lever back and cut loose with a long, awkward burst of lead. I aimed up from the floor intentionally for two reasons: To catch Bathory as he presented himself in the air—and I didn't want to spray bullets near Vicki and the kids.

Bathory obliged. His tattered cape snapped and rattled out behind him as he leapt. Our eyes locked, then he descended, fingers of both hands spread out before him like a series of death-inducing iron spikes.

But this time, I didn't miss.

A cacophony like giant popcorn poppers and fireworks erupted, and my machine gun rounds hit home, cutting across Bathory from chest to groin in mid-spring. The sheer force of the impacts held him in the air for only an extra millisecond, but since my brain was drenched in an adrenaline rush, the whole scene entered slow motion, highlighted by the white fangs in Bathory's mouth, the blood spewing from his throat and out into the air before him in a gory, red spray. And the absolute shock in his bloodshot eyes.

He made no sound as he came to an abrupt halt in midair—then face-planted hard, the vampire sprawled across the tiled floor only a foot in front of me.

I stood, but saw the Lady wave a pale hand in my direction again, so I dove to the side in a hurry. A disturbance of air so cold I could see the building frost surrounding the grapefruit shape of it went sailing just past my head with a whoosh.

This time I knelt to one knee and aimed my machine gun at Katrina. She put both hands together into a triangular pattern and sneered at me. I smiled back—and snap-shot a burst of lead.

The shot was on the mark. A half-dozen rounds aimed right across her chest and head in a narrow pattern.

The only problem was that I knew this because the rounds froze in the air in front of Katrina.

On instinct, I grabbed my 2011 pistol off the floor and slid over the side of the pool, a gun in each fist. No sooner had I gotten my head down below the edge of the ceramic than *crackle-snap*—my own bullets whizzed over me with the distinctive hornet sound I remembered so well from encountering rollergirl assassins.

I looked down at the children, hunched, bound, and terrified.

"Don't worry, I'm here to help," I said to the kids. It seemed a stupid thing to say after I said it, but in the heat of the moment, I wanted to reassure them. The youngest girl's face was streaked with tears, and her lips quivered, but she wasn't crying anymore. I smiled at her and glanced at the older pair of children again.

"See if you can get her loose," I said, and stood up to my full height searching the pool's rim for opponents. I fully expected Katrina, but I also knew damn well I hadn't ended the vampire.

As if in answer, Bathory appeared at the edge of the pool. He held a hand to his guts and was doing his best to hold inside the bloody mess I'd made with my machine gun.

"I haven't had a fight like this in centuries, boy, I'll give you that. But you will still die. And when I'm done, I'll feed on those little brats!" Bathory pointed a bony finger at the kids.

"This isn't a movie, motherfucker," I said, and aimed both of my weapons at the vampire.

But Bathory proved me correct, and unlike the typically flat-footed movie villain, he sprang back away from view before I could pull either trigger.

The older kids freed their youngest companion, then all three had their eyes locked on me. The teenage girl appeared as if she wanted to speak up, but I interrupted her by yelling out. "Vicki!" I took a deep breath. "Vicki, get down here!"

I wasn't so sure she could get away from the Ringmaster, or even if she fully recognized my voice, but my doubts were wiped away when I saw her appear at the opposite lip of the pool, plop her butt down on the edge, swing her bare feet over, then do a short run down to me and the kids. Her momentum was fast because Vicki was a good foot shorter than me and had to drop farther, so she dodged the kids but ended up running right to where I crouched.

I caught her in my arms, careful to not drop my guns or point them at her.

Vicki held on and corrected her balance until she stood firmly on the pool's basin. Once settled, we ended up eye to eye. My face was still covered in the wolf mask. Her hair was disheveled, but as red as I remembered it. The freckles across the bridge of her nose scrunched as she said, "Oh my God. It *is* you!"

Vicki practically grafted herself to me in a hug. She was still stronger than she looked.

"It's me," I replied lightly. I remained wary, looking up again, my weapons at the ready even as my arms surrounded Vicki's petite frame. "Let's get you home, eh?"

"You're still crazy. I can't believe this," Vicki answered, and she shook a few times with a mixture of giggling and terror.

"Bad habits," I said.

Vicki coughed a short laugh and looked up, first at me, then toward the top edges of the pool.

We were in a terrible situation. I knew it, and Vicki knew it better than me. I'd gotten the kids and her together in one spot, sure, but how in the hell was I going to get them out of the pool? Even if I sang again, it would be useless against the Ringmaster, Bathory, and the Lady.

Enemy reinforcements had to be coming. What about mine?

I triggered the comm unit still miraculously stuck into my ear and whispered, "Songbird here. Can anyone hear me?"

No response.

A few seconds later the Lady said, "He's got himself into a corner. And he's alone." Then she said, "I can keep you stuck down there as long as I want to, *Abaddon*."

Again with Abaddon. I didn't know what it meant, but I'd heard the term somewhere before.

"Fuck off, you cunt! You think I'm letting you have them? Don't know what you are, but I feel your fear! Come and take it!" Not appropriate language around kids, but can you blame me? And that last part, well, I *am* from Texas.

Katrina howled like a banshee.

"As much as I want to complete the sacrifices, my good judgment has gotten the better of me," the Ringmaster said.

I couldn't see him, but something in the Ringmaster's tone resonated defeat. Maybe I'd ruined his party? I could live with that. I could die knowing it, but I didn't plan to make that part easy.

"Fine, fine," the Lady replied. "We'll keep him contained. Find out where the rest of your useless guards are. Where *is* Aaron?"

I was so tempted to guess aloud that it was Aaron that I'd killed inside the boathouse, but the little crowd of kids I'd gathered gave me the good sense to not run my big mouth again. The cultists wanted them alive, but Katrina was not exactly the rational, calm super-villain. No telling what she might do if completely set off.

"Trapped," Vicki whispered.

I didn't respond. I didn't have an answer.

So, I bluffed.

"Let me get out of here with these kids, and I'll let you live," I yelled.

Bathory and Katrina laughed in unison. The Ringmaster was silent or had left the room. I couldn't sense his presence before, and still couldn't. Bathory remained a blank as well.

"Audacity," Katrina replied. "I admire that in a man. But we will kill those children before we allow them to leave."

"We'll eat them if they stay," Bathory taunted.

The faces of the kids went a new shade of white, and the little girl whimpered.

Vicki beat me to a reply. "You people are a *freak show*!"

The Lady and the vampire only laughed louder.

I raged inside at the sound of their cruelty and determined that if I charged up at Katrina and Bathory, Vicki might still be able to escape with the kids to the forest edge, then they might have a small chance of survival. Fan might find them in the chaos and run to the lake.

But the evening was not out of surprises yet.

Cu—Cú Chulainn, the enormous Irish Wolfhound alpha of Silana's pack in Austin—appeared literally out of thin air, in the pool next to me.

I imagine you can appreciate the level of amazement with which I responded to this, considering that by that point I'd already encountered two sorceresses, one vampire, a demon-infested cyborg, and a gaggle of sexually perverse death cultists.

All doubt of my own senses left in a split second when Cu stepped one paw forward and licked my face with a cow-sized tongue.

I also knew immediately what Cu wanted more than a jumbo milk bone, because whether I sensed it first or he conveyed it with his own mind, I couldn't rightly tell you, but Cu wanted to be petted. By the kids. All three kids. Right away.

"Loch, are you seeing a giant dog, too?" Vicki whispered as she scrunched a notch closer into my chest.

"Don't worry, he's a friend," I answered.

She reached out a hand and patted Cu on a furry shoulder almost as high as the top of her head.

"Pet the doggie, kids," I commanded. "Pet him right now. He won't bite you."

The two older kids gave me a look like I'd lost my mind, but the little girl, God bless her, went from fearful whimpering to a fresh shade of hopeful in that moment. She stood up then walked straight over to Cu. Cu turned to face the kids, licked the little girl, who giggled, and then he took two calm steps toward the others. I gently held Vicki as we both watched.

The kids were still just kids, despite the horrors of the temple, and they responded with a round of petting, probably half-expecting the magic dog to do a trick.

Funny thing? He *did*.

Cú Chulainn vanished. And so did the kids.

Poof.

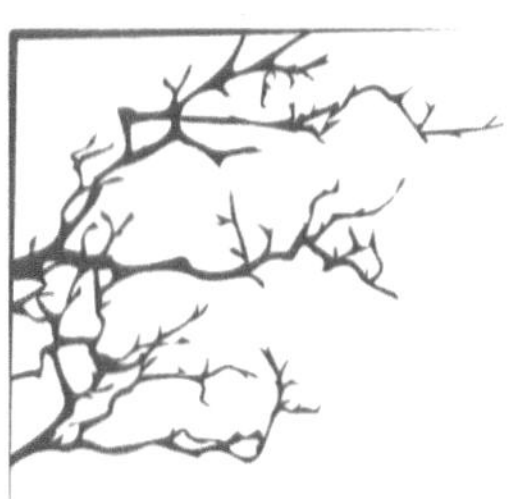

Chapter 29

I blinked a few times, but Cu and the kids were definitely gone. Vicki ran, slapping barefoot steps to where the quartet had been and waved both arms around wildly. She looked at me, her mouth hanging open.

I couldn't help myself. I laughed.

The kids were out of danger. I just knew it. Finally a win.

My new friends hadn't abandoned me in my time of most needy-need.

"Dog?" Katrina was outraged. "What dog!" The witch risked a shuffle to the edge of the pool and peered down at us. "They're gone," she cried. She stared at me, and I laughed again, even louder.

"Silana! This has to be Silana's doing!" Katrina smelled of impending death, but I anticipated it and pushed forward until I crouched defensively between her and Vicki. I aimed both my pistol and machine gun at the Lady, who thought better of her next action and, with a girlish squeak, retreated out of sight.

"Your damnable sister is here?" Bathory evidently knew of Silana.

"I thought I sensed her taint on this *Abaddon! Yes!*" Katrina fumed, but I still sensed more fear in her. "We should search the grounds. There's no telling what mischief her minions might be—"

A sound like a thunderclap made me flinch and reverberated inside the temple. Vicki grabbed fistfuls of my tux jacket from behind me.

"What was that?" she gasped.

"We're getting out of here," I replied, not really sure what the sound meant either, but I wasn't letting the distraction go to waste.

I turned, shoulder-holstered my 2011, swapped the machine gun to my left hand and scooped Vicki up with my right. I put the pendant to the test and sprang out of the pool in a bound.

My leap took me and Vicki out of the ceramic basin in such a high arc I howled, and Vicki let out a high-pitched yelp and clutched hard enough that her fingernails almost pierced my flesh through the fabric of my jacket.

I landed hard, but I held Vicki off the ground, so her feet dangled without striking the tile floor.

I turned then and faced off with the Lady and the vampire. The Ringmaster *was* gone. Cultist bodies formed a macabre patchwork on the temple floor, some wriggling like worms, some deathly still.

Bathory stood gazing at me slack-jawed. We must have mirrored one another in that moment. I was just as astonished by my leap. A rush of exhilaration filled me up to the tips of my flushed cheeks and ears.

With no hesitation this time, I fired a machine gun burst at the slobbering vampire. He side-stepped in a near invisible flash, but I didn't watch him recover. I scrambled for an exit.

A rumbling sounded from outside in the grand hallway leading from the Olympic pool conservatory, bar and terrace. It shook the floor, and I spun back around. All the electric lights in the temple went out, and the background music fell silent. The flickering of candles still cast macabre shadows in every direction, so we weren't in complete darkness, but my shoulders tensed. Something was definitely happening.

The Lady turned away from me to face the twin doors along the wall that led to the secret black entrance.

She cried out, "No!"

Waves of water crashed through both doors, crystal clear, frothing and churning as madly as tides pouring onto a stormy beach. The water seemed to flow together from both doors instantly and supernaturally into one wave, and along the edges of the heaving water there were—*sparkles.*

Mixed in with the roar of the rushing water were the sounds of giggling children.

Katrina didn't spring from the floor so much as she simply flew straight up into the air and then hovered a couple of stories above the evolving scene.

Bathory the vampire cursed, then rushed to the far end of the chamber and I lost sight of him in the shadows.

I ran away, too, Victoria tucked under my arm like an over-sized football, but as I fled, I risked a short look back.

The magic water scoured through the room, tumbling the squirming or cataleptic bodies of cultists over and over, some pushed outward away from the pool, others dumped roughly into the basin itself, disappearing over the edges as the waters worked to fill the entire temple like a flash flood. It doused candles and candelabras, one after another, and many tables overturned, creating the illusion that darkness was in hot pursuit and trying to swallow me and Vicki.

I punched through the huge curtains into the helicopter hangar where lights still shone brightly with electric power. The large, luxury helicopter sat on its landing pad, not a person anywhere in sight. That surprised me. I'd seen more than a few of the cultists stagger into the hangar to get away.

Down a short hallway to the immediate right was an open door that answered that question. All the same, I kept an eye open as we made our way deeper into the hangar. The ceiling was at least three stories above us and marked by only a few lights, so it was pretty dark that far up. In contrast, the room at our level was well lit by a series of wall lamps just higher than my head, all surrounding the helicopter in a wide circle.

It wasn't my plan to pilot the helicopter if that's what you're thinking. I didn't have pilot training, but I had other ideas.

"Search for switches or buttons, some sort of control panel," I said to Vicki.

"Okay," she agreed, and I set her down.

I looked all over. "There's gotta be a way to get the roof open. An elevator."

Vicki ran around the dimly lit hangar to one side, and I rushed along the other.

"Here!" Vicki smacked something on a long wall. I imagined a big red button. She was far enough away that even my eyes couldn't see what she manipulated in the shadows.

A gurgling sound made me turn. Waters seeped into the hangar from under the curtains. I sprang toward Vicki, and my feet caught extra air for a second before I landed, then I burst into a full run.

Overhead, a sharp metallic *crack* resounded, mixed in with the rush of the churning waters, and the roof split open to reveal the stars of the night sky.

Unfortunately, a harsh, incredibly loud alarm sounded, buzzing with every foot that the doors opened. A perfect four-four beat that would surely alert the entire Serenity Mere compound, if my gunfire hadn't already.

From the temple chamber Katrina screamed furiously again. I could only imagine what she faced, but the water was keeping her occupied. I couldn't sense her emotions from that distance.

Water continued to pour inside the hangar, but not in a torrent. Not yet.

"I think this one starts the elevator," Vicki offered. She pointed at a black lever with a t-shaped handle.

I nodded at her, then eyebrow'd the lever.

She immediately pushed the handle up—and small spotlights hidden under a series of metal hoods snapped on all around the perimeter of the circular landing pad.

I grabbed Vicki by the wrist. "Come on!"

As I ran, I couldn't help but notice the slappity-slap of Vicki's feet as she barely kept from being dragged behind me. My boots hardly made a whisper as I sprinted for the helicopter and the center of the landing pad. The Lady's pendant was doing its job.

The two of us reached the blue and black helicopter, then leaned against it for cover and support. Vicki tried to catch her breath.

We stared back toward the tall, curtained entrance—and the Lady burst through them. She flew straight in, up, spun around one-eighty in a swirl of her skirts, then motioned with both hands at a wave of water that pursued the witch.

The air in the tall chamber dropped to a bone-chill, and a large section of the water froze solid as it formed a wave at least eight feet high and a dozen across. Yet, despite Katrina's spell, more of the water kept coming.

A prerecorded voice filled the hangar: "Warning. The elevator will begin ascension in thirty seconds. Please stand clear of the landing area."

The Lady turned and fled from the sparkling wave as it crashed around the frozen pillar she'd created in its midst, reformed, and then continued pursuit. She spotted me and Vicki, lit up as we were by the spotlights on the landing pad.

I aimed my machine gun her way but didn't waste the ammo. The distance was too great, and I knew she was too fast. But I wanted to warn her off—and it worked.

The Lady glared at us for just a second and then looked into the night sky through the now almost completely open hangar doors. She flew away, up and through the opening, so lightning fast and at an angle so steep it defied every natural law I'd ever learned.

The laughter of a hundred children bounced in the hangar, and it made me look back at the curtains. The animated water fell flat and spread evenly on the hangar floor in a shrinking layer. Countless white lights pulled away from that tide and coalesced into a glowing sphere, the ball hovering and sparkling in front of the curtains. Then the tiny lights retreated out of sight, puffing apart the heavy drapery as if hit by a gale force blast.

The laughter went with them.

Of course, Vicki's childhood fascination with faeries went into overdrive. "Oh, my—those weren't. Those couldn't be... *Could they?*"

I grinned. "I'll find out for you."

Above us loomed the rusty moon, half-visible through the open roof. It hadn't reached its zenith, but the bloody sheen of it made the hairs on my neck stand up all the same.

Katrina's silhouette flew across that moonlight and then she halted and hovered. She reached up with both hands to her face, and her white mask fluttered like a dying butterfly down toward Vicki and me, bouncing lightly off the helicopter until it landed face-up on the platform.

"This isn't over, *Abaddon*," Katrina screamed. She flew up and away, then vanished northwest.

"Mother Mary," Vicki prayed and crossed herself.

I was about to respond, but another prerecorded warning interrupted. "The landing pad is now ascending. Please watch your step and keep clear of the edges." A jolt shook the floor beneath us as the entire platform began to rise.

Vicki's hands squeezed one of my own, and I looked down into her eyes. They were wet with tears. "How? How, Lochlan?" she asked in a shaky voice.

I cocked my head and grinned. "How what?"

"How did you find me? How—*did you do all of this?*"

"Your breadcrumb, *dork*," I answered.

Vicki laughed, her relief obvious, and she squeezed my hand tighter.

"And then I just followed this." I tapped my nose with an index finger and stared at the floor of the elevator as it steadily made its way up to ground level. "I had some help."

As the floor continued to rise ever upward, Vicki reached up to my face with both hands and touched my wolf mask. "Take this off," she demanded.

I'd forgotten about the stupid mask during all the violence, and was genuinely shocked it was still in place. "Oh, right." I allowed Vicki to push the mask up away from my nose and eyes. "I guess Halloween is over with." I'd worked all night to try to hide my identity, but nobody would see my face where we were. It didn't matter more than Vicki anyway, right then, right there.

"It *is* you," Vicki said as I helped peel the mask off.

"Yes, yes, it's *me*," I agreed for the second time. "What gave me away?"

Vicki smiled. "Are you kidding? I was at your vocal recital, remember? I'd know your voice anywhere, but *Ave Maria*? Of course, it was you." But her smile dwindled. "I'd thought I'd lost it. At first. Like *completely* lost it. These people. These *monsters*..."

We were only a few meters from the surface. I reached out and gently lifted a lock of Vicki's hair to reveal all of her face. "Won't touch you again," I promised.

I didn't toss the wolf mask away. Instead, I crumpled it up roughly in both hands and stuffed it into one of my pockets. Then, I unhooked the chain under my neck that kept my cloak attached and allowed it to float to the floor. I yanked the uncomfortable bow tie off my bloody tux shirt too. After that, I turned my back to Vicki and knelt. "Climb on," I demanded.

She didn't sound convinced. "I'm not six years old, Lochlan."

"And you can't keep up with me. Climb on. I'm gonna run like a mad dog."

Vicki capitulated and wrapped her arms around my neck and her legs tightly around my waist. I tucked my right arm under one of her thighs to make sure she was secure, and then I stood to my full height.

The landing pad and helicopter came level with the earth, grinding to a halt with a shake and several loud clanks. The whir and grind of the elevator silenced, along with the buzzing alarm and then was replaced with the sound of...sprinklers.

All around me and Vicki was a wide expanse of wet grass glistening in the moonlight.

The golf course. Happily, there wasn't an army of soldiers or vampires—or the Lady—waiting to greet us. I sighed in relief. "Hold on."

Vicki patted my chest just below my Adam's apple, then locked arms around my neck. "Giddy-up!"

I moved forward a little awkwardly at first with Vicki clinging to me and the wet grass sliding under every step, but, as I found my footing and used my left arm for balance, I picked up pace rapidly. The lighted windows of the Serenity Mere estate glowed to the north, no more than fifty yards away.

My feet were light beneath me. That struck me as odd considering how long it had been since I'd last rested. And again, I didn't make a sound as I ran, other than the flapping of what was left of my tux jacket.

There had to be more to it.

I pushed up hard as I took another step—and put a good three feet between my shoes and the ground, then sailed forward with nothing but air between me and the grass. I landed like a feather and continued running.

"Wow!" Vicki was loud and clear, her head only inches from my right ear. "Are you going to fly, too?"

I laughed and continued running west at a rise of hills outside the golf course perimeter. "I don't think so, but if you lose your grip, let me know."

"I'm too scared to let go."

In a few more yards I crossed a wide, paved set of lanes like I remembered from high school track meets. A running and biking trail, perhaps. I only gave it a cursory glance and kept going.

We reached the edge of the property in no time, but when we did, a new threat sounded.

Barking dogs were somewhere behind us. And getting louder.

"Oh, God," Vicki said. "Is that a wall? How high are we?"

It *was* a wall just ahead of us, with a carved stone railing on top, very much like the one I'd leaned on back outside the pool conservatory.

"Yeah. Shouldn't be a problem. Let me take a look."

The dogs' barking grew louder, frantic, and reverberated from both north and east.

"Better hurry," Vicki warned.

I moved to the railing to peer over the side. There was a lamppost about ten yards from where I stood. Light would have been helpful, but I didn't want to stand in it and make finding us easier for our pursuers.

In the moonlight, I could make out the bottom of the wall opposite us quite easily. I guessed the drop to be only about two stories. I thought about risking a jump, but I had no way of knowing how hard I'd land, even with the Lady's 'gift' around my neck. Not to mention Vicki on my back.

I had to decide.

"I'm climbing it," I said.

"Okay." The dogs were even louder. "They're coming! Go, go, go!"

I swung one leg over the railing, then the other, then I let go of Vicki so I could use both hands to scale down the side of the stone-bricked embankment. It was a sheer drop. Even if I had to plummet the second half of the climb, we'd survive. But if I broke something in the process...

I almost didn't notice the *noise* at first, between the barking of the dogs and my concentration on picking handholds. A snapping—like someone cracking a pencil in half—made me look up, just as I grabbed the side of a brick on the lower part of the railing. Vicki's grasp on my neck went slack, and she cried out.

"*Loch*—" She sounded hurt and frightened and then—*nothing*. Her hold on me failed completely, but I grabbed a pillar under the railing with one hand, then snatched at Vicki with the other—just in time to keep her from falling the two stories to the rough ground below. Something wet and warm was on the back of my neck, and the barking dogs were closing in.

I ran out of choices. I pulled Vicki up to my chest and let go of the railing, my legs out, ready to take the brunt of the impact.

But we landed lightly on the hillside that formed the base of the wall. I stirred up a few dead leaves, but there was no jolt to my bones, no breaking of my heels. I didn't even have to catch my footing when I landed.

The magic in the Lady's pendant had saved us from the fall, but I knew something more terrible had already happened.

"Vicki? Vicki! How bad is it?" I could hardly see in the wall's shadow, now that we were out of the moonlight. I lifted her in both arms. Her head was slumped backward. She didn't respond.

"Oh, *Jesus*. Jesus Christ, no!" I spun and ran straight west into the trees with Vicki in my arms, doing my best to shelter her from tree limbs and debris. Dogs must have reached the railing above because the barking became deafening.

I stopped and peered back up at the wall's summit. Bright flashlights flooded the ground at the base of the wall, and several men shouted at one another, but not in English.

I knelt behind a rise covered by many trees, then held Vicki up just enough so that a beam of moonlight illuminated her.

She had fresh, wet blood all over her head, neck, and right shoulder, and it seeped down into the white t-shirt she wore. I gasped in horror. Vicki was breathing, but barely.

"No! No-no-no! Not now! Not this way," I yelled.

The men and dogs erupted with a fresh barrage of shouts and barks when I made my presence known.

Tears stung my eyes, as I swung Vicki into a fireman's carry, then continued to retreat west down the hillside and through the trees, toward Lake Tahoe.

Everything had gone wrong.

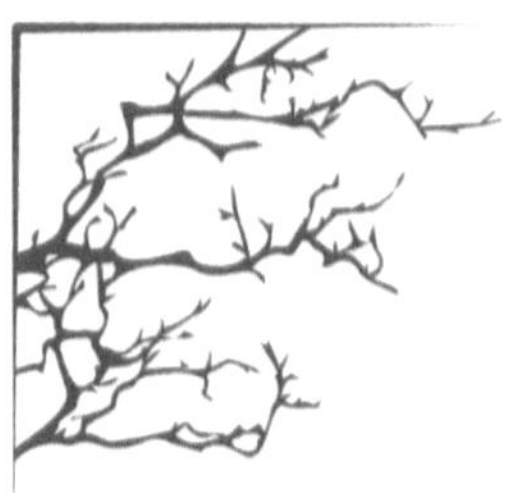

Chapter 30

There was little hope. I couldn't risk stopping to tend to Vicki. There were too many enemies in pursuit. Men and dogs—and maybe more monsters.

I crashed through short, low-hanging branches then pushed on for another thirty or forty yards with Vicki slung over my shoulder. At a long ridge in the treeline, I hesitated a moment because it would force me to go higher and risk being spotted from the wall we'd just fled.

A fresh round of shouts made me turn around. I saw a body fall from the railing. Two more men were on my side of the wall, I presumed on repelling rope. One scrambled back up to the outside of the stone railing while the other sprang away from the wall and repelled down toward the forest floor. The climber was moving fast and would be down in no time.

He didn't make it.

Off from my northwest came a burp, and the man on the rope spun upside down, dropped several feet, snagged in the line, then hung in place like a fly in a web.

Men at the top of the railing grabbed the one climbing back to them and hurriedly pulled him over the wall, then silhouettes scattered in all directions. There were more shouts of alarm—and above the din rose the barks and howls of maddened beasts.

Fan. It had to be Fan and her sniper's rifle.

I nodded grimly in appreciation, then thumbed my earpiece. "Songbird here. Need medical assistance urgently. Can anyone hear me?"

Nothing. Either my comm unit was dead or the Round Table was still blocking transmissions. I figured it was pointless, but I'd had to try, at least once more.

Fan's deadly shooting had delivered Vicki a tiny reprieve. I moved up the ridge ahead, just enough to benefit from more bloody moonlight, and then I examined my friend.

Victoria was in a very bad way. As best as I could tell, she'd been shot through the neck and shoulder and had serious head trauma. I wasn't sure how bad it was because her scalp and the hair at the back of her head were saturated and matted with blood. Head wounds bleed like wild, and the sight left me cold with fear.

What else could I do but pray?

I checked the machine pistol at my waist—still secure—then tore off my tux jacket, roughly ripped it with my bare hands, tore the lining out in strips, and then bandaged Vicki. I overdid it, if that was even possible under the circumstances, but I did, because I was near blind in the low light. I had to stop all the bleeding—or she was dead, and I kept telling myself that over and over again with every makeshift bandage I wrapped around her head and neck.

Vicki's neck was the worst. The spine was intact, but blood pulsed steadily from the gory wound, and I was fairly certain that an artery had been severed. She only had minutes to live if she didn't receive real help.

Her unconscious face appeared distant, serene. That was a small comfort. At least she wasn't awake and screaming in pain.

A thought occurred to me. *Fan might have a med kit.*

I lifted Vicki into a fireman's carry again, then ran as fast as I safely could in the direction of the rifle shots I'd heard, up and over the ridge where I'd bandaged Vicki. I bounded like an overgrown rabbit whenever there was a space clear enough between trees. Perhaps I didn't spring as far and as fast as Bathory the vampire could, but I came damned close to it. My leg strength combined with the Lady's magic necklace—and my panic for Vicki—gave me the superhuman edge I prayed would make the difference between life and death.

I veered westward more as I ran. I wasn't sure that Fan would find me first, or I'd find her, but I wanted to keep moving toward Lake Tahoe. If we got caught because I lingered too long in the shadow of Serenity Mere, I could end up not only losing Vicki, but Fan as well.

Surely Fan would see me first and adjust. She had the night vision gear. She was the pro. Not me.

The toe of my right foot caught in a root by the side of a wide oak tree, and I had to roughly catch my balance. Somehow, I didn't drop Vicki, and she gave no sign of waking from my rude handling.

I placed a fearful hand on her back and was rewarded with the slight sensation of her breathing. She shuddered once though, and I moved forward again with renewed vigor. She'd fallen into a state of shock, I was sure of it.

My breathing became labored after a couple more minutes of bounds and sprints. The nighttime woods were difficult and dangerous to traverse, taking heaping amounts of concentration and energy to avoid a calamitous stumble and fall—even with the support of the Lady's pendant—and I'd exerted myself for nearly twenty-four hours straight. Strong as I was, I knew my limitations were being sorely tested.

"Songbird!"

I stopped short and a cloud of leaves kicked into the air around me. I went to one knee. "Hawk," I responded, relieved, and gulped a breath.

Fan's goggled silhouette appeared between shrubs and trees directly ahead of me. Her rifle was slung across her back, but she had a pistol out and at the ready as she ran to us. She leaned forward, as if to fling herself at me in an embrace but stopped short when she saw the burden I carried.

Fan stammered, "Oh, God. Oh, Jesus. Is she—"

I cut her off. "She's alive...but it's bad. Real bad." I gently placed Vicki onto a clear patch of ground between the trees where fallen leaves formed a natural bed.

"Fuck. It's my fault. I... I didn't get the shooter in time. I saw him but—"

I reached out and grabbed Fan by an arm. "This *isn't* on *you*. You saved us back there!" Fan faced me and even in the shadowy light, I could make out her anguished expression. I could feel her emotions flow into me too, but I pushed them aside. "Do you have a first aid kit?"

Fan returned to pure soldier in a blink. "Yes. Hold on." She removed her rifle first, followed by a small backpack. From inside the pack, Fan produced a red medical kit adorned with a white cross. "What happened in there?" she asked. "When we lost contact I... I thought we'd lost you for good."

Fan kept her night vision gear on, so she needed no light to attend to Vicki. She held what appeared at first to be an ordinary syringe, but it was a plastic tube holding a series of tiny balls. She placed bare hands onto the bloody, makeshift bandages I'd applied to Vicki, then, in quick succession, she made injections into the wound along Vicki's neck, and then the one in her shoulder.

"What's that?" I asked.

"Combat wound sealant. Sponges that adapt and expand and seal off the bleeding. It's instant." Fan frowned. "She's lost a lot of blood, Lochlan. But she won't lose any more."

I'd unconsciously reached up to rub my neck, and my hand came away damp with Vicki's blood.

"Fuck," I whispered. "There were kids in there! I didn't have time to think. I—Silana's dog showed up. Out of *nothing*. Like magic."

"Cú Chulainn," Fan answered knowingly.

"Yeah, that's right."

"He can do that. She summoned him, and because he'd met you before, found you with no problem."

"I don't get it," I admitted.

Fan was applying fresh, sterile bandages to Vicki. "We're not meant to understand everything, I think. Lift her head. *Gently...*" I placed a hand under the base of Vicki's skull and lifted. Fan spun tape around Vicki's neck to hold a bandage in place. "Okay. You can put her down now."

Fan pulled more items from her med-kit. As she did, she continued trying to explain.

"Cu isn't a dog. At least, not a dog like *we* know. He looks like one, sure. But these beings take shape. Shape-change at will, some of them. I've just gotten used to it, I guess." Fan moved on to tape Vicki's shoulder bandage. "Hell, you might be able to do it, too."

"What? No. No way..."

"We'll see."

I seriously didn't know what to say.

Fan examined her handiwork. "All done here. Let's *go*."

Urgency hit me again. "Lead the way," I replied, then I lifted Vicki in my arms as I stood. She was still breathing, and I sensed no urgency in her as she slept—or my empathy had failed me—but I was relieved either way.

Vicki wasn't out of the fire yet, but her chances of survival had just leveled up.

The barking of dogs broke through the trees far to my left, back east, the way I'd escaped the Serenity Mere compound.

"Shit," Fan spat. "They have our scent." Fan moved deftly through the brush and branches ahead of me, her night gear giving her a clear advantage, so I followed in her footsteps.

"Just go. With you leading, I can move even faster," I urged.

Fan took off, her athleticism on full display for the first time. If the head wound she'd suffered a few hours earlier was slowing her down, I could only marvel.

I watched Fan's feet in the scattered and broken light of the moon and carefully emulated her every step, every motion and sidestep. It worked well enough that I almost caught up to her twice, even with the burden of Vicki held tightly to my chest, but I had to compensate for Vicki's weight every now and again to keep my balance, and that forced a more cautious pace.

Still, we kept well ahead of the dogs, and soon the waters of Lake Tahoe appeared at the base of the rolling, forested hills. Fan increased her speed as we ran down to meet it. I counted on her to get us to the rendezvous point since I no longer had my GPS on me, and I literally had my hands full even if I did.

"Just need a minute..." Fan stopped. Her breathing was hard and steady.

"Okay." I gently placed Vicki on the ground and checked to make sure her bandages hadn't been disturbed—and that she was still breathing.

She was.

Fan flipped a compass open on her palm, got our bearings, snapped it shut, then placed it back into the utility belt of her wet suit. "We're on track. Southwest from here and then we should run straight into the others," she whispered, and sat on a large tree root. She unsnapped a canteen from her belt. "After Cu took off, what then? How'd you escape?" She pushed her night vision goggles to her forehead, sipped from her canteen, and her eyes glinted in the dim moonlight as she watched me.

"I ran into Silana's sister." I scanned the dark woods that surrounded us. "And something else."

"What?"

"A vampire, I think. I guess. I'm pretty sure it was a vampire. I know how that sounds..." I half-expected Fan to laugh out loud, but, when I met her gaze, she'd let the canteen drop away from her open mouth. She lowered her eyes and pushed her hand out to offer me the water.

"Drink this quick—and then we're moving again. I've run into one of those before...and once was enough," Fan said in a hurry. Her fear was naked to me, and I couldn't blame her.

I accepted the water and kept checking around us, even as I drank one deep gulp after another. I handed back Fan's canteen, then reached down to pick up Vicki again.

"Craziest thing wasn't the vampire, or Silana's sister. I think Silana sent help, cast some sort of spell, I dunno. But water poured into the room where we were trapped. A sacrificial chamber. I'm sure they were gonna do terrible things to the kids. But this water...*it was alive.* And I swear there were... I can't believe I'm even saying this. There were *faeries.*"

This time Fan *did* laugh.

"That was *definitely* Silana's doing," Fan affirmed. She stood from her tree root. "Ready?"

I nodded and we took off southwest in a steady jog, the twinkling waters of the lake growing ever closer.

Fresh barks reminded us that the search dogs hadn't given up. Fan picked up the pace, but I kept up easily. I was feeling optimistic, and that fueled me.

You'd think I'd have recognized the warning signs by then.

A shadow flowed across the sky directly above us, and as I searched for the cause, another shadow bolted out of the dark recesses of the trees to my left. The black figure moved with inhuman speed, yet I cried out before it struck. "Look out!"

Fan was fast and nimble as hell, but this enemy was faster and had the initiative. She spun around at me, a shining, steel combat knife in her hand, but got hit in the flank by the shadow. Both tumbled over and over through leaves, twigs, and branches.

Fan cried out, and I took one step forward before moving to place Vicki on the ground. I did my best to do it fast but not so roughly it would harm my friend, but I also had to risk some speed to save Fan. I almost managed it, all things considered, but I couldn't hope to be fast enough.

It was the vampire again. He'd tracked us and escaped the temple and the wrath of the elemental waters.

He knocked Fan's knife from her hand and came up standing with her grappled before him, both of her wrists locked above her head in one of his fists. Bathory's other hand held—a *pistol*, pointed straight at my chest.

"*Don't*. Don't move, *Abaddon*. I *will* kill her, if you test me," the vampire said.

His ruptured midsection was tightly wrapped in layers of dark cloth.

The creature above us fluttered, its shadow strafing across the forest floor between Bathory and me.

I sensed her again in that moment. Katrina the Lady, and she let out a wicked laugh overhead.

Vicki lay unconscious just in front of me, so I put one hand up and took a step to the side of her, being careful to avoid approaching Bathory.

"Don't listen to him," Fan hissed as she kicked her legs behind her, trying to break free. Bathory was tall, and his spidery arms made it simple for him to avoid her futile kicks, infuriating Fan even more. "*Shoot him!*"

In trouble again with a repeat of tonight's duo of evil. That made me doubly pissed off. Vicki would die if she didn't get help soon. Fan would die if I made the wrong choice.

I needed time to think.

So, I stalled.

"What is it you want?" I asked.

The vampire, unmasked since our first encounter, had his gun trained on my head. He was no older in the face than me, but with paler skin. His features were European and handsome, his dark hair blackened in the shadows cast by the faint light of the moon.

For some reason he didn't pull the trigger. It might have been because my 2011 was pointed at his skull, a reflex I'd developed at some point—but I was sure this thing wasn't killable in the conventional manner, and I *was*, as far as I knew. Or it was that Bathory wanted something more important than my life.

"The girl at your feet, boy. She's what they gathered this whole affair for. Give her up and I'll let this one go," he shook Fan once for emphasis and she gagged, "Don't—and I'll kill them both."

I stared murderously at the creature. "You're really what I think you are?"

"Am I? Oh, you mean..." Bathory chuckled. "Yes. So, I assure you, I can and *will* make good on my threat. You're powerful, *Abaddon*, but you're not faster than my kind." The vampire noticed the rifle slung across Fan's shoulders. "Ah, so this is the little pest that shot so many of our guards. She's a real killer. And lovely, too. Almost as pretty as you. I'd *turn* her under different circumstances, but tonight's prize is Victoria."

I was about to reply, but saw something move behind the vampire, and not just another shadow from the witch flying overhead. I focused on the old oaks that loomed tall and wide beyond Bathory. An outstretched tree limb—or what I took for one in the darkness—swayed and centered on the vampire. There was a strong breeze in that moment, and I expected the bough to swing back.

It didn't.

The vampire noticed me looking past him. "What? Katrina?" Bathory glanced up once for a split second, then back at me, his black pistol still trained on my head as if held by a statue.

I opened my mouth, and in that second it happened.

The 'bough' came crashing down on top of Bathory with enough force to crumple him into a heap. His bones and skull made sick popping sounds as his face disappeared from view. The arm that held Fan tore off at the shoulder and dark gore spurted out. His gun-wielding hand drove downward at the dirt and fired once harmlessly. Luckily for Fan, the force of the strike was enough to protect her from both the bullet *and* the blood spray.

She somersaulted away from the carnage, then stopped just in front of Vicki's unconscious body.

A scream of outrage descended upon us from Katrina as she flew by in another low pass over the treetops.

Disgusted, I turned my pistol in her direction and fired two shots. I knew the chance of hitting her was next to nothing, but I wanted to make her think twice before she'd risk flying near us again.

A booming voice shouted, "Begone, Lilith! These children are not for you!"

When I looked back again at the carnage that had formerly been Bathory the vampire, Fan had already taken a few steps, and her shadow stretched out and met what I had mistaken for a tree.

The form that manifested out of the woods was twice my height and wider than the Bomber's front end. The shape of a man became clear as the moonlight illuminated his naked, insanely muscled upper body. He only wore a classical leather kilt down to his knees and ankle-tied sandals.

The giant stepped onto the form of Bathory and ground one foot the size of a portable fridge into the undead thing for good measure, then dropped the dead tree trunk he'd used to smash the vampire. Dead leaves and pine needles spouted up into the air, fluttering in all directions.

"Filthy things, vampires," the bearded giant grumbled. His voice was so deep it made my bones rattle.

I stared at him dumbly. In a few days chock full of insanity, this was the pinnacle moment.

"Conrad," Fan whispered.

"You've got a beard," I said stupidly.

The giant smiled down at us both, but his gaze shifted to Vicki. "Your friend?"

I found my voice after a second as Fan's declaration sunk in. "Yes. She's been shot."

"I stabilized her, but she's lost too much blood," Fan explained. "We need to hurry."

Conrad's giant face, similar in shape but not exactly like the one I was used to, grimaced. He reached down, then lifted Vicki up in both hands like a toddler, careful to cradle her head.

Frenzied dog barks added to the tension.

"There's no time to burn this thing." Conrad kicked at the vampire puddle as he cradled Vicki. "And the trees should not pay the price for its crimes." He spit on what was left of Bathory. "Follow," and he turned to the south to begin a fast walk. The giant's strides were so long I had to jog to keep up with him. Fan ran, sandwiched between us.

I had to ask. "How can anything come back from *that?*"

Conrad nodded. "It will take him some time. And it won't be pleasant."

"Huh," I grunted.

When we reached a clearing, Conrad ran full-out, and Fan and I both had to exert ourselves to keep up. I could still talk though, so I asked, "They called her Katrina. The witch or whatever that flying bitch is. Silana's evil sister. Right?"

"She goes by many names. But Lilith was her first," Conrad replied. Conrad knocked a branch out of his way as we reached more trees, and he slowed to a fast walk again. "Immortality often breeds anonymity."

That made sense. "Lilith sounds familiar. From college. Religious Studies, maybe?"

"Surely. She is a creature often discussed in Jewish myth. But she is quite real, as you've seen. A demon, vile and cruel beyond measure." Conrad began another jog as we entered a steeper downhill path.

"How could something—like that—be related to Silana," Fan asked.

"They are two of the eldest beings upon this plane, and they have a history. But in truth they're not sisters by blood. Not by any conscious design, so don't worry yourself upon that. My wife has the purest spirit. Pure enough to save *me*."

Conrad didn't explain further. After what Cu had done for the kids, I had no more doubts about Silana, and Fan didn't push the subject. However, another question occurred to me.

"You...you can't teleport, can you? Cú Chulainn appeared and saved some kids—"

"Unfortunately, no. I am but flesh and bone, like you," Conrad answered. "Cu is a powerful spirit. But even he...such a dimensional shift takes a lot." The giant's breathing was steady and heavy as we continued at a run. "He won't be back to aid us again tonight."

I nodded grimly.

"Hey! I need to create a doggie diversion. Only take a minute," Fan said. "Don't wait for me."

"No. I'll guard you. Go on, Conrad."

"Be quick," he answered, and then rumbled down the hill. The lake was only a few minutes in the distance.

Fan stopped, and we both caught our breath as she removed a small foil packet from a pouch on her belt. "This will stink like hell," she warned. She tore open the packet, then quickly poured some of the contents onto a nearby tree. She emptied the last of the powder onto another evergreen thirty feet from the first.

Stink is just a word. Think dead skunk. No, think ten dead skunks.

I gagged. "Good God..."

Fan smiled impishly. "*Run*, dummy."

"Absolutely," I agreed, then we chased after Conrad, but I slowed my pace to keep Fan close.

After a minute, I saw Conrad's bulk ahead of us. He was nearing the beach. There was a thick fog on the water below him, and the moonlight faded by the minute as the lunar eclipse approached, so I could see little else besides the tops of trees.

Unintentionally, at first, I reached out with my senses. Conrad remained determined and tireless. Vicki was barely there, but I detected a fine thread of confusion. She was caught in a dream. But she still lived.

Dogs broke my concentration with a fresh round of excited barks. They'd gained ground on us, but sounded different somehow.

Then the pack chasing us degenerated into whines and yipping.

"They've found the bait," Fan said deviously.

I smiled.

Just ahead, the fog upon the lake broke open like a cloud caught in a gust, and our motorboat appeared. Silana jumped lightly off the boat's deck and walked across the lake water as if it were a sheet of solid glass. In mere seconds, she reached Conrad and Vicki at the beach's forested edge.

Fan broke into a sprint, so I matched her.

Conrad placed Vicki onto the sand, and Silana moved her palms all across Vicki's still form in a circular pattern, sometimes rubbing her body lightly, other times lifting her hands a couple inches above the flesh but maintaining the same motion.

I was breathing roughly when I reached Vicki, but was careful not to interrupt Silana. Nobody spoke a word as she worked.

Fan tapped my shoulder, then herself, unslung her rifle, and moved off two dozen yards to a sentry position, just off the sand and behind a fallen tree.

I followed her example and checked the ammo in my guns. The machine pistol I'd taken had a single, nearly empty magazine. My 2011 wasn't much better off.

The dogs had finally gone silent. Whether that meant they'd run off or were being hushed by their handlers, I had no way of knowing, but I remained keenly uneasy. Most of that was my fear for Vicki, but a nagging paranoia kept my eyes on the sky, too. Lilith—Katrina, the Lady, *whatever*. I expected her to make another appearance.

Silana groaned, and I whipped my head around at her and Vicki. Conrad was kneeling as if ready for Silana to request his aid, an earnest look in his eyes that matched his aura.

I'd gotten used to reading emotions quickly, and now it was happening unconsciously.

The red tint from the slowly darkening moon overhead cast its deathly sheen over us all. A light breeze blew every so often across the lake, and crickets and toads all around joined into a sad chorus.

Something wasn't right.

Silana spoke to me in a soft voice. "I'm sorry, Lochlan." She looked up and her eyes were wet with tears. "She's dying."

"What?" I choked on a stuttering breath as a ball of emotion pushed up into my chest so hard that I thought my heart might burst. *"What?"*

I stepped to Vicki's side and dropped to my knees in the graveled sand. I reached out my left hand to place my palm over her forehead.

I don't know what I was expecting. I suppose I was desperate enough to pray more random, miraculous magic might raise Vicki up like I was Lancelot laying on hands.

But there wasn't magic. I could hardly register life in my friend. Her skin felt cool and her pallor was obvious even in the scant light of the eclipsing moon.

I asked, "Hospital?" I knew what the answer would be even as the word escaped my mouth.

"Not enough time," Conrad answered before Silana. "I'm very sorry."

Fan's feet appeared in the periphery of my vision as my eyes remained locked on Vicki's serene face. "We need to go," Fan said.

A firefly sputtered and blinked past Fan's ankles. *Even in death, there is life*, I thought.

Another firefly twinkled and bobbed nearby.

I raised my eyes and focused on the tiny golden glow, and a third firefly popped alight as I did—then zoomed by my face.

A wispy, childlike voice spoke in my left ear. "In death, there is life."

I turned and the golden light sputtered up and away a few inches—and then a tiny, perfect, humanoid limb extended from within the blinding ball, as clear as a doll's arm. It pointed a finger and my eyes followed. A dozen more gumball-sized, golden lights appeared all around Vicki's body.

"What's happening?" I whispered. I met Silana's gaze, and she smiled.

"I cannot save her, but I will not let her die," Silana answered. "This will require more energy." Silana's form blurred before me, and then she—*she changed.*

One second I gazed at human Silana, beautiful, tall and stately, and the very next there was what appeared to be a five-foot teenage girl before me, but absolutely not human.

The 'girl' had skin of blue and green, and her hair and nails grew instantly longer, shifting color between purple, blue, and back again. She wore little more than a shift of gossamer cloth that rustled and flowed with every touch of the wind. Everything about her was absolute perfection, a beauty so intense that I found my breath caught in my throat.

"Cloak us from prying eyes," Silana commanded, and instantly the fae creatures surrounding Vicki's face sprang outward to form a circle around our group. The world around us went away, or perhaps we went out of the world. Whatever happened, I could no longer see more than ten feet away. Crickets still chirped. The breeze still tickled my ears. But we were all behind a wall of absolute darkness. Even the sky above faded into nothing but total black.

Silana placed both of her sylvan hands upon Vicki's chest, and a white light formed and glowed below Silana's palms. This radiance seeped into Vicki's skin and then slowly, steadily Vicki's entire body became wreathed in a bright white light. The very antithesis of the umbra that protected us from detection.

Silana reached out her left hand. "Give me your hand, Lochlan Nohr."

I did as she asked. Her touch was impossibly light and very warm.

A sweet jolt of something—I can't describe it exactly—swept up my forearm, then into my right shoulder. Not pain yet not pleasure, I found myself relaxing, then a sleepiness tapped at my brain. After how much time I have no recollection of, I came back to myself staring at the freckles on Vicki's nose, lit by the intense white brilliance that covered her.

A trembling breath filled my lungs. My vision blurred.

And then Victoria Lott winked out of time and space, perfect nose and all.

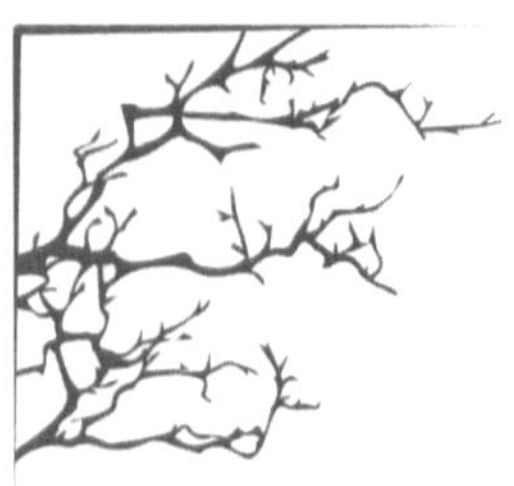

Chapter 31

Energy returned to my body quickly and cleared the fog from my brain. I knew Vicki had disappeared, but questions formed.

When I came fully back to myself, Silana and Conrad stood to either side of me, both back in human form and their traveling clothes. Fan was a few feet away, her rifle at the ready and her night vision goggles panning actively across the woods behind us.

The faeries and their cloak of darkness were gone.

I looked into Silana's deep eyes and asked, "Is she safe?"

Silana's lips curled into a tight smile. "*Oui.*"

"She'll live then?"

"She will sleep," Silana replied. "I placed her where no more harm may come to her and time has little meaning."

I shook my head in wonder. "I don't..."

"A pocket dimension. Much as my wife can shape-shift and help me transfer mass, she can craft and fold the very layers that exist all around us. It still amazes me, even after all these centuries," Conrad explained.

"It's nothing," Silana claimed. "It is good that I could draw upon you." Silana squeezed my right hand. "I was too drained from maintaining our glamour...to safely hide your friend by myself."

I managed a nod. It relieved me that Victoria was alive, but what Silana described was hardly different from a coma.

"I see." I sighed. "I failed her then. My stupid hero act—"

"*Chut!* We threw you to the wolves as much as you walked into the den. Without you, she would be dead! And those children...those children would be worse than dead!" Silana pulled my arm until I met her gaze again. "Few could have managed such a feat alone. Never doubt that!"

Fan interrupted. "Sorry, but we need to *go.*"

"She's right. We'll talk more later," Conrad said. "Everyone onto the boat."

Silana half-pushed me toward the boat as Conrad jogged into the lake waters up to the tops of his boots then pulled himself over the side and into the captain's seat. I walked to the boat next, but my mind was numb, so my strides were deliberate and unhurried, despite the danger.

I suppose, recalling, I was in shock.

When I reached the side of the boat, I spotted Sophie's drone. It was dormant but appeared to be in good condition. The bundle I'd thrown into the forest was on the corner of the deck next to it. I climbed onto the boat, then asked, "Sophie?"

"No contact with her since the wireless blocker activated. She's probably surveying the surrounding area through any remote means she can find. The drone has a built-in pigeon mode and returned with no issue. *There*." Conrad pointed at the deck. "Grab your gear."

I picked up the bundle. As I sorted through it and tugged my leather jacket on, an odd, chortling bird startled us all. The call came from the forested fringe along the beach.

Silana and Fan had reached the water's edge together and also turned to look in the direction of the bird call.

At the edge of the wood the willowy, unmasked figure of the Lady manifested from the depths of the shadowed brambles. Her dress had a moon-red hue to it. Or I imagined it. Either way, the image was haunting.

I went for my guns, but Conrad stopped me. "No. I think there's no more need for that, Lochlan. Fan, get in."

Silana didn't take her eyes off of her sister. "She wishes to speak with me. I won't be long."

"Are you sure?" Fan wasn't convinced. Her fingers caressed the stock of her rifle.

"If she wished to attack us, we would certainly be facing down a small army by now. Go on." Silana walked toward Lilith.

Fan took one last look through her scope before re-slinging her rifle over her back and shoulder. She entered the water, reached out, and I pulled her aboard.

"I don't like this," Fan whispered.

"They haven't encountered each other in many years. I don't expect an ambush but—you might be right. Be ready," Conrad warned.

That's all Fan needed to hear. She had her rifle back out and surveyed the length of the shoreline.

A couple hundred feet away, Silana and Lilith faced one another above the stony dunes. I half-expected a pack of rabid wolves or guards and their dogs to come leaping out of the trees, but all that I spotted in the night was the flight of two large, dark birds swooping and circling the vicinity before disappearing into the woods.

"What were those? Crows?" I asked.

"Ravens," Conrad replied. "Some of Lilith's eyes and ears."

I reached up to my chest and pinched the pendant between the cloth of my shirt.

Conrad hadn't started the speed boat's engines, so the natural sounds of lapping water, frogs, and insects seemed deafening as the three of us waited anxiously for Silana.

The two immortals didn't talk animatedly. The conversation between them appeared amiable from my vantage point, and that disturbed me. I'd been inside the temple and seen what I'd seen. Lilith had tried to murder me, and she surely would have taken part in all the sick rituals planned.

Yet, here was gentle Silana parleying with the demoness.

"What is she really? Lilith, I mean," I asked.

"The embodiment of corruption. The Mother of Vampires some say. Silana believes she is one of the Fallen. Those willful Powers that rebelled against the Creator." Conrad paused. "But in truth, after so many millennia, even Lilith is unsure how she came to be. She just is. Like my wife, they are both anomalies. And that is their bond."

The night grew darker. The blood moon was very near total eclipse. Nearby, Fan sat on a soft, white, cushioned seat, her rifle across her lap. Her legs swung anxiously. She was eager to leave.

So was I. I looked back at the forest.

With no parting gesture, Lilith turned and disappeared back into the trees behind her. Silana stood deathly still, watching her sister depart. Only Silana's hair, blowing lightly in the night's breeze, gave her aspect any life at all.

It was a sad sight.

Eventually she made her way back to the boat.

Conrad and I both lifted Silana aboard, but Conrad was the first to ask, "Well?"

Silana's countenance was somber but her emotions were in absolute flux.

"The war has begun," Silana said. "We must make plans to go home." Silana grimaced at her husband. "Europe will burn soon, then the rest of the world. We must do our part to safeguard who we can." She gazed at me next. "My greatest hope remains...that you will accompany us, *mon ami*. Lilith fears you. For good reason. And that fear will spread."

It was a lot to accept. Just days before I'd been a not-so-humble musician plying his craft. What was I now?

"We. Need. To. Go," Fan reiterated emphatically, and Silana smiled at her, tight-lipped and mournful.

"*Oui.*" Silana sat in a seat and then Conrad cranked up the motors.

Fan walked up and spoke into Conrad's ear. Soon he maneuvered our boat alongside a sharp outcropping of the rocky shore.

Fan jumped off the boat, splashed to the beach then fished out a well-hidden cache of her rented scuba tanks, fins, and other gear. When she was safely back on board, Conrad pointed our boat toward Incline Village and gunned the engines.

The cool mist of churned lake waters gave me some relief, even as I still chewed on Silana's warning and the ultimate fate of my wounded friend. So many questions. I'd fallen to the bottom of the proverbial rabbit hole, and hardly a shred of light showed the way out.

Vicki's parents. Would we tell them?

Goddammit.

The trip back to friendly shores was met with no interference, and hardly a word was spoken among us on the way.

Once docked, Fan and Conrad returned the boat's key and rented equipment via a drop box. I changed back to my jeans inside a public men's room. When I exited, I held a bundle of badly torn tuxedo clothing. On top was the crumpled wolf mask I'd stuffed into my pocket.

Conrad and Silana both noticed the mask immediately.

"You wore that?" Conrad asked.

"I did," I admitted.

Silana laughed.

I smirked at Silana, but who was I kidding. It *was* ironic.

"May I see it?" Conrad extended a hand.

"Sure." I handed Conrad the white plastic, sequined mask.

Fan joined us while Conrad examined the thing. After a minute, he held it in front of an outdoor light fixture near the rental shop's front door.

"What I thought," Conrad said. "Cutting-edge CIA and Mossad tech. It's designed to allow infrared facial recognition cams to record straight through..."

"Oh, great," I muttered.

"Ingenious really."

I huffed. "So what's the point? Everyone in attendance was part of the club. Well, except me."

Conrad lowered the mask away from the light, then turned to face us. "The point is blackmail," he said. "Many of those in attendance were new, I'm sure. Now they're cataloged and will do the bidding of the Round Table or risk being exposed as the predators they are. This is how most governments today are so heavily compromised."

I thought about that. "If we were to get our hands on that evidence..."

Conrad nodded. "Yes. I have discussed with Sophie before. It's a possibility. Which reminds me..." Conrad pulled out his phone as he stuffed my mask into his travel bag. "I'll keep this if you don't mind."

"Have at it."

Conrad dialed. "Secure line," he said to us. There was an immediate answer on the other side. "Yes. Yes, we're fine. I'm sorry we didn't contact you sooner." Conrad listened. "That's great news." He paused. "Shot. We've done all we can for her for now. I'll explain soon. Make sure the children are fed and get some sleep. I want them ready to return to their families in the morning." Conrad smiled. "Thank you, Sophie. You saved lives today... Yes, I'll tell the others. See you soon."

Conrad hung up. "Cu arrived back at the compound with three children. Safe and sound." He smiled at me.

"I love him," Silana said.

"Thank God," I added. "Yes, there were three. Hopefully, only three. I didn't sense or see any others."

"Good. But how did you manage it?" Conrad asked.

Silana and Fan both smiled at me. "We thought the worst when the communications died," Silana murmured.

"I thought I was dead, too. I had nothing left." I took a deep breath as I recalled the horrific scene in the temple. "So, I sang."

I received expressions of astonishment in response to that.

Conrad broke the silence. "Come. Tell us everything on the way back. Grab the bikes and follow us to the airport." He picked up his bag and slung it over a shoulder. "I'm damned proud of you." He smiled at Fan. "Both of you." He took Silana by the hand.

I had no response, but tried to smile back.

Fan poked me in the ribs when the couple walked away to the Rover. "They'll find a way," she said. "To save your friend."

I looked down at Fan and managed a grim smile, but words still wouldn't come out.

"Come on. I want to hear this tall tale before I pass out on the plane ride," Fan added, and she pulled me along to the parked motorcycles.

I filled everyone in on the details of the temple and the sacrifice pool, my fight with Bathory and Lilith, the ringmasters—and especially the Ringmaster who'd claimed to be Vicki's biological father—and, consequently, her mother's rapist.

"He collapsed in a heap when Vicki kneed him in the balls," I continued.

"Good for her," Fan said.

"Yeah, well, that's when I knew he wasn't my father."

He might have raped my mother, too, yet I doubted he was my biological dad. He was a runt compared to me.

There was silence on the comm.

I went on. "If we hadn't been surrounded, I'd've killed him. Still pissed off I didn't."

"Do not let that fester," Silana said. "We will catch him one day."

"I still have more questions," I said.

"*Oui?*"

"What's with the British accents? First on that thing inside Chiang—and then the Ringmaster."

My answer didn't come all at once.

"The Round Table was founded in Great Britain. Many of the central, most powerful members are of royal blood," Conrad answered first.

"In many ways, the British Empire never died," Silana added.

"Okay, but why did I hear some Middle Eastern speak from the guards that came after us? It sounded familiar but I'm no linguist."

Conrad asked, "Arabic?"

"No, I don't think so, but I was running...and pretty far away. And there were fucking dogs barking."

"*Hebrew*," Conrad said. "Mossad mercenaries."

"Wait, what? Why would they be involved?"

"It's not uncommon. They're well trained and loyal. Not only British are in the Round Table."

I was speechless.

"Okay. And Katrina, err, *Lilith*. She called me something strange." I recalled the syllables. "*Abaddon*. What the hell is that?"

Again, there was a sizable pause before Silana responded.

"Angel of Death," she said.

That took half a minute to sink in.

I finally asked, "Um, I'm sorry, what?"

Silana continued gently. "It is a Hebrew word. 'Angel of Death.' In Greek, *Apollyon*."

"That answers that question then," Conrad said.

I wasn't so sure. "What question?" I asked.

"What you are," Conrad replied. "Lilith would know better than anyone."

"That monster? Why?"

"Her brother... Her brother is Lucifer."

I almost steered my motorcycle off the Goddamned highway.

"You're serious?" I asked.

"I'd never joke about such a thing," Conrad said.

"I—" *What the fuck?*

Silana told me. "Your father is one of the Principalities, Lochlan. One of the Powers. Most commonly referred to as...'angels.' I suspected as much, honestly. But my sister knew it as soon as you opened your mouth." Silana let me chew on that for a few seconds before adding, "The rules have changed. You were either fathered by one of the Fallen—something unheard of in millennia—or even more astoundingly, your sire is from one of the Houses loyal to Him. And that has *never* happened before."

My mouth hung open.

"I need to process," I said finally.

"It's a lot, I know," Conrad said. "My father was a son of the Fallen. A *Nephilim*."

"We're...*cousins*," I said.

Conrad chuckled. "Yes."

"My angels," Silana added in an impish tone.

Fan had been listening quietly, taking it all in. "Holy shit," she whispered.

I nodded to myself.

"Holy shit," I echoed.

A huge question hit me. "Hold the fuck on! How in the hell did that happen? When? If I was conceived at the same time as Vicki..."

"Only your father knows," Silana said. "But I have ideas. Let it wait. We are almost to the airport. *Oui?*"

"Right at the light ahead," Conrad replied.

I shut up. I was tired and lightheaded. I wanted to load up the plane and get back to Austin ASAP. Feel my own bed under me again. Feel something...*anything*, normal.

I'd order a pizza the first chance I got.

"You okay?" It was Fan, asking without the comm line. We'd stopped side by side at an intersection, just behind Conrad's rented Land Rover.

I glanced over at her. "Yeah. Yeah, thanks. I'll be fine. It's just... I..."

"It's good, Loch. *You're* good."

I smiled under my helmet and nodded.

It *is* good. To know the truth. Right?

Conrad told us to load up our gear and motorbikes onto the jet. After that, we all piled into the Land Rover and headed to a nearby motel where the aircrew had registered for us. Three additional rooms were ready in our names.

The second I saw the queen-sized bed in my first-floor motel room, a wave of pure exhaustion hit me like a Mack truck. I'd pushed myself to the limit for days and by that point had been awake for nearly twenty-four hours straight. I closed the door to my room and flopped onto the bed, fully clothed.

A *knock-knock* pulled me alert just as I was about to doze off.

I raised my voice. "Who is it?"

"It's me." It was Fan.

I got up and opened the door.

Fan stood outside under the long walkway overhang in a simple lady T, bare feet, and black yoga pants.

"Did I wake you?" Fan asked softly.

"Almost," I said. "Everything okay?"

"Yeah, sure." She didn't convince me. Fan looked up. She'd been crying. "I started thinking about Dante..."

I cleared a path into my room and nodded toward the interior. "Come on."

WE SLEPT CURLED UP together until well past sunrise and awoke fully clothed, still on top of the bedspread.

The kicker? We'd slept right through the full lunar eclipse.

Fan returned to her room to shower, and I cleaned myself up before breakfast.

Everybody, including the flight crew, ate at a local greasy spoon recommended to us by the motel manager. They served me up bacon and pancakes—three triple stacks and a dozen crispy strips.

I'm sure Conrad suggested it because he wanted to relieve Courtney of server duty on the way home. Our flight attendant sat at a corner table, out of earshot from me, Captain Chomette and his copilot. Silana, Fan, and Conrad ate their breakfast at Courtney's table, alternating between eating and consoling her.

"She seems to be taking it better than I expected," I whispered to the two men at my table. I followed my comment with a swig of orange juice from a huge glass.

"She's dealt with loss before," the Captain said. "Many times."

"Hmm?" My mouth was full of bacon.

Nobody else in the humble mom-and-pop diner paid us any attention, so Captain Chomette answered easily, "She's one of *them*. A *fae*."

I swallowed the bacon. "Ah, okay." I cut and stabbed my second stack of pancakes with a fork. "I should get used to it."

"You will," the captain said.

"Yep," Gabriel agreed.

I set my fork down and sipped more coffee. "What about you two? Are you...?"

The captain and his copilot glanced at one another, then both scoffed.

"No."

"No."

Captain Chomette cut into his omelet and said, "We're just men. But our families have worked with them for generations."

"Huh," I grunted. "That makes sense, doesn't it?"

"There are many of us. Don't be too surprised when you meet them," Gabriel said.

"A whole army," Captain Chomette added.

The ramifications grew even as I killed another strip of bacon.

"That's good," I said. "We're gonna need an army."

The two pilots exchanged glances but added nothing else.

When breakfast was done, we all drove to the nearby airport and made final flight preparations to return to Austin.

This included the storage of a temporary coffin that housed Dante's body bag. Conrad insisted on handling that alone when only the pilots and I were left at the jet's rear ramp. I loaded Chiang's remains.

On the way home, I reminded Silana that she needed to call Pack so we could make good on our dinner promise. I also discussed the upcoming Friday night gig, because like it or not, I had responsibilities. I'd have to pretend that it was just another day in the life. None of the members of Trip the Shark would ever hear the tale. Ever know I'd rescued three kids—or that Victoria Lott lay tucked away like Sleeping Beauty.

I was fine with that. More than fine. None of my friends needed to learn the dark, ugly truth I'd barged my way into. In fact, the less they knew, the safer they'd be.

About halfway to Austin, I asked Silana another burning question.

"I need to know...," I said.

Silana smiled. "*Bien sûr.*"

"Why did they want Vicki? What the...what was the point?"

Silana sighed. "As a...child of one of their leaders, they must consider her to be a vessel. For a major ritual. From my brief talk with Lilith, she realized that fighting us for Victoria was futile, especially because she had been gravely wounded. My sister is evil, but she does not pursue simply for the sake of pursuit alone.

"Like you and Conrad, Victoria is a hybrid. But until my husband can safely examine her, we will not know exactly what."

I studied some clouds through the portal window above the couch. "This is fucking insane. All of it," I grumbled.

"Yes. It is," Silana agreed. "But there is a purpose to it all, too. *To all of us.* I'm sure of that."

Conrad spoke to me. "The Round Table is making new moves, but *you* showed up. *The wild card.* Broke up their little party. Your existence changes everything. I'm pretty damned sure the enemy broke the *rules* a while ago, or you wouldn't have been born." Conrad paused. "So, you're no accident, Lochlan. A Power stepped in for your mother and...here you are."

"What does that even mean? Did she consent to it?" Anger heated my blood.

Conrad thought about it. "I have no way of knowing for sure. Has she ever confided in you? Any hint of that day?"

"No, of course not. I had no reason to believe my mother'd ever been raped. But...she's shown signs of PTSD, off and on. That's why she's in the happy house again. But she keeps the details between her and her doctors private. Ever since...Dad's death..."

The irony of those last words hit me like a blow to the stomach. I went silent.

But my mind took the inevitable turn, because I'd touched on the worst subject.

"They were gonna rape the kids," I said. "Rape. Murder. *Jesus.* I've read the rumors on the Net—I think they were... There were tables. All along the walls. Buffet tables, I couldn't miss them. I've played enough weddings to know..."

"They were going to eat them," Conrad said, matter-of-factly. "The blood is collected and distributed. The more terror induced in the children, the more of a delicacy it is to these psychopaths." Despite his tone, Conrad was having a tough time with what he said. "The organs are harvested. Every shred of the child's body is used or consumed."

"I should have killed them! *All the motherfuckers!*"

The interior of the plane went dead silent.

"You do not know?" Silana's voice held genuine surprise.

"What?"

"You *did* kill many of them. With your voice. Many of the worst that did not escape in time—went mad and catatonic with fear and guilt. My sister told me they would be cleaning up your mess—and making political amends—for years to come, not being able to explain away what happened to their mortal proxies.

"An unfortunate few drowned as well."

Silana lifted an eyebrow at me.

"Where did all the water come from?" I asked.

"The pool," Silana said. "Lake faeries were more than happy to help, acting as my eyes. I bolstered their elemental control. Unfortunately, the vampire escaped—"

"He didn't get far," Conrad reminded us.

Silana smiled at her husband. "Evidently not."

"Faeries," I said. "Sure, why not?"

Silana laughed. "They are quite smitten with you."

"Great..." I cracked a half-smile. "Well, tell them I said 'Thank you.' For helping."

"I will," Silana said.

I had one more question that kept gnawing at me.

"Why were they all white? European. The kids. *Vicki.* Two blonde girls, one redheaded woman. All of them, even the boy, had light-colored eyes. Blue. Green. Even my mother. Vicki's, too. It doesn't feel random is what I'm saying. Am I reading too much into it?"

Silana nodded at Conrad, so he answered.

"It's not random. They prefer fair-skinned kids. Usually the younger, the better," Conrad said. "The especially gifted are prized above all others."

"What the fuck is that all about?" I asked

Conrad's tone grew dark. "Some very ancient rites. Humiliation rituals, and overt Satanism...that has only become more twisted, as evil always does. Too many young victims are forced into white slavery—for sex trafficking. And worse.

"It gets even more complicated when corrupt politicians and corporate heads are involved. It shouldn't surprise you that the U.S. is their most profitable hunting ground."

I sighed. "Nope. No, it doesn't. Corrupt fucking government. I'm feeling like half of everything I learned in school was either a lie or a diversion."

"At least half," Conrad said. "Remind me to tell you about the World Wars someday."

"*Conrad.* Don't overdo it, my love," Silana said. "His head is already spinning."

Conrad relented.

But then Silana added, "Sadly, this all connects to the civil wars that are brewing in Europe. We must return as soon as possible, before a spark kindles the flame."

I'd heard the news reports. Europe was in a bad way, the EU crumbling as more and more states concluded that economic union was disguising an untenable ideological agenda, and so they exited. Britain had led them.

I'd never been to Europe.

"I could go with you to France, but the band. And my mother..."

Silana assured me. "Oh, we would bring the band. We're arranging your tour. It was in our minds all along, remember?"

"Oh."

Conrad spoke up. "And as for your mother, we can arrange for her, too. She can come along, if you want. We'll take care of her, as you wish. The choices are yours. But she's already under our protection, I assure you."

"That...that's really kind of you. Thank you." I still worried though. "What about Vicki?"

Silana answered this time. "We will consult physicians. Only the finest. And our most loyal. When the time is right, I'll place her into their care—but not before they are absolutely prepared. She was almost gone, Lochlan. We will have next to no time left to spare when she is returned to this world."

"I'll supervise things personally," Conrad said.

"You're a doctor, too?"

"I've had a long time to learn many things, but I'm not practiced enough to carry out the procedures safely, not when there are better hands. But I'll provide all the additional machinery needed. And Sophie will assist in surgery."

Good news for a change.

"Sophie. Speaking of..." I looked up at the speakers running along places in the plane's ceiling. "Are you there? Sophie?"

But there was no reply.

"She's probably having trouble connecting to us at our current altitude. Nothing to worry about," Conrad said.

"Ah." I went back to the previous subject. "How long? Until the surgery I mean."

Conrad tilted his head then calculated. "Several weeks. Perhaps longer. Arrangements need to be made for Vicki's safety. And her immediate family's. Even the surgery will have to be done in secret."

"Her family. We can't tell them anything yet, can we?"

Conrad grimaced. "No. I'm sorry. The last thing we'd want is to endanger them with this knowledge. Though it might afford them some small hope...we still don't know if their daughter will survive."

That hurt. To realize the pain that Vicki's parents had to be suffering, wondering where she'd been taken to, what nightmares she was enduring.

At least I'd prevented the worst of it.

"I understand," I said. "Thank you both for trying so hard."

"Always," Silana answered.

"I only wish we could do more," Conrad said.

I accepted that. What more could I have done?

But it still felt like another loss. And I don't like losing, especially when people I care about are getting hurt.

I wouldn't forget it.

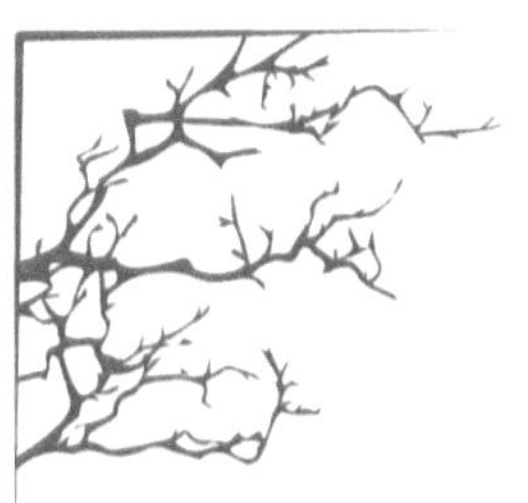

Chapter 32

"Oh my God! How are you? Didtheyfindyourfriend? Are you okay? *I've been messaging you all day and night!*"

Lois was happy to hear from me.

"I'm fine, I'm all right! Take a breath. I couldn't get to a phone for a while." That part wasn't a lie, but I went on. "We didn't find Vicki."

I wondered if I'd get too good at lying.

Lois didn't notice.

"I'm so sorry, Lochlan," she said.

I hesitated. "Yeah. It sucks." I knew I'd better change the subject. "But life...we've got the gig on Friday. The recording deal. I need to get back to *work...*"

"You're sure you're all right? I mean..."

"I'm dealing. Thanks. You're sweet. A great friend, but don't worry about me so much. We've got things to do." I tossed in a diversion. "There's talk of a European tour—"

"What? Are you kidding me?"

"Nope. Probably starts in France." I stabbed a guess, but it was pretty likely from what Silana had talked about. "Can you go with us?"

"Go—*are you kidding me?*"

I laughed out loud.

"I'll take that as 'yes' then."

"Yes? Oh my God! *Yes!* I—I can't—I can't even..."

"Breathe. In. Out."

"We're going to France!"

For the first time in what seemed like forever, I smiled a real smile.

It was Wednesday, just after noon, when our plane arrived back in Austin. Sunny. Not too warm. A perfect May day, and there was no rain in the forecast all the way through the weekend, but most importantly, none for Friday night's gig.

I called Pack right after I got off the phone with Lois, gave him the 'bad news,' then I helped arrange our belated dinner with Silana and Conrad.

Pack offered to call up the rest of the band to verify plans and I agreed. Gratefully.

After my phone calls, I went home to the apartment, and slept through the night and half of Thursday.

When I awoke, I found the best way to not get mired in worry over Vicki was worrying about Trip the Shark instead.

For a minute, I considered visiting Mom, but when I checked my saxophone cases, I was fresh out of tenor sax reeds. I needed to get to a shop to buy more boxes, so that's what I ended up doing, and Austin traffic chewed up a big chunk of the rest of my day.

Just before midnight, I checked out my YouTube feed and came across an international news story about three missing children who'd all mysteriously reappeared back on their parents' doorsteps, around the same time, but in three separate states, complete with unbelievable stories about a creepy cult, a magic dog, and a guardian angel.

"That was fast," I said to myself. I breathed a huge sigh of relief, allowed myself another smile, then finished a beer I'd picked up with my groceries.

There were reports about Vicki and her ongoing investigation, too, but I didn't torture myself by watching those. I was ripped up with guilt about it, but the beers helped.

Finally, Friday morning came. I loaded up the Bomber with my gig bags, sound effects rack, and microphone stand.

All members of Trip the Shark showed up early. Highly unusual. Even Jasmine was there ahead of me.

They were in good spirits, but I could tell they were uncomfortable around me because of it, so I put them at ease straight off.

"Vicki's still missing, but y'all don't need to walk on eggshells around me. Let's do what we do and have fun. I'm okay, I promise."

There was no response, only blank stares.

I lifted both eyebrows. "Cool?"

That got a few sheepish grins in return, and, finally, a chorus of agreement.

"And on that note..." I paused.

Tabor couldn't stand it. "What? Did we lose the contract? *We lost the contract!* Too good to be—"

"We're going to Europe."

Tabor almost dropped his guitar case. "Europe?"

"A tour?" Kat asked.

"For *real?*" That was Lindie.

"Yeah, we're headin' to France first. The dates haven't been set in stone...but soon. So get your calendars prepped. I confirmed this all last night."

Unsurprisingly, my band erupted into a riot of shouts and hugs.

I can't really explain how good it was to see my band so happy. Music life ain't easy, so this wasn't business-as-usual, and I stood back to enjoy the moment.

Once everybody calmed down a notch, we went over the upcoming night's set list, then set up our gear out of the way, along the side of the stage.

Except for the drums. Those would be used by the night's opening band.

Not long after, Lois walked through the back door of the club, right on time for the sound check.

"Hey, y'all," she said.

The band greeted Lois in chorus, but she came straight to me.

I gave her a bear hug squeeze, then put her down gently. "Good to see you, shorty."

Lois feigned outrage and soft-punched my belly. "You too, jerk. You guys ready?"

"Yup, pretty much." I turned to face everyone on stage. "Now that Lois is here, let's get the sound, and... *I'm treating for lunch!*"

Running Bear coughed loudly. "Whoa! What the hell?"

"Is the world ending?" Pack joked.

I almost said the wrong thing in response but caught myself.

"We ain't poor scrubs anymore, all right? So, let a guy splurge a little. Even on you band o' trolls!"

Pack pointed at me. "Ah, there's the real Loch. Had me worried for a second."

Laughing with the band felt like home. We got set, then sound-checked easily enough because Lois did her thing. (The girl's got a good ear, what can I say. I don't hire hacks.)

I informed everyone over barbecue that Lois was now an official part of the team and would be on the tour. That bit of info—and the BBQ—went down super well with Trip the Shark. So well that Lois was spontaneously lifted onto the shoulders of Pack and Running Bear and paraded around the restaurant like a Macy's princess.

After our happy meal, we went separate ways to chill before the midnight set. The split was into the usual duos and trios.

As for me, Lois insisted I hang out with her and give up all the details of my searches around Austin. We jumped in the Bomber and quickly found a local, air-conditioned coffee shop.

We jawed in that place for three hours.

I kept quiet about flying to Nevada or any of the insanity that had transpired there. I mentioned my UT campus finds and conversations, then I flat out lied about taking part in a police search. Not knowing how long I could keep the deception up, I gradually shifted our conversation to what visiting Silana and Conrad's house had been like.

Lois gobbled up the *Lifestyles of the Rich and Famous* stuff.

Soon enough it was time for me to grab Pack and head to dinner, so I dropped Lois off to replace him as hang-out buddy for Running Bear and Tabor. I told her about the never-ending queso bowl, to which Lois admitted she had a date with a fine cheese, and that I'd just have to get over her. Then she ran her smart ass inside the bar to join the guitarists.

"I like her," Pack said as he climbed into the Bomber. "Good people, and she makes sound-checks a snap."

"Yeah, she's awesome." I pulled out into East Austin traffic. "So, you ready to go muck it up with the mucky-mucks?"

"*Fuck yeah*. I still can't believe this...."

I nodded. "Believe me. I'm right there with ya." Oh, brother, was I.

Pack clasped his hands in the passenger seat, and I sensed his tension. "I'm sorry you didn't find your friend, man," he said. "There's still a chance. I pray to God every night."

I nodded at my kindhearted partner. "Thanks, Pack." I thought of Vicki, lost but not lost, in the ether, frozen in time. "There's *definitely* still a chance."

Pack changed the subject. "Sooooo. You and Lois..." He gave me a goofy grin.

"Wait. What? No. *No*, just...definitely not. Get that out of your head, okay? Just buddies is all. That's it."

"Ah, right. Right. Sorry. I just sort of assumed—"

"Drop it, Pack."

"Dropped, dropped."

But I saw why he might have assumed as much between me and Lois. I'd have to watch out for that. I didn't want to complicate touring, and certainly didn't want to mislead Lois.

Ironically, despite all of it, it was comfortably normal to be worrying about potential band drama, something so mundane in the grand scheme of things, after all the occult shit I'd just experienced.

DINNER WITH CONRAD and Silana would be a much-needed return to more of that normal, even if it was dinner at a mansion being served to us by a pair of immortal beings. But Pack didn't know that, so I reveled in his first reactions. His first sight of the house. His astonishment that the gate had a speaker system to let us in. His flirtation with Gloria, the now familiar voice on the other side of the gate's speaker. And his face-to-face meeting with Silana's dog pack.

Cu approached us with his train of dogs the second we exited the Bomber.

Pack joked, but he was genuinely nervous. "Is that a dog—*or a shaggy horse*? Did they feed it?"

I laughed. "It's fine, don't freak out. He's a buddy." I petted all the dogs surrounding us but reserved special attention for the huge wolfhound. Cu clumsily licked my hands as I reached out to ruffle his jowls.

I leaned in to whisper into a furry ear. "I owe you one, big guy. Thank you."

Cu smiled at me. A big, sloppy, doggie smile, with tongue dropping out the side of his snout.

"Cu, meet my pal, Paz. Paz, this is Cú Chulainn."

Cu half-sneezed and licked Pack's face in one long swipe.

"Okay. Not Cu for *Cujo*. Nice to meet you, too, I think..." Pack stammered. "Jesus, he's what? The biggest fucking dog ever?"

"Could be," I admitted. "Is your mom inside, Cu?"

Cu ruffed twice.

Pack took a step back. Cu was loud, even when he wasn't trying to be.

"I'd say that's an affirmative," Pack said.

"Yep. Come on." I patted Cu's nose. "See you later." I let the dog pack lick and sniff my other hand, down at my hip. "Later dogs."

Silana met us almost as soon as I rang the doorbell, but Conrad wasn't with her.

She beamed. "Paz, Lochlan. Please come in."

We entered the foyer. It was perfectly cool inside. Across the way, the two broad doors that lead to the outdoor pool were open, and a breeze was blowing. The entire hall and living room were bathed in warm, late afternoon sunlight.

After a few pleasantries and choices made about appropriate household footwear, Pack had both sandals set by a section of wall near the entrance. Silana took him by the hand and led us into her kitchen.

Something smelled delicious. A jambalaya recipe Silana had picked up in New Orleans. The hotter the better as far as Pack and I were concerned. Silana stirred a big pot with a wooden spoon, then invited us to sit around the pool, designed like two teardrops joined at irregular angles. Not gigantic like the one that Silana had emptied back at Serenity Mere, but still stately.

Unfortunately, there wasn't time for swimming before the gig.

We talked about things small and large. Silana filled Pack in on details of the Euro tour, to which he responded excitedly. Some of the info I hadn't heard yet either.

We'd be traveling in style. Security to be provided. Food catering. The best hotel accommodations filled.

It was going to be something to remember.

Fifteen minutes of chit-chat later, Conrad approached the pool from across the wooded yard that flanked the nearby river.

"Very sorry, gentlemen. I was preoccupied. I'm sure Silana has kept you entertained?"

"Enchanted," I said. Conrad gave me a knowing grin.

"I can't get over this place, Conrad," Pack said. "When I'm rich, I want one just like it."

We all laughed.

"Well, I'll help you design it," Conrad said. He was being serious.

"Holy...okay, sir. You've got a deal," Pack said.

The three of us talked briefly about Conrad's workshop while Silana went to get us all drinks. Conrad said he'd been putting the finishing touches on a gift for his wife. Something to help out in the kitchen.

Silana returned with a silver tray filled with beers poured into frosty, glass mugs, and one tall pitcher. Local brews from around Austin and enough in the pitcher to refill for a second round.

The suds were cold and fresh and tasted like paradise.

I'd almost forgotten, but there was business left to deal with, and so Pack reached into a leather tote he'd brought along. His hands emerged with his signed LMG contract.

"All signed and ready to go," he proclaimed.

"Excellent," Silana said, as she accepted the stack of papers. She checked the signature and then set the contract down on a nearby glass table. "Looks to be perfectly in order. How exciting! Soon we shall all be in my homelands, and I can't wait to show you around."

"It'll be good to see the coasts of Europe again," Conrad agreed.

Pack followed Conrad across the grounds for a tour of the property, down to the riverside and following the trails I remembered from my first visit, but, notably, Conrad left off a stop at the Workshop. Conrad and Silana pointed out the adjoining compound where LMG staff and security worked, and Pack just stared for a long moment, then he mouthed a 'wow' at me when nobody else was looking.

And that's pretty much how the early evening went. The jambalaya was delicious. The dinner conversation was happy and casual. Everyone was looking forward to the tour, and so Pack had no reason to suspect there was anything else to it.

When it was finally time to get to Emo's, to mingle and play our sets, Pack and I said our thank you's then headed out back to the Bomber.

There was one last thing on my mind. I waited for Pack to climb into the car, and as he and Silana made small talk, I leaned toward Conrad and asked, "I've been meaning to ask. Is Sophie all right? I know she probably was just being quiet but—"

"She was listening over dinner, I'm sure. She wanted me to tell you that she is very sorry about what happened. She's still getting used to the concept of death and suffering, Lochlan. It's...complicated for her. You understand."

I wasn't really sure I did. I mean, how could I really? But I said, "Yeah. Sure. Of course. She's...can she..." I inhaled deeply and finally finished in a whisper. "Can she feel? I mean, really *feel* anything?"

"You're wondering because you can't sense her emotions, right?"

"Well, yeah, there *is* that."

"It's difficult for me to know either. And I designed her. But she's extraordinary. My greatest achievement. Well, right up there anyway..."

Conrad didn't explain further, but added, "Let's just wait and see what happens."

I nodded. "Fair enough. I'd like to talk to her soon though."

"Oh, you will. I'll make sure of it."

"Good," I said, and then I walked over to the driver's side of the Bomber. "Thank you for the hospitality. See you at the club?"

Conrad nodded. "We'll be right behind you."

We arrived back at Emo's not long after sunset. Most of the band sat at the bar. Lois was chatting with Tabor, Running Bear, and Lindie when we interrupted.

"Hey-oh," I said.

"Oh, hey there," Lois said, a little too loudly, and I wondered if she'd maybe snuck a sip of something stronger than a Coke while I was gone.

As if to mark my thought, Lindie and the boys greeted us with a tip of their drinks.

Lois pointed out an archway that led to the dance floor and stage. "The Kettle Men are almost ready for set one. Looks like the crowd is already here, too." She gestured back over my shoulder toward the front doors.

Sure enough, a line had formed at the door, and money was exchanging hands with two tellers.

I nodded. "Gonna be a good night," I said. "Pack handed over his contract. That means the rest of you'll be getting yours collected soon."

"Things are moving fast," Running Bear said.

"Not fast enough for me," Tabor said. "When does the plane leave?"

"Soon as we've rerecorded our singles," Pack said in an exaggeratedly blasé manner.

"W-what?" Tabor stared at me with wide eyes.

"We're recording in a studio?" Lindie sounded breathless. "Please tell me we're getting engineered. Like the big kids..."

I dipped my brow at Pack and let him do the honors.

"We ab-so-fucking-lutely are! LMG just told us," Pack roared.

Lindie hopped off her bar stool. "Holy fuck!"

"Right on," Running Bear added.

"I guess Europe can wait a couple days," Tabor snarked, and he clapped Running Bear on the back.

"Relay the good news to the girls when they show up, but I'll be making announcements to the crowd later tonight anyway," I said. "So, I'd say—it's time to do a little *drinking*—and you fuckers are ahead of me. Bartender!"

Shark grabbed the drinks I sprung for, and then all of us roamed up into the balcony level for the two upcoming sets by the Kettle Men. The crowd of Austinites entering the club was quick to flock to the bar we'd retreated from, and more kept coming in.

Emo's is a popular place, so I was proud to know we were drawing a good chunk of the audience.

The Kettle Men carried a three-piece horn section along with the core band. I hadn't seen them play live before, but tagging horns garnered my immediate respect. Call it horn-bias if you will, but brass makes everything better. A mixture of ska and R&B, the Kettle Men delivered a slick first set of the night and got the crowd warmed up for us, good and hot.

Right around when the Kettle Men took their first set break, I stood alone among the listeners on the balcony level. I'd said a few hellos to familiar fans for sure, but up until that point I hadn't been chatted too often, at least not so often that I was ready to flee to the green room.

Turns out, I was glad I'd hung out and was looking over the railing at the front entrance, because someone caught my eye. And that doesn't happen every day.

She was a tall girl with jet black hair and a fair shade of eyes that sparkled in the light of lamps overhanging the cashiers. In gray jeans with blue cowboy boots and a small, black leather vest open to reveal a low-cut ladies t-shirt in white, her figure was, well, let's just say every red-blooded man nearby noticed. I thought a few might end up with whiplash.

Despite this, she appeared to have arrived at Emo's alone. My curiosity piqued, and I kept my eyes locked on her moves. The beautiful girl didn't walk straight to a bar, but instead found a spot in a corner and appeared to scan the crowd for someone. A boyfriend surely. Which made sense enough—there was no way a chick that hot would be out on a Friday night solo.

I still hadn't gotten a good look at her face from my angle upstairs, but right as I considered possibly moving for a better view, she looked up at the balcony to my left and panned her eyes in my direction.

The word 'perfection' gets overused too often, but let me tell you, when I saw this girl's face, that's the only word that came to mind. She made me a little nervous. Me. The Angel of Death.

She gazed straight into my eyes, and I must have had the dumbest expression on my face in that instant because she smiled. A big, shining, blinding smile.

I was sure I'd never seen this girl before, but she turned—and headed straight for the nearest stairway to the balcony level. I stepped back from the railing and took a gulp of confidence out of my beer bottle. She climbed the stairs, moved easily and gracefully through the crowd, turned again and aimed herself—right at me.

Just your imagination, fool, there's no way—

She walked up, the crowd on the balcony level parting for her as if she were royalty. In fact, she hardly noticed the surrounding people.

The girl stood in front of me, my back to a section of balcony, and I wasn't sure whether I felt more turned on or cornered. Her eyes were steel-gray and absolutely breathtaking up close, even in the low light of the club.

"You're Lochlan Nohr," she said simply.

I got a hold of myself. "I am. But we haven't met. I sure as hell'd remember."

She smiled again. "You really don't know me?"

I stared at her face and then sized her up and down. My usual boldness reasserted itself.

"Unless I was stoned out of my mind, there's pretty much no way I'd forget. I mean, *hello*..." I pointed an open hand at her.

"I'm not playing fair. You know my employers. LMG."

"Really? Oh, well shit. That's a sad surprise. So this ain't just a random thing. And here I was hoping you were a rabid fan looking to take advantage of me."

The beautiful girl laughed. A musical, amazing laugh.

"Now, why would I take advantage of you? I'll be working with you."

My heart sank.

"Fuck. Doesn't that just figure?" We both laughed.

"So, you like what you see then?"

It's a trap, I thought. "Um. I really shouldn't answer that."

"No. Please. I'd like to know. Just be honest."

I grimaced at her for a second. "Well, okay. Only since you're asking again, and because I'm almost sure nobody will fire me from my own band. Almost." I took a breath. "You are the hottest thing I've seen all night. Maybe all year." I met her eyes. She was the hottest thing I'd seen in ten years, but I didn't want to overdo it. "And I'm crying inside because you work for LMG."

I'd paid so little attention to the surrounding crowd that I didn't notice Silana and Conrad until they materialized out of my mental fog on either side of my new, lovely acquaintance.

"I see you found him," Conrad said to the girl.

"He's difficult to miss," Silana said. "Have you been properly introduced yet, Lochlan?"

I acknowledged my bosses. "Oh, hey you two. Um, no, we were just, um, getting to know one another. And I've just now realized I don't know your name...*Miss?*"

"Sophie," the beautiful girl said.

I chuckled. "That's...ironic. I know a Sophie..."

"I know you do." She grinned slyly at me.

"Lochlan, meet your new head of security, Sophie Carlisle."

"You're shitting me," I said. "*Our* Sophie?"

"I am. I'm sorry, Lochlan. They made me do it, but I must admit I enjoyed seeing your reaction to this new body." She turned to Conrad. "You must have done a superb job, sir. His heart rate increased rapidly with my approach."

"I, uh, *yeah*. Guilty as charged." Silana laughed as I grinned weakly at Conrad. "Wow. Mad skills. You've got mad skills, man," I said to him sincerely.

"Oh, I won't take all the credit. I used you as inspiration. Doesn't she look a tad related? To you, I mean." Conrad caressed his wife's shoulder. "And Silana added her extra bit of magic."

Sophie stood up straighter with an expectant look on her face.

"Ya know, she does, now that you mention it. It's the eyes," I replied.

"The ones I wanted," Sophie said. "Your eyes."

The club music playing through the speakers all around us covered our conversation. Nobody paid too much attention to us in my corner of the balcony, but a door to the green room was nearby, just in case.

Silana rubbed a hand along Sophie's back. "Sophie's finally free to see the world from our perspective."

"I'll be damned," I said. "Head of Security. Tabor's gonna have another heart attack, but yeah, I can see it. Why not? Happy for you, Sophie."

"*Thank you*, Lochlan." She put one palm on her chest. "I'll do my best."

"I know you will," I said. "Anyway, let's get into the green room, gang. I need a fresh beer, and y'all look thirsty to me. I mean...can you drink?" I looked wonderstruck at Sophie.

She laughed again. "Yes. I can metabolize all food and most liquids." Then Sophie's expression relaxed, and she looked more human than ever. "I'll have what you're having." And she winked.

I chuckled loudly. "Damn. Damn, damn, damn." I shook my head. "Come on, this way."

I turned to pull open the green room door, but a familiar voice stopped me.

"Is that where the free booze is stashed?"

I glanced over past Conrad and Silana. Fan Zhan sauntered up in high heels and a skin-tight, black and white dress. Striped, as if a mad genius had painted it on her. Let me tell you, it worked, whoever the designer was.

Right behind Fan, a young woman with light brown skin followed, lead lightly by Fan's fingers drifting behind her. She had big brown eyes, pretty ones like Fan's, but unlike Fan, this girl's hair was long and chestnut brown and wavy. She was a tiny thing, too, half a foot shorter than Fan, even in her high heels. She had a comfortable pair of blue jeans on, and a sparkling, red and silver blouse accented by a pair of silver necklaces and prominent earrings.

Fan pulled her date next to her. "Everyone, this is my friend Adriana. Adriana, this is Conrad, his wife Silana and this tall, handsome hunk is Lochlan Nohr."

"Hello. Nice to meet y'all. I've seen you play before, Lochlan. Can't wait to hear your band again," Adriana said.

I grinned at Adriana and then at Fan. "Well, thank you. You both look lovely."

Fan noticed Sophie. "I'm sorry," Fan said, "but I don't believe we've met."

Conrad took the lead. "Actually, you *have*, but not in person. Fan, this is Sophie."

I sensed and saw a pang of shock run across Fan's features, but to her usual professional credit, she adapted so quickly, hardly anyone besides me would have noticed.

"Sophie!" Fan took a step forward and embraced our shiny, new android in a hug. "So glad to finally meet the *real* you."

Sophie evidently caught the joke. "Yes, I'm a real girl after all," she said and shared a laugh with Fan.

"Sophie, Adriana," Fan concluded.

Once all the introductions were out of the way, I got back to the business at hand. Beer business.

"Follow me. I'll get us some drinks and then I'd better get ready."

Conrad and Silana fell in behind me as I opened the green room door. Fan and Adriana followed Sophie.

Trip the Shark filtered in and out of the green room as the Kettle Men played their second and final set, and I made introductions whenever I could. A friendly waitress took care of my guests' drinks, and I finished off another beer I'd pulled out of a nearby ice bucket. A small table between two couches had tortilla and potato chips, and those were snatched up by musicians and guests alike.

When I eventually readied to take my leave for the stage, I slung a neck strap over my head, then knelt down and removed my tenor and alto saxophones from their cases. It was good to have them in hand again.

"Just when I thought you couldn't get any sexier, you put those things on," Fan said. Adriana giggled.

I stood back up and clicked the tenor onto the end of my neck strap. The alto I held up in my left hand until I could deposit it on a stand. "It's what I'm here for. If y'all come out this way, you can find good spots near the side of the stage. They're reserved for guests."

My friends followed me out the other side of the green room to the curtained rear of the stage. It was loud as hell from the cheering crowd and the rumblings and horn blasts of the Kettle Men, so I pointed a finger to where everyone needed to go and nodded at a burly man in a black t-shirt adorned with SECURITY in big, white letters. He nodded back and motioned for everyone else to follow him.

All of Trip the Shark gathered at the rear of the stage, and waited patiently for our final stage prep before our midnight set. The band was all smiles and high spirits.

What a difference a day makes.

My mind wandered back to Lake Tahoe for a second, but I shoved the darkness aside and blew air into my alto sax to warm up the brass body. My saxes are always a great focus when I need it, and, after the Round Table, I definitely needed it.

Cheers and whistles from the crowd resounded after the last note from the Kettle Men. My band praised the guys as they exited the stage and popped through curtains to where we all stood, and the Kettle Men wished us a good set. Kirk, their leader, shook my hand and then moved off for the green room.

When Trip the Shark entered the stage to move our equipment into place, the crowd went a little wild. The band waved greetings. For me, that meant waving my alto sax, and that got another cheer. It made me smile again.

I set my saxophones onto a dual stand near my vocal mic and checked to make sure the sound was active. A single finger-tap did the trick. My wireless sax microphones were on. Green lights equal good.

Across the crowd, inside the sound booth, Lois gave me a thumbs up.

Once the stage was set, we all exited to wait out the few minutes until midnight. Then it was time for the real thing.

And the crowd let us hear it.

"*I love you, Jaz,*" a random girl shouted at Jasmine.

"I love Lochlan more!" yelled another random girl, pulling a lot of laughs out of the crowd.

"We love you, too," Jaz said into her center stage mic. *"How y'all feeling tonight, Austin?"*

The crowd erupted.

I turned around to face Lindie, Running Bear, Tabor, and Pack. They were ready. Kat on her drum kit met my eyes. With a single chin wag from me, Kat clicked drumsticks four times into our first song of the night.

Trip the Shark was loose again.

The midnight set brought me back to the place where I belonged. Back to the music.

After the first tune was over, I made announcements.

First, I gave up the news that LMG had signed us to a deal.

The crowd lost their minds.

Next, I announced we were to begin recording our first LMG album within just a few weeks.

The crowd blew up into hoots, whistles and hollering.

Finally, I announced Trip the Shark's first world tour would follow that, beginning in the early fall.

I almost went deaf from the response.

We quickly followed up with more of our originals, and then after our fourth song of the evening, I had something more important to say.

"As I'm sure most of you have heard by now, a professor out of UT was kidnapped over the past weekend." The crowd hushed itself. "What many of you probably don't know is Miss Victoria Lott is an old friend of mine." Many distraught responses to my revelation bounced around the large hall of the club. I put up my hands. "This isn't about me. I just want everyone to please pray for Vicki. She's a wonderful person, and I'm sure, a fantastic teacher. Why anyone would harm her...I'll never understand, but I know if we all...keep her in our hearts and minds, it'll help. Trust me on this. So please. Pray for Victoria."

I choked up as a legion of emotions washed into me, most my own but hundreds outside myself. I was moved close to tears and the crowd could tell. Shouts of encouragement and love hit the stage—and me.

I managed to get back in control. I wanted to do something special for the Austin crowd, and also as a tribute to Vicki, so I reached down for my alto sax.

"We've got the greatest fans in the world. God bless you all." Uncharacteristic of me to utter into a mic, but that last week had gotten to me. I wasn't the same man.

Literally.

I gave the crowd a minute to quiet down and then I continued.

"This one's for Vicki, everybody. It's something brand new," I said, and Kat clicked slowly into a blues inspired ballad I'd composed only a month before. "We'll call this one...*Sublime*."

The crowd roared and whistled but fell to a murmur when I blew out the first somber note from my alto.

The end of our second set also ended the night for me. I was spent, and, despite every attempt I'd made to keep it all a happy occasion, especially for our fans, I couldn't completely shake the past week's events.

I said my goodnights to the band, gave kudos all around and then I went outside the stage into the crowd to reunite with LMG. I shook many hands with fans and acquaintances on the way but managed to not take too long to find Ordo Severinus.

Fan and Adriana were sharing a tall drink decorated with orange slices. Sophie continued to gaze at the crowd like a child at her first sporting event, and Silana and Conrad were snuggled up against one another in a corner of a bar in the most open display of affection I'd yet seen between them.

"So, final verdict?" I asked. "The crowd seemed to be into it."

Sophie gave me a look I couldn't discern. "A strange kind of happy. There wasn't a dry eye in the place—that's the phrase—yet, the crowd was pleased. Yes. They were. Into it." She was learning.

"Your tribute. It was... I witnessed a performance of Beethoven, and I am not sure which left me more at a loss for words," Silana said seriously.

"Uh. That's a huge compliment. I...I'm sorry. I didn't try... I mean, I tried not to use my powers..." I ran out of words. I wasn't sure what I'd done or not done, really. I'd performed like any other night, but I'd released so much passion during the two sets, things might have gotten away from me.

Had I evolved so quickly since learning about my heritage?

"What are you talking about? You were amazing. The band was amazing. Here, you need this more than we do?" Fan offered me her tall, fruity glass.

I shook my head. "No, sorry, I'm good. Just tired. 'Fraid I should call it a night, guys. I need to be fresh for tomorrow. And gotta visit Mom in the morning." I hefted the alto sax case in my hand then pulled my tenor bag closer to my shoulder. "Be sure to update me as soon as a time is set for Dante's funeral, okay?"

"We will," Conrad said.

Fan suddenly hugged me. When she stepped back, I grinned at her girl-friend.

"It was a pleasure meeting you, Adriana," I said.

"I had a blast. We might be back tomorrow night? Maybe?" Adriana looked at Fan.

"We'll be here," Fan replied.

"Me, too," Sophie said.

Silana hugged me next, then I shook Conrad's hand.

"Get a good night's sleep," Silana said. "If you wish to stop by for lunch or dinner tomorrow, our door is always open."

"The way you cook, you should be careful about makin' offers to an eatin' man." I waved my alto case around. "Okay. I'm off. Thanks for helping make the night so special for me and the band."

But I wasn't done. Not quite.

"Sophie," I said, and opened my arms. The look on her face made me grin. Everyone grinned, even Adriana, though she wasn't in on what was really happening.

Sophie blinked and hesitated as if calculating a response. Then she smiled, too, and slowly entered my embrace, strong and—*human*.

We separated and for the first time since I'd met her, Sophie was speechless. Her eyes said all I needed, machine or not. She was *ours*. And I trusted her and Conrad to get the experiment right.

"Now I'm *really* out," I said. My new friends waved goodnight, and I escaped Emo's through a back door to the Bomber, loaded the trunk, then drove back to my apartment.

I left the radio off all the way home.

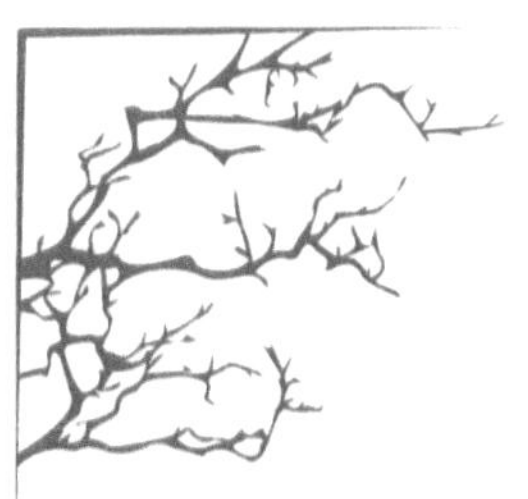

Epilogue

Saturday morning dawned with a smattering of rain that made it easy to lounge in my bed for an extra hour.

This time when I arose, all my juices were flowing right. I drank half of the orange juice carton in the fridge, showered, and then headed out the door. The drizzling rain had stopped completely.

I knew there wasn't much I could or would tell Mom about the last seventy-two hours, but I couldn't wait to see her. I'd at least tell her about last night, and about the tour and recording plans. She'd be excited for me, I knew.

But about Vicki? The rescued kids? I had to keep secrets, like it or not.

Traffic was relatively sparse, so I had an easy time of it, stopping at Groovy Biscuits for some breakfast takeout. Philly cheesesteak-covered biscuits for me and a veggie omelet for Mom, plus plastic cups of grapefruit juice to wash it all down.

Ten minutes later, I parked in front of the all-too-familiar Austin Waters Mental Health Hospital.

I walked up to the front desk to sign in and showed my bagged breakfast to nurse George.

"Whew, boy. That smells real good," George said.

"Does it? I hadn't noticed." I grinned.

George laughed.

I reached into the paper bag, pulled out a wrapped handful, and placed it on the counter in front of George.

"Whasthis?" he asked.

"Biscuit. Egg, cheese, and bacon. Enjoy."

George's eyes went wide. "You, sir, are a saint among men!"

"No problem," I said. "How's Mom doing?"

"She's been calm. She's asked about you. Probably a dozen times since your last visit. Better get in there."

I nodded. "Thanks, George."

He opened the biscuit's paper wrapping. "Thank *you*."

I made my way through the halls to Mom's room.

A small, green ball rolled out through the door to my mother's room when I was just feet away. Mittens the cat bounded through the doorway and onto the ball, teeth and claws gnawing at it as the little furry monster curled around the helpless toy.

She spotted me in a split second and popped up onto her four paws, meowed once, and padded straight up. I reached down to retrieve both her and her ball. The green toy I pushed into her front paws, and she happily grabbed the ball into a wrestler's clinch all over again, chewing it—and me—as I carried her with my breakfast-bag clenched in a fist and stroked the top of her head between her ears.

"Mom, I found a wild animal stalking the halls—"

I stopped cold in the doorway. Her room smelled different, like Mom's kitchen instead of a hospital ward.

Mom wasn't alone.

A man in simple khaki slacks, brown shoes, and a yellow polo shirt stood near the window that overlooked the hospital's backyard and fountain. My mother was close beside him.

Mom's face burst into a broad smile. "Here he *is*, Jerry! Lochlan, I finally get to introduce you..."

"Sorry about that. My fault. The toss got away from me," Jerry said and pointed at Mittens still nestled in the fold of my right arm.

I set Mittens down on the floor and let the green ball go rolling. The cat chased it under Mom's bed.

"Mom, I...think maybe you should come give me a hug."

"What? Oh, ha-ha." Mom did as I requested and when she let go of me, I held her firmly but lightly by a wrist, so she couldn't return to Jerry.

"Lucky?" I asked.

"Huh?" Jerry's brow wrinkled, but I'm sure he couldn't top the incredulous look I wore.

I mean, after all, I was staring at Lucky, the egg-salad hobo I'd met way back in Nevada. Sure, his clothing was different, and he wasn't wearing a floppy fishing hat, but there was no doubt that the man, this 'Jerry,' was the same one I'd conversed with near the cigar shop.

After a nervous moment, Jerry laughed out loud.

Mom wasn't laughing though. "Lochlan, don't be silly, his name is Jerry. He's an old friend. Why are you holding me? Let me go, Son."

"Mom..."

"Apologies, Lochlan. I sometimes forget that I appear for others as I last did. I'm not so used to making an appearance, you see," Lucky Jerry said, and just like that—his face changed into another man's and his entire body grew in stature to equal my height.

"There, hopefully that's better. You can let Tressa go. I assure you...I'm a friend. More than a friend, really," Jerry said.

I couldn't form words. Jerry was statuesque. With his jawline, defined brow, gray eyes, and black hair, staring at the man was like looking into a mirror.

But there was something different about his eyes. His eyes were old. Not a tired old, but centuries old. Eyes that had seen many stories. More stories than I could ever hope to know.

I let go of Mom. She rubbed her wrist for a moment and then walked between Jerry and me. She didn't notice any change in her friend. "Well, that's better. What's gotten into you? Honestly, I don't know what to think but...never mind. Lochlan, this is *Jerry*. Jerry this is my overprotective son, Lochlan. He's been away searching for a friend." Mom paused. "Oh, my goodness, which reminds me. *What happened?* Did you find her?"

I still couldn't speak. I stood there staring at my reflection in Jerry.

"He found her," Jerry said. "Give the boy a minute, Tressa. He's had a rough few days, and I'm afraid I'm not helping things at the moment."

Mom grew more concerned. "Lochlan, are you all right, baby? What happened?"

"Many things have changed, Tressa," Jerry said. He walked past my mother, stood before me and extended a hand.

"Lochlan, my name is Jeremiel."

I examined Jeremiel's hand.

"I've got so many questions," I said.

I took his hand and shook it. His *left* hand. It was a good handshake. Firm. Strong.

The tension in my spine went away the instant I touched him.

"I'll do my very best to answer. Anything I can," Jerry replied, and he looked down. "Also, you forgot these..." In his other hand he held out my lost blues harp and multi-tool.

I still held my bag of breakfast, or maybe I'd have taken my items back, but instead I just stared, dumbfounded. And that lasted I don't know how long.

Eventually, I could make thoughts again.

I met Jerry's gaze straight on, released his hand and arched an irritated eyebrow.

"Is it flat or not?" I asked. "And don't bullshit me this time."

Don't miss out!

Visit the website below and you can sign up to receive emails whenever John McDonough publishes a new book. There's no charge and no obligation.

https://books2read.com/r/B-A-JXCJ-QWFEB

BOOKS 2 READ

Connecting independent readers to independent writers.

About the Author

John McDonough was born in Denver, Colorado. The son of a playwright, he grew up surrounded by tall book shelves filled with historical tomes of ancient Rome and Greece, myths and legends. Some of his earliest memories include "reading" The Adventures of Tintin during Kindergarten nap-time (they were in French), and buying Detective Comics and X-Men for 15 cents. The love of music took hold early on, too, and while working toward his college English degree, he began playing in bands professionally, which continued for fifteen years. This was followed by a foray into the Corporate World, which lead to him finally realizing that he needed to escape and make writing his full-time job. Today, he lives in the Hill Country of Texas. Rumors of ghosts haunting the local football field have only inspired him to write faster.

Read more at john-mcdonough.com.

About the Publisher

Charming Dragon Press is the Texas-based indie imprint of author John Mc-Donough.

If you enjoyed this book, please consider leaving a review. Each review helps tremendously, both in spreading the word about the books, as well as helping the author better plan upcoming series releases.

Thank you.